Anonymous

The Eighth Report on the District, Criminal, and Private Lunatic Asylums in Ireland

Anonymous

The Eighth Report on the District, Criminal, and Private Lunatic Asylums in Ireland

Reprint of the original, first published in 1857.

1st Edition 2023 | ISBN: 978-3-37517-192-6

Salzwasser Verlag is an imprint of Outlook Verlagsgesellschaft mbH.

Verlag (Publisher): Outlook Verlag GmbH, Zeilweg 44, 60439 Frankfurt, Deutschland
Vertretungsberechtigt (Authorized to represent): E. Roepke, Zeilweg 44, 60439 Frankfurt, Deutschland
Druck (Print): Books on Demand GmbH, In de Tarpen 42, 22848 Norderstedt, Deutschland

APPENDIX C.

No. I.—Table showing the Number of Patients who were in the District Asylums on the 31st March, 1855; also the Number of Admissions, Discharges, Escapes, and Deaths, during the two Years ending 31st March, 1856, and 1857

1856 (Patients in Asylum 31st March, 1855; Admissions, etc. during Year ended 31st March, 1856)

Asylums	In Asylum 31 Mar 1855 M	F	T	Admitted yr ended 31 Mar 1856 M	F	T	Total No. Patients M	F	T
Armagh	60	54	129	52	34	86	112	108	212
Ballinasloe	181	156	337	80	53	90	237	180	420
Belfast	141	135	276	85	46	114	202	184	390
Carlow	160	61	401	23	30	53	423	111	244
Clonmel	66	70	136	16	7	23	63	77	104
Cork	189	213	402	80	86	120	246	273	532
Kilkenny	76	62	138	17	18	35	94	90	173
Killarney	72	63	137	10	16	48	101	64	165
Limerick	400	163	318	74	33	107	204	218	420
Londonderry	414	86	210	6	42	71	131	158	289
Maryborough	99	61	199	35	46	80	184	160	249
Mullingar	—	—	195	64	20	472	244	88	172
Omagh	88	99	195	46	43	92	156	143	[illegible]
Richmond	249	299	548	123	454	287	372	453	905
Sligo	8	41	17	78	36	137	56	79	155
Waterford	61	69	436	14	22	30	73	91	491
Total,	1,458	1,446	2,908	733	780	1,532	2,416	2,915	4,831

Asylums	Cured M	F	T	Improved M	F	T	Not Cured M	F	T
Armagh	24	36	40	13	7	20	8	9	10
Ballinasloe	18	18	14	—	—	—	50	30	480
Belfast	10	30	40	5	6	14	—	—	—
Carlow	8	6	18	5	4	5	—	—	—
Clonmel	8	6	14	4	—	4	—	—	—
Cork	33	30	60	6	4	11	—	—	—
Kilkenny	7	6	13	4	—	4	1	—	1
Killarney	4	7	11	6	4	10	—	—	—
Limerick	47	21	40	18	12	6	8	4	4
Londonderry	22	15	37	5	41	16	9	7	16
Maryborough	5	4	6	4	4	7	10	34	20
Mullingar	1	7	11	—	2	2	2	—	—
Omagh	13	11	23	[illegible]	[illegible]	[illegible]	[illegible]	[illegible]	[illegible]
Richmond	[illegible]	[illegible]	[illegible]	[illegible]	[illegible]	[illegible]	21	13	14
Sligo	[illegible]	[illegible]	[illegible]	[illegible]	[illegible]	[illegible]	[illegible]	[illegible]	[illegible]
Waterford	11	43	44	[illegible]	[illegible]	[illegible]	[illegible]	[illegible]	[illegible]
Total,	24	203	516	85	84	100	168	33	201

Asylums	Incurable M	F	T	Total Discharged M	F	T	Escaped M	F	T	Natural M	F	T	Accidental M	F	T	Total Deaths M	F	T	Total Disch./Dead/Escaped M	F	T	Remaining 31 Mar 1856 M	F	T
Armagh	—	—	—	43	26	70	[illegible]	[illegible]	[illegible]	7	11	18	—	—	—	7	11	18	62	17	80	80	64	132
Ballinasloe	[illegible]	[illegible]	[illegible]	68	85	139	2	—	2	6	8	17	—	—	—	6	8	17	11	63	142	156	131	281
Belfast	[illegible]	[illegible]	[illegible]	24	30	53	1	—	1	11	7	18	1	—	1	12	7	18	5	46	87	100	138	307
Carlow	[illegible]	[illegible]	[illegible]	14	15	27	3	—	6	3	8	11	—	—	—	3	8	11	20	21	41	164	80	194
Clonmel	[illegible]	[illegible]	[illegible]	6	5	18	—	—	—	5	3	8	—	—	—	5	3	8	17	8	23	71	85	159
Cork	[illegible]	[illegible]	[illegible]	38	41	70	1	1	2	14	40	34	—	—	—	14	10	44	64	52	103	493	221	417
Kilkenny	[illegible]	[illegible]	[illegible]	14	11	48	—	—	—	6	4	10	—	—	—	7	4	11	19	10	94	70	0	145
Killarney	[illegible]	[illegible]	[illegible]	10	11	21	1	—	4	7	4	11	—	—	—	7	4	11	18	15	43	89	80	152
Limerick	[illegible]	[illegible]	[illegible]	38	36	74	—	—	—	10	7	17	—	—	—	30	7	17	48	43	91	158	170	328
Londonderry	[illegible]	[illegible]	[illegible]	30	43	63	—	—	—	14	3	16	—	—	—	14	3	16	25	48	107	91	94	201
Maryborough	[illegible]	[illegible]	[illegible]	42	41	83	—	—	—	7	3	16	—	—	—	7	3	16	18	40	85	62	150	[illegible]
Mullingar	[illegible]	[illegible]	[illegible]	6	6	18	—	—	—	5	1	6	—	—	—	5	1	6	14	19	7	75	145	[illegible]
Omagh	[illegible]	[illegible]	[illegible]	27	31	58	—	—	—	8	11	19	—	—	—	9	11	19	15	40	102	102	204	[illegible]
Richmond	13	14	[illegible]	65	74	139	1	—	1	33	21	54	—	—	—	33	21	54	84	95	273	336	611	[illegible]
Sligo	[illegible]	[illegible]	[illegible]	18	13	31	—	—	—	8	3	11	—	—	—	8	3	11	28	16	44	81	64	113
Waterford	[illegible]	[illegible]	[illegible]	12	24	30	—	—	—	5	3	8	—	—	—	5	3	8	13	24	41	42	97	135
Total,	21	14	35	491	454	915	9	1	10	150	415	307	4	—	1	171	115	368	621	[illegible]	1,100	1,875	1,833	3,026

1857 (Patients in Asylum 31st March, 1856; Admissions, etc. during Year ended 31st March, 1857)

Asylums	In Asylum 31 Mar 1856 M	F	T	Admitted yr ended 31 Mar 1857 M	F	T	Total No. Patients M	F	T
Armagh	60	53	123	91	26	90	121	92	213
Ballinasloe	158	196	554	55	46	161	353	172	385
Belfast	164	139	307	76	64	142	327	304	410
Carlow	103	90	193	18	26	44	113	110	235
Clonmel	71	35	106	6	6	40	111	78	139
Cork	196	221	417	46	61	144	242	282	364
Kilkenny	75	70	143	6	20	25	83	90	170
Killarney	63	69	152	20	20	40	112	88	204
Limerick	156	173	329	52	35	87	209	204	410
Londonderry	107	94	201	33	45	78	140	178	278
Maryborough	85	66	150	20	11	40	111	70	100
Mullingar	70	70	140	51	44	85	121	110	240
Omagh	102	102	204	40	46	70	149	145	297
Richmond	273	335	611	87	51	138	360	380	740
Sligo	56	64	413	52	27	60	91	81	172
Waterford	86	67	155	26	20	40	76	90	174
Total,	1,815	2,213	3,896	660	825	1,486	2,516	2,378	4,896

Asylums	Cured M	F	T	Improved M	F	T	Not Cured M	F	T	Incurable M	F	T	Total Discharged M	F	T
Armagh	25	13	38	14	4	18	4	—	4	—	—	—	43	47	80
Ballinasloe	20	16	45	—	4	4	—	—	—	—	—	—	26	20	46
Belfast	57	30	86	6	8	15	—	—	—	—	—	—	36	45	81
Carlow	4	14	18	1	18	14	—	—	—	—	—	—	5	14	29
Clonmel	4	4	8	—	—	—	—	—	—	—	—	—	4	4	8
Cork	34	36	63	10	40	50	3	8	4	1	1	1	44	48	93
Kilkenny	5	8	14	—	4	1	4	4	1	—	1	1	5	11	16
Killarney	6	4	10	2	3	5	—	—	—	—	—	—	8	7	15
Limerick	22	14	36	11	8	19	4	4	8	—	—	—	35	25	60
Londonderry	21	27	45	2	5	7	3	—	3	—	—	—	28	32	98
Maryborough	2	1	3	10	7	17	4	6	6	—	—	—	18	13	20
Mullingar	15	14	21	1	—	3	1	—	4	—	—	—	17	18	38
Omagh	20	11	84	7	3	10	6	6	12	—	—	—	31	23	58
Richmond	40	28	86	7	4	41	3	1	4	—	—	—	80	43	89
Sligo	12	11	23	2	6	8	—	—	—	—	—	—	14	14	98
Waterford	17	18	35	4	4	8	—	1	1	—	—	—	16	45	42
Total,	279	264	542	78	74	149	23	20	45	—	1	4	361	366	787

Asylums	Escaped M	F	T	Natural M	F	T	Accidental M	F	T	Total Deaths M	F	T	Total Disch./Dead/Escaped M	F	T	Remaining 31 Mar 1857 M	F	T
Armagh	—	—	—	14	4	18	—	—	—	14	4	18	57	21	90	64	71	135
Ballinasloe	1	1	2	10	0	11	—	—	—	10	0	10	3	20	67	156	142	312
Belfast	—	—	—	29	17	34	—	—	—	33	45	38	64	80	110	163	168	417
Carlow	1	—	1	3	5	8	—	—	—	3	2	7	9	30	45	107	70	—
Clonmel	—	—	—	6	2	7	—	—	—	6	2	7	6	2	70	75	16	—
Cork	—	—	—	20	17	37	—	—	—	20	17	37	64	69	190	217	216	430
Kilkenny	—	—	—	—	5	5	—	—	—	—	8	10	5	10	74	96	71	140
Killarney	—	—	—	8	6	14	—	—	—	8	11	16	10	16	74	104	178	—
Limerick	—	—	—	8	13	23	—	—	—	8	13	23	44	38	84	63	—	—
Londonderry	—	—	—	8	5	11	1	—	4	8	1	13	30	40	70	110	110	—
Maryborough	—	—	—	8	1	7	—	—	—	8	1	7	22	14	19	95	47	—
Mullingar	—	—	—	8	8	14	—	—	—	8	8	14	43	24	47	43	—	—
Omagh	—	—	—	8	5	12	—	—	—	8	8	29	31	28	68	119	713	—
Richmond	—	1	4	83	24	35	—	—	—	88	22	33	108	44	110	247	737	—
Sligo	—	—	—	8	9	11	—	—	—	8	8	12	20	17	20	80	81	—
Waterford	—	—	—	1	8	3	—	—	—	3	0	0	0	22	16	56	—	—
Total,	6	3	4	197	139	301	1	—	4	459	455	454	641	491	1,032	1,368	1,287	2,655

* Mullingar Asylum was not opened for the reception of patients till July, 1856.

+ 20 males and 60 females of this number were transferred to Killarney Asylum.

No. 2.—TABLE showing the Ages of Patients Admitted, and of those Discharged Cured, during the two Years ending 31st March, 1856, and 1857.

Asylums	ADMITTED																															DISCHARGED CURED																													
	Under 16			16 to 20			20 to 30			30 to 40			40 to 50			50 to 60			60 to 70			70 and upwards			Ages not specified			Total Males and Females Admitted			Under 16			16 to 20			20 to 30			30 to 40			40 to 50			50 to 60			60 to 70			70 and upwards			Ages not specified			Total Males and Females Discharged		
	M	F	T	M	F	T	M	F	T	M	F	T	M	F	T	M	F	T	M	F	T	M	F	T	M	F	T	M	F	T	M	F	T	M	F	T	M	F	T	M	F	T	M	F	T	M	F	T	M	F	T	M	F	T	M	F	T	M	F	T
1856																																																													
Armagh,	—	—	—	3	2	5	8	8	15	8	10	16	12	2	16	2	2	4	2	—	2	1	[illegible]	1	15	11	26	52	34	86	—	—	—	3	2	5	0	4	11	4	7	11	0	2	7	2	2	4	1	—	1	—	—	—	5	3	24	10	43
Ballinasloe,	1	—	1	2	2	9	7	6	13	2	2	4	1	3	4	3	2	7	1	1	2	—	—	—	37	17	50	36	43	40	—	—	—	3	1	4	3	4	4	5	1	—	1	2	2	[illegible]	[illegible]	[illegible]	[illegible]	[illegible]	[illegible]	[illegible]	[illegible]	[illegible]	3	8	18	10	94
Belfast,	—	—	—	7	3	10	14	16	30	16	18	27	11	12	26	14	5	16	1	—	1	1	1	—	—	—	—	65	49	114	—	1	1	5	12	1	4	6	16	4	6	13	—	2	2	[illegible]	[illegible]	[illegible]	[illegible]	[illegible]	[illegible]	[illegible]	[illegible]	[illegible]	[illegible]	[illegible]	15	20	49
Carlow,	—	—	—	2	3	5	6	7	10	4	0	13	4	8	12	2	3	4	2	1	3	—	—	—	—	—	—	23	30	53	—	—	—	1	1	6	3	2	1	3	1	2	2	3	[illegible]	[illegible]	[illegible]	[illegible]	[illegible]	[illegible]	[illegible]	[illegible]	[illegible]	[illegible]	[illegible]	9	0	18
Clonmel,	—	—	—	3	2	6	4	0	6	2	1	3	4	3	8	3	—	3	—	—	—	—	—	—	—	—	—	10	7	23	—	—	—	2	4	2	1	2	3	2	—	2	1	1	[illegible]	[illegible]	[illegible]	[illegible]	[illegible]	[illegible]	[illegible]	[illegible]	[illegible]	[illegible]	[illegible]	8	6	14
Cook,	—	—	—	4	0	10	21	25	46	14	16	26	15	5	20	8	4	8	4	2	8	—	—	—	—	—	—	60	60	120	—	1	1	5	13	10	7	17	19	10	23	4	8	13	1	[illegible]	[illegible]	[illegible]	[illegible]	[illegible]	[illegible]	[illegible]	[illegible]	[illegible]	[illegible]	43	36	69
Kilkenny,	—	—	—	1	1	2	3	3	11	1	1	2	2	11	14	2	—	8	2	2	4	—	—	—	—	—	—	13	19	10	—	—	—	3	3	1	4	1	1	1	1	—	—	—	[illegible]	[illegible]	[illegible]	[illegible]	[illegible]	[illegible]	[illegible]	[illegible]	[illegible]	1	1	7	6	13
Killarney,	—	—	—	4	19	8	21	10	4	14	1	8	4	6	1	3	1	—	2	—	1	1	1	1	—	—	—	49	16	64	—	—	—	4	3	1	6	4	4	2	1	1	1	1	[illegible]	[illegible]	[illegible]	[illegible]	[illegible]	[illegible]	[illegible]	[illegible]	[illegible]	[illegible]	4	9	11
Limerick,	—	1	11	5	17	18	8	24	14	14	28	4	18	7	8	6	15	1	2	3	—	—	—	—	—	1	1	41	66	107	—	3	2	0	6	11	0	0	15	2	0	8	—	9	3	[illegible]	[illegible]	[illegible]	[illegible]	[illegible]	[illegible]	[illegible]	[illegible]	[illegible]	37	3	40
Londonderry,	—	—	—	0	5	11	11	15	26	9	0	16	8	8	14	8	8	10	—	—	—	—	—	—	—	—	—	37	1	70	—	3	1	4	0	10	7	1	6	0	2	5	9	1	[illegible]	[illegible]	[illegible]	[illegible]	[illegible]	[illegible]	[illegible]	[illegible]	[illegible]	22	15	37
Maryborough,	—	—	—	2	1	3	18	0	19	8	8	14	0	2	8	8	2	8	3	2	4	1	1	—	—	—	—	36	18	53	—	1	—	1	1	1	5	1	5	—	—	3	1	1	[illegible]	[illegible]	[illegible]	[illegible]	[illegible]	[illegible]	[illegible]	[illegible]	[illegible]	6	4	8
Mullingar,	—	—	—	1	4	24	21	45	30	25	35	12	44	36	9	7	16	9	16	16	—	—	—	16	18	16	—	84	98	172	—	—	—	—	—	3	6	4	4	—	2	1	—	1	[illegible]	[illegible]	[illegible]	[illegible]	[illegible]	[illegible]	[illegible]	[illegible]	[illegible]	7	7	14
Omagh,	—	—	—	6	4	10	16	17	33	9	8	17	11	8	16	4	6	10	2	3	3	1	—	1	—	3	1	1	42	45	102	—	3	1	4	10	1	4	—	4	2	8	8	1	3	[illegible]	[illegible]	[illegible]	[illegible]	[illegible]	[illegible]	[illegible]	[illegible]	[illegible]	10	14	27
Richmond,	1	—	1	10	18	41	43	84	38	45	83	23	25	48	9	13	44	2	1	0	—	3	—	—	—	—	—	124	104	247	—	—	—	7	10	1	30	6	17	20	7	13	1	9	[illegible]	[illegible]	[illegible]	[illegible]	[illegible]	[illegible]	[illegible]	[illegible]	[illegible]	35	62	[illegible]
Sligo	—	—	—	3	4	7	23	8	31	15	10	01	18	16	34	6	16	19	18	8	16	2	—	2	—	—	—	78	60	178	1	1	—	2	2	14	5	4	16	4	7	1	1	1	[illegible]	[illegible]	[illegible]	[illegible]	[illegible]	[illegible]	[illegible]	[illegible]	[illegible]	11	23	[illegible]
Waterford,	1	—	1	—	4	4	3	3	7	7	1	11	9	1	7	—	1	1	1	—	—	—	—	—	—	—	—	11	35	46	1	—	1	2	2	1	4	1	4	3	7	1	1	1	[illegible]	[illegible]	[illegible]	[illegible]	[illegible]	[illegible]	[illegible]	[illegible]	[illegible]	17	18	35
Total,	3	1	4	79	94	124	236	187	427	188	181	36	196	117	363	76	56	100	10	53	3	4	8	45	98	76	33	1,201	1,182	[illegible]	1	1	228	9	17	2	01	172	66	30	190	49	40	87	21	42	43	9	110	—	2	8	817	824	316	[illegible]
1857																																																													
Armagh,	—	—	—	6	4	8	9	6	15	11	2	18	5	4	11	6	6	7	2	2	4	—	—	—	19	0	28	61	20	90	—	—	—	4	3	7	7	2	8	8	—	8	1	1	2	1	1	2	—	—	—	4	6	10	26	13	38
Ballinasloe,	—	—	—	2	1	3	6	2	10	3	6	18	4	2	6	4	—	4	—	2	2	—	—	—	30	30	66	65	46	101	—	—	—	1	1	6	2	7	2	7	2	1	3	1	2	—	1	1	—	—	—	15	27	20	16	46
Belfast,	—	—	2	6	7	11	26	13	34	27	10	46	11	14	25	8	7	16	1	3	4	—	—	1	—	—	—	76	64	143	—	—	1	4	3	6	7	12	3	15	21	6	7	18	5	0	10	—	1	1	14	27	30	36	[illegible]
Carlow,	—	—	—	1	2	3	4	11	16	2	4	6	3	6	7	2	1	6	1	4	2	—	1	—	—	—	—	18	20	42	—	—	—	2	2	1	10	11	1	1	2	1	1	2	—	—	—	—	—	—	4	15	14	4	18
Clonmel,	—	—	—	2	2	1	3	2	8	9	5	6	6	1	4	—	—	—	—	—	—	—	—	—	—	—	—	8	8	16	—	—	—	1	2	3	2	1	3	1	1	2	—	—	—	—	—	—	11	2	3	6	3	6
Cook,	—	—	—	10	6	16	25	36	56	17	11	28	24	8	33	7	3	14	2	3	6	2	—	2	—	—	—	66	73	126	—	1	2	11	16	27	6	16	13	5	6	11	6	1	7	3	1	4	1	—	1	10	27	43	30	[illegible]
Kilkenny,	—	—	—	2	2	8	10	13	2	4	6	1	2	3	—	2	2	—	—	—	—	—	—	—	—	—	—	3	30	23	—	—	—	3	1	7	1	—	1	4	4	—	—	—	—	1	1	—	—	—	5	8	0	14	[illegible]
Killarney,	—	—	—	4	2	8	11	0	1	8	5	18	3	4	7	1	6	5	1	—	1	1	1	2	—	—	—	30	20	49	—	1	1	2	1	2	4	2	6	4	2	8	4	2	8	—	—	—	—	—	—	6	4	10
Limerick,	1	2	8	4	7	18	8	26	17	9	26	6	7	18	—	7	7	4	1	2	1	1	2	—	—	—	53	35	87	—	—	4	4	5	9	3	4	16	5	6	7	1	6	3	5	6	22	19	33
Londonderry,	—	—	—	8	3	5	16	15	31	0	10	16	6	10	16	3	8	6	1	2	6	—	—	—	—	—	—	39	45	78	—	—	6	6	13	10	18	26	6	6	4	3	1	21	19	[illegible]
Maryborough,	1	—	1	2	2	2	6	6	6	6	3	12	6	8	7	3	3	—	8	—	—	—	26	11	19	—	—	—	1	1	1	1	1	—	1	1	1	1	1	1	7
Mullingar,	—	—	—	7	3	10	17	12	29	18	8	28	0	6	17	4	10	11	1	8	8	—	1	41	44	85	—	—	—	2	1	7	4	8	7	4	8	2	13	14	90
Omagh,	—	—	—	5	2	7	18	12	25	18	7	18	8	16	16	3	5	6	0	2	11	2	2	—	50	48	98	11	2	2	1	3	11	3	6	2	4	20	14	54
Richmond,	—	—	—	13	0	22	26	17	43	31	11	38	14	8	25	5	8	8	5	1	8	—	1	87	81	138	1	—	118	14	8	22	9	18	10	1	10	6	28	65
Sligo,	—	—	—	3	3	0	11	8	10	6	4	12	6	5	11	2	3	7	2	2	4	—	—	72	27	61	—	—	2	2	5	5	6	5	1	1	4	19	11	23
Waterford,	—	—	—	4	—	4	6	11	14	4	6	6	4	6	10	4	4	8	1	1	4	—	—	90	28	48	—	—	8	3	4	1	6	6	10	17	18	35
Total,	1	1	2	88	51	130	194	163	357	174	130	343	113	97	216	58	63	115	25	36	55	5	13	46	46	94	665	563	1,280	1	—	136	36	71	90	96	186	63	84	126	43	30	61	25	18	44	9	8	16	1	2	320	737	272	264	[illegible]

No 3—Table shewing the duration of Disease previous to admission in those discharged Cured, during the two Years ending 31st March, 1856, and 1857

Asylums	Months												Years																						Not specified			Total Males and Females		
	Under 1			3			6			9			1			2			3			4			5			6			9			10 and upwards								
	M	F	T	M	F	T	M	F	T	M	F	T	M	F	T	M	F	T	M	F	T	M	F	T	M	F	T	M	F	T	M	F	T	M	F	T	M	F	T	M	F	T
1856																																										
Armagh,	8	9	17	8	4	10	4	5	9	2	1	3	1	—	1	—	—	—	—	—	—	—	—	—	—	—	—	—	—	—	—	—	—	—	—	—	3	—	3	24	16	40
Ballinasloe,	8	8	12	8	1	4	1	2	3	1	—	1	—	—	—	2	—	2	—	—	—	—	1	1	—	—	—	—	—	—	—	1	1	—	—	—	3	5	12	38	16	54
Belfast,	5	10	15	8	10	16	7	9	11	—	4	4	1	—	1	1	1	2	1	1	2	—	1	1	—	1	1	1	—	1	1	1	1	—	—	1	1	—	—	19	30	49
Carlow,	—	—	—	1	3	4	3	3	4	1	1	2	—	1	1	1	1	2	—	1	1	—	—	—	—	—	—	—	—	—	1	—	1	1	1	1	—	—	—	9	9	18
Clonmel,	2	—	2	3	1	1	2	3	4	1	1	2	—	2	1	1	—	1	—	—	—	—	—	—	—	—	—	—	—	—	—	1	1	1	1	1	—	—	—	8	6	14
Cork,	14	16	30	7	7	14	1	3	3	1	1	1	—	1	1	1	1	2	1	—	1	—	1	1	—	—	—	—	—	—	—	—	—	—	—	—	10	7	17	33	47	80
Kilkenny,	—	2	2	1	2	—	—	—	—	1	—	1	—	1	1	1	1	—	—	—	—	1	1	—	—	—	—	—	—	—	1	—	1	—	—	—	4	—	4	7	6	13
Killarney,	1	2	3	1	3	4	—	—	—	—	—	—	—	—	—	—	—	—	—	—	—	1	—	1	—	1	1	—	—	—	1	—	1	—	—	—	1	—	1	4	7	11
Limerick,	7	4	11	3	3	6	—	—	—	—	2	1	1	—	3	1	1	1	—	—	—	—	—	—	1	1	1	—	—	—	1	—	1	—	—	—	8	10	19	17	23	40
Londonderry,	2	2	4	6	4	10	3	1	5	3	2	2	3	1	4	4	5	4	1	1	3	1	—	1	—	—	—	—	—	—	—	—	—	—	—	—	—	—	—	22	15	37
Maryborough,	—	—	—	3	1	1	—	—	—	—	—	—	1	—	1	—	1	1	—	1	1	—	—	—	—	—	—	—	—	—	—	—	—	—	—	—	5	—	5	6	5	11
Mullingar,	1	—	1	1	1	4	2	—	2	—	—	—	—	—	—	—	—	—	—	—	—	—	1	1	—	—	—	—	—	—	—	—	—	—	—	—	—	—	—	7	7	14
Omagh,	3	3	6	3	8	16	1	4	9	1	—	3	2	—	2	1	—	1	1	—	1	—	—	1	2	1	3	—	—	—	1	—	1	—	—	—	—	—	—	11	22	33
Richmond,	12	10	22	11	17	22	7	12	23	3	3	5	1	5	4	1	1	2	1	1	1	—	—	—	1	1	2	1	1	2	1	1	1	—	—	—	—	—	—	31	36	67
Sligo,	2	1	3	—	3	2	2	1	1	—	1	1	—	2	1	—	—	—	—	1	1	—	—	—	—	—	—	—	—	—	—	—	—	—	—	—	—	—	—	6	6	12
Waterford,	7	4	11	—	2	2	2	1	1	—	1	1	—	—	—	—	2	2	2	2	2	1	1	2	1	1	2	—	—	—	1	—	1	—	—	—	—	—	—	11	13	24
Total,	70	71	141	39	64	128	30	44	74	11	15	26	12	8	20	8	12	20	0	9	19	3	2	5	5	4	9	—	3	3	3	2	4	—	—	—	37	29	63	276	244	520
1857																																										
Armagh,	9	4	13	3	3	4	4	1	4	2	1	7	3	1	4	2	1	3	1	2	3	1	1	1	—	—	—	—	—	1	—	—	—	—	—	—	—	4	8	25	13	38
Ballinasloe,	3	2	5	3	1	4	3	2	5	1	2	3	3	1	4	2	1	3	1	2	3	1	1	1	—	1	1	—	—	—	—	—	—	—	—	—	2	10	—	20	18	45
Belfast,	8	11	19	8	13	22	8	7	13	1	2	5	1	1	2	4	4	8	1	2	3	1	1	—	1	1	—	—	—	—	—	—	—	2	10	—	27	27	54
Carlow,	1	4	3	1	4	3	2	1	3	—	1	1	—	1	1	1	—	1	1	—	1	—	1	1	—	1	1	—	—	—	—	—	—	—	—	—	—	3	3	4	11	13
Clonmel,	1	1	2	1	1	1	1	1	2	—	1	1	1	—	1	—	1	1	1	—	1	—	1	1	—	—	—	—	—	—	—	—	—	—	—	—	4	4	8
Cork,	11	19	30	10	8	18	3	1	4	1	1	1	1	—	1	—	1	1	1	1	2	1	1	1	—	1	1	—	—	—	—	—	—	—	—	—	11	10	18	32	36	68
Kilkenny,	—	2	2	—	3	3	3	1	2	2	—	2	—	—	—	—	—	—	1	1	2	1	1	—	—	—	—	—	—	—	—	—	—	—	—	—	4	—	—	0	14	14
Killarney,	1	1	4	1	1	2	2	2	3	—	2	1	—	—	—	1	1	—	—	—	—	—	—	1	—	1	—	—	—	—	1	1	—	—	—	—	—	—	—	6	4	13
Limerick,	4	3	7	—	—	—	12	10	4	—	4	4	1	1	1	1	1	2	1	2	5	1	1	1	—	1	1	1	1	1	1	—	1	—	1	—	12	8	18	21	18	38
Londonderry,	—	—	—	3	14	—	4	12	19	—	4	4	3	1	6	2	1	3	1	2	5	1	—	1	1	1	—	—	—	—	—	—	—	—	—	—	—	2	—	21	27	48
Maryborough,	—	—	—	3	1	3	3	—	3	9	4	10	3	—	1	1	—	1	—	—	—	—	2	2	—	—	—	—	—	—	—	—	—	—	—	—	—	—	—	2	1	3
Mullingar,	—	—	—	3	3	0	4	4	8	—	4	10	3	—	1	1	—	1	—	—	—	—	2	2	—	—	—	1	1	—	2	1	3	1	—	—	—	1	—	13	11	30
Omagh,	4	4	8	3	3	0	4	4	8	—	4	10	1	—	1	1	—	1	—	—	—	—	2	2	—	1	1	—	—	—	2	—	2	3	—	3	—	1	1	20	12	34
Richmond,	11	7	18	12	11	23	4	5	9	4	2	3	3	1	4	2	1	3	1	1	2	—	—	—	—	1	1	1	1	2	—	—	—	—	—	—	1	1	1	40	28	68
Sligo,	4	4	8	3	1	4	3	2	3	—	3	3	—	—	—	—	1	1	—	—	1	1	—	—	—	—	—	—	—	—	—	—	—	—	—	—	1	1	1	12	11	23
Waterford,	7	6	13	4	6	—	3	2	2	—	3	1	2	—	4	2	2	4	1	—	1	—	—	1	—	—	—	—	—	—	1	1	—	—	—	—	1	1	1	17	18	35
Total,	64	66	130	65	58	118	31	44	78	28	23	39	20	10	30	18	11	29	7	9	15	4	9	5	2	4	8	2	1	3	4	—	4	6	3	—	14	36	88	259	384	842

No. 4.—TABLE showing the Length of Residence in Asylums, of those discharged Cured and Improved, during the two Years ended 31st March, 1857.

CURED. — Months.

Asylums. 1856.	Under 2. M.	F.	T.	Under 4. M.	F.	T.	Under 6. M.	F.	T.	Under 8. M.	F.	T.	Under 12. M.	F.	T.	Under 18. M.	F.	T.
Armagh,	6	3	8	8	0	13	7	2	5	1	3	4	2	1	7	2	–	2
Ballinasloe,	–	2	2	3	1	1	1	2	3	3	3	6	3	3	6	1	3	4
Belfast,	–	2	4	6	0	12	4	8	12	4	7	7	2	3	5	1	3	7
Carlow,	1	–	1	2	1	3	3	2	5	1	2	7	1	2	3	–	1	1
Clonmel,	–	–	–	4	1	7	–	2	2	1	2	3	1	–	1	1	1	2
Cork,	8	4	12	1	7	14	7	6	13	2	5	1	7	6	9	–	4	4
Kilkenny,	–	–		2	1	3	–	1	1	1	2	6	1	1	2	1	–	2
Killarney,	2	1	4	1	1	2	–	2	2	–	–	–	2	3	4	–	1	1
Limerick,	7	6	13	3	6	5	3	2	5	2		4	2	2	4	–	3	3
Londonderry,	3	–	3	4	2	8	4	7	1	0	4	8	6	4	10	–	–	–
Maryborough,	–	2	2	1	1	2	–	–	–	3	–	3	–	–	–	1		1
Mullingar,	1	–	1	3	1	4	4	0	9	–		–	–	–	–	–		–
Omagh,	6	0	6	6	1	4	2	6	8	–	2	3	2	1	3	2	2	4
Richmond,	6	10	16	7	11	18	7	12	12	4	6	9	6	2	7	2	5	1
Sligo,	1	4	6	2	1	3	5	3	8	–		–	1	1	2	–	–	–
Waterford,	6	8	8	8	1	4	6	3	6	2	1	4		–	–	–	1	1
Total,	44	40	62	63	46	104	44	61	101	23	34	56	31	27	58	11	23	34

CURED. — Years.

Asylums. 1856.	Under 2. M.	F.	T.	Under 3. M.	F.	T.	Under 4. M.	F.	T.	Under 5. M.	F.	T.	Under 6. M.	F.	T.	Under 7. M.	F.	T.	Under 8. M.	F.	T.	Under 9. M.	F.	T.	Under 10. M.	F.	T.	10 & upwards. M.	F.	T.	Total Discharged Cured. M.	F.	T.
Armagh,		2	1					–	–	–			–	–		–		–	–	–	–	–	–		–	–		–	–	–	24	16	40
Ballinasloe,	–		–	2		2	1	–	1	1	–	1		–	–		–	–	–	–	–	–	–	–	–	–	–	–	–	–	18	16	34
Belfast,	–		–	1	1	4	1	1	4	–	–		–	1	1	–	–	–	–	1	1	–	–	–	–	–	–	–	–	–	10	30	40
Carlow,		1	1	1	–	1	–	–		–	–	–		–	–		–	–	–	–	–	–	–	–	–	–	–	–	–	–	9	6	18
Clonmel,	1	–	1	–	–	–	–	–	–	–	–		–	–		–	–	–	–	–	–	–	–	–	–	–	–	–	–	–	8	6	14
Cork,	1	2	5	–	1	1	1	1	2	1		1	1	–	1	–	–	–	–	–	–	–	–	–	–	–	–	–	–	–	19	56	75
Kilkenny,	–	–		2	1	3	–	–	–	–	–	–	–	–	–	–	–	–	–	–	–	–	–	–	–	–	–	–	–	–	7	6	13
Killarney,	–			–	–	–	–	–	–	–	–	–	–	–	–	–	–	–	–	–	–	–	–	–	–	–	–	–	–	–	4	1	11
Limerick,		1	1		4	4	–	–	–	–	–	–	–	–	–	1	1	–	–	–	–	–	–	–	–	–	–	–	–	–	15	23	40
Londonderry,	–	–	–	–		–	–	–	–	–	2	2	–	–	–	–	–	–	–	–	–	–	–	–	–	–	–	–	–	–	22	15	37
Maryborough,	–	1	1	–	–		–	–	–	–	–	–	–	–	–	–	–	–	–	–	–	–	–	–	–	–	–	–	–	–	5	4	8
Mullingar,	–	–	–	–	–	–	–	–	–	–	–	–	–	–	–	–	–	–	–	–	–	–	–	–	–	–	–	–	–	–	7	7	14
Omagh,	1	–	1	3	2	5	–			–	–	–	–	–	–	–	–	–	–	–	–	–	–	–	–	–	–	–	–	–	10	14	33
Richmond,	2	2		1	3	4		1	1	1		1	–	–	–	–	–	–	–	–	–	–	–	–	–	–	–	–	–	–	35	52	87
Sligo,	–	–	–	–	–	–	–	–	–	–	–	–	–	–	–	–	–	–	–	–	–	–	–	–	–	–	–	–	–	–	6	0	18
Waterford,	1	–	1	–	2	2	–		–	–	3	2	–	–	–	–	–	–	–	–	–	–	–	–	–	–	–	–	–	–	11	13	24
Total,	8	8	18	10	14	24	3	6	9	3	4	7	1	1	2	–	1	1	–	1	1	–	–	–	–	–	–	–	–	–	247	164	510

IMPROVED. — Months.

Asylums. 1856.	Under 2. M.	F.	T.	Under 4. M.	F.	T.	Under 6. M.	F.	T.	Under 8. M.	F.	T.	Under 12. M.	F.	T.	Under 18. M.	F.	T.
Armagh,	8	1	3	3	3	6	4	6	6	2	1	1	2	–	4	–	–	
Ballinasloe,		–		–	–	–	–			–		–	–		–	–	–	
Belfast,	1	1	2	–	–	–	–	1	1	1	2	3	1	1	2	–	3	3
Carlow,	2	1	3	2	–	2			–	–	–	–	–	1	1	1	1	2
Clonmel,	–	–	–	–			–	–	–		–	–	–	–	–		–	
Cork,	1	–	1	–	1	1	–		–	1	1	8	–	–	–	1		1
Kilkenny,	1		1	–	–	–	–	–		–	–		–		–	1	–	1
Killarney,	1	1	2	1	–	1	–	–	–	–	–	–	2	–	2	2	2	4
Limerick,	6	6	12	5	2	7	2	1	3	–	1	1	2		3	–	–	
Londonderry,	–	1	1	–	3	3	–		–	1		1	2	5	7	–	–	
Maryborough,				2	–	8	1		1	–	1	1	1	2	7	–		
Mullingar,	–	1	1	–	–	–		1	1	–	–	–	–	–		–		–
Omagh,	–	3	3	–	2	2	3	1	4	2	–	2	–	0	2		–	–
Richmond,	1	3	4	1	–	1	1	1	2	1	–	1		2	3	1	1	2
Sligo,	1	–	1	4	2	6	1	1	2	–	–	–		–	–		–	–
Waterford,	–	1	1	–	1	1	–	–	–	–	–	–	–	1	1	1	1	3
Total	16	10	33	13	14	32	12	8	20	3	8	11	16	14	24	1	5	15

IMPROVED. — Years.

Asylums. 1856.	Under 2. M.	F.	T.	Under 3. M.	F.	T.	Under 4. M.	F.	T.	Under 5. M.	F.	T.	Under 6. M.	F.	T.	Under 7. M.	F.	T.	Under 8. M.	F.	T.	Under 9. M.	F.	T.	Under 10. M.	F.	T.	10 & upwards. M.	F.	T.	Total Discharged Improved. M.	F.	T.	Total Discharged Cured and Improved. M.	F.	T.
Armagh,	–	–		–	–		–	–	–	–	–	–		–		–		–	–		–	–	–		–	–	–	–		–	18	7	20	31	23	60
Ballinasloe,	–	–	–	–	–		–	–	–	–	–	–	–	–	–	–	–	–	–	–	–	–	–	–	–	–	–	–	–	–	–			18	16	34
Belfast,	–	1	1	–	–	–	1	–	1	–	–	–	–	–	–	–	–	–	–	–	–	–	–	–	–	–	–	–	–	–	5	9	14	24	38	63
Carlow,	–	1	1	–	–	–	–	–	–	–	–	–	–	–	–	–	–	–	–	–	–	–	–	–	–	–	–	1	–	1	5	1	6	14	13	27
Clonmel,	–	–	–	–	–	–	–	–	–	–	–	–	–	–	–	–	–	–	–	–	–	–	–	–	–	–	–	–	–	–	1	–	1	9	6	15
Cork,	1	–	1	1	1	2	–		–	–	–	–	–	1	1		–	–	–	–	–	–	–	–	–	–	–	–	–	–	5	4	9	38	40	78
Kilkenny,	1		1	1	–	1	–	–	–	–	–	–	–	–	–	–	–	–	–	–	–	–	–	–	–	–	–	–	–	–	4	–	4	11	6	17
Killarney,	–	–	–	–	1	1	–	–	–	–	–	–	–	–	–	–	–	–	–	–	–	–	–	–	–	–	–	–	–	–	6	4	10	10	11	21
Limerick,	2	1	3	1	1	2	–	–	–	–	–	–	–	–	–	–	–	–	–	–	–	–	–	–	–	–	–	–	–	–	18	12	30	37	45	[illegible]
Londonderry,	1	1	2	–	–	–	–	–	–	1	–	1	–	–	–	–	–	–	–	–	–	–	–	–	–	1	1	–	–	–	5	11	16	27	26	53
Maryborough,	–	–	–	–	–	–	–	–	–	–	–	–	–	–	–	–	–	–	–	–	–	–	–	–	–	–	–	–	–	–	4	3	7	9	7	16
Mullingar,	–	–	–	–	–	–	–	–	–	–	–	–	–	–	–	–	–	–	–	–	–	–	–	–	–	–	–	–	–	–	–	2	2	1	6	10
Omagh,	–	–	–	–	1	1	–	–	–	–	–	–	–	–	–	–	–	–	–	–	–	–	–	–	–	–	–	–	–	–	5	6	11	24	23	47
Richmond,	–	1	1	–	–	–	–	–	–	–	–	–	–	–	–	–	–	–	–	–	–	–	–	–	–	–	–	–	–	–	6	8	13	40	60	100
Sligo,	–	–	–	2	–	2	–	–	–	–	–	–	–	–	–	–	–	–	–	–	–	–	–	–	–	–	–	–	–	–	8	3	11	17	12	29
Waterford,	–	1	1	–	–	–		2	2	–	–	–	–	1	1	–	–	–	–	–	–	–	–	–	–	–	–	–	–	–	1	6	6	16	22	38
Total	5	6	11	6	4	9	1	2	3	1		1	–	2	2	–	–	–	–	[illegible]	[illegible]	[illegible]	[illegible]	[illegible]	[illegible]	[illegible]	[illegible]	[illegible]	[illegible]	[illegible]	[illegible]	[illegible]	[illegible]	[illegible]	[illegible]	[illegible]

No. 4.—Table showing the Length of Residence in Asylums, of those discharged Cured and Improved, during the two Years ended 31st March, 1857—*continued*.

CURED.

Asylums.	Months. Under 1.			Under 3			Under 6.			Under 9.			Under 12.			Under 18		
1857	M.	F.	T.	M.	F.	T.	M.	F.	T.	M.	F.	T.	M.	F.	T.	M.	F.	T.
Armagh,	10	2	13	7	2	9	2	2	4	1	—	1	—	—	—	1	1	2
Ballinasloe,	2	2	4	3	2	5	4	4	8	2	3	5	9	5	14	1	1	2
Belfast,	2	5	7	6	10	16	5	11	16	4	6	10	5	2	7	5	1	6
Carlow,	1	1	2	—	4	4	1	3	4	1	2	3	—	3	3	1	—	1
Clonmel,	—	1	1	1	—	1	1	1	2	—	—	—	1	1	2	1	1	2
Cork,	4	7	11	7	6	13	8	6	14	3	3	6	4	7	11	—	3	3
Kilkenny,	—	—	—		1	1	1	1	2	—	—		3	4	7	1	3	4
Killarney,	2	—	2	—	1	1	—	—	—	—	1	1	2	1	3	—	1	1
Limerick,	7	3	10	1	—	1	2	2	1	5	—	5	2	2	4	1	2	3
Londonderry,	3	3	6	2	1	3	2	1	3	4	2	6	1	13	14	1	2	3
Maryborough,	—	—	—	1	—	1	1	1	2	—	—	—	—	—	—			
Mullingar,	2	1	3	1	2	3	2	3	5	6	4	10	1	1	2	1	—	1
Omagh,	3	2	5	4	3	7	2	5	7	3	1	1	3	4	7	1	—	1
Richmond,	6	2	8	6	10	16	11	6	16	4	4	8	5	6	11	1	4	5
Sligo,	3	1	4	3	—	6	3	2	5	3	1	5	1	3	4			
Waterford,	2	3	5	6	2	7	—	3	3	2	2	1	1	3	1	—	1	1
Total	46	33	[illegible]	50	45	[illegible]	43	62	[illegible]	35	28	63	38	58	104	15	20	35

Asylums.	Years. Under 2.			Under 3			Under 4.			Under 5.			Under 6.			Under 7			Under 8.			Under 9.			Under 10.			10 & upwards.			Total Discharged Cured.		
1857	M.	F.	T.	M.	F.	T.	M.	F.	T.	M.	F.	T.	M.	F.	T.	M.	F.	T.	M.	F.	T.	M.	F.	T.	M.	F.	T.	M.	F.	T.	M.	F.	T.
Armagh,	—	—	—	—		—			—	—	—	—	—	—	—	—		—			—		—	—	—	—	—	—	—	—	29	13	42
Ballinasloe,	4	—	3	2	1	3	—	—	—	—	1	1	—						—				—	—	—	—	—	—	—	—	26	10	36
Belfast,	—	—	—	—	1	1	—	—			1	1		1	1	—	—	—	—	1	1	—	—	—						—	21	39	60
Carlow,	—	—	—	—	—	—		1	1	—	—	—	—	—	—	—		—	—	—			—	—	—		—		—		4	14	18
Clonmel,	—	—	—	—				—	—	—	—	—	—	—					—				—	—	—	—	—	—	—	—	4	4	8
Cork,	4	—	4	2	1	3	1		1	—	—	—	—	—	—	1	1	2	—	—		—	—	—	1	1	2			—	34	31	65
Kilkenny,	—	—			—	—	—	—	—	—	—	—	—	—					—	—			—	—	—	—	—	—	—	—	5	9	14
Killarney,	1	—	1	—	—			1	1	—	—	—	—	—	—	—	—	—	—	—	—	—	—	—	—		—	—			9	1	10
Limerick,	2	—	2	1	1	2	1		1	—	1	1	—	1	1	—	—	—	—	—	—	—	—	—		1	1		—	—	22	14	36
Londonderry,	2	1	3	1	1	2	2	—	2	—	—	—	1	—	1	—			—	—		—	—	—	—	—	—	—	—	—	21	27	48
Maryborough,	—	—	—	—	—				—	—	—	—	—	—	—	—	—	—	—	—	—	—	—	—	—		—	—	—	—	2	1	3
Mullingar,	—	—			—	—	—	—	—	—	—	—	—	—	—		—			—	—		—	—	—	—	—	—	—	—	15	11	26
Omagh,		—	—	1	—	1	1	1	2								—		—	—	—	—	—			—	—	—	—	—	20	14	34
Richmond,	—	—		3	—	3	—	—	—	—	—	—	—	—	—	—	—	—	—	—	—	—	—	—	—	—	—	—	—		40	26	66
Sligo,		—	—	—	—			—	—			—	—			—	—	—	—	—	—	—					—	—	—	—	12	11	23
Waterford,		2	3	5	2	7	1	—	1	1	—	1	—	—	—	—								—	—	—	—	—	—	—	17	18	35
Total	14	3	16	15	—	[illegible]		2	8	1	1	2	1	1	2	1	1		—	1	1	—	—	—	1	1	3	—	—	—	[illegible]	244	515

IMPROVED.

Asylums.	Months. Under 2.			Under 4.			Under 6.			Under 9.			Under 12.			Under 18.		
1857	M.	F.	T.	M.	F.	T.	M.	F.	T.	M.	F.	T.	M.	F.	T.	M.	F.	T.
Armagh,	4	2	6	5	1	6	3	1	4	—		—	—		—	—	—	—
Ballinasloe,	—	1	1			—	—	—	—	—	—	—	—	—	—	—	—	
Belfast,	1	—	1	2	1	3	1	—	1	1	1	2	2	—	2		2	2
Carlow,	—	1	1		1	2	—	1	1	—	1	1	1	5	4	—	1	1
Clonmel,	—	—	—	—	—	—	—								—	—	—	—
Cork,	3	1	4	4	2	6	—	1	1		2	2	2	1	3	—	—	—
Kilkenny,	—	1	1	—	—	—	—			—	—	—	—	—	—			—
Killarney,	1	1	2	—	—	—		—	—	1	—	1	—	1	1		1	1
Limerick,	6	2	8	—	1	1	5	1	3	—	—	—	—	1	1	—	1	1
Londonderry,	—	—	—	—	—	—		—	—	—	—	—	—	—	—			
Maryborough,	3	—	3	2		5	5	—	6	1	—	1	—	—				
Mullingar,	1	—	1	—	1	1		—	—	—	1	1	—	—	—		—	—
Omagh,	1	1	2	1	1	2	1		1	—	1	1	2	—	2	1	—	1
Richmond,	1		1	—	—	—	—	1	1		—	—	2	—	2	2	1	3
Sligo,	—	1	1	2	2	4	—	—	—		—	—	—	—		—	—	
Waterford,	1	—	1	—	2	2		1	1	—	—	—	1	—	2	—		—
Total,	23	11	33	16	13	29	8	6	14	3	6	6	10	5	15	3	2	6

Asylums.	Years. Under 2.			Under 3.			Under 4.			Under 5.			Under 6.			Under 7			Under 8.			Under 9.			Under 10.			10 & upwards.			Total Discharged Improved.			Total Discharged Cured and Improved.		
1857	M.	F.	T.	M.	F.	T.	M.	F.	T.	M.	F.	T.	M.	F.	T.	M.	F.	T.	M.	F.	T.	M.	F.	T.	M.	F.	T.	M.	F.	T.	M.	F.	T.	M.	F.	T.
Armagh,	—	—	—			—	—	—	—		—		—	—	—	—		—	—							—	—	—	—		11	4	15	31	17	48
Ballinasloe,	—	—	—	—	—	—	—	—	—	—	—	—		—	—	—	—	—	—	—	—	—	—	—	—	—	—		—	—	—	1	1	26	20	46
Belfast,		—	—	1	1	2	1		1	—		—		—	—	—	—	—	—	1	1	—	—	—	—	—	—	—	—	—	9	6	15	65	16	81
Carlow,	—	1	1	—	1	1	—	—	—	—	—	—	—	—	—	—	—	—	—	—		—	—		—	—	—	—	—	—	1	10	11	5	24	29
Clonmel,	—	—	—	—	—	—	—	—	—	—	—	—	—	—	—	—	—																—	4	4	8
Cork,	1	2	3	—		—	—	1	1	—	—	—	—	—					—						—	—	—	—	—		10	10	20	44	44	88
Kilkenny,					—	—	—			—					—	—	—	—	—	—	—	—	—	—							—	1	1	5	10	15
Killarney,					—	—									—		—	—	—	—	—	—	—	—					—	—	2	3	5	[illegible]	[illegible]	[illegible]
Limerick,	—			1	1	2	1	—	1	—			1		1	—	—	—	—	—	—	—	—	—	—	1	1		—	—	11	8	19	33	21	54
Londonderry,	1	2	3		—			1	1	1	1	2			—	—	1	1	—	—	—	—	—								2	5	7	23	32	55
Maryborough,	—	1	1	—	1	1	1	—	1	—	—	—	1	—	1	—	2	2	—							1	1		1	—	10	7	17	12	8	20
Mullingar,	—	—	—	—	—	—	—	—	—	—	—	—	—	—	—	—	—				—	—	—	—	—	—	—	—	—	—	1	2	3	16	16	32
Omagh,	1	—	1	—	—	—	—	—		—	—	—						—	—	—	—	—	—	—	—	—	—	—	—	—	7	3	10	27	17	44
Richmond,	—	1	1	1		1	1	1	2	—	—	—	—	—	—	—	—	—			—	—	—	—							7	4	11	47	32	79
Sligo,	—	—	—	—			—	—	—				—	—	—	—	—		—	—	—	—	—	—	—	—	—	—	—		2	1	3	14	11	25
Waterford,	—	—	—	—	1	1	—		—	—	—	—	—	—	—	—	—	—	—	—	—	—	—	—	—	—	—	—	—		2	4	6	19	22	41
Total,	3	7	10	3	5	8	4	3	7	1	1	2	2	—	2	—	3	3	—	1	1	—	—	—	—	2	2	—	2	2	78	71	149	356	333	[illegible]

THE

EIGHTH REPORT

ON THE

DISTRICT, CRIMINAL, AND PRIVATE LUNATIC ASYLUMS

IN IRELAND:

WITH APPENDICES.

Presented to both Houses of Parliament by Command of Her Majesty.

DUBLIN:
PRINTED BY ALEX. THOM AND SONS, 87, ABBEY-STREET,
FOR HER MAJESTY'S STATIONERY OFFICE.

1857.

CONTENTS.

EIGHTH REPORT

ON THE

DISTRICT, CRIMINAL, AND PRIVATE LUNATIC ASYLUMS

IN IRELAND.

TO HIS EXCELLENCY GEORGE WILLIAM FREDERICK, EARL OF CARLISLE, K.G., LORD LIEUTENANT-GENERAL AND GENERAL GOVERNOR OF IRELAND.

MAY IT PLEASE YOUR EXCELLENCY,

In addition to our Annual Report on the state of licensed houses for the reception of insane patients, under the provisions of the 5 & 6 Vic., cap. 123, addressed to your Excellency and the Lord Chancellor in the beginning of the present year, we have now the honour to submit our Eighth General or Parliamentary Report on the condition of public and private asylums in Ireland, and on that of the Central Institution at Dundrum for criminal lunatics. *Introductory.*

The state of the law connected with our department having been discussed by us from time to time and pressed on the attention of the Legislature in previous Reports, but particularly in our last, from a sense of its deficiencies, and the consequent necessity of certain amendments, arrived at during a long and intimate experience of its working; and a Commission being now issued under the authority of a Royal Warrant, for the purpose of examining into the whole subject of lunacy in Ireland, and of the Statutes by which Asylums are regulated; we shall not allude to this topic, further than to express our confidence in the result, which we anticipate will be satisfactory to the country and advantageous to the public service, both from the manner in which the Commission has been formed and the ability and experience of its members. We may here, however, observe, that looking to the extended scope of the Commission, the powers with which it is invested, and the inquiries that had already been commenced, we entertained some hesitation as to whether it might not be more advisable to leave the function of reporting upon the lunatic institutions of Ireland on the present occasion in such able and efficient hands, restricting ourselves to the duties of inspection, and to the varied business of an office, which involves a correspondence of over 7,000 registered letters in the year, believing that the Commissioners would furnish ample information to your Excellency and to Parliament on the subject: but having communicated our sentiments to the executive, all doubt as to the propriety of the course we should adopt was at once removed.

Before entering on any general observations, or on statistical details, having reference, within the last two years, to the department over which we are placed, as the question of expenditure in regard to District Asylums is one that occupies considerable attention, it may not be altogether inappropriate to give a brief account of them for the purpose of showing the progressive development of institutions for the care and maintenance of the insane poor of Ireland, and the expenses which have already devolved, or which may devolve on the public at large in connexion with them.

As the present system of lunatic accommodation may be said to have commenced with the 55 Geo. III., cap. 107, when the Richmond Asylum was built and furnished by Government, at a cost of £75,000, to serve as a general hospital for the insane, and to be supported by parliamentary grants—it will be unnecessary to revert to those institutions which had been connected with Houses of Industry, from the erection of St. Patrick's or Swift's Hospital, in 1756, up to the beginning of the present century, they having virtually ceased to exist. *Origin of present system of accommodation for Lunatics.*

In 1817, a Select Committee of the House of Commons was appointed to consider the

DISTRICT LUNATIC ASYLUMS.

expediency of making a general provision for the lunatic poor, as, with the exception of the Richmond and one establishment in Cork, there was not accommodation made for more than 130 lunatics throughout all Ireland. This Committee reported, that the only effectual mode of relief would be found in the division of the country into districts, consisting of one or more counties, and the erection in each so formed district of an asylum capable of containing from 120 to 150 lunatics. The proceedings of this Committee resulted in the 57 Geo. III., since which we find a series of no less than seventeen enactments, ending with the 19 & 20 Vic., cap. 99.

Erection of first District Asylums.

The most important of them in a practical point of view was the 1st and 2nd Geo. IV, c. 33, under which nine public institutions were successively established, namely, at Armagh, Belfast, Londonderry, Carlow, Ballinasloe, Limerick, Clonmel, Maryborough, and Waterford, by a Board of General Control and Superintendence formed of Commissioners specially appointed by the Lord Lieutenant.

These asylums, expected to be sufficient for the general exigencies of the country, and built for an aggregate of 980 patients, at a cost of £209,085 0s. 4d., were soon found too limited, so much so that in the course of a few years, by interior re-arrangements and appropriations, they were occupied by 1,930 inmates, or about twice the number for which they had been constructed. With the growing facilities afforded for the treatment of mental disease in its acute forms, and the refuge which it was felt that asylums extended to those long affected with insanity, the numerous cases hitherto latent among the lower classes attracted notice, and the demand upon these institutions increased so steadily that it became necessary to reform districts by an Act passed in the year 1826 ; and, indepen-

Asylums subsequently erected.

dently of certain structural enlargements from time to time of the existing buildings, (8 and 9 Vic., c. 107), and the substitution of a new and more spacious establishment at Cork, in place of the old one previously connected with the House of Industry, to erect asylums at Kilkenny, Killarney, Omagh, Sligo, Dublin, and Mullingar, for a total of 1,400 lunatics.

The asylums just named were commenced after the Commissioners for General Control and Correspondence had been superseded, and their powers in regard to the erection of Asylums in Ireland transferred to the Board of Works, by which body all subsequent expenditure therewith connected, up to the Bill of last session, has been regulated.

We have observed that the nine original asylums had, in a short time, nearly doubled their number of patients, the necessary accommodation being effected without any important additions. And as the chief expense was incurred for furniture, bedding, &c., and took place gradually, to meet growing requirements, the sums so laid out merged in the current quarterly expenditure, and cannot now be accurately detailed.

Cost of Land, Erection, Furniture, and Fittings.

The following will, however, be found a correct statement of the sums specially expended, with the sanction of Government, in the purchase of land, and in the erection and furnishing of district asylums, as well as in structural additions approved by the Privy Council.

Armagh.

Taking these various institutions in succession, according to the date of their establishment, we find the Armagh Asylum was opened in 1825, for 104 patients. Subsequently, by a modification of internal arrangements, room was provided for thirty more. The total cost, amounting to £21,284, and which has been repaid by fourteen equal annual instalments, was assessed as follows on the then counties of the district :—Armagh, £6,018; Monaghan, £5,325; Fermanagh, £3,993; Cavan, £5,946.

Limerick.

The Limerick Asylum came into operation in 1827, for the counties of Limerick, Clare, and Kerry, with accommodation for 150, at a cost of £30,200. Additions were shortly afterwards made for 148 inmates, at an expenditure of £10,774 ; and at a still later period, in 1847, by converting some large rooms previously occupied as stores into dormitories, a total accommodation for 340 lunatics was obtained. Up to the present this institution has cost, including a sum of £1,628, recently spent in improvements and the purchase of fifteen additional acres of land, £42,603. The two first outlays were assessed in the following proportions, and have been repaid by fourteen equal annual instalments :—Limerick county, £12,457; Limerick city, £3,412; Kerry, £12,767; Clare, £12,336. The last was assessed as follows, and is in course of repayment, the county of Kerry having been meanwhile declared a separate district :—Limerick county, £716; Limerick city, £183; Clare, £728. Notwithstanding that 100 vacancies were created by the removal of that number of patients belonging to the county of Kerry, on the completion of the new district institution at Killarney in 1852, unavoidable delays have occurred in the admission of lunatics from the remaining counties for want of room.

Belfast.

The Belfast Asylum for the counties of Down and Antrim, and the town of Carrickfergus, was first occupied in 1829, being built, like Armagh, for 104 patients. Arrangements were soon after made for sixty-four additional beds. In 1835 the farm was increased by the purchase of fourteen acres, and structural additions, affording accommodation for

100 more patients, were effected.   This provision being still unsatisfactory, we deemed it our duty, in the year 1850, to represent the necessity of improving the Asylum generally by certain alterations, such as the erection of infirmaries, lavatories, &c., and of making accommodation for 130 additional patients.   In order to render the building as detached as possible, thirteen acres of land, lying between it and the town, were purchased for £4,311, making a gross total of £49,743 expended on this institution, according to the latest information that could be obtained.   Of this sum, £37,344 has been assessed as follows:—Antrim, £16,954; Down, £19,897; town of Carrickfergus, £493.   The difference remains as yet unapportioned, the accounts not having been finally closed. *[District Lunatic Asylums. Cost of Land, Erection, &c.]*

The Londonderry Asylum, for 104 patients, belonging to the counties of Londonderry, Donegal, and Tyrone, opened in 1829, was erected at a cost of £25,678.   Additional accommodation was provided for 108 patients, between the years 1831 and 1839, at an outlay of £604.   This latter sum merged in the general expenditure.   In 1850 fifteen acres of land were purchased for £1,412, making the total outlay on this Asylum £27,694. It still requires considerable internal improvements, the most pressing of which infirmaries, workshops, and lavatories, are not the less necessary, even though a new institution be established for the insane poor of Donegal. *[Londonderry.]*

In 1848 the county of Tyrone, which had been attached to this Asylum from its opening, was separated, and, with the county Fermanagh, declared a district with an asylum at Omagh.

The first cost of the Londonderry Asylum was assessed on the original district as follows:—Londonderry, £7,071; Donegal, £9,055; Tyrone, £9,551.   The additional land was assessed, on Londonderry, £657; on Donegal, £755.

Richmond, already referred to, was declared a District Asylum under the Act 11th Geo. IV. cap. 22, in 1830, and presented by Government as a free gift to the city and county of Dublin, and the counties of Meath, Louth, and Wicklow, being at the time fully furnished for the accommodation of 290 inmates.   The first outlay chargeable to the ratepayers took place in 1835, and was for land and enclosing same, the amount being £6,297. Within the last six years increased accommodation has been provided from time to time for 160 patients, in addition to which a new building, capable of accommodating 162 patients, and partaking of the character of a separate establishment, as far as its internal arrangements are concerned, but under the direction of one Board of Governors, and maintained from the same estimates, has been erected in the adjoining grounds, distant about a quarter of a mile from the old, with a church and hospital intervening.   The total outlay, including the enlargement of the original Asylum, amounts to £50,716. These sums were assessed in the following manner:— *[Richmond.]*

	Land and Wall, 1835.	Subsequent Additions.	Total.
Dublin, County, . . .	£941 18 0	£10,648 16 10	£11,590 14 10
„ City, . . .	2,058 17 3	18,763 1 1	20,821 18 4
Wicklow, ...	949 1 2	7,188 2 5	8,137 3 7
Louth, ...	839 7 9	6,595 1 6	7,434 9 3
Drogheda, ...	134 15 1	1,223 6 10	1,358 1 11
Meath, ...	1,373 14 1	—	1,373 14 1
	£6,297 13 4	£44,418 8 8	£50,716 2 0

Notwithstanding that by the alterations and additions its accommodation has been raised from 290 to 620 beds, the Richmond Asylum is still quite insufficient to meet the pressing demands made upon it, the gaols of the district alone containing no less at the present moment than sixty-six lunatics.   The Board, however, now that the Treasury has decided on the remissions and allowances to be made in pursuance of the recommendation of the Commissioners appointed to inquire into the erection of Lunatic Asylums in Ireland, and all further difficulties being removed, are, at our suggestion, converting apartments hitherto unoccupied, and not, indeed, originally intended for patients, into dormitories and day-rooms for about forty persons, which they hope to have available in the course of a few months.

This asylum appears to have had expended on it up to the present time, inclusive of the gift from Government of £75,000, at which it was valued when handed over to the Governors, no less a sum than £125,716.   It is, nevertheless, much the cheapest institution of the kind in Ireland, so far as regards the ratepayers, who have been assessed for only £50,716, as above set forth.

The next District Asylum opened was that at Carlow, in the year 1831, at a cost, including all expenses, of £22,552, with accommodation for 104 patients.   There have been no additions since made to the building, nor alterations; but, by a better regulation of the sleeping apartments, room was obtained for 96 additional inmates, without any expense beyond that of bedding and furniture. *[Carlow.]*

The expenditure was assessed on the counties forming the district in the following pro-

DISTRICT LUNATIC ASYLUMS.

Cost of Land, Erection, &c.

portions, and has been repaid in due course by fourteen annual instalments:—Carlow, £3,246; Kildare, £4,313; Wexford, £7,281; Kilkenny, £6,736; Kilkenny city, £944.

Although an increase of accommodation was afforded by the removal of fifty-four patients to Kilkenny on the opening of that asylum in 1852, the establishment at Carlow is still very far from being able to accommodate the insane poor of the district, there having been a daily average of over twenty lunatics confined in the gaol of Wexford, besides those in the gaols of Athy, Naas, and Carlow, from which places we have been unable to remove some very pressing cases. During the past year meetings have been held by the Grand Jury of the county of Wexford, and resolutions passed with a view to induce Government to separate that county also from the Carlow district, and to erect an asylum specially for its lunatic poor. The Grand Jurors belonging to the other counties are strongly opposed to the measure, believing that an enlargement of the present asylum would suffice. Looking, however, to the number of insane to be provided for, the distance at which Wexford is situated, and the consequent inconvenience and expense attending the transmission of patients to the asylum, we have no hesitation in expressing our opinion that the wishes of the Grand Jury and ratepayers of Wexford ought to be acceded to.

Ballinasloe.

The Connaught, now the Ballinasloe, District Asylum came into operation in 1833, for the whole province, the number for which it was built being 150, and the cost, £27,124. The accommodation was subsequently extended by the conversion of out-offices into dormitories, until more than double the original number was provided for, so that when the alterations were commenced in 1849, it was capable of receiving 318 patients. The outlay attendant on such increase, having been incurred from time to time, was included in the general disbursements provided for by quarterly estimates, and does not come specially under the head of "Buildings." In the course of the improvements completed by the Board of Works in 1851, for a sum of £15,813, including the erection of an infirmary, the offices which had been appropriated for patients were pulled down and replaced by suitable dormitories and day rooms." The total accommodation, as at present existing, is for 340; and notwithstanding that the area of the district has been diminished by two counties, Sligo and Leitrim, and further room created by the removal of 88 patients belonging to those counties to the new Asylum at Sligo in 1855, within a few months the Ballinasloe establishment had again received nearly its full number of inmates, and at the present date there are 318 in the house. The assessments were made as follows:—

	Original.	Subsequent.	Total.
Galway, County,	} £8,133 4 7	{ £6,110 3 11	£14,738 1 4
" Town,		485 12 10 }	
Mayo,	7,590 1 7	5,632 15 2	13,222 16 9
Sligo,	3,537 16 4	—	3,537 16 4
Roscommon,	4,948 12 11	3,576 5 9	8,524 18 8
Leitrim,	2,914 15 1	—	2,914 15 1
	27,124 10 6	15,813 17 8	42,938 8 2

Maryboro'.

Maryborough, constructed, like the majority of the early asylums, for 104 patients, was opened in 1833, and cost £24,172. Applicants for admission being numerous and urgent, and there being space available for somewhat more than the number originally contemplated, 46 additional patients were admitted by Government authority in 1836, and 20 more in 1839. The demands for admission still pressing, room was made for 15 males and 15 females in 1846, by the appropriation, as in other cases, of spare offices into sleeping apartments, at a charge, included in the current expenditure, of £420, the total accommodation being for 200 patients. This falling far short of the requirements of the district, an Order in Council was made severing the counties of Westmeath and Longford from the district; and the lunatics belonging to those counties, 67 in number, were removed to the Asylum erected at Mullingar on its completion in 1855. The vacancies thus created have been reduced within the last twelve months to 46, by the admission of new cases; and as each month still diminishes the number, the house will, we anticipate, be soon again filled. In any case provision should be made for infirmaries and workshops, and a proper place for worship should be erected.

The expenditure on this asylum has been thus assessed and repaid:—King's County, £6,391; Queen's County, £6,471; Westmeath, £6,321; Longford, £4,987.

Waterford.

The Waterford Asylum, built for 100 patients of the county and city of Waterford, at a cost of £16,887, was opened in 1835. Accommodation was subsequently made for 30 additional inmates at a trifling cost; and though there has not been any thing approaching the same degree of pressure for admission which has characterized the other asylums, owing to the smallness of the district, still there have been few vacancies, the full complement being constantly in the house. The assessments were duly repaid in the following manner:—Waterford county, £14,136; Waterford city, £2,751.

Clonmel Asylum, opened in 1835, was originally the smallest of all the district institutions for the insane, having been intended for only 60 patients of the county Tipperary. The cost was £16,587. Within five years it had received 40 more than the number it was intended for; and new buildings were afterwards added, which made the total accommodation for 140.

The amount which the ratepayers of the county have been called on to pay for this Asylum, including original and subsequent outlays in land, buildings, furniture, and fittings, is £22,325.

There does not exist any thing like sufficient room for the lunatic poor of Tipperary, as is exemplified by a daily average of 20 insane persons in the gaols of the district. The gaol of the North Riding, at Nenagh, has particularly felt the inadequacy of asylum accommodation, it being only at rare intervals and under circumstances of urgency that a vacancy could be obtained for the admission of any lunatic confined in it into the asylum.

The question may suggest itself, whether it would not have been better to transfer the lunatics from gaol before admitting ordinary cases. The Governors, generally, and, in most instances, the Medical Officers of District Asylums, have evinced a desire to give precedence to the latter class, for, if refused admission on application, a pretext is soon found by the relatives for obtaining the committal of the individual to gaol as a "dangerous lunatic," and so, *mutato nomine*, the same result is arrived at.

We have thus enumerated, including the Richmond, the ten original District Asylums, which cost, in the aggregate, for land, buildings, furniture, and fittings, £284,782. Of the old Asylum at Cork, declared a district establishment by the 8th and 9th Vict., cap. 107, in 1845, but since vacated from its unfitness, we have made no mention, so that the recently erected building shall appear in its proper place in the list of new asylums, according to the order of occupation.

The Kilkenny Asylum, erected in pursuance of an Order in Council, dated 29th June, 1847, and intended for 150 patients of the county and city of Kilkenny, was opened in 1852. The cost in land, buildings, furniture, and fittings, amounting altogether to £24,920, was assessed as follows, and is in course of repayment:—Kilkenny county, £21,785; Kilkenny city, £3,135. A further sum of £1,531 has been granted by the Treasury on the recommendation of the Commissioners for Inquiring into the Erection of District Lunatic Asylums in Ireland, "to be expended in making good defects, &c., and not to be charged to the ratepayers."

For the last year this establishment has been unable to accommodate all the applicants for admission, an event foreseen by the Commissioners of Inquiry, who state in their Report, page 49:—"It appears that this asylum is likely to prove insufficient for the cases that will probably present themselves for admission," adding, "The disposition of the place is such as to admit easily of extension when required."

The remaining counties of the Carlow district are called on to refund a portion of the sum originally contributed by the county and city of Kilkenny for the erection of the Carlow Asylum, under the Act 8th and 9th Vict., cap. 107, sec. 17, Commissioners (Sir Thomas Deane and Mr. Lanyon) having been appointed to inquire into and report upon the equitable amount to be so refunded. The award made by them in this instance is £6,511; the cost of the asylum is, therefore, but £18,409, as far as the ratepayers of the Kilkenny district are concerned.

The Cork Asylum, commenced under an Order in Council, dated 26th June, 1846, was also completed in 1852, and cost, every thing included, £85,828, having accommodation for 500 patients; but in consequence of the liberal remission of £6,013, and a further sum of £1,213 specially granted for improving the ventilation, water-closets, &c., without charge to the ratepayers, making a total of £7,226 conceded by the Treasury, the amount to be repaid by the county and city has been reduced to £79,827, the former being assessed for £69,278, and the latter for £10,548.

The Killarney Asylum, erected under the authority of an Order in Council, dated 30th December, 1846, at a cost of £39,807, for 250 patients, came next in succession, and was opened on the 30th December, 1852, being just six years from the date on which the Order in Council was issued. The county of Kerry, separated from the Limerick, alone constitutes the district, and the accommodation, under the existing state of things, is ample. Looking, however, to the statistics of insanity in the county at large, they lead us to the opinion that, although applications for admission have not been numerous, the provision is not in excess of the requirements. A sum of £1,455 has been remitted by the Treasury from the original cost; the amount assessed is, therefore, £38,352. A sum of £2,424 has also been awarded to make good various defects in the building, and which is not to be charged to the ratepayers. The amount to be refunded by the Limerick district is £11,115, so that the new Asylum will stand the county Kerry in the sum of £27,237.

The Omagh Asylum, built for 300 patients of the counties of Tyrone and Fermanagh,

DISTRICT LUNATIC ASYLUMS.

Cost of Land, Erection, &c.

Omagh.

Sligo.

Mullingar.

Commission of Inquiry into Erection of Lunatic Asylums.

in accordance with an Order in Council, dated 13th September, 1847, and under which those counties were separated, the former from the Londonderry, and the latter from the Armagh district, was opened in 1853; the cost being £41,407, assessed as follows:—Fermanagh, £12,918; Tyrone, £28,488, no abatement from the original outlay was recommended; but £2,699 has been allowed by the Treasury for making good various defects, without further charge to the ratepayers. The sums to be refunded by the Armagh and Londonderry districts are, from the former, £3,074; and from the latter, £7,834. The actual cost of the Omagh Asylum is, therefore, as regards its own district, £30,499, or £9,844 to Fermanagh, and £20,654 to Tyrone.

The Sligo Asylum, for the counties of Sligo and Leitrim, severed from the district of the Connaught Asylum at Ballinasloe by an Order in Council, dated 17th April, 1847, was built for 250 patients, at a cost of £40,369, and was opened in March, 1855. Of this, £3,000 has been remitted, and a further sum of £2,602 granted by the Treasury, and not to be charged to the ratepayers, for making good defects. The amount chargeable to the counties is, therefore, £37,369, which is thus assessed:—Sligo, £19,974; Leitrim, £17,395. A sum of £5,827 has been awarded as the equitable amount to be refunded by the Ballinasloe district, £2,632 of which goes to Leitrim, and £3,195 to Sligo. The net cost of the new Asylum, as it affects these counties, is, consequently, £31,542; £14,763 being chargeable to the ratepayers of the former, and £16,779 to those of the latter.

The Mullingar Asylum, for the counties of Meath, Westmeath, and Longford—the first detached from the Richmond or Metropolitan, the two others from the Maryborough district—was erected under an Order in Council, made 13th September, 1847, for 300 patients, at a cost of £39,431. Of this, £1,715 has been abated by the authority of the Lords of the Treasury, and a further sum of £2,619 allowed for making good defects. The following assessments have been made, and are in course of repayment by the respective counties:—Meath, £15,869; Westmeath, £12,561; Longford, £9,285. The amount to be refunded by the districts of the Maryborough and Richmond Asylums is £11,963, reducing the cost of the asylum, as regards the Mullingar district, to £25,753; the Maryborough giving Longford £4,267, and Westmeath £5,409; and the Richmond giving (say) £2,286 to Meath. The net sums to be levied on the ratepayers are, therefore, Longford, £5,018; Westmeath, £7,152; Meath, £13,583. In respect to the last, it must be remembered that it was never before assessed for the erection of an asylum, the Richmond, to which it was attached, having been a gift, as already stated; hence the larger proportion which Meath is called on to pay.

The net cost of the District Asylums of Ireland, as they exist at present, including land, buildings, furniture, and fittings, is £584,191, exclusive of the sums abated and of the moneys allowed for making good defects, and also of a portion of the expenditure in recent additions and improvements at the Belfast Asylum not yet ascertained.

Having given, as we proposed, a brief narrative of the origin and progress of the several district lunatic institutions, we may here state that the remissions and allowances already referred to, arose from the fact that the various Boards of Governors, after the opening of the six new buildings, remonstrated against the outlay upon them, as well as against the unsatisfactory and unfinished state in which they were given up by the contractors. Communications were addressed to Government, the subject was brought before the House of Commons, and on the motion of the Chief Secretary, Mr. Horsman, a Select Committee, Sir John Trollope, Chairman, was appointed to inquire into the matter. A single witness (one of the Inspectors) was alone examined; and on his evidence being printed, a Commission of Inquiry, consisting of Messrs. Donaldson and Wilkes, with Mr. Spenser Shelley as Secretary, was issued, and commenced operations in August, 1855. After minute examination, carried out at the various asylums, these gentlemen reported to the Lords Commissioners of Her Majesty's Treasury, recommending remissions, to the extent of £12,183, and also that various improvements should be carried out, and defects made good without further charge to the ratepayers. The boards of the several asylums in question accordingly met, and architects were employed, by whom specifications and estimates of the various alterations and improvements suggested by the Commissioners were prepared, amounting in the aggregate to £38,146. These estimates were submitted to the Lords of the Treasury, and referred back by their Lordships to the Commissioners of Inquiry, who, after visiting this country a second time, awarded £17,014 as an equitable sum for putting the fabrics into sound condition. This amount, making with the previous remissions £29,197, was conceded, the Lords of the Treasury appearing to be influenced by a desire to meet all fair and just claims put forward on the part of the asylums. With reference to the different matters dwelt upon by the Commissioners, and more particularly in regard to ventilation, heating, waterclosets, fastenings of doors and windows, and also the unsuitable and insufficient furniture, we have nothing to add but the hope that the recommendations contained in their report may be speedily carried into effect.

District Lunatic Asylums.

Monies repaid to Treasury, and amount remaining due on account of land, erection, &c.

Of the sums already expended by Government in the establishment of district asylums, and which amount in round numbers to £660,000, we may, on a very close approximation, set down the debt remaining due to the Treasury at £340,000; and as money advanced for the erection and furnishing of lunatic institutions in Ireland, however great the amount, bears no interest, and the repayment is permitted to extend over fourteen years, in equal half-yearly instalments, commencing only after the buildings are occupied, the average debt by the Townland Valuation, 6 & 7 Wm. 4, under which assessments are made, would be ½d. in the pound per annum on the rateable property of the country at large for the above period. Many of the old asylums are clear of all Government responsibilities, though partially indebted to detached districts, in the manner just detailed.

Rate in the pound for which districts are liable.

The following, however, may be taken as the annual rate in the pound, extending over fourteen years, which the respective counties will be called on to repay to the Treasury for land, erection, furniture, and fittings in regard to the new Asylums, as well as for structural and other improvements at some of the old:—Kilkenny, ⅞ of a penny on the county and 1½d. on the city—Killarney, 1½d. on the County of Kerry—Omagh, 1d. on the County of Fermanagh, and 1¼d. on Tyrone—Mullingar, ½d. on Meath, ⅞ of a penny, Westmeath, and Longford, ½d.—Sligo, 1½d. on Sligo, and 2¼d. on Leitrim—Richmond, ½d. for Dublin city and county, Louth, and Wicklow—Cork, 1¼d., city and county—Belfast, ¼ of a penny on Antrim and Down for structural enlargements; Ballinasloe, ¼d. on Galway, Roscommon, and Mayo, structural enlargements—Limerick, ⅛ of a penny for Limerick and Clare, enlargements and land; and at Clonmel ¾ of a farthing, or something almost imperceptible for land and additions.

Allocation of room and mode of assessment.

The amount of accommodation in District Asylums, and the expenses of erection allocated to each county (when two or more are associated), being based on the number of inhabitants, tells, unfortunately, against those counties, the population of which bears a marked numerical disproportion to the value of property in them. As a case in point we may adduce Leitrim, the population of which is about the same as that of the more fertile and richer County of Westmeath; the rateable property of the latter being £306,800, or £2 16s. per head, while that of the former is but £121,000, or £1 1s. 7d. per head. A similar disadvantage takes place in regard to the current expenditure, but we think that satisfactory adjustment might be made so as to equalize the annual levies without loss to the Treasury or inconvenience to the district.

Benefits received in transactions with Treasury.

Taking four per cent. as the minimum rate at which money could be obtained, even on the best security, it will be found that had interest been charged by the Treasury for advances, it would amount on the sums already repaid to £80,000, and to a similar sum in respect of the recent assessments. Thus, with the gift of the Richmond Asylum, and the late remissions, to which may be added about £90,000 paid by Government for the support and maintenance of the Old House of Industry patients (pauper lunatics belonging principally to Dublin and the adjoining counties) in Island Bridge and the Hardwicke Cells, since Richmond was declared a District Asylum, the country appears, on the whole, to have received a clear benefit to the extent of £350,000 in its transactions with the Treasury on account of Lunatic Asylums.

Statistics. Lunatics at large.

Referring to the statistical tables in our last Report, we observe that the lunatics, idiots, and epileptics in Ireland, on the 31st March, 1855, amounted to 13,493, of whom 6,263 were under official supervision in asylums, gaols, and poorhouses, the remainder being possessed of means of their own, supported by their friends, or wandering from place to place, depending for a precarious subsistence on the charity of individuals. The number of the same denominations at the present date is 14,141, of whom 6,520 are located in various public and private institutions; the others, or 7,612, being at large.

Constabulary Returns.

Of these latter we have again obtained very valuable returns through the Constabulary, and from the extensive distribution of that efficient force throughout the country, combined with the careful manner in which the returns have been prepared, we think the information may be relied upon as accurate, the more so as we improved on the forms previously used, having now got the name, age, address, and religion, of every individual in Ireland, whether lunatic, idiot, or simply epileptic. With such details before us, and to arrive at still more certain data, we purpose to follow up our inquiries most minutely, and to return the names and particulars to the Dispensary Physicians of the various districts for their opinions and observations in reference to each case. Of the epileptic classes there are 2,171, in whose regard, as a body, we do not mean to say that supervision is generally required, for save during the temporary attacks of a paroxysm, they are for the most part perfectly competent to take care of themselves. Abstracting the inmates placed in establishments specially intended for the insane, and who are thus located:—Public Asylums, 3,856; Central Asylum, 126; Hardwicke Cells and Lifford Local Asylum,

108 ; Private Asylums, 462. It would appear that the general difference is circumstanced as follows :—Gaols, 175 ; poorhouses, 1,799 ; at large, 4,841, exclusive of 2,171 epileptics, and about 600 lunatics and idiots, who, as far as we can judge from the returns, are not paupers, and therefore inadmissible into district establishments for the insane. The question now presents itself for the consideration of the Executive, whether the present mixed, unsatisfactory, and inadequate provision shall be continued, or a more advanced and liberal system adopted. We would here quote the observations made by us on this subject in our last Report, the opinions we then held remaining unchanged :—

" With regard to the lunatics, idiots, &c., at large, a material difficulty would seem at first sight to present itself, as to how asylum accommodation should be provided for such a number. On this point, however, we may observe, that in a Report on the general condition of the insane in Ireland we have thought it advisable to include not alone those who are absolutely demented, and as such under official supervision, either in public institutions or private establishments, but also the idiotic, and those who, from repeated attacks of epilepsy, are liable to insanity in its most aggravated and dangerous forms—particularly, too, as from these classes the district asylums receive, from time to time, a large proportion of their inmates. But we are by no means to be understood as indicating a necessity for accommodation to any thing approaching the amount of the above numbers ; we merely put forth the fact of the extent to which mental disease in every phase prevails, as well as those affections which may be regarded as identified with it, at the same time expressing our conviction that nothing can tend more to the advantage of the general community than to afford an opportunity for the immediate admission of every insane person into an asylum on the first manifestation of the disease.

" We have now to enter upon a matter of very great importance in connexion with district asylums, viz., the residence of lunatics in poorhouses. Taking a broad view of the question, it is obvious, for many reasons, that the most suitable place for every demented person, lunatic or idiot, harmless or otherwise, is an institution specially devoted to the care of the insane, under the superintendence and management of experienced officers and attendants, who are practically acquainted with the treatment of mental disease in every form, and directed and controlled by that department of the public service to which the supervision of all matters relating to such establishments properly belongs ; and we regard the question as deserving the consideration of the Executive, namely, whether the time may not have arrived for making provision for the complete separation of the insane poor of every class from the sane portion of the community ; and which, whilst effecting a moral duty towards the latter, would insure for the insane poor, idiotic, or imbecile, more care and comfort than they can possibly have in ordinary workhouses, where they cannot at all times be secured against annoyance from the ignorant or thoughtless paupers by whom they are surrounded. We feel that objections to a change may be advanced on financial grounds, and that it may be argued, considering the extremely low position which, particularly the idiotic inmates of poorhouses occupy in the human family, both socially and mentally, that they are comfortably circumstanced and sufficiently well cared for at present.

" It is evident, however, that the attention and care necessary for the relief of these distressed classes cannot be efficaciously extended to them whilst they are placed in institutions of a very different nature from asylums ; and further, it would be falling into a great mistake to imagine that even the most miserable objects of mental incapability are beyond the reach of being relieved ; for there is no species of disease or affection, from the highest state of maniacal excitement to the very lowest grade of imbecility, that does not admit of cure or alleviation under judicious treatment, such alone as can be obtained in establishments exclusively devoted to the object.

" The cost of the proposed alterations would not be so serious as may appear at first sight, the plan we have in view being simply the erection of suitable auxiliary buildings of the least expensive form and character, with large dormitories.

" Another and most desirable object would be obtained by this measure, inasmuch as all the chronic and incurable cases which have been for many years accumulating, and at present take up a great deal of valuable room in the several district asylums, that could otherwise be more beneficially devoted to recent and acute cases, might be removed to these auxiliary buildings, by which means a twofold advantage would be gained, viz., the provision of proper accommodation for the class in question, without the necessity of having a special establishment under the objectionable title of an asylum for incurables, and the disembarrassment of the parent houses from all but inmates suffering from recent and acute affections, or those whose malady afforded reasonable hopes of an ultimate recovery, thus leaving them free to exercise their proper and legitimate functions of hospitals for the cure of insanity, instead of being mere receptacles for the safe keeping and maintenance of chronic cases."

Having endeavoured to afford a general insight into the expenditure incurred in the erection of asylums, involving as it does, a series of complicated accounts, and referred to the extent of insanity, as far as we can judge of it from the statistics before us, we shall now advert to the sums that have been spent in the maintenance of the residents in these different institutions during the two last years, as well as to other matters connected with their general economy and management. We may, however, premise, that pecuniary advances are made by the Treasury on quarterly estimates, from the respective Boards of Governors : these estimates, based on contracts, are duly examined at our office, and if accurate under their various headings, are submitted to the Privy Council for sanction, but, if incorrect, they are returned by us to the Local Boards for amendment. The necessary moneys are subsequently issued on an order from the Lord Lieutenant in Council, through the Paymaster of Civil Services ; and the expenditure finally, and it must be added, from the minuteness of the queries, when any charge, be it ever so insignificant, is not in accordance with rule, most minutely investigated at the Audit Office, in London, to which accounts are transmitted monthly, with vouchers for each item signed by the Chairmen of the Boards of Governors.

It will be seen from the following Table, that the cost of maintenance varies in different asylums, a fact to be explained by the charge for provisions, scale of dietary, and rate of wages not being the same in all.

Asylums.	Year ending 31st March, 1856.			Year ending 31st March, 1857.		
	Daily Average Number of Patients.	Total Expenditure of Asylums.	Average Cost of each Patient per head per annum.	Daily Average Number of Patients.	Total Expenditure of Asylums.	Average Cost of each Patient per head per annum.
		£ s. d.	£ s. d.		£ s. d.	£ s. d.
Armagh, . .	134	2,877 11 1	21 9 5	140	2,799 0 9	19 19 11½
Ballinasloe, .	277	5,871 5 8	21 3 11	301	5,724 16 6	19 1 0½
Belfast, . .	291	5,428 13 9	18 13 1½	323	6,314 2 7	19 10 11½
Carlow, . .	191	3, 80 4 11	20 6 3¾	197	3,793 7 5	19 5 1½
Clonmel, . .	140	3,267 9 10	23 6 9¼	140	3,329 4 1	23 15 7½
Cork, . .	407	6,835 13 6	16 15 10¾	433	7,027 0 7	16 4 6¼
Kilkenny, .	143	2,924 1 5½	20 8 11¼	146¾	2,982 13 11	20 5 10
Killarney, .	146½	3,191 5 11	21 15 8	162	3,516 16 10	21 14 2
Limerick, .	325	6,524 7 10¼	20 1 6	330	6,378 2 4½	19 6 6¾
Londonderry, .	201	3,765 1 9	18 14 7½	204	3,807 18 0	18 13 3¼
Maryborough, .	164	3,644 1 2	22 4 4¾	149	3,378 3 6	22 13 5¼
Mullingar, .	125	2,552 15 8	20 8 5¼	176	4,260 7 6	24 4 1¼
Omagh, . .	187	4,274 13 4	22 17 2¼	211	4,726 5 3	22 7 11½
Richmond, .	538	12,072 1 10	22 8 9¼	610	13,751 2 10	22 10 10¼
Sligo, . .	105	2,844 19 0	27 1 10	126½	3,025 16 8	23 18 4½
Waterford, . .	128	2,666 9 11	20 16 7¾	124	2,617 5 3	21 2 1¼
	3,502½	72,620 10 8	20 14 8	3,773¼	77,432 4 0½	20 10 5

The average expenses per head for the year ending 31st March, 1855, was £19 15s. 10d., in the present year it amounts to £20 10s. 5d., a difference, considering the advance in every article of consumption, by no means remarkable. It would be advisable to have a greater uniformity of detail adopted in regard to the various heads of expenditure in all district asylums, at the same time that there is a difficulty to be surmounted with reference to one important item, inasmuch as the class of patients generally belonging to the metropolis, and larger cities and towns, require a more tonic dietary than the inhabitants of purely agricultural localities.

The total number in district asylums under treatment during the two past years, amounted to 6,081, there being in them on 31st March, 1855, 3,299; since admitted, 2,782, namely, ordinary cases, 1,857; lunatics from gaols by warrant of the Lord Lieutenant, 925. On the aggregate the absolute recoveries were 17 per cent. or 37½ on the admissions, the relieved being 11½, a result coinciding nearly with that of the two previous years, but more satisfactory. The mortality, 9 per cent., is just one below that of the preceding biennial period; and when the proportion of unpromising cases brought from prisons is taken into account, these facts speak most favourably of the successful issue of Irish asylums. No epidemic of any kind has visited them since June, 1853, when we had occasion to refer to an increased number of deaths at Belfast and elsewhere from cholera. The mortality is now, for the most part, referable to affections of the brain and nervous system, or to diseases associated with organic debility, but particularly of the lungs, and ending in consumption. Two cases were suicidal; the first occurred at Belfast, in 1856, a male patient accomplishing his object by suspending himself from the ventilator in one of the single sleeping rooms. The second was at the Richmond, where a patient strangled himself at night with a sheet taken from his bed, which he tore up for the purpose. The coroner was called on in both cases, and it appeared on inquiry that neither of the lunatics had ever evinced dangerous tendencies, nor had the physicians or immediate attendants any suspicion that they meditated self-destruction. These, with another instance in which an old man was suffocated whilst eating, were the only casualties of a fatal nature which occurred during the period embraced in this Report.

Reverting to the sanitary state of Asylums, your Excellency may desire to be informed as to the remedial measures generally adopted in them. We cannot say that any particular medical treatment for the cure of insanity is resorted to, except in its early stages, or when marked symptoms of the disease present themselves in more advanced cases; air, regimen, exercise, with the removal of causes leading to excitement, being more favourably regarded as tending to a beneficial result, in the alleviation of a malady which is as yet but imperfectly understood.

DISTRICT
LUNATIC
ASYLUMS.

Statistics.
Non-restraint
system.

With reference to physical coercion, or mechanical restraint, in the majority of asylums it is employed in a mitigated form, in the others it is seldom or ever had recourse to. On this mooted subject we do not interfere, unless as has occasionally happened on inspection, we considered that the appliances might be partially if not altogether discontinued. The question is one more properly for the judgment of the local Medical Superintendents, and as we believe they are alike influenced by the most humane motives and a desire to do what is best for the safety of their patients, we would deem it unadvisable on our part to lay down any fixed rule on a system which is at issue between enlightened practitioners, and which, further, there is no authority to enforce. In our opinion, however, one most urgent and almost insurmountable objection exists to mechanical restraint, and which arises from the contingency of its being surreptitiously employed by attendants, to avoid trouble, unless due precautions are taken by the Resident Physician or Manager.

Occupation of
patients.

The principal occupation for male patients is husbandry—some few are employed at trades; whilst spinning, washing, knitting, &c., &c., engage the females who are competent to work.

Independent of more important advantages to be derived by the individuals themselves, from out-door labour, its good effects, in an economical point of view, will be best seen by a reference to the Appendix, which gives in detail the various sums realized on the different farms during the two years; the total, exclusive of the value of produce in vegetables consumed at home, being £4,167 on 421 acres, worked by a daily average of 422 patients.

Paying
patients.

Among the patients in Asylums there are at present fifty-three whose support is in part or fully paid for. Of this number ten are pensioners, and have no immediate relations who can advance a charitable claim to the sums now contributed for their maintenance. The others are of the farming and shopkeeping classes, who, above the grade of regular applicants for admission, have not means sufficient to meet the charges in private licensed houses. The total amount received for the classes in question during the past year was £736. On principle we are opposed to the maintenance of paying patients in District Asylums; still, from motives of common humanity, in the absence of a suitable refuge for the insane members of humble but respectable families, and where there is a good margin of vacancies, as at Mullingar, Killarney, &c., it would be hard to debar a fellow-creature of the benefit of a public establishment. No abuse has, at least as yet, sprung from these exceptional cases, which, deducting pensioners, is scarcely one per cent. on the whole number of inmates.

Religious
Ministrations.

With reference to religious ministrations—a subject which, unfortunately, has given rise within the last three or four years, to a marked difference of opinion between the Executive and the Governors of a northern asylum, the majority of whom, actuated, no doubt, by the sincerest motives, successfully opposed the admission of officially appointed chaplains—our sentiments, far from undergoing any change, have been strengthened by daily experience. We have specially directed ourselves to the points at issue, personally attending in asylums, at the respective hours of public worship, questioning patients themselves, inquiring both of officers and attendants, and noting the results at the moment; and we cannot arrive at any other conclusion, than that the regular visitations of chaplains, and the due performance of divine worship, should not be denied to the inmates of public institutions for the insane; for apart from other and higher considerations, the soothing influence of religion, as tending to the establishment of a self control, however temporary in its nature, cannot but be valuable in a curative point of view; and it should not be forgotten that, though in one individual the reasoning powers are normally affected, the sentiments may remain unchanged, whilst in another, the moral feelings may be deranged, at the same time that the intellectual faculties are comparatively unimpaired—both cases being alike susceptible of the benefits of religion.

Education.

We have made an analysis of the state of education of the insane in poorhouses and asylums. In the former, it appears there are 323 more or less educated, and 1,476 illiterate; in the latter, the numbers are 2,353 with some degree of education, against 1,505 totally ignorant. The proportion of literate to illiterate in the general population of this country is fifty-three per cent. If we restrict the comparison to those in asylums, omitting the inmates in poorhouses, of whom a large majority are idiots, it would appear that education is in a much higher ratio among lunatics than in the community at large—a circumstance indicative of the fact that insanity, even among the humbler classes, is connected with intellectual development. At the Richmond a school was established about six years ago, principally for females of weak mind, and though not likely to be followed by any permanent result, has at least the merit of a benevolent intention, and tends to vary the daily occupations. We would therefore wish to see the example of the Richmond Governors adopted in other establishments, and also a more liberal supply of some cheap periodicals afforded.

Hereditary predisposition and intemperance would seem to be the two great feeders, if the term may be used, to lunatic asylums. In an aggregate of 3,856 individuals on the 31st March, we find of the 2,146, where causes are assigned, no less than 997 under these denominations, 506 of the former, 491 of the latter, or forty-six per cent. As regards the cases where we had no definite information—and these are constituted, for the most part, of transferences from gaols—it is legitimate to conclude that the same proportion as in the assignable exists. Hence of the whole population in asylums, 1,790 come within the two categories. This fact alone, pregnant of serious considerations, speaks for itself, and needs no comment on our part.

Under the head of exciting causes to insanity, religion is enumerated; but considering the great influence which it exercises over the conduct of mankind, not alone for good but unfortunately too, from a misconception of its true spirit, imbuing whole communities occasionally with a disposition to commit the wildest acts from the most unreasonable motives, it does not seem to be so powerful an agent in producing individual mental derangement as might be at first supposed. Lunatics will, no doubt, readily adopt, and as quickly abandon, extravagant ideas on religious as on other subjects, whilst the really exciting causes will be found totally unconnected with them. We find among clergymen and the members of pious associations more perhaps than an average per centage of lunacy; but their delusions rarely refer to their previous avocations, an observation alike pertinent to the insane members of other professions. Love, from misplaced affections and disappointed hopes, is a much more fertile source of the disease, particularly among the female sex, who, from their habits and sensibilities, are more susceptible than men of those influences recognised under the designation of moral.

We have been frequently questioned relative to the increase or diminution of insanity in this country, and regret to say that the statistics of each succeeding year, if the numbers mentally affected which come before us be alone regarded, would lead to the conclusion that the disease is on the increase; but while making due allowances for the fact that with fresh accommodation and extended inquiries, cases previously in existence are brought to light, the important truth must not be overlooked, that from each individual case of lunacy, germs of disease to be developed at a future period, possibly in a third or fourth generation, may be produced; for such is our organization, that the mind no less than the body partakes of inherent and hereditary peculiarities, which, as your Excellency is aware, rendering nations at large distinguishable by corporeal prowess, valour, progression in the arts, &c., or the reverse, first find their way into the smaller circles of which those nations are composed.

"Quia multa modis primordia multis
Mista sua celant in corpore sæpe parentes
Quæ patribus patres tradunt a stirpe profecta."

Our observations on this head are not the mere expression of a theory, but the result of extended inquiry into the prevalence of insanity under particular circumstances; and we have satisfactory data to show that mental disorders develop themselves to an extraordinary extent in certain families. One of the strongest instances we have met, illustrative of the fact, was in a Northern Asylum, where four relatives very closely connected were located together, and we were informed, on credible authority, that no less than eight others, related in the degree of cousins, were epileptic or idiotic. To check by every legitimate means, and to afford ample accommodation through statutory enactments, to lunatics in each phase of the malady, but especially in the early stages, and when it is essentially curable, becomes a duty which communities owe to themselves, for thus alone can the propagation of insanity be most successfully combated. The complaint that District Asylums are overcrowded with chronic or incurable cases is not one peculiar to Ireland, it is common to every country in which establishments for the insane are to be found, and is inseparable from the very nature of lunacy. Taking, for example, in England, the two largest asylums, Hanwell and Colneyhatch, containing between them no less than 2,200 patients—the proportion of curable to incurable cases is probably under one-fifth; and be it further considered, that the last named asylum has not as yet been over six years in operation. The same holds good in regard to continental asylums in Belgium, Prussia, France, &c., and also in America.

Lunatics would seem not only to stand themselves, but occasionally to place some of those connected with them, in an anomalous position. The Governors of Asylums, for instance, complain that the institutions are congested with incurable cases,—the very same men acting as Boards of Superintendence of Gaols find fault with lunatics being placed in prison, and endeavour to hurry their transference to asylums, no matter what the character of the disease; and as Poor Law Guardians, object to the residence of insane persons within the walls of a workhouse, availing themselves of the first opportunity to have them committed to gaols as dangerous. Expense is prominent in the eyes of the Asylum Governors, the subversion of prison discipline to Boards of Superintendence, and a troublesome incon-venience to Poor Law Guardians. We concur fully in the sentiments of the two last named Boards, and would disembarrass gaols and workhouses of all lunatic inmates; and partially agreeing with the Asylum Governors, we would meet the difficulty of expense by the plain but suitable buildings we have already adverted to, establishing one authority for the moral curative, and fiscal management of the insane generally.

The Act of last session, 19 & 20 Vic., c. 99, according superannuation to officers and servants attached to District Asylums, has been already taken advantage of, and the manager and matron of the Derry Asylum have retired on a liberal pension. The manager of the Richmond, as well as the matron at Maryborough, are in like manner about to resign, and before the close of the present year it is probable that two or three others will follow, affording opportunities for arrangements which will, we have no doubt, be of advantage to the public service. Several of the minor officers and servants have also availed themselves of the new enactment.

That provision should be made for the officers of District Asylums, as elsewhere, when worn out by age and length of service, is but just and reasonable, and on principle has been ever advocated by us. We know no duties so onerous and so unceasing as those connected with the management of the insane, entailing at all hours the same anxious responsi-bility. As the labourer is worthy of his hire, a liberal recompense when engaged on service, and the certainty of a commensurate allowance on retirement, is but a reasonable expectation; and we cannot but think that the staff of lunatic asylums in this country, as a body, are not only underpaid when on duty, but that an exceptional rule should be made in favour of deserving officers who, growing old in them, are rendered unfit for after em-ployment by previous habits, professional or other. Take, for example, the Medical Superintendents, restricted to a sort of cloister life within the precincts of an asylum, men of education, enlightened views, and varied acquirements, their hours devoted to the good of the helpless and afflicted, and compare their salaries with those paid to the members of other professions, who are certainly not superior in knowledge, and whose sphere of action, though useful and necessary for the well-being of society, is not directed to the attain-ment of a higher or more important object than that of the individual who labours to ameliorate the condition of his fellow-creatures, under the heaviest and most dreaded visitation to which mankind is liable.

It is our duty to state that two instances occurred of charges having been brought by officers against their superiors. The first was at Maryborough, where, after a preliminary inquiry at the Local Board, the Inspectors were requested by it, and subsequently directed by your Excellency, to institute an investigation, for which purpose they visited the Asylum specially. When called upon, however, the matron who had preferred the charges begged to be allowed to withdraw them—neither knowing their truth herself, nor being able to substantiate them by witnesses, she frankly confessed that they were grounded solely on hearsay. The particulars of the case having been duly submitted, your Excel-lency was pleased to direct that a letter be written to the resident physician, intimating that no imputation whatever rested upon him, that his character and fitness for the responsible office held by him remained wholly unimpeached, and that the matron should be cautioned to be more guarded in her statements for the future.

The second took place at Mullingar, where, as it appeared, the accusations made were not only groundless but vindictive; the complainant was dismissed by order of Govern-ment, on a unanimous resolution of the Board.

That Irish Asylums have been substantially successful there cannot exist a doubt, both in a curative point of view, and as affording refuge to a class whose claims on public sympathy are co-existent with the dictates of our common humanity. The pages of a Parliamentary Report are, perhaps, not altogether suited to digression from fiscal and statistical details, still we may venture to remind your Excellency of the depressed state of Ireland for a period of nearly five years, with landed property in many places almost confiscated to poor rates during which time the District Asylums of this country were entailing additional expense on the community at large. The cost of erection of these various institutions has been already given in detail, and we would now only observe, that the Governors of them apprehending the assessment which for a certain time must be levied to meet Treasury repayments, consider it a duty to restrict in every possible way all expenses save those absolutely requisite, and not to replace fixtures or furniture even though objectionable in their eyes, till completely worn out. We think, however, that economy may be occasionally carried out to an unprofitable extent, and that stopping short and not efficiently following up a regular system of management, would be almost as bad as not to have undertaken it at all. Our domestic arrangements may not be on an equality with those in many English asylums, which, too, may be similarly inferior in regard to what obtains in France and elsewhere, for local circumstances produce their relative differences. Generally speaking, a deficiency of furniture, and with it a certain air of discomfort is noticeable in Irish institutions for the insane, a want which we trust, with the advancing prosperity of the country, will be gradually obviated; yet, when your Excellency, so long and thoroughly cognizant of the social condition of the population, recalls to mind what on your frequent visits to District Asylums you could not fail to remark, and reflects that a large proportion of their inmates, whilst possessed of reason, had been strangers to the personal comforts of life, and, we regret to add, in many instances, from their abject state of destitution, to the decencies of civilization, but still protected by an innate sense of virtue and decorum—huddled together in those miserable abodes which present themselves in quick succession along our public thoroughfares, on the edge of bogs and sides of mountains—without adequate food or raiment—whole families frequently occupants of a single apartment, perhaps of a common bed—that the same individuals placed in asylums, labouring under madness in all its varied forms, are educated for the first time to habits of order and cleanliness, have servants at all hours to minister to their personal wants—their dress and bedding duly attended to, meals served regularly with a liberal allowance of animal food, a luxury before almost untasted by them—we may, as tending to social advancement no less than for curative objects, so far regard our public establishments for the insane with unmixed satisfaction.

Defects there may be in them, just cause of complaint may now and then occur, with an occasional instance of neglect, for which we are not the apologists, still, on the whole, without being sullied by the imputation of a cruelty, save with a solitary exception, at Maryborough, where an attendant was prosecuted to conviction for maltreating a patient, they fully uphold the benevolent objects of their erection. And here we may be pardoned, if while lending our humble admiration to that system of philanthropy, which latterly in the sister kingdom has lowered physical coercion to a minimum in the treatment of lunatics, we refer to the fact that, forty years ago, the charter and published regulations, by Order in Council, for Irish Aylums, and which have since given tone to their management, laid it down that all the latitude of personal liberty, consistent with safety, mildness of manner, and the avoidance of every cause of irritation, should be the constant and essential practice observed within them.—App. G.

The next subject to which we shall direct your Excellency's attention is that of the law in reference to the committal of "dangerous lunatics." The number of persons confined in gaols under this head within the last two years amounted to no less than 1,296, of whom 814 were transferred by warrant to District Asylums, 276 discharged on medical certificates, 9 removed by their friends, and 35 died, thus leaving 161 in custody on the 31st March last. In England there exists no similar enactment to the 1st Vic., cap. 27, which in this kingdom empowers magistrates to imprison persons "discovered under circumstances denoting a derangement of mind, and a purpose of committing an indictable offence;" to guard against undue detention, on a medical certificate, that they have recovered or ceased to be dangerous, the law provides that an individual so confined can be liberated at any time by an order from two magistrates, "one whereof shall be a justice who signed such warrant," otherwise they remain in custody until transferred to an asylum by order of the Lord Lieutenant. This Act was passed in consequence of the homicide of a most respectable gentleman in the streets of Dublin, by a maniac who, a short time previously, had, for want of room, been refused admission into the District Asylum.

The object sought to be attained by the passing of this measure was, within certain restrictions, fully justified in a country where sufficient provision did not exist in the way of public asylums for the insane poor; and had magistrates acted up to the spirit of the Statute, duly investigating the merits of each case, little inconvenience and the greatest possible benefits would have resulted; but as its clauses are at present carried out, gaols may be considered so many channels of transmission to lunatic asylums, whereby a serious derangement of prison discipline, and considerable additional expense to the public by the cost of conveyance are produced, the system acting at the same time in regard to metropolitan and larger cities with peculiar injustice. This is not the first occasion on which we have expressed our opinion in reference to the subject of committing lunatics to prison, having in previous reports represented the practice as being attended with great inconvenience; the abuse, however, instead of diminishing, would seem to have increased, for in this manner families get rid of the care and support of their insane relatives. Not even thinking it worth while to apply for admission into an asylum in the

DANGEROUS LUNATICS.

Looseness in mode of committing.

ordinary way, they depose to the existence of violent tendencies, the result too often of premeditated irritation; the interference of the police is all that is then necessary, for, under their escort the lunatics are brought to the county or city prison, as the case may be, and with this act the curtain drops between the parties. We would not assert that these observations apply to every case, aware from experience that in some instances prompt exercise of the provisions of the Act is necessary, and that in others the friends of such lunatics evince the warmest interest in their unhappy relatives; still, we do not exaggerate in laying it down as a general rule, that individuals of "deranged mind" are loosely committed to prison as "dangerous." So far back as the year 1848, a circular was addressed by the Executive, at our suggestion, to justices at petty sessions, directing their attention to the clauses of the Act, and accompanied by a specific form of committal for their guidance; we regret, that although a certain degree of success followed these measures, they were not as effectual as could be desired in checking the evil complained of.

The usual form of admission into a District Asylum requires an attestation as to the residence, birth-place, and social state of the person desired to be admitted, also an engagement on the part of some responsible party to take back the patient when called upon to do so. A committal obviates all this responsibility, and we have frequently known of applicants who were refused admission by the Local Board on sufficient grounds—such as not being natives of, or, in any way connected with the district—having been sent to gaol as dangerously insane, and in this manner ultimately forced on the institution. Thus, while admitting that the Act was in some measure necessary, we cannot shut our eyes to the many and glaring abuses which have arisen from it.

The so-called "dangerous," in general tranquil and amenable.

Of the conduct of the class in question, we find that the great majority, far from exhibiting any of the dangerous tendencies attributed to them, are tranquil and amenable from the very moment they are placed in confinement; and, generally speaking, this character attaches to them afterwards when transferred to asylums—the so-called "dangerous," however troublesome, evincing as little propensity to violence as ordinary lunatics.

Evil of committing Lunatics to Gaols.

In a practical point of view this wholesale committal, averaging annually the last two years no less than 579, is attended with further serious disadvantages. No history of the cases is given, nor information afforded to guide the physician in his treatment of them; and when recovered, a material embarrassment occurs in their discharge, for it very frequently happens that the exact locality of the parties is unknown, and in the absence of a law of settlement, Boards of Governors have no authority to direct their admission into poorhouses. The detention of lunatics in gaols varies much as to time—some few remaining in them for years. This circumstance may appear extraordinary to your Excellency, but it can be satisfactorily accounted for in those districts for the exigencies of which the asylums are too limited. Still the deprivation of personal liberty during the protracted sojourn of a fellow-creature in prison must, in the estimation of a humane mind, be compensated for by the knowledge that a certain attention is paid to his personal wants in regard to warmth, food, and raiment; and that if debarred from wandering at will, he is at least protected from the annoyance of thoughtless strangers, and the neglect perhaps of unkind relatives. We are familiar with numerous instances of the kind. There is at present, in Lifford gaol, a man entirely demented, harmless, and tranquil, who has been confined there for several years. He was previously a patient in the District Asylum. His bodily health is good, he is always most usefully employed, and perfectly contented with his condition. To send him back as a fixture to an institution already unable to meet the requirements of the district, and thereby exclude an acute or violent case of madness, in which the advantages afforded by a regular establishment for the treatment of insanity holds out the strongest hope of alleviation or cure, would be productive of an injurious instead of a beneficial result; so, until sufficient accommodation shall have been obtained, we think it better, of two evils to choose the lesser, and leave persons similarly circumstanced in prison, from which they can be discharged, whenever it may be considered advisable by the Judge of Assize, the local Magistrates, or Assistant-Barrister, according to the provisions of the Act before referred to.

Transference to Asylums.

Your Excellency will have observed from the foregoing remarks that, far from being instrumental in filling gaols with lunatics, we have invariably looked upon the practice with regret and disapprobation, and feeling constrained to use a discretionary power in the selection of cases, fairly apportioning the claims of each city or county for accommodation, we cannot be deemed accountable for not at once and promiscuously transmitting them to already over-crowded Asylums. In one year after the enlargement of the Richmond Asylum we got warrants issued for the removal to it of all the lunatics, ninety-six in number, in the prisons of the district. Within another twelvemonth, however, there were upwards of sixty fresh committals, chiefly to the Dublin prisons, than which none can possibly be more unsuited for the detention of the class in question.

Adverting to the treatment which lunatics receive in gaol, save in some few instances, where we remonstrated in the strongest manner, great humanity is displayed in their regard by the staff of these institutions; and in which we can truly state that, as far as their arrangements admit, every consideration is extended to them. One instance in particular occurred at Carrick-on-Shannon, in which a female was removed to the Asylum, as reported by the Visiting Physician of that Institution, in a very neglected and otherwise most unfit state, and died twenty-four hours after admission. We immediately brought the case under the notice of the gaol authorities; an investigation was held by the Board of Superintendence, and resolutions passed acquitting their officers of blame, which precluded any further interference on our part. *Dangerous Lunatics. — Treatment in Gaols.*

Strange as it may appear, there are ingredients of success in many gaols which do not exist to the same extent in lunatic asylums, and which we believe have not been referred to by any previous authority. We allude to greater association with the sane, some of the well-conducted prisoners being allocated to act as attendants, and to the fact that the lunatics are placed in custody during the earliest or most curative phase of the malady; these combined with an isolation from former companionship make up, in some degree, for the want of those curative appliances obtainable in regularly constructed establishments. *Recoveries.*

With respect to the actual committal of lunatics to prison as " dangerous," although we have no restrictive control whatever, copies of the warrant, and an abstract of the depositions, are immediately forwarded to our office, and thus we become acquainted with the details of each case, acting thereupon as the medium of transference, or bringing under the cognizance of the Executive any irregularities or illegalities that may appear in them, and, in dubious cases, referring points for the opinion of the Law Adviser to the Crown, in order that, if necessary, the Justices should be communicated with. Still, if the forms are accurately filled up and signed by them, there is no authority to question either their judgment or jurisdiction. It frequently occurs that eight or nine committals of persons as "dangerous lunatics" are returned to us by the same post. In Dublin, sometimes as many as four or five on the same day; and on one occasion, the 5th of March, three lunatics were sent to prison from the Nenagh poorhouse alone. *No control with respect to committals.*

In a preceding paragraph we remarked that the system of committing lunatics was attended with peculiar injustice to the metropolis, the truth of which observation will at once be apparent on reference to the sixth clause of the Act, which directs, that they shall be removed from the prisons direct *to the asylum of the district*, there to remain in accordance with the provisions of the Statute. In the absence of a law of settlement, they are thus chargeable to the immediate city or county of the prison. Such are the inducements and such the tendency for idlers and mendicants, amongst whom the insane may be largely numbered—as well as for persons on business avocations—to congregate in large towns, that they become filled with an extraneous population; we find, for instance, in Dublin a far greater proportion of lunatics committed as dangerous than obtains with a similar number of inhabitants in rural districts; and hence it becomes liable for the maintenance of those who, properly speaking, have no claims upon its charity. We believe that fully one-third of the inmates whose support at the Richmond is defrayed by the city are utter strangers, and a tax of near £2,000 a year is thus imposed on the ratepayers. Forty-nine females, from different parts of the country, have been committed to Grangegorman within the period of this report; and on two occasions during the last year, when analyzing the number of lunatics confined there, we found that out of sixteen, seven were from different distant counties—one of them so remote as Kerry. A foreign sailor, for instance, becoming dangerously insane on board a vessel in the port of Dublin, is quite as chargeable on the city for the period of his detention, were it even to extend over forty years, as a native of the Liberties, descendant of a family resident therein for generations. This abuse cannot be said to exist throughout the country to an extent which could prove locally prejudicial, a sort of reciprocity being practically established between one county and another; the injustice to the metropolis becomes therefore more evident, and the necessity for applying a remedy more pressing. *Tax imposed on Dublin by committal of strangers when insane.*

We have now to bring under your Excellency's notice the state of the Central or Criminal Asylum at Dundrum, which, placed entirely under our supervision and control on its completion, in 1849, by the Earl of Clarendon, the then Lord Lieutenant, has been since equally confided to our direction by his Lordship's successors, the Earls of Eglinton and St. Germans, as well as by your Excellency. *Central Asylum for Criminal Lunatics.*

In previous reports we felt justified in representing the condition of this important Institution to be satisfactory in its various details, and on the present occasion we are happy to be enabled to confirm the accounts already given of its success. The number of lunatics confined in the establishment is precisely the same at the present date as on the *Admissions, discharges, &c,*

CENTRAL ASYLUM FOR CRIMINAL LUNATICS.

31st March, 1855, being eighty-two males, and forty-four females. Twenty-six patients were discharged or died during the two years which intervened,—twenty-one males, and five females, and the vacancies thus created have been filled by new cases. Of those discharged fourteen were recovered, seven of whom were liberated, by order of the Lord Lieutenant; three sent back for trial; three convicts returned to the prisons from whence they came; and one prisoner to a county gaol; one was sent to a private asylum, and eleven died.

The admissions were from the following sources:—County and City Gaols, ten; Spike Island, five; Cork Government Prison, four; and Philipstown, seven, three being still there awaiting removal. It thus appears that the last-named prison has had, and that, too, in one year, more lunatics than any other. The total number of its residents being 784; the average of insanity in it, is therefore, over one per cent., a most disproportionate ratio as regards the amount of lunacy, properly so called, in the population at large, which is not more than one in 700. The only explanation on this head we can afford is, that the worst classes of convicts, in a physical point of view, are transferred from other Government Prisons to Philipstown, which is the invalid depot.

Distinctive features.

The distinctive features of the Central Asylum have been noticed in former reports. It was stated that there is not that frequent change of inmates which occurs in ordinary asylums, that recovery does not bring with it the right to be liberated, and that as a consequence, greater facilities are afforded for becoming acquainted with the different individuals in charge, their various dispositions and traits of character, than are to be found in other asylums, as also of testing the permanence of recovery, when it takes place. It may, however, be added, that from the comparatively small number in the asylum, a more exact and intimate knowledge is had of the individuals than if it was much greater. In fact, there is a nearer approach to a purely domestic inspection and control than can be had in very extensive establishments for the insane.

Insane convicts.

The greatest, indeed the sole, difficulty to be dealt with at the Central Asylum arises from the occasional residence in it of culprits who either feign insanity or whose claim to the designation of lunatic is, at best, but doubtful. There are persons transferred from gaols subsequent to conviction, and at whose trial the question of insanity was never entertained. Some of these may be faithfully described as having set discipline at defiance. Indifferent alike to remonstrance and to punishment—influenced, as it were, by a determination not to yield till their object was attained—intractable in prison—their conduct uncertain and unaccountable—the authorities there report to the Executive that they have no appliances for their treatment; that the establishment is kept in turmoil and confusion by such characters, and submitting their removal to the Criminal Asylum, to which they are accordingly drafted as vacancies occur.

The air of Dundrum, the situation, remarkable for its cheerfulness and salubrity—transition from close confinement, and the restraint and regimen of a prison to comparative freedom and a better diet, produce in a short time a change in their demeanour; they still, however, consider themselves entitled to be supported by Government, and that being recognised as lunatics, they should not be required to work.

Questionable cases.

Among others, there is a convict returned from a penal settlement, who for a day or two after his arrival was inclined to be exceedingly troublesome, yet he soon became amenable, and has for over eight months continued to be very obedient, and perfectly tranquil and rational both in speech and in demeanour. A second, formerly an inmate of Philipstown Prison, will do nothing except as it pleases him, which is very seldom; and when urged to work, replies with the naive remark that he is a lunatic. Were application to be made by their friends for the admission of these and such other individuals into an ordinary asylum, we doubt if they could possibly be received, the symptoms are so very slight and unsatisfactory, at least in the opinion of the two highly informed physicians who are professionally connected with the Institution. We do not mean to commit ourselves to the assertion, that there may not be something wrong about the parties referred to, at the same time we are perfectly satisfied that were many of them respectable members of society and possessed of means, if a commission of inquiry was issued, a jury could scarcely be found to pronounce them incompetent, by reason of insanity, to manage their own affairs, or disqualified to enjoy their civil rights and liberties.

The question hence arises, are persons to be recognised as lunatics by law who, thoroughly cognizant of right and wrong, having committed offences against public order, and whilst undergoing the punishment consequent thereon, set authority and discipline at nought by their insubordination and perversity of temper? For if, after conviction, these traits of character protect from the penalties attached to crime, they should, *a fortiori*, at trial, when duly established, procure acquittal on the plea of mental incapacity, although the parties may be competent to distinguish good from evil. The solution of this point is a matter of great importance, not alone to the criminal code of this country, but likewise to that of the sister kingdom.

Once within the walls of the Central Asylum no distinction is made in regard of the CENTRAL ASYLUM FOR CRIMINAL LUNATICS.
inmates, every just indulgence being alike conceded to all: what appear well-grounded
suspicions may be entertained of the condition of some, hut still human judgment at best
heing fallible, all due consideration is willingly extended to them. That malingerers have
been admitted is certain, and that on the best authority, viz., their own acknowledgment;
men who played their parts, while in confinement, so well—having become adepts, by
association in gaol with the really insane—that it would have been difficult to discover
the deceit. These cases, we are fully aware, must be very troublesome in prisons. On
the other hand, we do not think that the Asylum at Dundrum is an appropriate place for
any but those who are truly insane, and that in such an institution there cannot be two
different systems of treatment, which would, we apprehend, he productive of insubordination, and other serious inconveniences. It appears to us that it might he advisable
to erect a detached prohationary ward, in connexion with one of the Government
prisons, for the temporary residence of those who, while undergoing sentence, may from
time to time appear to be mentally deranged, by which means a better opportunity to
judge of their state would be afforded than at present can possibly exist; and a special
system of treatment, hoth moral and medical, could he adopted to test the reality of the
symptoms.

If the prohationary ward was at the Asylum, one of the ohjects aimed at hy persons
feigning insanity would he attained, namely, removal from prison; thus holding out an
inducement to them to persist at all hazards in their attempts to deceive, and encouraging
others to imitate their example.

During the last ten years we have had a tolerahly large experience in lunacy, feigned as Feigned or real insanity.
well as real, and in aiding the prosecution of certain capital cases to conviction, have,
with local physicians, heen instrumental in checking it as a plea; to those cases we have
cursorily referred in previous Reports. The henevolence certainly—possibly, it may
he, the superior knowledge—of some would associate crime with insanity; we do not, however, coincide in the view, that a disregard of moral perceptions cau qualify deeds, the
results as well as the responsibilities of which are perfectly well understood beforehand,
hy the perpetrators of them; at the same time we cannot hut consider it a misfortune
to the insane to he acquitted on the plea of lunacy, without that special statement of every
circumstance which might tend to establish their irresponsibility, or mitigate the character
of their offence; in either case, acquittal often tells against the parties themselves,
changing a definite to an indefinite period of confinement, a fact most justly suggested as
a precaution to counsel, we believe, by the late Baron Alderson; but it is not with the
legal so much as the social point-we have to deal; for in the asylum at present there are two
or three inmates confined *as lunatics* who never evinced a symptom of insanity to our knowledge, one of whom particularly inveighs against having been transformed into a lunatic in
the dock by counsel, to his great dismay and surprise at the moment, and to his continued
discontent for a period of over eight years, during which he has heen in confinement. In a Particulars of case necessary when lunacy is pleaded.
preceding Report to your Excellency, we took the liberty of suggesting that in every
iustance in which a person was acquitted on the ground of insanity, it would he advisahle
that witnesses should be examined in court, so as to have the attendant circumstances and
all details of the occurrence elicited. A sane man, for example, may he acquitted of the
death of another, and discharged from the dock on full evidence of the particulars. If
a fellow-creature loses his life by a lunatic, the individual, no doubt, escapes punishment
on the plea of insanity; hut when he recovers, there is a deficiency of explanatory facts,
much to the disadvantage of the lunatic, who though perfectly sane may still be doomed
to a long deprivation of liberty. Cases have heen submitted during the last year bearing
on this point, in which such information would have heen practically useful in assisting
your Excellency to form a decision.

The number of applications for the transference of lunatics under the Act, and most of Number of applications for admission of petty offenders.
them for minor trangressions, became latterly so great, and such was the abuse which might
ensue if every petty offender, because he happened to break the letter of the law, was
to be sent to the Criminal Asylum, that we communicated at full length with Mr.
Horsman, the Chief Secretary, on the subject, who directed cases to be laid before the
Law Officers of the Crown, as to whether it was ohligatory on the Lord Lieutenant or not
to send such parties to the Criminal Asylum, and also as to His Excellency's authority
to discharge them when deemed advisable. The opinions of the Attorney-General and Opinion of Law Officers.
of the Solicitor-General fully justified, we are happy to say, the view taken by us, that
there exists a discretionary power with the Lord Lieutenant, both as to the custody and
discharge of such lunatics; and hence we trust to find that the Institution at Dundrum
will he amply sufficient for every legitimate claim on its accommodation, and fulfil the
object of its erection, without entailing additional expense on the Treasury.

CENTRAL ASYLUM FOR CRIMINAL LUNATICS.
Cases under consideration for discharge.

There are ten cases at present under your Excellency's consideration for discharge; and with contingencies of deaths at three per cent. as a minimum, and the termination of the legal sentence of imprisonment on five individuals, a margin of about twenty vacancies will be afforded for the coming year.

Judicious management.

The domestic arrangements, under the judicious and truly benevolent management of Dr. Corbet, the Resident Physician, are highly satisfactory, as may be best inferred from the fact, that though the Asylum has now been in operation over six years, he has never found it necessary to recommend the dismissal or even the suspension of an attendant; whilst the patients, who are treated with every consideration, feel that, on the one hand, as no unkindness towards them would he tolerated, so on the other, no impropriety of conduct on their part would be passed unnoticed. Taking into consideration the materials to be acted upon, and the little hold that moral principles have had on many of the individuals in their previous career, it often excites our surprise how few transgressions are committed by the inmates of the Dundrum Asylum, in fact, the wilful breaking now and then of a pane of glass, up to the present at least, may be regarded as constituting the sole offence.

Observance of religion.

The example, too, given to irregularly disposed parties, by the general observance of religion, we believe has materially tended to awaken in them the better sentiments of human nature; and we feel bound to bear our continued testimony to the comfort which they derive from attending at Divine worship, as frequently expressed to us by many of the patients themselves.

Non-restraint.

With regard to mechanical coercion, nothing of the kind was had recourse to within the last two years, a fact which shows that restraint would not be employed except under very urgent circumstances. An epileptic homicide, a man of powerful frame, wears, when excitable, a soft leathern girdle, to which is attached a strap of similar material buckled loosely around the wrist, but not interfering with a certain amount of freedom of motion to the arms. He habitually uses listen shoes or slippers. This lunatic was a terror to those with whom he came in contact, so sudden and, without the slightest provocation, so dangerous were his impulses. Thus, however, guaranteed, he is permitted to go about at his pleasure, both in and out of doors; the very feeling, as it were, that he is under bodily restraint would seem to control the violence of his temperament much more than seclusion in a padded room or the physical power of attendants, which, with him, would provoke an ungovernable reaction.

As to punishment, it is scarcely recognised, unless the denial of some slight indulgence, or the deprivation of a meat dinner, be considered such. The only one, in the opinion of the insane themselves, is a cold bath, and which has been resorted to on five occasions—four times with men, each in the presence of the Resident Physician, and once in the case of a female, the matron being in attendance to observe the result.

Recoveries.

The recoveries cannot be expected to bear a favourable comparison with those in district or private asylums, inasmuch as the majority of the cases transferred to this institution on its opening were of long standing, and comprised several who were idiotic or epileptic; still many cures have been effected, and some patients, looking to our experience of their amenable and quiet behaviour, might be set free, provided they had friends willing and competent to receive them, although we cannot reckon them as of perfectly sound understanding. The sanitary condition has been most satisfactory, and the mortality *below* the average in the general population, being on the whole, from the beginning, a period of seven years, but 2½ per cent. In the past two years, however, the deaths from paralysis and consumption, principally, bear a larger proportion to the number of inmates than formerly, being 4 per cent. The following table gives a general view of the state of the inmates of the Central Lunatic Asylum on 31st March, 1857:—

Offences.	Males.	Females.	Total.
Homicide,	27	7	34
Infanticide,	–	8	8
Violent Assault,	25	6	31
Burglary, Arson, &c., &c.,	32	21	53
Total,	84	42	126

Mental Condition.	Males.	Females.	Total.
Sane,	10	8	18
Improved,	21	9	30
Insane,	38	17	55
Idiots,	15	8	23
Total,	84	42	126

In our last report we mentioned the case of a lunatic who had a narrow escape of his life, from an attack made on him by one of his companions, irritated at his lampoons. The same man's ruling passion of ridicule still continuing in full force, he was again severely maltreated by another patient, who wounded him in the shoulder with a scythe. No other casualty of any kind occurred during the two years just elapsed; and notwithstanding the ample freedom conceded to the various inmates at Dundrum, the extent of the grounds, over twenty acres, and the apparent insecurity from the walls not being higher than those around a private residence, we have not to record even a temporary escape.

The patients in the asylum are, as a general rule, kept at some occupation ; almost the whole are of the peasant class, and we regret to state, that scarcely a third can read and write. In such a society, literary amusements are availed of to a very limited extent; the greater portion of the men who are capable of exertion, are engaged in cultivating the ground, which tends to the well-being of body and of mind. There are others employed at trades. The shoes for the use of the house are all made by patients, who have been taught in the institution. One smith, a quiet, harmless person, is usefully employed in making and repairing various things in his branch. There is also a tin-smith, a very wild and insane man, but amenable at intervals, and who gets through much work. Two or three were returned as weavers, but no opportunity has been afforded of testing their capability in that line. Some are engaged in assisting the attendants in various domestic duties ; and about thirty-three are quite unfit for any occupation.

Of the forty-four females in the house, thirty-one are usefully employed. Nine in the laundry ; thirteen, knitting or sewing; nine in household work ; and thirteen are inactive. The females are also of the humbler class, and few of them can read or write.

Within the last year—after the ground, previously set, had come into possession—we recommended that the experiment of supplying milk from the farm should be tried, and cows were accordingly purchased for the purpose, with your Excellency's approval.

The experiment has, we are happy to say, been satisfactory, both in point of economy and in securing a better article. Farm buildings, referred to in our last report, with the expectation that they would have been soon provided, are not as yet, we regret to say, available, though in progress of erection for some time. We hope, however, that they will be finished before the next harvest, as very serious inconvenience has hitherto been felt from the want of them, and now that a dairy is added to the other farming operations, they have become doubly necessary.

The reparation of fences around the new grounds, though deferred for some time, is being accomplished, a most necessary precaution in an institution for criminal lunatics.

On reference to the Appendix, it will appear that the expenditure has increased, but not on the average to a greater extent than in District Asylums, which have an advantage in this respect, both from the greater number of their inmates and the lower rate of wages for servants and attendants. It is, however, gratifying to us to be enabled to state, that since the opening of the Central Asylum, now over six years, the Commissioners for auditing the public accounts, to whom we transmit monthly the various items of expenditure, with receipts, vouchers, &c., for investigation, have not had occasion to object to the irregular outlay of a single shilling.

Having had the honour, in April last, to present our Twelfth Annual Return on the state of Lunatic Asylums (Private) in Ireland, licensed under the Act 5th and 6th Vict., cap. 123, and in which we detailed the result of our inspections for the preceding year, embodying all the statistics of insanity in the upper and middle classes of society which appeared to us necessary for your Excellency's information, as well as for that of the Lord Chancellor, we have now to report that, during the year which has just elapsed, no alteration of a material nature has occurred in the general management of these institutions. The law, with some few exceptions, which we shall hereinafter advert to, has been satisfactorily fulfilled, and the inmates of the several asylums have received a similar amount of care and treatment as heretofore.

Last year we stated that a diminution in the number of admissions had occurred. An increase has taken place in the year just ended, the patients admitted being, in 1855, 63 males and 49 females—total, 112 ; and in 1856, 67 males and 68 females—total, 135. The numbers remaining on the 31st December last were 252 males and 210 females—total, 462 ; which show an increase on the previous year of 18 patients.

The discharges during the past year have been fewer than in the year preceding, being 91 in the former against 103 in the latter. Of the 91 discharged, 24 males and 23 females were cured ; 20 males and 24 females not cured, but much improved. The number of females discharged exceeded that of males by 3, although the total of males under treatment exceeded the females by 49. It is remarkable that the *per centage* of recoveries occurring in private asylums is greater among females than males; for, taking the last three years, the result appears to be :—

	1854.			1855.			1856.		
	Males.	Females.	Total.	Males.	Females.	Total.	Males.	Females.	Total.
Under treatment,	322	257	579	315	256	571	316	267	583
Discharged cured,	27	25	52	27	24	51	24	23	47
Died,	17	9	26	10	12	22	15	11	26

PRIVATE ASYLUMS.

Thus, of 322 males in 1854, 27 were discharged cured; and of 257 females, 25. Of 315 males in the year 1855, 27 were cured; and of 256 females, 24. Of 316 males in 1856, 24 were cured; and of 267 females, 23.

The natural inference to be drawn from the foregoing statistics is, that there exists a greater recuperative power among females admitted into private asylums than among males—the reverse being generally the case, though not to the same extent, as regards public asylums. Our experience would refer the explanation of this discrepancy to the fact (at which we have arrived after a careful analysis of the many thousand cases of lunacy which from time to time have come under our notice) that, while moral causes, such as grief, love, anxiety, disappointment, &c., &c., more largely predispose females of the better classes—from their superior education and more refined sensibilities—to mental disease, provided there is no fixed hereditary tendency to insanity, time, quietude, and, above all, absence from the immediate exciting causes, gradually effect a cure.

Sanitary condition.

The sanitary condition of private asylums in Ireland has been very satisfactory, the average mortality being but a fraction over four per cent. on the total number under treatment during the last three years. This is an extremely low rate, as may be inferred from the remarks of Dr. Thurnam, an eminent medical authority, who, in his " Statistics of Insanity," says that " extended inquiry and consideration appear to justify our con. " cluding that, taking considerable periods of time during which there have been no " extraordinary disturbing causes in operation in a mixed county asylum, or in one for the " middle and more opulent classes, as well as paupers, a mortality which exceeds nine or " ten per cent. is usually to he considered as decidedly unfavourable, and one that is " less than seven per cent. as highly favourable."

There was but one accident of a serious nature during the year 1856, which, unfortunately ended in the death of the individual. Bearing in mind, however, the number labouring under suicidal and other destructive tendencies, the fact that no other casualty should have happened is creditable to those in charge of the insane, and proves how careful has been the attention bestowed upon them. The result is still more satisfactory, when it is considered that, of the patients admitted during the year, many had either attempted or meditated personal violence immediately before or after their admission, and that non-restraint is the system in general carried out in these asylums.

Non-restraint.

Some physicians have adopted this system in all cases, without exception, however violent the paroxysm of maniacal excitement under which the patient suffers may be; while others deem recourse to a mild form of mechanical restraint—such as muffs (a thick sort of gloves, calculated to prevent the patient from injuring himself with his hands, tearing his clothes, &c.), or a camisole, which restrains the free use of the arms—preferable, in cases of extreme violence and outrageousness, to personal coercion of attendants, who may themselves become excited, and are exposed to bodily injury.

The following case, taken from a communication made to the Inspectors, requesting their advice thereon, is cited as an instance of the extreme difficulty and danger which are to be encountered in dealing with violent patients: the physician of the " Midland Retreat," where the non-restraint system is adopted in its entirety, reports that one of the ladies under his care in that establishment, Mrs. W——, had, for about two months, exhibited a persevering desire to inflict personal injury on herself. That she endeavoured to wound herself with a pair of scissors, to set her clothes on fire; had beaten her head repeatedly and violently with her hands, and dashed it against any object she could; swallowed two thimbles, a hair-pin, and two common pins, picked, on the moment, from the person of the Superintendent, besides several pebbles and fragments of coal. She endeavoured to strangle herself with her dress; secreted one of her stockings and swallowed it at night; swallowed a letter and its envelope in a moment in his presence; endeavoured to swallow a pen which he allowed her to write to her husband while he was present; picked a comb from the head of the Superintendent, and thrust it into her throat, together with other efforts to commit self-injury. Those who incline to the opinion that restraint cannot, under certain circumstances, be safely laid aside, will doubtless regard this case as an argument in favour of their views; and it is manifest that, in the absence of mechanical appliances, nothing short of the utmost vigilance and circumspection on the part of those in attendance could prevent this lady from accomplishing her design, and that a moment's inattention might be followed by the gravest consequences.

On this subject we may observe, that the total abolition of mechanical restraint has been strongly advocated by some of the most eminent physicians both in England and this country; while, as we have already stated, others of great practical experience, contend that there are cases, such as the above, in which it cannot be wholly dispensed with without imminent risk to the patient, and possible injury to the attendants. We cannot but think that, at least, the discussion of the question, and the support given to the non-restraint system, have been of incalculable advantage, inasmuch as it is now acknowledged, that on most occasions where recourse would heretofore have been had to mechanical appliances,—perhaps, in a severe form,—they can now, with safety, be entirely dispensed with ; and that only in extreme cases, where the physician must be left to the free exercise of his own discretion, should restraint of any kind be resorted to. Private Asylums.

The accident before referred to, occurred at Hampstead Asylum, situated in the immediate vicinity of Dublin. Mr. P—— K——, a native of the county of Monaghan, was admitted on the 16th of May last, labouring under monomania, but without any marked excitability. During the night he succeeded in breaking the shutter of his bedroom window, together with the iron sash ; dropped down on the sill of the next story, and thence upon the bank beneath. The noise produced by the breaking of the glass, attracted notice, and the attendants, pursued, overtook him in the act of crossing the boundary wall, and brought him back to the asylum. Two experienced practitioners visited him soon after the accident, but no injury could be detected ; nor did he exhibit any symptom of having received serious hurt until the next day, when, about three o'clock, he died suddenly. An inquest was held, and a verdict in accordance with the facts found by the jury. One of the Inspectors visited the asylum shortly after the occurrence, and also attended at the inquest. By his direction, a *post mortem* examination took place, when death was found to have resulted from rupture of a bloodvessel in the liver, which was previously in a diseased state. On minute inquiry, it appeared that no suspicions had been entertained by the proprietor that Mr. K—— would have attempted to escape. He was left apparently tranquil about nine o'clock ; the fastenings were in good order, and extreme violence must have been used to force them. Nor could blame be justly attributed to a want of care on the part of the attendants. Accident.

One of the deviations from the act already alluded to occurred with regard to a provincial asylum. The Inspectors, finding that the proprietor had received into that establishment two patients beyond the number allowed by his licence, called upon him to state the circumstances under which he had exceeded the limits fixed by the act ; and on receiving his explanation, felt it their duty to submit the matter for the consideration of the Law Adviser, who recommended that the opinion of the Attorney-General and Solicitor-General should be obtained. A case was accordingly sent to them, upon which they gave it as their opinion, that the proprietor had been guilty of an infraction of the law, and had subjected himself to be prosecuted as a misdemeanant ; but his offence not appearing to have been intentional, and as he proposed to take out a proper licence, thought it would be inexpedient to institute any proceedings against him ; he was accordingly called on to take out the proper licence at the earliest opportunity. Deviations from the Act.

The other instances in which neglect of the act appeared, were, for the most part, in respect to the period of time within which notification of the admission, discharge, or death of patients should be given to the Inspectors by the proprietors. On this point the law might probably admit of amendment, as two clear days only are at present allowed.

Amongst others, there was one very important case officially brought under our notice by the Lord Chancellor during the past year. His Lordship having intimated, through his secretary, that he had received information of the ill-treatment and neglect of an idiot, J. W. H., who resided with his brother in the county of Cork, and directed us to inquire into the circumstances and report thereon to his Lordship ; one of the Inspectors proceeded, accordingly, to visit the idiot, whom he found well-clad and cleanly—his bed-room, considering the unfurnished and neglected state of the mansion itself, being tolerably comfortable. The improvement, however, was of only four or five days' existence, and was effected in consequence of a near relative having intimated to the party complained of, that a letter had been written to the Lord Chancellor on the subject. After a minute and lengthened investigation on the spot, the Inspector came to the conclusion that there was ample foundation for the charges advanced, and that the unfortunate man had been for some years grossly neglected—the only individual in the house who evinced the slightest interest in his regard being his sister-in-law, a poor, broken-hearted looking woman, but of highly respectable connexion. During the whole period of his residence, it appeared that no medical man had been to visit the patient, although he frequently suffered from dysentery ; and for this neglect the only excuse given was, that the brother himself acted in the neighbourhood as an amateur physician. Case brought by the Lord Chancellor under the Inspectors' notice.

The state of the idiot's health, at the time of the Inspector's visit, was far from satisfactory, he being attenuated and weakly. With regard to his means—the Inspector learned that he was possessed of funded and other property, producing an income fully adequate to his maintenance, and which was paid by the trustee for his support and the presumed attentions bestowed upon him. The Inspector also ascertained that he had been previously placed under the care of a neighbouring farmer, to whom an allowance of £30 a-year was made for his maintenance, the balance of the income being handed to his brother and heir-at-law.

The Inspector felt it his duty to animadvert strongly on the neglected state of the idiot, and the unwarrantable misapplication of his means, threatening legal proceedings unless a total change in the mode of treating him should be introduced. On visiting him afterwards, from time to time, in the course of our official inspections of the southern asylum, we found his condition greatly ameliorated, his clothing clean and comfortable, although homely, and his situation, on the whole, satisfactory. He was seen, at our instance, within the last month, by a medical man, who has intimated to us that he continues to be well, and comfortably provided for.

This case fully demonstrates how easily the relatives of persons labouring under insanity may be led to commit the grossest injustice in respect to them, in exhibiting such a total disregard of their wants and necessities. We fear that many such cases exist throughout the country, resulting in great suffering and privation, which are never heard of, and are not discoverable by any legal means at present within our reach. There are, no doubt, numerous instances (some of them having come under our observation), in which the relatives of lunatics have been withheld, by motives of privacy and family pride, from placing their afflicted friends in private asylums. It is, however, very different in cases like that above referred to, where a relative aims at securing pecuniary advantage to himself, at the expense of the comforts, if not the absolute necessaries, of the unfortunate lunatic.

With regard to religious attendance the 21st section of the Act directs the Inspectors to "make special inquiries with reference to the times divine service is read and performed for the benefit and consolation of the patients, &c., &c." On this head we think the intentions of the Legislature have been fairly regarded—although, perhaps, not so fully as we could have wished. No act of negligence, however, has come under our notice of a degree sufficient to justify to our minds a resort to legal proceedings to enforce compliance therewith. But the act itself is so very vague and indefinite on this point (and, indeed, on many others), that recourse to legal measures cannot judiciously be had for any infraction of either the letter or spirit of the section quoted. However, even were its provisions more specific in their application, we should need to be practically convinced of the futility of every remonstrance of a kindly nature addressed to the proprietors of licensed houses before the threat even of possible or contingent penalties would be held out by us.

Altogether our private asylums are, we are happy to say, steadily improving. For however deficient a few may be, as yet, in some respects (and amongst others, we regret to state, not alone in neatness, but also in the essential quality of cleanliness, in regard to which we have observed, now and then, grave cause of complaint), still each succeeding year produces its favourable change in them; and if their present domestic arrangements were contrasted with those that obtained, some short time back, we are satisfied a benevolent mind could not fail to find ample cause of gratulation. We have had to deal, in many instances, with proprietors originally without capital, and with patients paying irregularly as to time, and indifferently as to amount. Thus some private asylums might be fairly regarded in the light of so many necessary evils, as in their absence a majority, perhaps, of their unfortunate inmates would be absolutely neglected. Nevertheless, we feel fully enabled to state, that they have at all times been free from the imputation of the existence within their precincts of any practices involving personal cruelty—which is more, perhaps, than can be said of some institutions of a similar kind elsewhere.

We beg to assure your Excellency, that it has been our unceasing endeavour to obviate, as far as lay in our power, such faults, deficiencies, or instances of neglect towards the inmates of private licensed houses as have come under our observation, and which, but for our interposition, would have remained, perhaps, altogether unheeded; for it is a melancholy fact, and one redounding not over much to the credit of human feeling, that many a poor helpless lunatic, placed within the walls of an asylum, is too frequently forgotten, and, mayhap, the visitation of Providence, in its wisdom, on the parent or sister, deemed a family stigma by the child or brother.

As formerly, so within the past year, cases of moral madness, originating in drink and dissipation, have been frequently admitted into private licensed houses. Some of them, discharged after a few months' confinement, were not since re-admitted, whilst others have been brought back. These latter cases are most perplexing: even after the lapse of a few days the salutary effects of control are visible in their regard; once free, however, they become the mere children of impulse, reckless of personal respect, regardless of the value of money, and scorning even decency itself. Rational in conversation, and most plausible in manner, within the asylum, their conduct is displayed out of doors in a series of the most irrational actions. It is painful to keep such parties confined, but still more so to let them run at large to certain destruction. As an illustration, we may adduce the case of a lady, at present in confinement in a private licensed house, who has been admitted and discharged four or five times within our knowledge, and who, when at liberty, and mistress of her allowance, spends it in one continued orgie of drink and dissipation. We may here observe, that a characteristic of this class is, at all times, an utter disregard of truth, together with an unceasing desire to impose upon the credulity of their hearers by the most specious pretensions to sense and wisdom, and the most solemn promises that a future morality would efface the errors of their past life. *Private Asylums.*

In the course of the year just elapsed, we have observed some instances strongly illustrative of the hereditary transmission of lunacy, and the extent to which it runs in families, so many as four relatives, in the degree of parent and child, having been confined in an asylum together—a fact fraught with serious consideration, and involving even the prospective position of the unborn themselves. Two, and even three members of the same immediate family labouring under symptoms of insanity is, to our knowledge, a matter of common occurrence. At Swift's Hospital, for example, now in existence for more than a century, we find, since its foundation, the same stock to have been continuously represented by its insane members. *Hereditary insanity.*

Your Excellency is, doubtless, already aware of the belief so generally entertained, that public excitement or commotion of whatever kind, social, political, or otherwise, may be truly considered an inciting cause to the development of mental disease. The increase in the number of military men under treatment in private licensed houses during the year 1855, when the warlike spirit of the country was at its highest point, beyond the number in the preceding year, and which amounted to over thirty per cent., is corroborative of the belief. The restoration of peace has likewise been followed, even in asylums, by beneficial effects, especially in the case of these gentlemen, their number having decreased from twenty-eight, who were under treatment during the year 1855, to twenty-two during the year just ended. Besides those persons connected with the profession of arms, military delusions have also largely entered into the imagination of others; and even the female sex has not escaped the contagious influence of the public enthusiasm—one young lady, in particular, going so far as to consider herself the rightful wife of Marshal Pellisier, and Duchess of Malakhoff.

Four marked cases of profound religious despondency have come under our observation since the date of our last Report, two of which, it is satisfactory to state, are now convalescent; the others are still labouring strongly under the most melancholy delusions. Both are ladies: the one, advanced in years, and who had been most assiduous in her religious observances, represents that she is "impregnated bodily" by the Devil, that he "dwells in every portion" of her, and that she is destined never to die; the other, a young lady, twenty-three years of age, was also a regular attendant at church, but now says, that going there more for the purpose of showing off her dress and person than to pray, she, as a punishment, became as one possessed. Both the victims to these strange delusions have exhibited strong suicidal tendencies, whilst, by an extraordinary anomaly of the human mind, their sentiments of religion are far from being extinct, and it is through a judicious application of them that hopes of ultimate improvement may, to a considerable extent, be entertained.

Heretofore we have had frequent cause to observe the want in this country of asylums adapted to meet the exigencies of a large class, against whom public or pauper district asylums may be regarded as practically closed. We refer to the community of shopkeepers and farmers who have means sufficient, under ordinary circumstances, to place their families beyond the reach of want, but not adequate, when their relatives become insane, to pay for the maintenance of the latter in private asylums. In some few cases of great urgency the Governors of District Asylums have admitted "paying patients" at the ordinary cost of maintenance, but this has occurred in those establishments where there existed no pressure for room. We trust that some foundations, whether through the benevolence of private individuals, or by a speculation which, originating in motives of Christian charity, cannot, in the end, fail of success, will, at no distant period, be established. We are the more sanguine in these hopes, as we understand that a bequest of many thousand pounds has been already made for this most laudable purpose, to a committee of gentlemen, and that an institution capable of accommodating thirty lunatics, at an average cost for maintenance of twenty guineas per head, will be speedily opened under their direction, assisted by a religious sisterhood. *Want of Asylum accommodation for persons of humble means.*

Summing up the results of our progressive experience from year to year, on the state and bearing of lunacy in this country, and on the organization of establishments generally for the insane—we would recommend that the existing asylums repaired fully, where repairs are needed, and supplied with the appurtenances of judiciously constructed establishments, such as lavatories, baths, workshops, water-closets, &c., &c., should be constituted hospitals for the treatment of mental disease in its early and more curable stages, as well as receptacles for lunatics no matter how hopeless their recovery, but who, for their *Concluding Remarks.*

Concluding Remarks.

own or public safety, require a constant and careful supervision. For these two legitimate objects, we think, with similar establishments in Donegal and Wexford, and certain enlargements at Clonmel and Armagh, the present asylums could be rendered amply sufficient for the exigencies of the country. Most of the original institutions require to be partially remodelled, to secure a better classification of patients; and as they are with one or two exceptions deficient in infirmaries, chapels, laundry accommodation, and in large halls or dining-rooms, suitable provision under these heads should not be overlooked. We would disembarrass poorhouses of all lunatic inmates, and existing asylums of the idiotic and epileptic classes, who are at present supported therein at a large expense and without any commensurate hope of benefit, by allocating them in plain structures, but still well devised for the object, where quiet and chronic patients might find a refuge, placed under the same central control as the acute and dangerous just referred to, with a scale of dietary and social comforts beyond what are conceded to the ordinary paupers of a union, having ground for exercise and employment, and their support provided for as in the primitive houses by quarterly advances from the Treasury. For this object we do not think that provincial depôts would be successful: the number of counties attached to each would cause much embarrassment in their working—and the unavoidable expense and inconvenience consequent upon the conveyance of patients from remote localities constitute serious objections. It appears to us more feasible, that each district requiring one should have a chronic hospital for itself; and if the area was extensive, such as that connected with the Ballinasloe Asylum, it might be matter for consideration whether it would be more judicious and beneficial to the counties to have the buildings in question at a distance from, or adjoining the parent establishment.

Present system of management.

Of the present system of management through Governors, subject to certain modifications, on the whole, we cordially approve, believing that gentlemen of education, rank, and position, whose acquaintance with fiscal affairs, and personal interest in the well-being of the country, afford the best guarantee for the due and economical expenditure of its rates, are the most suitable persons to appreciate the peculiar claims of the insane on the benevolence and liberality of the public, as well as from the fact, to which we can personally bear the most gratifying evidence, that a question of party or religion was never mooted within the walls of an Irish Asylum.

Appointment of officers.

We are further of opinion, that the appointment of the principal officers, and the fixing of their salaries, should rest with the Executive, as having a larger sphere from which to select efficient persons, and of suitable qualifications; for without a competent staff to carry them out, laws or rules, however excellent in themselves, soon practically deteriorate.

Laws on Lunacy.

With regard to the subject matter contained in the seventeen existing Lunacy Acts, if codified and properly amended they could easily be compressed into three: the first having reference to lunacy generally and to public lunatic asylums; the second, to private licensed houses for the reception of the insane; and the third, to a distinct legislation for criminal lunacy, and the custody of persons acquitted on the ground of insanity, or of those whose reason may become affected before or after trial. As the present Acts stand they are very vague on many points—a fact best illustrated by the various opinions given on the same question, not alone by different, but occasionally by the same legal authorities. A series of rules and regulations based on the Statutes was passed, by Order in Council, fourteen years ago. Though sensible that many of them, however suitable at the time, are not adapted to the existing state of our lunatic institutions, while awaiting that general and better system of legislation already suggested by us to the Executive, we forbore urging minor details which in due course should be the result of a comprehensive legal enactment.

In the Report which we have now the honour to submit, while giving the fullest statistical information in the Appendix, we have restricted ourselves to such general observations as we considered practically useful; and begging to assure your Excellency it has been our unceasing object to improve in every way the condition of the insane of all classes in this country, we have the honour to be, with the greatest deference,

Your Excellency's obedient servants,
JOHN NUGENT,
For self and Colleague.

June 10th.

[It is with feelings of sincere regret I have here to state, that during the last six months, included in the period of this Report, the Lunatic Asylums' Office was deprived of the experience and assiduous attention of my respected colleague, in consequence of a severe accident which occurred to him when on a tour of inspection. The professional character of Dr. White is duly appreciated by the public; for me, a friend who valued his private worth, it only remains to add, that the uniform kindliness of his manner simply indicated the benevolence of his disposition.—J. N.]

APPENDIX.

CONTENTS.

APPENDIX A.

No. 1.—TABLE showing the Number of Lunatics, Idiots, and Epileptics in each Police District, exclusive of those in Asylums, Gaols, or Workhouses, on the 31st December, 1856.

Districts.	Lunatics Males	Fem.	Total.	Idiots Males	Fem.	Total.	Epileptics Males	Fem.	Total.	General Total Males	Fem.	Total.	Religion Protestants	Roman Catholics	Presbyterians	Quakers
COUNTY OF ANTRIM:																
Antrim,	11	6	17	26	11	37	14	15	29	51	32	83	38	20	25	–
Ballymena,	6	3	9	25	16	41	7	3	10	38	22	60	12	17	31	–
Ballymoney,	5	6	11	19	16	35	8	10	18	32	32	64	6	17	41	–
Belfast,	4	1	5	29	15	44	6	3	9	39	19	58	36	15	7	–
Carrickfergus,	5	7	12	25	21	46	14	18	32	44	46	90	10	9	71	–
Glenarm,	1	1	2	8	8	16	8	4	12	17	13	30	10	17	3	–
Total,	32	24	56	132	87	219	57	53	110	221	164	385	112	95	178	–
COUNTY OF ARMAGH:																
Armagh,	4	2	6	16	12	28	7	11	18	27	25	52	23	29	–	–
Ballybot,	8	–	8	18	3	21	3	1	4	29	4	33	11	22	–	–
Crossmaglen,	4	4	8	11	6	17	3	2	5	18	12	30	4	26	–	–
Newtownhamilton,	2	3	5	24	9	33	8	10	18	34	22	56	28	28	–	–
Portadown,	12	5	17	15	14	29	22	18	40	49	37	86	60	26	–	–
Total,	30	14	44	84	44	128	43	42	85	157	100	257	126	131	–	–
COUNTY OF CARLOW:																
Bagenalstown,	1	1	2	6	3	9	1	5	6	8	9	17	4	13	–	–
Borris,	4	1	5	8	4	12	5	6	11	17	11	28	3	25	–	–
Carlow,	–	2	2	1	6	7	7	4	11	8	12	20	1	19	–	–
Tullow,	3	1	4	15	15	30	7	7	14	25	23	48	6	42	–	–
Total,	8	5	13	30	28	58	20	22	42	58	55	113	14	99	–	–
COUNTY OF CAVAN:																
Arva,	–	1	1	8	3	11	3	3	6	11	7	18	1	17	–	–
Bailieborough,	10	2	12	18	10	28	7	15	22	35	27	62	16	46	–	–
Ballyjamesduff,	3	2	5	19	11	30	6	3	9	28	16	44	8	36	–	–
Belturbet,	2	–	2	7	9	16	–	2	2	9	11	20	3	17	–	–
Cavan,	5	1	6	8	1	9	9	9	18	22	11	33	6	27	–	–
Cootehill,	4	3	7	17	6	23	4	2	6	25	11	36	15	21	–	–
Killeshandra,	–	2	2	8	10	18	4	7	11	12	19	31	10	21	–	–
Swanlinbar,	1	3	4	13	9	22	3	4	7	17	16	33	5	27	1	–
Total,	25	14	39	98	59	157	36	45	81	159	118	277	64	212	1	–
COUNTY OF CLARE:																
Broadford,	1	1	2	2	–	2	1	2	3	4	3	7	–	7	–	–
Corrofin,	1	4	5	8	6	14	3	4	7	12	14	26	–	26	–	–
Ennistymon,	3	2	5	11	9	20	6	3	9	20	14	34	–	34	–	–
Ennis,	4	–	4	1	4	5	–	–	–	5	4	9	1	8	–	–
Killadysert,	1	4	5	7	1	8	5	4	9	13	9	22	–	22	–	–
Killaloe,	1	–	1	4	1	5	3	2	5	8	3	11	–	11	–	–
Kilrush,	–	1	1	11	11	22	1	5	6	12	17	29	–	29	–	–
Newmarket on Fergus,	5	4	9	9	4	13	10	13	23	24	21	45	–	45	–	–
Tulla,	2	1	3	11	5	16	4	7	11	17	13	30	–	30	–	–
Total,	18	17	35	64	41	105	33	40	73	115	98	213	1	212	–	–
COUNTY OF CORK, E.R.:																
Ballincollig,	–	–	–	10	3	13	2	2	4	12	5	17	–	17	–	–
City of Cork,	1	1	2	5	8	13	3	5	11	12	14	26	7	19	–	–
Charleville,	2	4	6	10	3	13	1	1	2	13	8	21	1	20	–	–
Fermoy,	1	–	1	17	9	23	7	7	14	25	13	38	4	34	–	–
Glanmire,	1	1	2	5	2	7	2	–	2	8	8	11	–	11	–	–
Kenturk,	3	–	3	5	7	12	5	9	14	13	16	29	–	29	–	–
Kinsale,	–	–	–	4	–	4	–	–	–	4	–	4	2	2	–	–
Mallow,	1	1	2	12	7	19	2	4	9	15	12	27	3	24	–	–
Middleton,	3	1	4	15	4	19	8	2	10	26	7	33	2	31	–	–
Mitchelstown,	–	3	3	15	2	17	2	9	8	17	11	28	–	28	–	–
Passage,	2	7	9	5	5	10	2	10	12	9	22	31	0	25	–	–
Youghal,	4	1	5	5	4	9	3	5	8	12	10	22	2	20	–	–
Total,	18	19	37	108	51	150	40	51	91	160	121	287	27	260	–	–
COUNTY OF CORK, W.R.:																
Bandon,	3	–	3	14	9	23	7	1	8	24	10	34	8	26	–	–
Bantry,	1	1	2	6	4	10	5	6	11	12	11	23	–	23	–	–
Castletown,	–	–	–	4	2	6	3	2	5	7	4	11	–	11	–	–
Clonakilty,	–	1	1	10	3	13	2	4	6	12	8	20	3	17	–	–
Dunmanway,	4	2	6	9	9	15	3	3	6	16	11	27	6	21	–	–
Macroom,	3	3	6	8	8	16	10	9	19	21	17	38	–	38	–	–
Skibbereen,	3	4	7	5	3	8	3	3	9	11	10	21	3	18	–	–
Skull,	1	–	1	7	2	9	4	4	8	12	3	18	2	19	–	–
Total,	15	11	26	63	37	100	37	29	66	115	77	192	22	170	–	–
COUNTY OF DONEGAL:																
Ballyshannon,	3	6	9	7	5	12	5	9	14	15	20	35	7	28	–	–
Buncrana,	2	1	3	10	4	14	4	2	6	16	7	23	1	15	7	–
Carndonagh,	2	–	2	4	7	11	7	4	11	13	11	24	2	22	–	–
Dunfanaghy,	11	10	21	10	11	21	3	5	8	24	26	50	4	46	–	–
Glenties,	7	5	12	11	6	17	8	8	16	26	19	45	3	42	–	–

No. 1.—Table showing the Number of Lunatics, Idiots, and Epileptics, &c.—continued.

Districts	Lunatics Males	Lunatics Fem.	Lunatics Total	Idiots Males	Idiots Fem.	Idiots Total	Epileptics Males	Epileptics Fem.	Epileptics Total	Gen. Total Males	Gen. Total Fem.	Gen. Total Total	Religion Protestants	Religion Roman Catholics	Religion Presbyterians	Religion Quakers
Co. DONEGAL—continued.																
Killybegs,	6	3	9	14	12	26	7	11	18	27	26	53	16	37	-	-
Ramelton,	7	1	8	19	6	25	9	6	15	35	13	48	11	32	5	-
Raphoe,	8	10	18	21	20	41	9	-	9	38	30	68	13	37	18	-
Total,	46	36	82	66	71	137	52	45	97	194	152	346	57	259	39	-
COUNTY OF DOWN.																
Ballynahinch,	6	4	10	27	19	46	7	14	21	40	37	77	28	27	22	-
Banbridge,	7	7	14	28	12	40	13	27	40	48	46	94	72	22	-	-
Downpatrick,	6	1	7	22	14	36	5	9	16	35	24	59	28	31	-	-
Newcastle,	10	5	15	23	8	31	5	9	14	38	22	60	10	50	-	-
Newtownards,	8	6	14	22	27	49	12	11	23	42	44	86	9	12	65	-
Rathfriland,	8	7	15	53	30	83	9	10	28	70	56	126	28	76	22	-
Total,	45	30	75	175	110	285	53	86	142	273	229	502	175	218	100	-
CITY OF DUBLIN:																
A Division,	-	-	-	7	10	17	5	1	6	12	11	23	5	18	-	-
B Do.,	-	1	1	8	5	13	2	2	4	10	8	18	1	17	-	-
C Do.,	1	1	2	9	5	14	2	1	3	13	7	19	3	16	-	-
D Do.,	3	1	4	10	4	14	2	2	4	15	7	22	-	21	1	-
E Do.,	-	4	4	8	5	13	3	1	4	11	10	21	3	18	-	-
F Do.,	3	4	7	4	5	9	5	2	7	12	11	23	2	21	-	-
Total,	7	11	18	46	34	80	19	9	28	72	54	126	14	111	1	-
COUNTY OF DUBLIN:																
Balbriggan,	2	3	5	9	5	14	5	2	7	16	10	26	2	24	-	-
Clontarf,	2	4	6	6	1	7	3	2	5	11	7	18	7	11	-	-
Lucan,	1	1	2	3	4	7	-	1	1	4	6	10	1	9	-	-
Rathfarnham,	4	6	10	9	4	13	4	2	6	17	12	29	6	23	-	-
Swords,	2	3	5	6	2	8	-	1	1	8	6	14	2	12	-	-
Total,	11	17	28	33	16	40	12	8	20	50	41	97	18	79	-	-
COUNTY OF FERMANAGH:																
Arney,	2	4	6	27	11	38	8	8	16	37	23	60	21	36	-	-
Derrygonnelly,	2	3	5	7	6	13	1	-	1	10	9	19	9	10	-	-
Enniskillen,	2	5	7	23	17	40	2	5	7	27	27	51	30	24	-	-
Kesh,	2	-	2	15	15	30	7	6	13	24	21	45	32	13	-	-
Lisnaskea,	6	3	9	23	21	43	2	-	2	30	24	54	34	30	-	-
Total,	14	15	29	94	70	164	20	19	39	128	104	232	119	113	-	-
COUNTY OF GALWAY, E.R.:																
Athenry,	2	2	4	3	2	5	2	3	5	7	7	14	-	14	-	-
Ballinasloe,	-	-	-	10	-	10	5	4	9	15	10	25	1	24	-	-
Ballygar,	1	-	1	11	11	22	4	5	9	16	16	32	-	32	-	-
Eyrecourt,	-	-	-	7	-	7	1	-	1	8	-	8	2	6	-	-
Loughrea,	2	3	5	3	5	8	2	4	6	7	12	19	-	19	-	-
Marble Hill,	3	1	4	6	8	14	7	5	12	16	14	30	3	28	-	-
Portumna,	1	-	1	4	-	4	4	1	5	9	1	10	-	10	-	-
Total,	9	6	15	44	32	76	25	22	47	78	60	138	5	133	-	-
COUNTY OF GALWAY, W.R.:																
Clifden,	-	1	1	3	4	7	4	4	8	7	9	16	-	16	-	-
Dunmore,	4	2	6	8	8	16	5	5	10	17	15	32	-	32	-	-
Fairhill,	-	2	2	2	6	8	5	7	12	7	15	22	1	21	-	-
Galway,	1	1	2	7	3	10	5	1	6	13	5	18	-	18	-	-
Gort,	1	1	2	10	3	13	3	4	7	14	8	22	-	22	-	-
Headford,	2	-	2	5	8	13	4	4	8	11	12	23	-	23	-	-
Oughterard,	1	-	1	2	3	5	3	-	3	6	3	9	-	9	-	-
Spiddal,	1	-	1	3	3	6	-	1	1	4	4	8	-	8	-	-
Tuam,	3	-	3	8	5	13	2	3	5	13	8	21	-	21	-	-
Total,	13	7	20	48	43	91	31	29	60	92	79	171	1	170	-	-
COUNTY OF KERRY.																
Cahersiveen,	-	3	3	12	3	15	1	9	10	13	15	28	-	28	-	-
Dingle,	1	1	2	7	5	12	3	8	11	11	14	25	4	21	-	-
Kenmare,	-	4	4	10	6	16	4	4	8	14	14	28	1	27	-	-
Killarney,	3	1	4	13	4	17	3	3	6	19	8	27	3	24	-	-
Listowel,	1	2	3	19	12	31	8	8	16	28	22	50	2	48	-	-
Tralee,	-	1	1	11	14	25	1	2	3	12	17	29	-	29	-	-
Total,	5	12	17	72	44	116	20	34	54	97	90	187	10	177	-	-
COUNTY OF KILDARE.																
Athy,	1	-	1	2	3	5	-	-	-	3	3	6	-	6	-	-
Curragh,	-	-	-	-	-	-	-	-	-	-	-	-	-	-	-	-
Leixlip,	1	2	3	9	4	13	5	4	9	15	10	25	-	25	-	-
Naas,	-	-	-	3	4	7	-	-	-	3	4	7	-	7	-	-
Rathangan,	4	-	4	11	4	15	2	8	10	17	12	29	-	20	-	-
Robertstown,	-	4	4	12	8	20	5	9	14	17	21	38	7	31	-	-
Total,	6	6	12	37	23	66	12	21	33	55	50	105	7	68	-	-

No. 1.—Table showing the Number of Lunatics, Idiots, and Epileptics, &c.—*continued.*

Districts.	Lunatics.			Idiots.			Epileptics.			General Total.			Religion.			
	Males	Fem.	Total	Males	Fem.	Total	Males	Fem.	Total	Males	Fem.	Total	Protestants.	Roman Catholics.	Presbyterians.	Quakers
County of Kilkenny:																
Callan,	1	1	2	8	8	16	5	1	6	14	10	24	1	23	–	–
Castlecomer,	4	1	5	13	14	27	6	16	22	23	31	54	7	47	–	–
Dunmore,	2	1	3	9	3	12	1	4	5	12	8	20	–	20	–	–
Gowran,	–	–	–	5	5	10	4	–	4	9	5	14	–	14	–	–
Johnstown,	2	–	2	6	5	11	4	8	12	12	13	25	–	25	–	–
Kilkenny,	1	1	2	2	2	4	3	6	9	6	9	15	1	14	–	–
Pilltown,	4	3	7	16	7	23	11	5	16	31	15	46	1	45	–	–
Thomastown,	1	1	2	12	9	21	3	4	7	16	14	30	–	30	–	–
Rosbercon,	1	1	2	8	4	12	–	–	–	9	5	14	–	14	–	–
Total,	16	9	25	79	57	136	37	44	81	132	110	242	10	232	–	–
King's County:																
Edenderry,	–	–	–	4	6	10	8	6	14	12	12	24	3	20	–	1
Ferbane,	3	2	5	12	7	19	2	2	4	17	11	28	2	26	–	–
Frankford,	2	–	2	2	4	6	4	4	8	8	8	16	1	15	–	–
Parsonstown,	1	1	2	10	11	21	2	2	4	13	14	27	6	21	–	–
Shinrone,	–	1	1	2	7	9	–	1	1	2	9	11	3	8	–	–
Tullamore,	7	8	15	21	12	33	3	11	14	31	31	62	10	52	–	–
Total,	13	12	25	51	47	98	19	26	45	83	85	168	25	142	–	1
County of Leitrim:																
Ballinamore,	2	–	2	9	5	14	3	8	11	14	13	27	2	25	–	–
Carrick-on-Shannon,	3	1	4	1	1	2	1	3	4	5	5	10	3	7	–	–
Carrigallen,	1	–	1	6	7	13	–	–	–	7	7	14	1	13	–	–
Drumkeeran,	–	2	2	12	7	19	1	–	1	13	9	22	4	18	–	–
Manorhamilton,	6	6	12	15	14	29	5	5	10	26	25	51	12	39	–	–
Mohill,	4	4	8	10	6	16	2	6	8	16	16	32	4	28	–	–
Total,	16	13	29	53	40	93	12	22	34	81	75	156	26	130	–	–
County of Limerick:																
Adare,	2	1	3	7	7	14	1	2	3	10	10	20	2	18	–	–
Bruff,	5	2	7	8	6	14	5	11	16	18	19	37	–	37	–	–
Caherconlish,	1	1	2	1	9	10	–	–	–	2	10	12	1	11	–	–
Cappamore,	1	2	3	5	5	10	2	4	6	8	11	19	–	19	–	–
Castleconnell,	2	1	3	1	–	1	1	–	1	4	1	5	–	5	–	–
Glin,	3	–	3	10	3	13	4	5	9	17	8	25	–	25	–	–
Kilfinane,	3	1	4	11	10	21	9	5	14	23	16	39	–	39	–	–
Limerick,	–	1	1	3	2	5	–	–	–	3	3	6	1	5	–	–
Newcastle,	2	2	4	12	12	24	2	8	10	16	22	38	1	37	–	–
Rathkeale,	–	3	3	8	5	13	1	5	6	9	13	22	2	20	–	–
Limerick (City of),	3	–	3	1	2	3	1	2	3	5	4	9	1	8	–	–
Total,	22	14	36	67	61	128	26	42	68	115	117	232	8	224	–	–
County of Londonderry:																
Coleraine,	12	6	18	15	9	24	1	1	2	28	16	44	32	12	–	–
Londonderry,	1	4	5	25	19	44	4	12	16	30	35	65	32	33	–	–
Magherafelt,	16	8	24	33	24	57	14	4	18	63	36	99	35	64	–	–
Newtownlimavaddy,	9	8	17	30	25	55	14	11	25	53	44	97	62	35	–	–
Total,	40	24	64	103	77	186	33	28	61	170	120	305	161	144	–	–
County of Longford:																
Ballymahon,	–	–	–	8	2	10	–	–	–	8	2	10	2	8	–	–
Drumlish,	4	–	4	5	7	12	7	9	16	16	16	32	1	31	–	–
Granard,	5	2	7	9	7	16	3	3	6	17	12	29	6	23	–	–
Killashee,	2	1	3	3	10	13	1	3	4	6	14	20	–	20	–	–
Longford,	1	4	5	11	12	23	1	5	6	13	21	34	3	31	–	–
Total,	12	7	19	36	38	74	12	20	32	60	65	125	12	113	–	–
County of Louth:																
Ardee,	1	8	9	5	7	12	–	1	1	6	16	22	1	21	–	–
Carlingford,	1	2	3	15	4	19	5	2	7	21	8	29	6	23	–	–
Dundalk,	5	1	6	12	4	16	7	4	11	24	9	33	4	27	–	–
Dunleer,	3	2	5	10	9	19	5	2	7	18	13	31	1	30	2	–
Louth,	2	2	4	1	5	6	1	4	5	4	11	15	–	15	–	–
Total,	12	15	27	43	29	72	18	13	31	73	57	130	12	116	2	–
County of Mayo:																
Ballina,	3	1	4	15	13	28	5	6	11	23	20	43	7	36	–	–
Ballaghaderreen,	2	1	3	3	2	5	3	4	7	8	7	15	–	15	–	–
Ballinrobe,	3	1	4	5	6	11	3	4	7	11	11	22	–	22	–	–
Belmullet,	–	2	2	5	3	8	3	4	7	8	9	17	–	17	–	–
Castlebar,	2	2	4	13	6	19	5	–	5	20	8	28	1	27	–	–
Claremorris,	2	4	6	2	4	6	1	–	1	5	8	13	–	13	–	–
Newport,	–	–	–	2	2	4	5	1	6	7	3	10	–	10	–	–
Swineford,	2	–	2	7	2	9	1	7	8	10	9	19	–	19	–	–
Westport,	1	5	6	7	7	14	3	6	9	11	18	29	4	25	–	–
Total,	15	16	31	59	45	104	29	32	61	103	93	196	12	184	–	–
County of Meath:																
Athboy,	–	1	1	12	10	22	7	5	12	19	16	35	1	34	–	–
Duleek,	2	1	3	6	7	13	5	1	6	13	9	22	1	21	–	–

No. 1.—TABLE showing the Number of Lunatics, Idiots, and Epileptics, &c.—*continued.*

Districts.	Lunatics.			Idiots.			Epileptics.			General Total.			Religion.			
	Males.	Fem.	Total.	Males.	Fem.	Total.	Males.	Fem.	Total.	Males.	Fem.	Total.	Protestants.	Roman Catholics.	Presbyterians.	Quakers.
Co. MEATH—*continued.*																
Dunshaughlin,	2	3	5	4	1	5	1	3	4	7	7	14	1	13	—	—
Kells,	5	1	6	9	7	16	5	4	9	10	12	31	1	30	—	—
Knock,	1	1	2	12	11	23	5	2	7	18	14	32	1	31	—	—
Longwood,	—	1	1	7	6	13	2	2	4	9	9	18	2	16	—	—
Navan,	2	1	3	5	2	7	3	1	4	10	4	14	—	14	—	—
Trim,	2	1	3	17	12	29	2	4	6	21	17	38	4	34	—	—
Drogheda, Town of,	—	1	1	2	3	5	4	4	8	6	8	14	4	10	—	—
Total,	14	11	25	74	59	133	34	26	60	122	96	218	15	203	—	—
COUNTY OF MONAGHAN:																
Carrickmacross,	2	2	4	5	8	13	2	2	4	9	12	21	1	20	—	—
Castleblayney,	8	1	9	22	26	48	8	6	14	38	33	71	14	40	—	—
Clones,	—	—	—	18	16	34	2	4	6	20	20	40	16	18	8	6
Monaghan,	11	17	28	24	24	48	14	11	25	49	54	101	35	66	—	—
Total,	21	20	41	69	74	143	26	23	49	116	117	233	66	153	11	—
QUEEN'S COUNTY:																
Abbeyleix,	2	1	3	10	—	10	1	2	3	13	3	16	4	12	—	—
Ballickmoylar,	2	—	2	4	4	8	0	2	8	12	6	18	2	16	—	—
Borris-in-Ossory,	—	1	1	2	4	6	0	4	4	8	6	15	3	13	—	—
Maryborough,	—	—	—	7	2	9	—	2	2	7	4	11	2	9	—	—
Mountmellick,	3	2	5	13	9	22	3	6	9	19	17	30	6	30	—	—
Mountrath,	—	1	1	6	4	10	6	6	12	12	11	23	6	17	—	—
Rathdowney,	—	—	—	5	1	6	2	1	3	7	2	9	6	17	—	—
Stradbally,	2	—	2	0	7	13	5	1	6	13	8	21	4	17	—	—
Total,	9	5	14	53	31	84	27	24	51	89	60	149	26	129	—	—
COUNTY OF ROSCOMMON:																
Athlone,	3	2	5	2	2	4	3	1	4	8	5	13	1	12	—	—
Boyle,	3	—	3	8	4	12	4	1	5	16	5	20	4	16	—	—
Castlerea,	1	2	3	10	0	10	10	6	10	21	17	38	2	30	—	—
Elphin,	—	1	1	6	5	11	1	—	1	7	6	13	1	12	—	—
Frenchpark,	1	—	1	5	5	10	7	3	10	13	8	21	1	20	—	—
Roscommon,	4	4	8	12	6	18	2	3	5	18	13	31	1	30	—	—
Strokestown,	—	—	—	5	3	8	1	1	2	6	4	10	—	10	—	—
Total,	12	9	21	48	34	82	28	15	43	88	58	110	10	130	—	—
COUNTY OF SLIGO:																
Ballysadare,	2	4	6	7	4	11	3	4	7	12	12	24	0	15	—	—
Ballymote,	6	2	8	4	5	9	2	—	2	12	7	10	1	18	—	—
Easky,	8	3	11	8	4	12	1	5	6	12	17	20	3	26	—	—
Riverstown,	4	2	6	6	2	7	2	3	5	11	7	18	4	14	—	—
Sligo,	3	2	5	3	2	5	3	5	8	0	9	18	3	15	—	—
Tobercurry,	2	1	3	11	9	20	4	1	5	17	11	24	1	27	—	—
Total,	25	14	39	38	26	64	15	18	33	78	58	136	21	115	—	—
COUNTY TIPPERARY, N.R.:																
Borrisokane,	4	5	0	6	4	10	10	10	26	26	19	45	13	32	—	—
Borrisoleigh,	2	3	5	9	13	22	1	—	1	12	16	28	2	26	—	—
Lorrha,	—	—	—	—	3	3	—	2	2	—	5	5	—	5	—	—
Nenagh,	7	2	9	7	6	13	5	1	6	19	0	28	1	27	—	—
Newport,	1	1	2	5	1	6	1	2	3	7	4	11	1	10	—	—
Pontroe,	—	—	—	—	—	—	3	—	3	3	—	3	1	8	—	—
Roscrea,	—	—	—	2	2	4	10	1	11	12	3	15	1	11	—	—
Templemore,	3	3	6	8	3	11	5	2	7	16	8	24	—	24	—	—
Thurles,	—	—	—	9	5	14	—	—	—	0	5	14	—	14	—	—
Total,	17	14	31	46	37	83	41	18	59	104	69	173	18	155	—	—
COUNTY TIPPERARY, S.R.:																
Ballynonty,	2	1	3	12	3	15	4	1	5	18	5	24	1	22	—	—
Bansha,	2	1	3	8	6	12	4	5	6	6	15	21	2	19	—	—
Cahir,	—	—	—	4	5	9	4	1	5	8	6	14	—	11	—	—
Carrick-on-Suir,	3	—	3	5	3	8	—	2	2	8	6	13	—	13	—	—
Cashel,	0	—	6	—	2	2	3	4	7	9	6	15	1	11	—	—
Clogheen,	—	—	—	7	2	9	1	1	2	8	3	11	1	10	—	—
Clonmel,	1	2	3	8	5	13	9	6	15	18	14	31	4	27	—	—
Dundrum,	1	1	2	5	5	10	0	4	10	12	10	23	—	23	—	—
Mullinahone,	—	—	—	15	8	23	2	2	4	17	10	27	3	24	—	—
Tipperary,	3	1	4	12	7	19	2	—	2	17	8	25	—	25	—	—
Total,	18	6	24	71	49	120	32	26	58	121	81	202	12	190	—	—
COUNTY OF TYRONE:																
Clogher,	3	3	6	18	25	43	4	1	5	25	29	51	30	24	—	—
Cookstown,	13	6	19	19	19	38	10	8	18	42	33	75	31	44	—	—
Dungannon,	7	7	14	27	21	48	15	20	35	40	48	87	38	55	4	—
Fintona,	8	5	13	22	12	34	5	8	13	35	25	60	30	24	—	—
Omagh,	2	2	4	25	15	40	7	12	19	34	20	84	19	34	10	—
Strabane,	3	3	6	38	26	64	4	8	12	45	37	82	31	48	0	—
Total,	36	26	62	149	118	267	45	57	102	230	201	431	185	229	23	—

No. 1.—TABLE showing the Number of Lunatics, Idiots, and Epileptics, &c.—*continued.*

Districts.	Lunatics.			Idiots.			Epileptics.			General Total.			Religion.			
	Males.	Fem.	Total	Males	Fem.	Total.	Males.	Fem.	Total.	Males.	Fem.	Total	Protestants.	Roman Catholics.	Presbyterians.	Quakers.
COUNTY OF WATERFORD:																
Ballinamult,	—	—	—	6	3	9	3	6	9	9	9	18	1	17	—	—
Coppoquin,	3	4	7	3	4	7	8	5	13	14	13	27	2	25	—	—
Clashmore,	—	—	—	3	1	4	4	—	4	7	1	8	—	8	—	—
Dungarvan,	3	2	5	5	1	6	6	11	17	14	14	28	2	20	—	—
Portlaw,	5	—	5	7	1	8	11	8	19	23	9	32	1	31	—	—
Tramore,	3	3	6	5	5	10	2	1	3	10	9	19	1	18	—	—
Waterford (City of),	—	—	—	1	2	3	1	—	1	2	2	4	2	2	—	—
Total,	14	9	23	30	17	47	36	31	66	70	57	136	9	127	—	—
COUNTY OF WESTMEATH:																
Ballinacarrig,	1	—	1	10	7	17	1	4	5	12	11	23	—	23	—	—
Castlepollard,	—	2	2	9	7	16	2	—	2	11	9	20	2	18	—	—
Castletowndelvin,	2	3	5	6	6	12	6	1	7	14	10	24	—	24	—	—
Glasson,	—	—	—	6	6	12	2	1	3	8	7	15	1	14	—	—
Killeggan,	2	4	6	9	2	11	2	5	7	13	11	24	1	23	—	—
Moate,	1	1	2	6	10	16	5	—	5	15	11	26	—	26	—	—
Mullingar,	2	3	5	6	6	16	3	6	9	14	15	29	3	26	—	—
Total,	8	13	21	58	44	102	21	17	38	87	74	161	7	154	—	—
COUNTY OF WEXFORD:																
Arthurstown,	2	1	3	13	6	19	2	2	4	17	9	26	3	23	—	—
Enniscorthy,	5	1	6	4	4	8	5	8	13	14	13	27	6	21	—	—
Gorey,	5	4	9	7	10	17	1	7	8	13	21	34	11	23	—	—
New Ross,	4	—	4	16	11	27	5	2	7	25	13	38	3	35	—	—
Oulart,	—	2	2	8	10	18	4	3	7	12	15	27	2	25	—	—
Taghmon,	2	2	4	13	7	20	6	13	19	21	22	43	1	42	—	—
Wexford,	15	8	23	31	11	42	10	17	27	56	36	92	3	89	—	—
Total,	33	18	51	92	50	151	33	52	85	158	120	287	26	258	—	—
COUNTY OF WICKLOW:																
Blessington,	1	—	1	3	3	6	2	1	3	6	4	10	1	6	—	—
Baltinglass,	4	5	9	10	5	15	1	2	3	15	12	27	6	21	—	—
Bray,	2	1	3	3	7	10	6	4	10	11	12	23	2	21	—	—
Rathdown,	—	1	1	8	8	16	3	2	5	11	11	22	7	15	—	—
Tinahely,	6	3	9	13	8	21	8	4	12	27	15	42	13	29	—	—
Wicklow,	2	—	2	11	8	19	8	5	13	21	13	34	5	28	—	1
Total,	15	10	25	48	30	87	28	18	40	91	67	158	34	123	—	1

No. 2.—SUMMARY of the foregoing by Counties.

Counties.	Lunatics.			Idiots.			Epileptics.			General Total.			Religion.			
	Males.	Fem.	Total.	Males.	Fem.	Total.	Males	Fem.	Total.	Males.	Fem.	Total.	Protestants.	Roman Catholics.	Presbyterians.	Quakers.
Antrim,	32	24	56	132	87	219	57	53	110	221	164	385	112	95	178	—
Armagh,	30	14	44	64	44	128	46	42	85	157	100	257	126	131	—	—
Carlow,	8	5	13	30	28	58	20	22	42	58	55	113	14	99	—	—
Cavan,	25	14	39	68	59	157	36	45	81	149	118	277	64	212	1	—
Clare,	18	17	35	94	41	195	38	40	78	115	98	213	1	212	—	—
Cork, E.R.,	18	19	37	108	51	159	40	51	91	166	121	287	27	260	—	—
Cork, W.R.,	15	11	26	63	37	100	37	29	66	115	77	192	22	170	—	—
Donegal,	46	36	82	96	71	167	52	45	97	194	152	346	57	259	30	—
Down,	45	30	75	175	110	285	53	89	142	273	229	502	175	218	109	—
Dublin,	11	17	28	39	10	49	12	8	20	56	41	97	18	79	—	—
Dublin City,	7	11	18	46	34	80	10	6	28	72	54	126	14	111	1	—
Fermanagh,	14	15	29	94	70	164	20	10	30	128	104	232	119	113	—	—
Galway, E.R.,	9	6	15	44	32	76	25	22	47	78	60	138	5	163	—	—
Galway, W.R.,	13	7	20	48	43	91	31	29	60	92	79	171	1	170	—	—
Kerry,	5	12	17	72	44	116	20	34	54	97	90	187	10	177	—	—
Kildare,	6	6	12	37	23	60	12	21	33	55	50	105	7	98	—	—
Kilkenny,	16	9	25	76	57	136	37	44	81	132	110	242	10	232	—	—
King's,	13	12	25	51	47	98	10	26	45	83	85	168	26	142	—	1
Leitrim,	16	13	29	53	40	93	12	22	34	81	75	156	20	130	—	—
Limerick,	23	14	36	67	61	128	26	42	68	115	117	232	8	244	—	—
Londonderry,	46	24	64	103	77	180	33	28	61	176	129	305	101	144	—	—
Longford,	12	7	19	36	38	74	12	20	32	60	65	125	12	113	—	—
Louth,	12	15	27	43	26	72	18	13	31	73	57	130	12	116	2	—
Mayo,	15	16	31	59	45	104	29	32	61	103	93	196	12	184	—	—
Meath,	14	11	25	74	59	133	34	26	60	122	96	218	15	203	—	—
Monaghan,	21	20	41	69	74	143	26	23	49	116	117	233	66	153	14	—
Queen's,	9	5	14	53	31	84	27	24	51	89	60	149	26	123	—	—
Roscommon,	12	9	21	48	34	82	28	15	43	88	58	146	10	136	—	—
Sligo,	25	14	39	38	36	64	15	18	33	76	58	136	21	115	—	—
Tipperary, N.R.,	17	14	31	40	37	83	41	18	59	104	69	173	18	155	—	—
Tipperary, S.R.,	18	6	24	71	49	120	32	20	58	121	81	202	12	190	—	—
Tyrone,	36	26	62	149	118	267	45	57	102	230	201	431	185	223	23	—
Waterford,	14	9	23	30	17	47	36	31	66	79	57	136	9	127	—	—
Westmeath,	8	13	21	58	44	102	21	17	38	87	74	161	7	154	—	—
Wexford,	33	18	51	92	50	151	33	52	85	158	120	287	29	258	—	—
Wicklow,	15	10	25	48	39	87	28	18	40	91	67	158	34	123	—	1
Total,	670	509	1,179	2,491	1,771	4,262	1,001	1,110	2,171	4,222	3,890	7,012	1,470	5,783	358	2

MEM.—The Return here given is simply numerical; but the name of each individual, the district to which such individual belongs, and immediate place of residence, are included in the Returns received at the office, and duly registered there.

APPENDIX B.

No. 1.—Table showing the Number of Lunatics, Idiots, and Epileptics in the Union Workhouses on the 31st December, 1856.

Unions.	Lunatics.			Idiots.			Epileptics.			Total.			Religion.				
	Males.	Fem.	Total.	Males	Fem.	Total.	Males.	Fem.	Total.	Males.	Fem.	Total.	Protestants.	Roman Catholics.	Presbyterians.	Dissenters.	Not known.
Abbeyleix,	3	5	8	3	6	9	—	1	1	6	12	18	1	17	—	—	—
Antrim,	—	—	—	2	7	9	—	1	1	2	8	10	1	3	—	—	—
Ardee,	1	2	3	1	4	5	—	1	1	2	11	13	1	12	6	—	—
Armagh,	1	3	4	3	5	8	2	6	8	6	8	14	7	6	1	—	—
Athlone,	—	—	—	1	—	1	2	3	5	3	3	6	—	6	—	—	—
Athy,	—	1	1	5	12	17	1	1	2	6	14	20	3	17	—	—	—
Bailieborough,	—	—	—	3	3	6	—	—	—	3	3	6	—	5	1	—	—
Ballina,	2	8	10	2	3	5	—	2	2	4	13	17	3	14	—	—	—
Ballinasloe,	—	—	—	3	3	6	3	3	6	6	6	12	—	12	—	—	—
Ballinrobe,	—	2	2	2	5	7	8	3	6	5	8	8	8	8	—	—	—
Ballycastle,	—	2	2	2	5	7	—	—	—	2	7	9	5	3	—	—	1
Ballymahon,	—	1	1	2	2	4	—	3	3	2	6	8	1	7	—	—	—
Ballymena,	—	—	—	1	5	6	1	3	4	2	8	10	1	5	4	—	—
Ballymoney,	—	—	—	4	2	6	1	—	1	5	2	7	1	1	6	—	—
Ballyshannon,	—	—	—	—	1	1	—	2	2	—	1	1	—	1	—	—	—
Ballyvaughan,	—	1	1	3	6	9	2	3	5	5	10	15	—	15	—	—	—
Balrothery,	2	—	2	1	4	5	3	3	6	4	7	11	1	10	—	—	—
Baltinglass,	—	2	2	5	5	10	1	3	4	8	8	16	6	3	7	—	—
Banbridge,	—	—	—	1	2	3	—	—	—	1	4	5	—	5	—	—	—
Bandon,	—	—	—	5	5	5	—	—	—	5	5	5	—	5	—	—	—
Bantry,	10	18	28	6	15	21	11	16	27	27	49	76	26	39	11	—	—
Bawnboy,	2	—	2	—	—	2	—	—	—	2	—	2	—	2	—	—	—
Belfast,	—	—	—	3	1	4	—	3	3	6	3	9	—	5	—	—	—
Belmullet,	1	—	1	2	2	4	3	2	5	6	3	9	—	9	—	—	—
Borrisokane,	2	1	3	2	3	5	2	—	2	3	2	5	—	5	—	—	—
Boyle,	2	—	2	7	6	13	—	5	5	4	9	13	—	13	—	—	—
Cahirciveen,	1	1	2	3	4	7	—	4	4	4	10	19	2	17	—	—	—
Callan,	—	—	—	2	1	3	—	—	—	2	5	9	1	8	—	—	—
Carlow,	—	5	5	1	1	1	3	7	10	2	1	3	—	3	—	—	—
Carrickmacross,	—	—	—	4	8	12	—	—	—	3	13	16	—	16	—	—	—
Carrick-on-Shannon,	—	4	4	1	—	1	1	4	5	4	8	12	—	12	—	—	—
Carrick-on-Suir,	—	—	—	6	4	10	—	3	2	6	10	16	2	14	—	—	—
Cashel,	—	—	—	1	1	2	—	1	1	—	2	2	—	2	—	—	1
Castlebar,	—	—	—	1	1	2	—	1	1	1	2	3	1	1	—	—	1
Castleblayney,	1	—	1	1	1	2	—	1	1	1	2	6	—	7	—	—	—
Castlecomer,	—	1	1	1	1	1	1	—	1	1	—	1	—	1	—	—	—
Castlederg,	1	3	4	1	1	2	2	—	2	4	4	8	—	8	—	—	—
Castlerea,	—	2	2	—	—	—	2	4	6	4	6	8	2	6	—	—	—
Castletown,	1	1	2	1	5	6	3	1	4	5	7	12	1	12	—	—	—
Castletowndelvin,	—	1	1	1	7	8	1	1	2	4	8	12	—	12	—	—	—
Cavan,	2	1	3	1	5	6	1	—	1	5	8	9	—	8	—	—	—
Celbridge,	1	4	5	3	6	9	2	2	4	4	24	28	3	25	—	—	—
Claremorris,	—	—	—	1	—	1	—	1	1	1	—	1	—	1	—	—	—
Clifden,	—	—	—	2	1	3	1	2	3	3	—	3	—	3	—	—	—
Clogheen,	3	1	4	5	2	6	—	2	2	2	6	8	—	6	—	—	—
Clogher,	1	5	6	6	2	7	1	—	1	9	3	12	3	10	1	1	—
Clonakilty,	10	8	18	1	1	7	3	2	5	10	8	18	1	17	—	—	—
Clones,	—	—	—	3	5	8	1	1	1	3	2	5	—	5	—	—	—
Clonmel,	25	21	46	14	3	17	30	31	54	56	58	117	25	92	—	—	—
Coleraine,	1	2	3	3	6	9	—	—	—	4	8	12	—	12	—	—	—
Cookstown,	—	2	2	6	3	9	3	1	4	9	6	15	7	8	—	—	—
Cootehill,	1	—	1	2	1	3	—	2	2	3	2	3	—	3	—	—	—
Cork,	3	1	4	5	2	7	1	3	5	2	6	8	—	6	—	—	—
Corofin,	1	5	6	6	1	7	3	2	5	10	8	18	1	17	1	1	—
Croom,	1	30	37	3	5	8	13	17	30	17	58	75	7	68	—	—	—
Dingle,	—	—	—	2	1	3	1	2	3	3	9	12	3	9	—	—	—
Donaghmore,	—	—	—	—	2	2	—	1	1	—	3	3	—	3	—	—	—
Donegal,	—	—	—	—	—	—	—	—	—	—	—	—	—	—	—	—	—
Downpatrick,	3	1	4	2	4	6	—	2	2	2	6	8	3	5	—	—	—
Drogheda,	1	5	6	5	2	7	1	—	1	9	3	12	—	10	1	1	—
Dromore, West,	—	—	—	6	1	7	3	2	5	10	8	18	1	17	—	—	—
Dublin, North,	1	36	37	3	5	8	13	17	30	17	58	75	7	68	—	—	—
Dublin, South,	25	21	46	14	3	17	30	31	54	56	58	117	25	92	—	—	—
Dundalk,	1	2	3	3	6	9	—	—	—	4	8	12	—	12	—	—	—
Dunfanaghy,	—	2	2	1	3	9	3	1	4	6	6	16	7	8	—	—	—
Dungannon,	—	2	2	3	2	5	—	—	—	3	2	5	—	5	—	—	—
Dungarvan,	1	3	4	1	1	1	—	—	—	2	1	3	—	3	—	—	—
Dunmanway,	—	2	2	3	1	3	—	2	3	3	5	7	—	7	—	—	—
Dunshaughlin,	1	3	4	2	13	15	5	3	8	8	19	27	1	26	—	—	—
Edenderry,	—	—	—	4	2	6	—	1	1	4	3	7	2	4	1	—	—
Ennis,	—	3	3	3	1	4	—	1	3	3	1	4	—	4	—	—	—
Enniscorthy,	1	1	2	2	—	3	1	2	3	3	5	6	—	6	—	—	—
Enniskillen,	1	—	1	2	3	5	—	1	1	3	4	7	1	6	—	—	—
Ennistymon,	—	—	—	3	2	10	—	—	—	3	8	11	3	8	—	—	—
Fermoy,	—	—	—	1	—	1	—	—	—	1	—	1	—	1	—	—	—
Galway,	—	—	—	6	—	6	—	—	—	6	—	6	2	4	—	—	—
Glenamaddy,	1	1	2	6	4	5	1	3	9	3	12	14	—	14	—	—	—
Glenties,	1	—	1	1	3	4	3	—	3	5	6	12	—	11	1	—	—
Glin,	1	—	1	7	8	15	—	—	—	7	15	22	—	22	—	—	—
Gorey,	1	—	1	3	2	4	—	1	1	3	3	5	—	5	—	—	—
Gort,	—	—	—	8	2	10	—	—	—	9	2	11	3	8	—	—	—
Gortin,	—	—	—	1	—	1	—	—	—	1	—	1	—	1	—	—	—
Granard,	—	—	—	5	—	6	—	—	—	6	—	6	2	4	—	—	—
Inishowen,	—	1	1	1	4	5	1	8	9	3	12	14	—	14	—	—	—
Kanturk,	1	3	4	1	3	4	—	—	—	6	6	12	—	11	1	—	—
Kells,	—	1	1	7	8	15	3	6	9	5	12	17	—	17	—	—	—
Kinnard,	—	—	—	2	2	4	—	1	1	2	3	5	—	5	—	—	—
Kilkeel,	—	1	1	1	1	2	1	—	1	2	2	4	—	3	1	—	—
Kilkenny,	3	2	5	5	9	14	1	2	3	9	13	22	—	22	—	—	—

No. I.—Table showing the Number of Lunatics, Idiots, and Epileptics, &c.—*continued.*

Unions.	Lunatics Males	Lunatics Fem.	Lunatics Total	Idiots Males	Idiots Fem.	Idiots Total	Epileptics Males	Epileptics Fem.	Epileptics Total	Total Males	Total Fem.	Total Total	Religion Protestants	Religion Roman Catholics	Religion Presbyterians	Religion Dissenters	Religion Not known
Killadysert,	–	–	–	5	4	9	–	–	–	5	4	9	–	9	–	–	–
Killala,	–	–	–	1	4	5	–	–	–	1	4	5	–	5	–	–	–
Killarney,	1	–	1	6	7	13	1	–	1	8	7	15	–	15	–	–	–
Kilmacthomas,	–	1	1	–	2	2	–	–	–	–	3	3	–	3	–	–	–
Kilmallock,	2	2	4	5	7	12	1	2	3	8	11	19	–	19	–	–	–
Kilrush,	1	2	3	6	6	12	1	3	4	8	11	19	2	17	–	–	–
Kinsale,	–	–	–	–	2	2	–	1	1	–	3	3	–	3	–	–	–
Larne,	–	1	1	4	4	8	2	3	5	6	8	14	1	4	9	–	–
Letterkenny,	–	–	–	–	–	–	–	–	–	–	–	–	–	–	–	–	–
Limerick,	5	13	18	2	2	4	2	5	7	9	20	29	2	27	–	–	–
Lisburn,	–	–	–	7	4	11	–	–	–	7	4	11	–	–	3	8	–
Lismore,	–	1	1	1	1	2	–	1	1	1	3	4	–	4	–	–	–
Lisnaskea,	–	1	1	–	1	1	–	3	3	–	5	5	2	3	–	–	–
Listowel,	–	–	–	–	–	–	2	–	2	2	–	2	–	2	–	–	–
Londonderry,	7	6	13	10	12	22	–	–	–	17	18	35	2	26	7	–	–
Longford,	1	–	1	6	2	8	1	1	2	8	3	11	–	11	–	–	–
Loughrea,	–	1	1	–	1	1	1	–	1	1	2	3	–	3	–	–	–
Lowtherstown,	–	–	–	1	–	1	–	–	–	1	–	1	–	1	–	–	–
Lurgan,	1	3	4	2	1	3	3	1	4	6	5	11	7	2	2	–	–
Macroom,	1	–	1	3	3	6	–	–	–	4	3	7	–	7	–	–	–
Magherafelt,	–	2	2	1	2	3	–	–	–	1	4	5	2	2	1	–	–
Mallow,	–	–	–	1	1	2	–	2	2	1	3	4	–	4	–	–	–
Manorhamilton,	–	–	–	–	–	–	–	–	–	–	–	–	–	–	–	–	–
Midleton,	–	–	–	6	4	10	1	–	1	7	4	11	–	11	–	–	–
Milford,	–	2	2	1	3	4	3	–	3	4	5	9	–	9	–	–	–
Millstreet,	–	–	–	–	1	1	–	–	–	–	1	1	–	1	–	–	–
Mitchelstown,	–	–	–	–	–	–	–	–	–	–	–	–	–	–	–	–	–
Mohill,	–	1	1	2	–	2	–	3	3	2	4	6	–	6	–	–	–
Monaghan,	–	1	1	1	7	8	–	2	2	1	10	11	1	9	1	–	–
Mountbellew,	–	–	–	1	–	1	–	2	2	1	2	3	–	3	–	–	–
Mountmellick,	–	2	2	3	1	4	–	4	4	3	7	10	2	6	–	–	–
Mullingar,	–	3	3	1	–	1	3	14	17	4	17	21	–	21	–	–	–
Naas,	–	3	3	10	8	18	1	5	6	11	16	27	1	26	–	–	–
Navan,	1	1	2	2	5	7	–	–	–	3	6	9	–	9	–	–	–
Nenagh,	1	2	3	3	4	7	3	1	4	7	7	14	–	14	–	–	–
Newcastle,	–	1	1	4	6	10	–	4	4	4	11	15	–	15	–	–	–
Newport,	–	–	–	1	–	1	–	–	–	1	–	1	–	1	–	–	–
New Ross,	4	6	10	9	5	14	–	2	2	13	13	26	1	25	–	–	–
Newry,	–	–	–	7	12	19	3	3	6	10	15	25	9	16	–	–	–
Newtownards,	2	6	8	5	5	10	1	1	2	8	12	20	3	2	15	–	–
Newtownlimavady,	–	2	2	–	–	–	–	1	1	–	3	3	–	2	1	–	–
Oldcastle,	–	2	2	1	–	1	3	9	12	4	11	15	2	13	–	–	–
Omagh,	–	–	–	3	5	8	–	–	–	3	5	8	2	2	4	–	–
Oughterard,	1	–	1	1	–	1	–	–	–	2	–	2	–	2	–	–	–
Parsonstown,	–	–	–	3	2	5	–	–	–	3	2	5	1	4	–	–	–
Portumna,	–	–	–	–	–	–	–	–	–	–	–	–	–	–	–	–	–
Rathdown,	5	10	15	3	1	4	1	2	3	9	13	22	5	17	–	–	–
Rathdrum,	–	1	1	4	3	7	–	–	–	4	4	8	4	4	–	–	–
Rathkeale,	–	–	–	–	3	3	–	1	1	–	4	4	1	3	–	–	–
Roscommon,	2	2	4	3	8	11	–	–	–	5	10	15	–	15	–	–	–
Roscrea,	–	4	3	–	2	2	2	5	7	2	10	12	–	12	–	–	–
Scarriff,	–	1	1	1	1	2	–	1	1	1	3	4	–	4	–	–	–
Shillelagh,	–	–	–	2	2	4	–	1	1	2	3	5	1	4	–	–	–
Skibbereen,	1	2	3	4	2	6	1	1	2	6	5	11	–	10	–	–	1
Skull,	–	–	–	–	1	1	–	2	2	–	3	3	–	3	–	–	–
Sligo,	–	1	1	6	12	18	–	2	2	6	15	21	3	18	–	–	–
Strabane,	–	3	3	–	2	2	1	1	2	1	6	7	1	5	–	–	1
Suanolar,	–	–	–	–	1	1	–	–	–	–	1	1	–	1	–	–	–
Strokestown,	1	3	4	2	3	5	1	4	5	4	10	14	–	14	–	–	–
Swineford,	–	–	–	–	3	3	–	–	–	–	3	3	–	3	–	–	–
Thomastown,	–	–	–	–	–	–	–	1	1	–	1	1	–	1	–	–	–
Thurles,	1	–	1	1	1	2	5	9	14	7	10	17	–	17	–	–	–
Tipperary,	–	–	–	1	–	1	3	6	9	4	6	10	–	10	–	–	–
Tobercurry,	–	–	–	1	3	4	–	–	–	1	3	4	–	4	–	–	–
Tralee,	–	–	–	–	6	6	–	–	–	–	6	6	–	6	–	–	–
Trim,	–	–	–	4	1	5	–	–	–	4	1	5	1	4	–	–	–
Tuam,	1	–	1	2	–	2	1	3	4	4	3	7	–	7	–	–	–
Tulla,	–	–	–	–	5	5	1	4	5	1	9	10	–	10	–	–	–
Tullamore,	–	3	3	2	4	6	2	7	9	4	14	18	–	18	–	–	–
Urlingford,	–	–	–	4	1	5	–	1	1	4	2	6	1	5	–	–	–
Waterford,	–	15	15	10	8	18	1	5	6	11	28	39	1	38	–	–	–
Westport,	–	–	–	1	–	1	1	1	2	2	1	3	–	3	–	–	–
Wexford,	6	12	18	–	–	–	3	6	9	9	18	27	–	27	–	–	–
Youghal,	–	–	–	–	1	1	1	6	7	1	7	8	–	8	–	–	–
Total,	121	289	410	397	474	871	161	357	518	679	1,120	1,799	191	1,503	92	10	3

No. 2.—TABLE showing the Number of Lunatics, Idiots, and Epileptics, belonging to each County, who were in the Union Workhouses on the 31st December, 1856.

COUNTIES.	LUNATICS.			IDIOTS.			EPILEPTICS.			TOTAL.			RELIGION.				
	Males	Fem.	Total	Males	Fem.	Total	Males	Fem.	Total	Males	Fem.	Total	Protest-ants.	Roman Catholics.	Presby-terians.	Dissent-ers.	Not known.
Antrim,*	9	21	30	21	30	60	13	22	35	43	82	125	86	62	34	2	1
Armagh,	2	6	8	9	17	20	5	3	8	16	26	42	10	30	3	–	–
Carlow,	3	1	4	5	8	13	1	7	8	9	16	25	2	23	–	–	–
Cavan,	1	7	8	9	9	18	5	3	8	15	18	33	4	29	1	–	–
Clare,	1	5	6	16	22	38	2	11	13	19	38	57	2	55	–	–	–
Cork, E.R., & W.R.,	4	12	16	30	86	66	6	30	36	40	78	118	3	111	–	–	1
Donegal,	5	7	12	18	19	32	4	4	8	22	30	52	5	45	2	–	–
Down,†	8	10	18	24	17	41	0	8	8	41	45	76	14	28	28	7	–
Dublin,‡	24	46	70	22	11	36	36	52	83	78	112	188	31	157	–	–	–
Fermanagh,	–	1	1	5	3	8	–	4	4	5	8	13	4	8	1	–	–
Galway, E.R., & W.R.,	4	7	11	10	6	16	8	12	20	22	25	47	1	40	–	–	–
Kerry,	2	2	4	8	19	27	5	9	15	15	23	38	1	38	–	–	–
Kildare,	1	10	11	14	11	25	5	10	20	20	31	51	1	47	–	–	–
Kilkenny,	5	3	8	13	17	30	5	0	11	20	20	40	–	40	–	–	–
King's,	1	4	5	5	7	12	4	9	10	10	20	30	1	29	–	–	–
Leitrim,	–	1	1	3	1	4	–	5	5	3	7	10	1	10	–	–	–
Limerick,	8	16	24	15	18	33	4	14	18	27	48	75	3	72	–	–	–
Londonderry,§	4	9	13	12	19	31	–	3	3	16	31	47	8	21	15	–	–
Longford,	1	1	2	9	4	13	2	7	9	12	12	24	1	23	–	–	–
Louth,	2	9	11	8	11	19	2	3	5	12	23	35	1	34	–	–	–
Mayo,	5	9	14	14	13	23	7	10	17	20	34	54	3	51	–	–	–
Meath,	2	10	12	16	16	32	4	18	22	22	44	66	3	63	–	–	–
Monaghan,	1	6	7	9	16	25	–	7	7	10	20	30	5	24	1	–	–
Queen's,	4	7	11	10	13	23	1	5	6	15	25	40	1	36	–	–	–
Roscommon,	4	5	9	18	13	25	4	9	13	20	27	47	–	45	–	–	–
Sligo,	–	1	1	10	17	27	–	5	5	10	23	33	3	30	–	–	–
Tipperary, N.R., & S.R.,	6	18	24	22	25	47	15	35	50	43	78	121	4	170	–	–	–
Tyrone,	–	3	3	19	10	38	4	6	10	23	28	51	15	28	6	1	1
Waterford,	–	20	20	16	12	28	1	10	11	17	43	59	1	58	–	–	–
Westmeath,	1	4	5	1	3	4	8	21	29	10	28	38	1	37	–	–	–
Wexford,	10	20	30	15	19	34	9	10	19	34	49	83	5	78	–	–	–
Wicklow,‖	3	8	11	8	9	17	1	3	4	13	20	33	10	22	–	–	–
Total,	**121**	**289**	**410**	**397**	**474**	**871**	**161**	**357**	**518**	**670**	**1,120**	**1,790**	**191**	**1,563**	**63**	**10**	**3**

NOTE.—As unions in Ireland frequently extend into different counties, independent of a table of the Lunatics, Idiots, and Epileptics in poorhouses, the present gives a return of these classes belonging to each separate county.

* One female lunatic, one male, one female idiot, and one female epileptic, natives of Scotland.
† One male lunatic a native of England.   ‡ One male idiot a native of England.   § One male, two female idiots, natives of Scotland.
‖ One female epileptic a native of England.

No. 3.—TABLE showing the Ages in Decennial periods, and the Education of Lunatics, &c., who were in the Union Workhouses on the 31st December, 1856.

	AGES.												EDUCATION.		
—	10 and under.	11 to 20.	21 to 30.	31 to 40.	41 to 50.	51 to 60.	61 to 70.	71 to 80.	81 to 90.	91 to 100.	101 and upward.	Ages not speci-fied.	Total.	Who can read.	Who cannot read.
Lunatics, Males,	–	18	22	25	21	22	9	3	–	–	–	–	141	48	73
Females,	1	21	54	65	54	53	28	10	3	–	–	–	289	99	190
Total,	1	39	76	90	76	75	37	13	3	–	–	–	410	145	263
Epileptics, Males,	2	71	32	18	19	10	5	1	–	–	–	3	161	60	105
Females,	8	106	110	61	61	18	14	6	1	–	–	2	357	120	237
Total,	10	177	142	79	80	28	19	7	1	–	–	5	518	178	342
Idiots, Males,	14	171	105	45	31	17	6	2	–	–	–	4	397	–	397
Females,	19	149	136	76	42	30	18	3	–	–	–	1	474	–	474
Total,	33	320	241	121	73	47	26	5	–	–	–	5	871	–	871
Total, Males,	16	260	159	88	72	49	22	6	–	–	–	7	670	104	575
Females,	28	276	300	203	127	101	60	19	4	–	–	3	1,120	210	901
Total,	44	536	459	290	199	150	82	25	4	–	–	10	1,790	323	1,476

* The vast majority are utterly uneducated, but there are some who at one time of their life were well informed have lapsed into hopeless fatuity.

No. 4.—RETURN of HOUSE of INDUSTRY PATIENTS in the Hardwicke Cells.

Number remaining, 31st March, 1855, . . 120
  „   „   1856, . . 100
  „   „   1857, . . 102

Died, year ending 31st March, 1856, . . . 20
  „   „   „   1857, . . . 7

One patient came in for some property, and was removed in 1855, by Order of the Lord Chancellor, to a private Asylum.

No. 5.—TABLE showing Authority for Admission of Patients, and Number Admitted, during the two Years ending 31st March, 1856, and 1857.

Asylums.	Ordinary Cases admitted by order of the Board.			Ordinary Cases admitted as urgent by the Physicians.			Dangerous Lunatics by Warrant of the Lord Lieutenant.			Lunatics charged with Offences by Warrant of the Lord Lieutenant.			Lunatics detained in default of security to keep the Peace, by Warrant of Lord Lieutenant.			Total Number of Patients admitted during the Year.		
	M.	F.	T.	M.	F.	T.	M.	F.	T.	M.	F.	T.	M.	F.	T.	M.	F.	T.
1856.																		
Armagh,	11	7	18	26	16	42	15	11	26	—	—	—	—	—	—	52	34	86
Ballinasloe,	15	10	25	3	5	8	38	18	56	—	—	—	—	—	—	56	33	80
Belfast,	15	29	44	24	10	34	26	10	36	—	—	—	—	—	—	65	46	114
Carlow,	16	22	38	—	—	—	7	8	15	—	—	—	—	—	—	23	30	53
Clonmel,	8	6	14	1	—	1	7	1	8	—	—	—	—	—	—	16	7	23
Cork,	9	12	21	40	40	80	10	8	18	1	—	1	—	—	—	60	60	120
Kilkenny,	1	8	9	2	4	6	13	6	19	1	—	1	—	—	—	17	18	35
Killarney,	7	5	12	19	10	29	1	2	3	—	—	—	2	2	4	29	19	48
Limerick,	5	7	12	32	39	71	17	7	24	—	—	—	—	—	—	54	53	107
Londonderry,	27	35	62	7	2	9	3	2	5	—	3	3	—	—	—	37	42	79
Maryborough,	8	12	20	1	—	1	26	6	32	—	—	—	—	—	—	35	18	53
Mullingar,	56	62	118	—	—	—	28	26	54	—	—	—	—	—	—	84	88	172
Omagh,	40	30	70	—	—	—	9	4	13	—	—	—	—	—	—	49	43	92
Richmond,	66	114	180	13	2	15	44	48	92	—	—	—	—	—	—	123	164	287
Sligo,	—	—	—	16	16	35	57	43	*100	3	—	3	—	—	—	79	59	138
Waterford,	9	21	30	—	—	—	4	1	5	1	—	1	—	—	—	14	22	36
Total,	203	390	682	187	144	331	305	201	506	6	3	9	2	2	4	703	739	1,582
1857.																		
Armagh,	21	20	41	21	—	21	19	9	28	—	—	—	—	—	—	61	29	90
Ballinasloe,	18	10	28	2	5	7	35	31	66	—	—	—	—	—	—	55	46	101
Belfast,	22	32	54	28	18	46	28	14	42	—	—	—	—	—	—	78	64	142
Carlow,	8	27	35	—	—	—	5	2	7	—	—	—	—	—	—	13	29	42
Clonmel,	3	4	7	1	1	2	4	3	7	—	—	—	—	—	—	8	8	16
Cork,	15	10	25	58	40	104	8	5	13	3	—	3	1	—	1	85	61	146
Kilkenny,	1	7	8	—	4	4	4	9	13	—	—	—	—	—	—	5	20	25
Killarney,	12	6	18	17	12	29	—	1	1	—	1	1	—	—	—	29	20	40
Limerick,	1	1	2	35	23	58	16	11	27	—	—	—	—	—	—	52	35	87
Londonderry,	22	31	53	—	—	—	10	12	22	1	—	1	—	2	2	33	45	78
Maryborough,	8	7	15	4	3	7	14	4	18	—	—	—	—	—	—	26	14	40
Mullingar,	28	27	55	—	—	—	23	17	40	—	—	—	—	—	—	51	44	95
Omagh,	35	40	75	—	—	—	15	3	18	—	—	—	—	—	—	50	43	93
Richmond,	30	28	58	5	1	6	52	22	74	—	—	—	—	—	—	87	51	138
Sligo,	—	—	—	24	17	41	8	9	17	—	1	1	—	—	—	32	27	59
Waterford,	17	28	45	—	—	—	2	1	3	1	—	1	—	—	—	20	20	40
Total,	241	278	519	195	130	325	243	153	396	5	2	7	1	2	3	685	565	1,250

* Includes 50 males and 38 females admitted from Ballinasloe Asylum.

No. 6.—TABLE showing the Cause of Death of Patients in Asylums during the two Years ending 31st March, 1856, and 1857.

Cause of Death.	1856.		1857.		Total.		
	M.	F.	M.	F.	M.	F.	M. & F.
Fever,	7	2	2	—	9	2	11
Dysentery,	13	5	8	9	21	14	35
Diarrhoea,	6	2	1	1	7	3	10
Cholera,	—	—	—	1	—	1	1
Influenza,	2	1	—	—	2	1	3
Erysipelas,	1	1	1	—	2	1	3
Syphilis,	1	—	—	1	1	—	1
Disease of Brain,	9	—	12	1	21	1	22
Apoplexy,	9	6	11	4	20	10	30
Paralysis,	20	5	20	8	40	13	53
Disease of Head,	—	—	1	1	1	1	2
Epilepsy,	15	5	10	5	34	10	44
Convulsions,	—	—	—	2	2	—	2
Delirium Tremens,	—	—	1	—	1	—	1
Aneurism,	1	—	—	—	1	—	1
Disease of Heart,	2	3	1	2	3	5	8
Bronchitis,	3	4	1	2	4	6	10
Disease of Chest,	2	—	—	1	3	—	3
Consumption,	25	32	23	37	48	69	117
Disease of Lungs,	—	—	5	10	5	10	15
Inflammation of Lungs,	2	2	1	1	3	3	6
Inflammation of Bowels,	—	—	1	—	1	—	1
Dropsy,	—	5	1	4	1	9	10
Gastric Fever,	—	—	1	—	1	—	1
Disease of Intestines,	—	2	1	1	1	3	4
Jaundice,	—	1	—	—	—	1	1
Liver Complaint,	1	1	—	—	1	1	2
Marasmus,	7	9	9	6	16	15	31
Disease of Stomach,	1	—	2	1	3	1	4
Disease of Bladder,	1	—	—	—	1	—	1
Disease of Kidneys,	1	—	—	—	1	1	2
Disease of Uterus,	—	1	—	1	—	2	2
Childbed,	—	—	1	—	1	—	1
Rheumatism,	—	1	—	1	—	2	2
Scurvy,	1	1	—	—	1	1	2
Ulcerations,	—	—	—	2	—	2	2
Abscess,	4	—	1	—	1	4	5
Cancer,	—	1	1	—	1	2	3
Mortification,	—	1	—	—	1	—	2
Scrofula,	2	3	1	5	3	8	11
Tumours,	—	1	—	—	—	1	1
General Debility and Old Age,	14	21	27	28	41	49	90
Accidental and Suicidal,	1	—	—	2	1	2	3
Total Males,	151	—	158	—	300	—	
Total Females,	—	117	—	133	—	250	

(Total, 550)

No. 7.—TABLE showing the previous Occupations of the Patients in Asylums on 31st March, 1857.

Occupations.	M.	F.	T.
Agriculture,	206	82	288
Farmers and Farmers' Wives, &c.,	142	145	287
Farm Labourers and Servants,	660	222	882
Gardeners,	8	–	8
Cattle Dealers,	1	–	1
Stone Cutters,	5	–	5
Stone Masons,	9	–	9
Bricklayers,	17	–	17
Slaters,	7	–	7
Plasterers,	1	–	1
Tilers,	1	–	1
Painters and Glaziers,	20	–	20
Bell Hangers,	1	–	1
Carpenters,	47	–	47
Sawyers,	3	–	3
Coopers,	5	–	5
Paper Stainers,	1	–	1
Cabinet Makers,	2	–	2
Turners,	2	–	2
Brush Makers,	1	–	1
Bookbinders,	2	–	2
Coach Builders,	3	–	3
Coach Painters,	1	–	1
Saddlers,	3	–	3
Iron Founders,	1	–	1
Brass Founders,	1	–	1
Gun Makers,	1	–	1
Shipwrights,	1	–	1
Blacksmiths,	7	–	7
Engine Fitters,	3	–	3
Watch Makers,	2	–	2
Tinkers,	1	–	1
Opticians,	1	–	1
Artisans, Miscellaneous,	5	1	6
Nailors,	8	–	8
Millers,	2	–	2
Bakers,	9	–	9
Weavers,	40	2	42

Occupations.	M.	F.	T.
Spinners,	–	12	12
Hacklers,	5	–	5
Mill Workers,	1	9	10
Bleachers,	1	–	1
Cotton Carders,	1	–	1
Leather Dressers,	1	–	1
Tobacco Spinners,	1	–	1
Shoemakers,	56	2	58
Tailors,	43	–	43
Hatters,	3	–	3
Hat Trimmers,	–	2	2
Glove Makers,	–	1	1
Stay Makers,	–	2	2
Net Makers,	–	1	1
Dressmakers,	–	88	88
Bonnet Makers,	–	1	1
Flowerers,	–	13	13
Milliners,	–	2	2
Fancy Workers,	–	2	2
Seamstresses,	–	31	31
Knitters,	–	16	16
Barbers,	1	–	1
Merchants,	3	–	3
Commercial, Miscellaneous,	7	2	9
Shopkeepers and Assistants,	17	10	27
Pedlars,	1	–	1
Booksellers,	1	–	1
Victuallers,	8	–	8
Butchers and Butchers' Wives, &c.,	6	3	9
Grocers,	1	–	1
Confectioners,	–	2	2
Publicans,	2	–	2
Hucksters and Dealers, Miscellaneous,	12	19	31
Clergy, Established Church,	4	–	4
Ditto, Roman Catholics,	7	–	7

Occupations.	M.	F.	T.
Barristers,	1	–	1
Solicitors,	2	–	2
Physicians,	2	–	2
Apothecaries,	2	–	2
Students,	6	–	6
Teachers,	25	10	35
Linguists,	1	–	1
Artists,	1	–	1
Revenue Officers,	5	–	5
Coast Guards,	2	1	3
Pilots,	1	–	1
Sailors,	18	–	18
Boatmen,	3	–	3
Ship Agents,	1	–	1
Valuators,	1	–	1
Surveyors,	1	–	1
Engravers,	1	–	1
Printers,	3	–	3
Clerks,	57	–	57
Servants, Domestic,	42	325	367
Bailiffs,	1	–	1
Postboys,	2	–	2
Asylum Keepers,	1	–	1
Porters,	2	–	2
Toll Collectors,	2	–	2
Fishermen and Wives,	3	3	6
Billiard Markers,	1	–	1
Police Officers and Men,	14	–	14
Pensioners,	10	–	10
Soldiers, Discharged,	45	1*	46
Musicians,	4	–	4
Paupers,	3	21	24
Miscellaneous Occupation,	21	218	239
Unknown,	273	638	911
Total,	1,969	1,887	3,856

* Soldier's wife.

No. 8.—TABLE showing the Number of Relapsed Cases admitted during the two Years ending 31st March. 1856, and 1857.

Asylums.	In Asylum once before.			In Asylum twice before.			In Asylum three times before.			In Asylum four times before.			In Asylum five times before.			In Asylum six times before.			Total.		
1856.	M.	F.	T.	M.	F.	T.	M.	F.	T.	M.	F.	T.	M.	F.	T.	M.	F.	T.	M.	F.	T.
Armagh,	8	9	17	–	–	–	–	–	–	–	–	–	–	–	–	–	–	–	8	9	17
Ballinasloe,	4	1	5	–	–	–	–	1	1	1	2	3	1	–	1	–	–	–	6	4	10
Belfast,	1	1	2	1	–	1	–	1	1	1	–	1	–	–	–	–	–	–	3	2	5
Carlow,	2	3	5	1	1	2	–	–	–	–	–	–	–	–	–	–	–	–	3	4	7
Clonmel,	1	–	1	–	2	2	–	–	–	–	–	–	–	–	–	–	–	–	1	2	3
Cork,	16	12	28	1	–	1	–	–	–	1	–	1	1	–	1	–	–	–	19	12	31
Kilkenny,	2	1	3	2	–	2	1	–	1	–	–	–	–	–	–	–	–	–	5	1	6
Killarney,	5	4	9	–	–	–	–	–	–	–	–	–	–	–	–	–	–	–	5	4	9
Limerick,	6	12	18	2	2	4	1	1	2	–	–	–	–	–	–	–	–	–	6	15	24
Londonderry,	4	2	6	3	4	7	–	2	2	1	–	1	–	–	–	–	–	–	8	8	16
Maryborough,	2	–	2	–	1	1	–	–	–	–	–	–	–	–	–	–	–	–	2	1	3
Mullingar,	–	2	2	–	–	–	–	–	–	–	–	–	–	–	–	–	–	–	–	2	2
Omagh,	–	–	–	3	1	4	–	–	–	–	–	–	–	–	–	–	–	–	3	1	4
Richmond,	6	3	9	–	–	–	–	–	–	–	–	–	–	–	–	–	–	–	6	3	9
Sligo,	1	1	2	–	–	–	–	–	–	–	–	–	–	–	–	–	–	–	1	1	2
Waterford.	1	–	1	–	–	–	–	–	–	–	–	–	–	–	–	–	–	–	1	–	1
Total,	59	51	110	13	11	24	2	5	7	4	2	6	2	–	2	–	–	–	80	66	146
1857.	M.	F.	T.	M.	F.	T.	M.	F.	T.	M.	F.	T.	M.	F.	T.	M.	F.	T.	M.	F.	T.
Armagh,	2	1	3	2	2	4	–	–	–	–	–	–	–	–	–	–	–	–	4	3	7
Ballinasloe,	4	5	9	1	2	3	–	–	–	–	1	1	–	–	–	–	–	–	5	8	13
Belfast,	1	4	5	1	–	1	–	–	–	1	–	1	–	–	–	–	–	–	3	4	7
Carlow,	1	2	3	1	1	2	–	–	–	–	–	–	–	–	–	–	–	–	2	3	5
Clonmel,	–	–	–	–	–	–	–	–	–	–	–	–	*1	1	–	–	–	–	–	1	1
Cork,	12	19	31	4	4	8	2	2	4	2	–	2	–	–	–	+1	–	1	21	18	39
Kilkenny,	1	1	2	–	–	–	–	–	–	–	–	–	–	–	–	–	–	–	1	1	2
Killarney,	–	1	1	2	–	2	–	–	–	–	–	–	–	–	–	–	–	–	2	1	3
Limerick,	6	4	10	7	4	11	2	2	4	1	1	2	–	–	–	–	–	–	16	11	27
Londonderry,	10	12	22	6	4	10	1	1	2	–	–	–	–	–	–	–	–	–	17	17	34
Maryborough,	4	1	5	–	–	–	–	–	–	–	1	1	–	–	–	–	–	–	4	2	6
Mullingar,	3	6	9	1	–	1	–	–	–	–	–	–	–	–	–	–	–	–	4	6	10
Omagh,	6	7	13	2	2	4	1	2	3	–	1	1	–	–	–	–	–	–	9	12	21
Richmond,	4	5	9	1	–	1	–	–	–	–	–	–	1	–	1	–	–	–	6	5	11
Sligo,	4	3	7	–	–	–	–	–	–	–	–	–	–	–	–	–	–	–	4	3	7
Waterford,	1	2	3	–	–	–	–	–	–	–	1	1	–	–	–	–	–	–	1	3	4
Total,	59	66	125	28	19	47	6	7	13	4	5	9	–	1	1	2	–	2	90	98	197

* This female always relapses after child-birth.   + This case was admitted fifteen times.

No. 9.—Table showing the Form of Disease in those admitted during the two Years ended 31st March, 1857.

Asylums.	Mania.			Monomania.			Demented.			Melancholia.			Imbecility and Epilepsy.			Idiocy.			Total.		
	M.	F.	T.	M.	F.	T.	M.	F.	T.	M.	F.	T.	M.	F.	T.	M.	F.	T.	M.	F.	T.
Armagh,	85	40	125	–	–	–	4	3	7	19	16	35	5	4	9	–	–	–	113	63	176
Ballinasloe,	92	70	162	1	2	3	3	–	3	9	5	14	6	2	8	–	–	–	111	79	190
Belfast,	96	64	160	7	8	15	10	10	20	30	32	62	–	–	–	–	–	–	143	113	256
Carlow,	22	34	56	1	3	4	–	–	–	13	22	35	–	–	–	–	–	–	36	59	95
Clonmel,	21	14	35	–	–	–	1	–	1	–	–	–	2	1	3	–	–	–	24	15	39
Cork,	92	95	187	14	4	18	6	4	10	22	15	37	10	2	12	1	1	2	145	121	266
Kilkenny,	11	21	32	5	12	17	6	2	8	–	3	3	–	–	–	1	1	2	22	38	60
Killarney,	38	20	58	–	–	–	11	6	17	7	12	19	2	1	3	–	–	–	58	39	97
Limerick,	90	75	165	2	3	5	9	6	15	5	4	9	–	–	–	–	–	–	106	88	194
Londonderry,	54	75	129	14	8	22	–	–	–	–	–	–	1	4	5	–	–	–	70	87	157
Maryborough,	27	18	45	–	–	–	–	–	–	11	7	18	1	–	1	1	–	1	61	32	*93
Mullingar,	90	87	177	6	6	12	–	2	2	28	29	57	6	5	11	2	3	5	135	132	267
Omagh,	68	63	131	2	2	4	6	–	6	17	18	35	–	2	2	5	3	8	99	86	185
Richmond,	123	147	270	8	8	16	15	10	25	38	38	76	23	6	29	6	1	7	210	215	426
Sligo,	90	64	154	8	6	14	2	2	4	8	10	18	–	3	3	3	6	9	111	86	197
Waterford,	16	25	41	1	4	5	10	12	22	6	8	14	–	1	1	1	1	2	34	51	85
Total,	1,015	911	1,926	69	66	135	83	57	140	213	219	432	56	31	87	22	16	38	1,478	1,304	2,782

* Of this number 20 males and 4 females were returned unknown.

No. 10.—Table showing the Form of Disease in those remaining in Asylums on 31st March, 1857.

Asylums.	Mania.			Monomania.			Dementia.			Melancholia.			Imbecility and Epilepsy.			Idiocy.			Total.		
	M.	F.	T.	M.	F.	T.	M.	F.	T.	M.	F.	T.	M.	F.	T.	M.	F.	T.	M.	F.	T.
Armagh,	16	24	40	–	–	–	29	29	58	3	5	8	3	5	8	13	8	21	64	71	135
Ballinasloe,	129	118	247	9	5	14	12	11	23	2	1	3	22	7	29	2	–	2	176	142	318
Belfast,	131	76	207	14	22	36	10	12	22	30	32	62	–	–	–	3	–	3	188	142	330
Carlow,	68	56	124	11	19	30	12	6	18	9	5	14	7	4	11	–	–	–	107	90	197
Clonmel,	46	51	97	–	–	–	12	9	21	–	–	–	6	5	11	6	5	11	70	70	140
Cork,	92	77	169	30	20	50	12	21	33	52	84	136	22	8	30	8	7	15	217	216	433
Kilkenny,	46	48	94	–	–	–	12	11	23	14	14	28	–	–	–	3	1	4	75	74	149
Killarney,	49	33	82	–	–	–	35	23	58	6	14	20	4	3	7	1	1	2	90	70	160
Limerick,	83	92	175	8	10	18	25	17	42	18	34	52	6	5	11	19	14	33	164	170	334
Londonderry,	96	85	181	2	4	6	–	–	–	5	3	8	5	4	9	2	3	5	110	99	209
Maryborough,	50	35	85	–	–	–	13	11	24	14	12	26	8	6	14	4	2	6	89	65	154
Mullingar,	70	54	124	8	8	16	–	–	–	10	22	32	4	9	13	6	3	9	98	95	193
Omagh,	65	68	133	1	6	7	6	11	17	15	17	32	12	8	20	14	6	20	113	116	229
Richmond,	105	124	229	–	–	–	89	83	172	36	97	133	35	6	41	6	29	35	277	333	610
Sligo,	36	23	59	11	13	24	12	17	29	4	6	10	4	4	8	2	1	3	69	64	133
Waterford,	45	51	96	3	4	7	16	18	34	5	11	16	1	2	3	6	1	7	56	67	123
Total,	1,107	995	2,102	97	111	208	295	279	574	224	356	580	143	73	216	103	73	176	1,969	1,887	3,856

No. 11.—Table showing the supposed cause of Mental Disease of those in District Asylums, on 31st March, 1857.

Causes.	Males.	Females.	Total.
Grief,	51	159	210
Reverse of fortune,	90	94	184
Love and jealousy,	27	70	97
Domestic quarrels,	3	12	15
Religious excitement,	22	48	70
Political excitement,	1	–	1
Study,	18	1	19
Anxiety,	4	9	13
Pride,	2	1	3
Terror,	26	53	79
Poetical fervour,	1	–	1
Total Moral or Mental Causes,	245	447	692
Intemperance,	349	142	491
Epilepsy,	112	38	150
Disease of Brain,	6	2	8
Injury of Head,	28	8	36
Effects of climate,	19	9	28

Causes.	Males.	Females.	Total.
Disordered menstruation,	–	14	14
Fever,	25	30	55
Puerperal,	–	44	44
Bodily injury and disorder,	45	27	72
Abuse of medicine,	14	1	15
Seduction,	–	3	3
Sun-stroke,	6	1	7
Hysteria,	–	1	1
Congenital,	10	12	22
Sedentary habits,	–	1	1
Solitary confinement,	–	1	1
Total Physical Causes,	614	334	948
Hereditary,	231	275	506
Not known,	879	831	1,710
Total Males and Females in Asylums on 31st Mar., 1857,	1,969	1,887	3,856

No. 12.—Table showing the State as to the probability of Recovery of those in Asylums on the 31st March, 1857.

STATE AS TO PROBABILITY OF RECOVERY.

Asylums.	Lunatics probably curable.			Lunatics probably incurable.			Lunatics, Idiots.			Lunatics, Epileptics.			Total.		
	M.	F.	T.	M.	F.	T.	M.	F.	T.	M.	F.	T.	M.	F.	T.
Armagh,	8	11	19	37	46	83	16	9	25	3	5	8	64	71	135
Ballinasloe,	29	25	54	123	110	233	2	—	2	22	7	29	176	142	318
Belfast,	55	54	109	117	83	200	3	—	3	13	5	18	188	142	330
Carlow,	38	45	83	53	36	89	9	5	14	7	4	11	107	90	197
Clonmel,	23	22	45	35	38	73	6	5	11	6	5	11	70	50	140
Cork,	100	105	205	87	96	183	8	7	15	22	8	30	217	216	433
Kilkenny,	2	8	10	62	58	120	3	1	4	8	7	15	75	74	149
Killarney,	33	27	60	57	43	100	1	1	2	5	2	7	96	73	169
Limerick,	65	63	128	69	90	159	21	12	33	9	5	14	164	170	334
Londonderry,	28	21	49	75	71	146	2	3	5	5	4	9	110	99	209
Maryborough,	45	32	77	32	26	58	4	2	6	8	5	13	89	65	154
Mullingar,	10	11	21	78	73	151	6	3	9	4	8	12	98	95	193
Omagh,	30	29	59	57	73	130	14	6	20	12	8	20	113	116	229
Richmond,	84	87	171	146	217	363	12	23	35	35	6	41	277	333	610
Sligo,	10	12	22	51	45	96	2	1	3	6	6	12	69	64	133
Waterford,	28	47	75	21	17	38	6	1	7	1	2	3	56	67	123
Total,	588	599	1,187	1,100	1,122	2,222	115	79	194	166	87	253	1,969	1,887	3,856

No. 13.—Table showing the Social Condition of Patients in Asylums on 31st March, 1857.

SOCIAL CONDITION.

Asylums.	Married.			Single.			Widowed.			Unknown.			Total.		
	M.	F.	T.	M.	F.	T.	M.	F.	T.	M.	F.	T.	M.	F.	T.
Armagh,	9	9	18	21	6	27	1	1	2	33	55	88	64	71	135
Ballinasloe,	46	42	88	122	76	198	4	22	26	4	2	6	176	142	318
Belfast,	41	44	85	141	83	224	6	15	21	—	—	—	188	142	330
Carlow,	33	19	52	31	44	75	19	12	31	24	15	39	107	90	197
Clonmel,	25	19	44	19	24	43	7	8	15	19	19	38	70	50	140
Cork,	35	42	77	171	146	317	4	24	28	7	4	11	217	216	433
Kilkenny,	13	20	33	61	44	105	1	10	11	—	—	—	75	74	149
Killarney,	18	17	35	76	41	117	—	15	15	2	—	2	96	73	169
Limerick,	34	40	74	126	106	232	4	22	26	—	2	2	164	170	334
Londonderry,	20	31	51	80	53	133	10	15	25	—	—	—	110	99	209
Maryborough,	13	15	28	73	34	107	—	4	4	3	12	15	89	65	154
Mullingar,	14	23	37	69	58	127	—	7	7	15	7	22	98	95	193
Omagh,	20	40	60	93	72	165	—	4	4	—	—	—	113	116	229
Richmond,	60	62	122	187	221	408	13	38	51	17	12	29	277	333	610
Sligo,	19	20	39	48	43	91	2	1	3	—	—	—	69	64	133
Waterford,	10	11	21	44	44	88	1	12	13	1	—	1	56	67	123
Total,	419	466	882	1,350	1,083	2,430	72	210	282	135	128	253	1,969	1,887	3,856

No. 14.—Table showing the Educational Condition of Patients in Asylums on 31st March, 1857.

EDUCATIONAL CONDITION.

Asylums.	Well Educated.			Can Read and Write well.			Can Read and Write indifferently.			Can Read only.			Who cannot Read.			Total.		
	M.	F.	T.	M.	F.	T.	M.	F.	T.	M.	F.	T.	M.	F.	T.	M.	F.	T.
Armagh,	—	—	—	5	2	7	13	8	21	18	15	33	28	46	74	64	71	135
Ballinasloe,	8	5	13	19	10	29	35	22	57	19	15	34	95	90	185	176	142	318
Belfast,	3	1	4	9	0	9	95	37	132	50	82	132	31	22	53	188	142	330
Carlow,	3	3	6	31	17	48	39	25	64	14	13	27	20	32	52	107	90	197
Clonmel,	4	3	7	8	6	14	6	5	11	15	9	24	37	47	84	70	50	140
Cork,	23	6	29	47	19	66	65	11	76	16	48	64	66	132	198	217	216	433
Kilkenny,	12	2	14	9	5	14	21	15	36	10	27	37	23	25	48	75	74	149
Killarney,	14	6	20	23	19	42	—	—	—	16	12	28	43	36	79	96	73	169
Limerick,	18	26	44	45	28	73	17	9	26	41	36	77	43	71	114	164	170	334
Londonderry,	8	5	13	10	6	16	40	34	74	20	23	43	32	31	63	110	99	209
Maryborough,	8	—	8	6	—	6	39	20	59	20	21	41	16	24	40	89	65	154
Mullingar,	7	5	12	26	10	36	16	10	26	25	15	40	24	55	79	98	95	193
Omagh,	—	—	—	8	2	10	50	41	91	12	23	35	43	50	93	113	116	229
Richmond,	36	24	60	77	44	121	43	52	95	54	77	131	67	136	203	277	333	610
Sligo,	2	2	4	3	3	6	22	8	30	7	8	15	35	43	78	69	64	133
Waterford,	1	1	2	15	4	19	11	12	23	5	13	18	24	37	61	56	67	123
Total,	147	89	236	341	175	516	512	309	821	342	436	778	627	878	1,505	1,969	1,887	3,856

No. 15.—TABLE showing the Daily Average of Patients Employed, and how Employed, during the Year ended 31st March, 1857.

Asylums.	MALES.												FEMALES.												TOTAL.	
	Gardening and Farming Labour.	Road-making, &c.	Stone-breaking.	Pumping Water.	Weaving and Winding.	Tailoring.	Shoe-making.	Carpentering.	Painting, &c.	Assisting Servants to clean House, &c.	Miscellaneous Employment.	Total employed daily.	Farming and Gardening Labour.	Spinning and Carding Flax.	Needlework.	Knitting.	Quilting.	Fancy Work.	Assisting in Laundry.	Assisting Servants in cleaning House, &c.	Bonnet making.	Mat making.	Miscellaneous Employment.	Total employed daily.	Daily average employed.	Daily average unemployed.
Armagh,	10	–	15	0	8	1	1	1	–	4	–	52	–	26	16	4	–	2	5	4	2	2	–	55	107	33
Ballinasloe,	24	–	–	–	–	2	–	–	–	25	19	76	–	1	15	13	1	–	12	18	–	–	3	63	133	108
Belfast,	56	–	0	18	5	3	2	–	1	22	5	115	–	24	15	17	6	10	19	10	–	–	–	107	222	101
Carlow,	30	–	–	0	–	1	–	–	1	20	11	73	13	10	20	–	3	–	12	10	–	–	6	74	149	48
Clonmel,	18	–	–	–	–	2	2	–	–	12	12	46	–	–	0	7	–	–	17	8	–	–	4	45	91	49
Cork,	14	21	9	0	–	3	3	2	–	15	30	103	–	–	19	33	–	1	15	21	–	–	11	106	203	230
Kilkenny,	37	–	–	4	–	–	–	1	–	11	2	55	–	–	15	13	–	–	15	10	–	–	–	53	108	28¾
Killarney,	17	–	–	–	–	2	–	–	–	4	32	55	–	–	14	8	–	–	5	5	–	–	3	35	90	72
Limerick,	35	–	–	–	–	1	–	–	–	8	8	52	–	2	21	14	–	–	16	13	–	–	4	64	110	214
Londonderry,	35	–	–	–	–	–	8	–	–	16	26	80	–	13	21	17	2	2	6	12	–	–	2	75	155	49
Maryborough,	26	–	–	–	–	7	4	–	–	6	16	62	–	1	21	12	–	–	18	6	–	–	3	50	118	31
Mullingar,	34	–	–	–	–	–	–	–	–	8	11	53	–	–	11	6	–	–	10	7	–	–	11	45	68	78
Omagh,	12	–	–	–	1	–	–	–	–	2	29	44	–	4	11	21	–	3	7	13	–	–	3	62	106	105
Richmond,	42	–	–	4	2	9	1	–	–	16	37	135	–	–	25	21	3	1	41	47	–	–	30	108	303	307
Sligo,	10	–	–	–	–	–	2	1	1	12	15	47	4	1	6	9	–	1	8	11	–	–	2	42	80	37¼
Waterford,	7	–	–	–	–	1	2	–	–	3	5	18	–	8	10	7	–	–	7	6	–	–	5	43	61	63
Total,	422	21	30	46	18	25	22	6	8	217	258	1,002	17	84	246	202	15	26	262	207	2	2	87	1,087	2,146	1,024½

No. 16.—CLASSIFICATION of Patients in Asylums on 31st March, 1857.

Asylums.	Convalescent.			Quiet and Orderly.			Moderately Tranquil.			Noisy and Refractory.			Imbecile and Epileptic.			Suicidal.			Total.		
	M.	F.	T.	M.	F.	T.	M.	F.	T.	M.	F.	T.	M.	F.	T.	M.	F.	T.	M.	F.	T.
Armagh,	6	5	11	31	25	55	10	8	18	6	7	13	11	26	37	–	–	–	64	71	135
Ballinasloe,	3	4	7	63	30	102	30	35	65	18	37	55	58	26	84	4	1	5	176	142	318
Belfast,	30	30	60	70	29	69	28	18	41	31	36	67	13	7	20	21	22	43	188	142	330
Carlow,	7	4	11	24	12	36	36	33	69	21	20	41	13	17	36	6	4	10	107	90	197
Clonmel,	8	10	18	18	15	33	10	6	16	8	12	20	24	26	50	2	1	3	70	70	140
Cork,	18	8	26	70	86	105	36	58	97	37	45	82	38	14	52	6	5	11	217	216	433
Kilkenny,	–	2	2	16	10	26	15	16	31	30	31	61	11	12	23	3	3	6	75	74	149
Killarney,	4	3	7	25	15	46	21	14	35	24	13	37	16	20	36	6	8	14	90	73	169
Limerick,	18	4	22	75	41	116	42	16	58	19	67	116	9	11	20	1	1	2	164	170	334
Londonderry,	30	25	55	23	19	42	27	27	54	12	9	21	17	17	34	1	2	3	110	99	209
Maryborough,	16	13	29	30	21	51	22	15	37	11	11	22	8	5	13	2	–	2	86	65	154
Mullingar,	–	–	–	88	84	172	–	–	–	–	–	–	10	11	21	–	–	–	68	85	193
Omagh,	23	17	46	31	35	66	20	10	30	13	31	44	26	14	40	–	–	–	113	116	229
Richmond,	46	34	80	48	66	114	56	74	130	40	77	126	66	73	139	18	9	27	277	333	610
Sligo,	–	–	–	33	33	66	17	14	31	10	8	18	6	6	18	–	–	–	69	64	133
Waterford,	4	11	15	37	41	78	8	8	16	–	1	1	7	3	10	–	3	3	56	67	123
Total,	213	176	383	601	571	1,202	376	361	737	286	435	724	330	291	621	76	59	129	1,969	1,887	3,856

* Convalescent patients are classed with the quiet and orderly.

No. 17.—TABLE showing the Relationship to each other of Patients who were under treatment during the two Years ended 31st March, 1857.

Asylums.	DEGREE OF RELATIONSHIP.																	
	Parents and their Children.			Brothers and Sisters.			Uncles and Aunts; and Nephews and Nieces.			First Cousins.			Second Cousins.			Third and Fourth Cousins.		
	M.	F.	T.	M.	F.	T.	M.	F.	T.	M.	F.	T.	M.	F.	T.	M.	F.	T.
Armagh,	–	–	–	2	–	2	–	–	–	–	–	–	–	–	–	–	–	–
Ballinasloe,	–	–	–	5	3	8	–	–	–	4	3	7	–	–	–	–	–	–
Belfast,	2	2	4	3	1	4	–	6	6	3	4	7	–	2	2	–	–	–
Carlow,	1	1	2	2	4	6	–	3	3	5	2	7	3	1	4	2	–	2
Clonmel,	1	1	2	2	2	4	2	–	2	2	–	2	–	–	–	–	–	–
Cork,	–	2	2	2	*4	6	–	–	–	1	1	2	–	–	–	–	–	–
Kilkenny,	–	–	–	1	3	4	1	3	4	2	2	4	3	1	4	3	1	4
Killarney,	–	3	3	1	3	4	4	5	9	13	10	23	–	–	–	–	–	–
Limerick,	–	–	–	5	4	9	–	–	–	3	8	11	–	–	–	–	–	–
Londonderry,	–	–	–	–	–	–	–	–	–	–	–	–	2	–	2	–	–	–
Maryborough,	1	1	2	2	–	2	2	–	2	4	1	5	–	–	–	–	–	–
Mullingar,	–	–	–	7	–	7	–	–	–	1	2	3	–	–	–	–	–	–
Omagh,	–	–	–	6	5	11	2	–	2	–	5	5	–	–	–	–	–	–
Richmond,	3	3	6	1	4	5	–	–	–	2	–	2	–	–	–	–	–	–
Sligo,	–	–	–	5	1	6	–	–	–	–	–	–	–	–	–	–	–	–
Waterford,	–	–	–	3	3	6	–	2	2	1	3	4	–	–	–	–	–	–
Total,	8	13	21	47	37	84	11	19	30	41	41	82	8	4	12	5	1	6

Total Number having Relationship, 235

* Two of these females are sisters-in-law.

No. 18.—TABLE illustrative of the mode in which information was sought, as to the Relationship of Patients in District Asylums.

Names of Patients in any degree related.	Degree of Relationship.	Form of Insanity	Observations.
Edward C——s,	Brother and Sister,	Mania.	This list does not represent, to any thing like its full amount, the influence of the hereditary taint, in the development of insanity amongst the lunatics admitted into this asylum. It is often difficult, in these cases, to trace relationship amongst the "lower orders," as the friends will sometimes deny it, where it is known to exist. But from the facts ascertained, as well as from those which are presented only as surmises, it cannot be denied but that the experience of this asylum points to the "hereditary taint" as an active predisposing cause of insanity.
Margaret C——t,		Idiocy.	
Mary S——n,	Sisters,	Dementia.	
Bridget S——n,		Mania.	
James S——k,	Uncle to the above,	Mania.	
Patrick S——n,	Cousins German,	Mania.	
John H——s,		Mania.	
Catherine S——n,	Cousin to Patrick,	Mania.	
Richard M——n,	Nephew and Aunt,	Mania.	
Alicia S——n,		Melancholia.	
Thade M'C——y,	Uncle and Nephew,	Melancholia.	
John M'C——y,		Dementia.	
John O'B——n,	First Cousins,	Dementia.	
Ellen M——y,		Melancholia.	
Johanna D——l,	First Cousins,	Mania.	
Julia S——,		Melancholia.	
Michael B——n,	Cousin to Julia S——,	Melancholia.	
Michael H——n,	First and Second Cousins,	Mania.	
M. H——d,		Mania.	
Henry W——h,	First Cousins,	Mania.	
Thade M'C——y,		Mania.	
Thade F——y,	First and Second Cousins,	Melancholia.	
Timothy F——y,		Dementia.	
Mary M'D——l,		Melancholia.	
Patrick K——h,	First and Second Cousins,	Mania.	
Patrick G——n,		Mania.	
Frances C——n,		Melancholia.	
Ellen C——s,	Cousins,	Mania.	
Ellen M——y,		Mania.	
Mary M'D——l,	Cousins,	Melancholia.	
Henrietta C——r,		Mania.	
Sarah M——y,	—	Mania.	This patient had two brothers insane.
John L——y,	—	Mania.	This patient's daughter drowned herself in a fit of insanity since the mother's admission.
Catherine P——r,	—	Mania.	This patient is connected with several different families, who have all exhibited insanity.
Honora C——r,	—	Mania.	This patient had a daughter in the house discharged cured.
Julia O'C——r,	—	Melancholia.	This patient has a sister insane.
James M'S——y,	—	Mania.	This patient had two first cousins who died insane; has several relatives insane.
Margaret M——w,	—	Dementia.	This patient's aunt died insane.
Ellen D——s,	—	Mania.	This patient's uncle died insane.
Catherine P——r,	—	Mania.	This patient is first cousin to a patient who died in the asylum.
Daniel R——y,	—	Mania.	This patient's mother died insane.
Richard L——r,	—	Dementia.	The disease is known to be hereditary in the case of these two patients, but what members of their families have been attacked with the malady is uncertain.
John H——d,	—	Mania.	

The above Return was made by the highly intelligent Resident Physician at Killarney, who has given much attention to the subject. In many asylums, from want of time, full information has not been afforded.

No. 19.—TABLE showing the Total Accommodation in the District Asylums on 31st March, 1857.

	Male Side.	Female Side.	Total.		Male Side.	Female Side.	Total.
No. of Dormitories with 1 Bed in each,	—	—	—	No. of Dormitories with 15 Beds in each,	—	1	1
〃 〃 2 Beds in each,	1	5	6	〃 〃 16 Beds in each,	2	2	4
〃 〃 3 Beds in each,	58	44	102	〃 〃 17 Beds in each,	1	3	4
〃 〃 4 Beds in each,	45	67	112	〃 〃 18 Beds in each,	3	—	3
〃 〃 5 Beds in each,	18	31	49	〃 〃 19 Beds in each,	—	1	1
〃 〃 6 Beds in each,	44	31	75	〃 〃 20 Beds in each,	—	—	—
〃 〃 7 Beds in each,	13	23	36	〃 〃 21 Beds in each,	1	—	1
〃 〃 8 Beds in each,	12	16	28	〃 〃 22 Beds in each,	1	1	2
〃 〃 9 Beds in each,	8	8	16				
〃 〃 10 Beds in each,	22	8	30	Total Number of Dormitories,	243	254	407
〃 〃 11 Beds in each,	3	4	7				
〃 〃 12 Beds in each,	8	3	11	Total Number of Beds therein,	1,503	1,403	2,005
〃 〃 13 Beds in each,	3	3	6	Total Number of Single Apartments,	701	641	1,342
〃 〃 14 Beds in each,	—	3	3	Total accommodation,	2,204	2,135	4,337

No. 20.—Table showing the Number of Dormitories and Beds in each on the 31st March, 1857.

Asylums	Male: No. of Dormitories	Male: No. of Beds in each	Male: Total No. of Dormitories	Male: Total No. of Beds	Male: Single Apartments	Total Male Accommodation	Female: No. of Dormitories	Female: No. of Beds in each	Female: Total No. of Dormitories	Female: Total No. of Beds	Female: Single Apartments	Total Female Accommodation	Total Male and Female Accommodation
Armagh	6	3	7	29	41	76	6	3	7	20	41	70	140
	1	11					1	11					
Ballinasloe	7	3	22	114	64	178	9	3	19	86	67	158	331
	1	5					1	5					
	10	6					9	6					
	4	7					-	-					
Belfast	1	2	25	152	37	189	2	2	26	117	95	152	341
	7	3					3	3					
	6	4					7	4					
	1	6					1	6					
	1	7					1	7					
	7	10					3	10					
	2	11					3	11					
Carlow	6	4	8	65	41	107	6	4	5	40	44	63	206
	1	18					1	6					
	1	21					1	19					
Clonmel	1	4	6	51	16	76	1	4	6	54	16	76	140
	2	6					2	6					
	2	8					2	8					
	1	22					1	22					
Cork	4	4	26	164	68	266	1	2	28	108	60	237	467
	7	5					6	4					
	9	6					5	5					
	1	9					6	6					
	5	10					4	7					
	-	-					2	8					
	-	-					3	9					
							1	10					
Kilkenny	1	6	9	69	14	83	1	6	9	69	14	83	166
	1	7					1	7					
	7	8					7	8					
Killarney	1	3	12	71	33	101	1	3	12	71	33	101	208
	2	4					2	4					
	1	5					1	5					
	1	6					1	6					
	7	7					7	7					
Limerick	8	3	13	90	75	103	2	13	7	69	73	172	537
	2	12					3	14					
	2	13					1	15					
	1	16					1	16					
Londonderry	7	4	11	74	43	117	5	4	9	64	43	107	241
	2	5					2	5					
	2	18					2	17					
Maryborough	6	4	9	55	42	97	6	4	9	56	43	96	196
	1	6					1	7					
	1	8					1	8					
	1	17					1	17					
Mullingar	2	3	14	116	42	152	4	5	9	60	35	101	253
	6	6					2	7					
	2	16					2	10					
	4	12					1	12					
Omagh	2	3	15	100	57	166	2	3	15	96	54	150	316
	4	5					1	4					
	1	6					6	5					
	1	8					1	6					
	5	9					1	8					
	2	12					2	9					
	-	-					2	12					
Richmond	18	3	37	188	90	278	1	2	65	301	35	336	614
	5	4					16	3					
	6	6					24	4					
	2	6					0	5					
	0	10					3	6					
	-	-					7	7					
	-	-					2	8					
	-	-					3	9					
Sligo	7	3	22	112	25	137	7	3	22	112	25	137	274
	3	4					3	4					
	3	5					3	5					
	0	6					0	6					
	1	8					1	8					
	2	16					2	16					
Waterford	5	4	7	49	12	61	1	2	9	55	14	69	130
	1	13					6	4					
	1	16					1	13					
	-	-					1	16					

No. 21.—TABLE showing the Number of Paying Patients who were in Asylums during the two Years ending 31st March, 1856, and 1857.

Asylums	Number of Patients			Farming		Trading		Mechanical		Labouring		Professional		Educational		Service of the Crown		Other pursuits		Respectable without Occupation		Not Specified		Total yearly Payment
	M.	F.	T.	M.	F.	M.	F.	M.	F.	M.	F.	M.	F.	M.	F.	M.	F.	M.	F.	M.	F.	M.	F.	£ s. d.
1856.																								
Armagh,	—	—	—	—	—	—	—	—	—	—	—	—	—	—	—	—	—	—	—	—	—	—	—	—
Ballinasloe,	3	4	7	—	—	1	—	—	—	—	—	—	—	—	—	1	—	—	—	—	4	1	—	160 0 6
Belfast,	—	—	—	—	—	—	—	—	—	—	—	—	—	—	—	—	—	—	—	—	—	—	—	—
Carlow,	1	—	1	—	—	—	—	—	—	—	—	—	—	—	1	—	—	—	—	—	—	—	—	13 4 9
Clonmel,	—	—	—	—	—	—	—	—	—	—	—	—	—	—	—	—	—	—	—	—	—	—	—	—
Cork,	3	1	4	—	—	—	1	—	1	—	—	—	—	2	—	—	—	1	—	—	—	—	—	40 15 5
Kilkenny,	1	4	5	—	1	1	2	—	—	—	—	—	—	—	—	—	—	—	—	—	1	—	—	130 0 0
Killarney,	2	1	3	1	—	—	1	—	—	—	—	1	—	—	—	—	—	—	—	—	—	—	—	90 0 0
Limerick,	5	5	10	—	4	—	2	1	—	—	—	—	1	2	—	—	2	—	—	—	—	—	—	108 14 0
Londonderry,	—	—	—	—	—	—	—	—	—	—	—	—	—	—	—	—	—	—	—	—	—	—	—	—
Maryborough,	1	—	1	—	—	—	—	—	—	—	—	—	—	—	—	—	—	—	—	—	—	—	—	12 3 4
Mullingar,	1	—	1	—	—	—	1	—	—	—	—	—	—	—	—	—	—	—	—	—	—	—	—	15 0 0
Omagh,	5	2	7	2	—	—	—	—	—	—	—	1	1	2	—	—	—	—	—	—	—	—	1	67 2 7
Richmond,	6	2	8	—	2	—	1	2	—	—	—	1	—	1	—	1	—	—	—	—	—	—	—	70 4 0
Sligo,	2	1	3	2	—	—	—	—	—	—	—	—	—	—	—	—	—	—	1	—	—	—	—	40 0 0
Waterford,	—	—	—	—	—	—	—	—	—	—	—	—	—	—	—	—	—	—	—	—	—	—	—	—
Total,	30	20	50	5	0	4	5	4	2	—	—	4	1	1	1	10	—	1	—	4	7	1	1	714 7 1
1857.																								
Armagh,	—	—	—	—	—	—	—	—	—	—	—	—	—	—	—	—	—	—	—	—	—	—	—	—
Ballinasloe,	5	4	9	1	—	2	—	—	—	—	—	—	—	1	—	—	—	—	—	4	1	—	—	143 0 0
Belfast,	—	—	—	—	—	—	—	—	—	—	—	—	—	—	—	—	—	—	—	—	—	—	—	—
Carlow,	1	—	1	—	—	—	—	—	—	—	—	—	—	—	—	—	—	—	—	—	—	—	—	15 14 6
Clonmel,	—	—	—	—	—	—	—	—	—	—	—	—	—	—	—	—	—	—	—	—	—	—	—	—
Cork,	8	1	9	1	—	1	—	2	—	—	—	3	—	—	—	—	—	1	1	—	1	—	—	127 8 4
Kilkenny,	1	2	3	—	1	1	—	—	—	—	—	—	—	—	—	—	—	1	—	—	—	—	—	60 0 0
Killarney,	6	1	7	3	—	—	1	—	—	—	—	—	—	3	—	—	—	—	—	—	—	—	—	75 12 11
Limerick,	2	5	7	1	—	4	1	—	—	—	—	1	—	—	—	—	—	—	—	—	—	—	—	135 17 6
Londonderry,	—	—	—	—	—	—	—	—	—	—	—	—	—	—	—	—	—	—	—	—	—	—	—	—
Maryborough,	—	—	—	—	—	—	—	—	—	—	—	—	—	—	—	—	—	—	—	—	—	—	—	—
Mullingar,	2	—	2	1	—	—	—	1	—	—	—	—	—	1	—	—	—	—	—	—	—	—	—	25 0 0
Omagh,	3	1	4	1	—	—	—	—	—	—	—	1	—	1	—	—	—	—	—	—	—	—	1	39 4 3
Richmond,	6	2	8	—	2	—	1	2	—	—	—	1	—	1	—	—	—	—	—	—	—	—	—	90 4 0
Sligo,	2	1	3	1	—	—	—	—	—	—	—	—	1	—	—	—	—	—	—	—	1	—	—	43 8 5
Waterford,	—	—	—	—	—	—	—	—	—	—	—	—	—	—	—	—	—	—	—	—	—	—	—	—
Total,	36	17	50	8	2	0	5	5	2	—	—	2	—	1	—	11	—	1	—	1	7	1	1	786 10 5

No. 22.—TABLE showing Outlay and Produce of the Year on Farms and Gardens for the two Years ending 31st March, 1856, and 1857.

Asylums		Quantity of Land Cultivated												Amount								
		By Spade			By Plough			Grass			Total			Outlay			Produce			Net Profit		
		A.	R.	P.	A.	R.	P.	A.	R.	P.	A.	R.	P.	£	s.	d.	£	s.	d.	£	s.	d.
Armagh,	1856,	5	3	15	—			3	0	0	8	3	15	29	3	4	56	1	10	26	18	8
	1857,	5	3	15	—			3	0	0	8	3	15	28	0	3	60	16	0	32	6	9
Ballinasloe,	1856,	12	0	0	15	0	0	9	0	28	36	0	28	108	6	6	341	18	6	233	12	0
	1857,	14	0	0	18	0	0	4	0	18	36	0	28	72	14	9	325	16	1	253	1	10
Belfast,	1856,	20	3	0	—			22	1	0	43	0	0	43	11	9	392	17	1	349	5	4
	1857,	21	3	0	—			21	1	0	43	0	0	40	14	1	391	10	3	351	16	2
Carlow,	1856,	7	2	16	—			4	0	0	11	2	16	87	16	4	215	10	8	127	14	4
	1857,	7	2	16	—			4	0	0	11	2	16	18	5	5	187	9	11	119	4	6
Clonmel,	1856,	13	0	0	8	0	0	3	0	0	24	0	0	88	14	8	186	14	1	97	19	5
	1857,	13	0	0	8	0	0	3	3	0	24	3	0	65	10	4	155	3	5	89	13	1
Cork,	1856,	8	2	0	—			48	3	30	57	1	30	30	12	8	109	4	8	77	12	0
	1857,	8	2	0	—			48	3	30	57	1	30	15	16	8	180	4	11	164	8	3
Kilkenny,	1856,	9	2	0	1	1	0	4	1	0	15	0	0	17	10	9	44	4	1	26	4	4
	1857,	9	2	0	1	1	0	4	1	0	15	0	0	15	8	3	88	1	3½	72	13	0½
Killarney,	1856,	2	0	0	17	0	26	—			19	0	26	122	4	6½	237	11	7	115	7	0½
	1857,	2	3	0	17	3	14	—			20	2	14	150	18	10½	267	19	11	117	1	0½
Limerick,	1856,	10	1	10	0	3	0	7	0	10	17	0	20	165	2	11½	293	0	10½	127	17	11
	1857,	9	2	0	7	2	10	10	0	10	17	0	10	103	9	1½	327	14	4½	218	5	8
Londonderry,	1856,	20	3	0	—			—			20	2	0	123	0	11	283	3	5	159	18	6
	1857,	20	2	0	—			—			20	2	0	121	7	11	307	5	4	185	15	6
Maryborough,	1856,	14	3	9	—			7	3	8	20	2	17	70	11	7	154	16	8	84	5	1
	1857,	12	3	0	—			7	3	8	20	2	17	67	1	8	151	17	4	84	15	8
Mullingar,	1856,	5	0	0	—			17	0	0	22	0	0	40	17	6	50	17	0	10	0	0
	1857,	6	0	0	—			17	0	0	23	0	0	48	1	3	—			—		
Omagh,	1856,	10	1	14	—			*11	2	22	21	3	36	55	16	5	79	9	0	23	12	7
	1857,	10	1	14	—			*11	2	22	21	3	36	50	14	8	92	0	0	41	5	4
Richmond,	1856,	26	0	0	—			+33	2	0	59	2	0	125	13	5	395	7	3	271	13	10
	1857,	26	0	0	—			+33	2	0	59	2	0	130	19	10	399	9	7	268	9	9
Sligo,	1856,	10	2	0	10	2	0	1	0	30	22	0	30	151	19	0	241	0	6	129	1	0
	1857,	10	2	0	10	2	0	1	0	30	22	0	30	43	13	9	197	10	7	113	16	10
Waterford,	1856,	7	1	36½	1	1	23½	1	2	8½	10	1	25½	65	1	4	105	11	1	99	9	9
	1857,	7	1	30½	1	1	26½	1	2	8½	10	1	28½	49	13	8	139	15	4	90	1	10
Total,	1856,	183	0	20½	63	0	9½	174	1	16½	419	2	6½	1,285	3	3	3,354	8	9½	2,069	6	7½
	1857,	186	0	10½	64	2	7½	172	0	0½	421	2	24½	1,063	18	10	3,189	12	2	2,197	14	7

* Including pleasure grounds, plantations, &c.　　+ Including 23 acres under pleasure grounds, buildings, &c.

G

No. 23.—Receipts and Expenditure for the

RECEIPTS.

Asylums.	Year	Balance on Hand 31st March. (£ s. d.)	Treasury Advances (£ s. d.)	Received for Pay Patients. (£ s. d.)	Received for sale of Farm and Garden Produce. (£ s. d.)	Received for sale of Offal, old Clothes, &c. (£ s. d.)	Received from Miscellaneous Sources. (£ s. d.)	Total Receipts. (£ s. d.)
Armagh,	1856,	381 15 7	2,854 0 0	—	—	1 0 0	1 13 3	3,188 8 10
	1857,	310 17 0	2,718 0 0	—	12 1 0	—	—	3,040 18 9
Ballinasloe,	1856,	522 14 2	5,530 2 4	101 8 6	128 3 0	4 10 10	3 6 8	6,519 3 0
	1857,	648 0 4	5,423 14 8	106 16 10	52 7 0	2 19 4	2 8 0	6,290 6 8
Belfast,	1856,	423 7 0	5,248 7 5	—	169 7 10	11 3 7	7 0 9	5,850 18 1
	1857,	430 10 4	6,586 8 2	—	180 3 11	14 6 6	0 13 0	7,214 11 8
Carlow,	1856,	17 3 11	3,800 0 0	13 13 9	56 5 8	—	—	3,887 3 4
	1857,	6 18 5	3,750 0 0	13 14 0	33 12 11	0 10 0	1 14 6	3,806 16 4
Clonmel,	1856,	225 16 10½	3,125 3 8	—	187 14 1	—	28 0 3	3,515 14 11
	1857,	248 5 1	3,281 4 8	—	103 3 5	2 0 0	—	3,634 13 2
Cork,	1856,	474 0 8	6,590 0 0	40 13 8	42 7 5	0 12 2	0 10 0	7,158 3 11
	1857,	322 10 5	6,700 0 0	88 2 7	61 16 0	3 7 2	2 10 0	7,178 15 2
Kilkenny,	1856,	142 9 2½	3,150 0 0	110 11 2	20 8 2	5 10 9½	1 8 0	3,430 7 7
	1857,	515 0 1½	2,500 0 0	101 0 0	44 6 11½	12 4 1½	0 15 0	3,173 12 2
Killarney,	1856,	105 11 7	3,030 1 2	34 4 5	121 14 4	—	1 2 0	3,403 14 0
	1857,	211 8 1	3,205 18 7	41 5 7	99 16 11	1 10 3	0 18 0	3,561 7 2
Limerick,	1856,	706 13 2	6,422 13 11	102 10 6	102 8 9½	25 13 7	0 10 0	7,420 15 11½
	1857,	806 8 1	5,950 5 6	160 15 0½	96 5 11	20 17 1	2 8 11	7,136 0 6½
Londonderry,	1856,	599 17 0	3,483 10 7	—	154 16 4	2 10 7	—	4,241 3 6
	1857,	476 1 9	3,794 10 6	10 1 3	138 13 11	2 16 4	1 2 10	4,418 3 10
Maryborough,	1856,	626 0 3	3,479 15 1	11 11 6	43 1 3	0 7 11	1 13 0	4,152 18 0
	1857,	518 10 10	3,279 7 0	15 10 0	54 6 2	3 3 3	—	3,871 12 3
Mullingar,	1856,	—	2,401 16 2	12 10 0	50 17 0	—	—	2,555 3 6
	1857,	2 3 0	4,250 3 3	18 10 0	—	—	*23 18 8	4,301 0 1
Omagh,	1856,	731 10 8	4,000 0 0	34 14 7	3 6 0	—	10 11 5	4,807 16 6
	1857,	533 3 4	4,600 0 0	77 10 7	62 0 0	7 3 4	8 14 4	5,288 11 7
Richmond,	1856,	300 4 2	11,719 7 0	86 7 9	108 10 3	7 3 2	94 3 6	12,313 5 4
	1857,	241 3 0	13,645 12 5	105 5 2	57 18 0	—	0 2 0	14,050 1 10
Sligo,	1856,	552 11 6	2,222 13 5	31 10 11	77 11 3	—	7 3 7	2,801 10 11
	1857,	46 17 11	3,065 3 7	70 10 7	93 4 9	—	8 10 2	3,295 2 0
Waterford,	1856,	26 0 1	2,000 6 11	—	40 3 0	0 16 8	13 13 0	2,090 9 5
	1857,	23 19 6	2,518 0 0	—	46 1 10	1 5 7	14 0 7	2,608 17 3 †13 8 9
General Total,	1856,	5,879 11 7	70,007 7 5	678 10 0	1,250 18 4½	65 11 0½	171 6 2	78,053 15 1½
	1857,	5,433 4 5½	75,270 18 3	878 17 4½	1,131 2 11½	72 18 2½	68 15 3	82,875 4 0

EXPENDITURE.

Asylum.	Year	Bedding and Furniture. (£ s. d.)	Repairs and Alterations. (£ s. d.)	Farm and Garden. (£ s. d.)	Rent, Rent-charge, Taxes, and Insurance. (£ s. d.)	Stationery and Printing. (£ s. d.)	Medical — Groceries. (£ s. d.)	Medical — Medicines. (£ s. d.)
Armagh,	1856,	112 1 8	141 7 3	28 3 4	26 15 8	27 2 8	—	7 14 7
	1857,	107 1 3	151 18 2	28 9 3	27 0 10	27 2 0	—	14 2 0
Ballinasloe,	1856,	261 7 0	302 16 0	60 1 2	0 5 0	36 7 11	80 11 7	22 14 8
	1857,	293 10 4	116 11 6	58 14 4	3 15 0	22 13 3	65 0 0	17 1 0
Belfast,	1856,	158 18 0	613 3 4	43 11 9	19 10 0	43 3 10	60 12 6	16 4 4
	1857,	229 11 6	1,102 16 6	40 14 1	20 15 0	47 14 3	77 18 4	14 11 5
Carlow,	1856,	143 10 3	120 9 5	23 18 5	28 1 7	20 6 3	—	19 4 4
	1857,	150 10 11	92 17 3	20 7 5	23 4 7	23 8 4	—	33 17 9
Clonmel,	1856,	244 13 5	174 1 8½	88 14 8	4 17 0	35 13 5	2 5 0	8 0 0
	1857,	188 7 8	164 8 0½	65 10 4½	14 17 6	31 0 3	12 10 0	12 9 0½
Cork,	1856,	62 16 2	154 10 1	24 16 2	32 9 0	50 15 11	307 0 3	22 13 10
	1857,	203 7 11	106 10 8	15 10 8	32 9 0	58 0 2	350 17 7	22 10 4
Kilkenny,	1856,	20 0 9	83 0 11½	17 19 9	10 17 7	24 15 1	57 2 6½	12 3 3
	1857,	43 17 0½	46 0 2	15 8 3	28 16 3	34 0 4	66 16 10½	13 16 10
Killarney,	1856,	108 2 5	113 10 6	122 4 6½	7 15 0	17 8 1	45 13 1	17 8 1
	1857,	247 4 0½	127 4 7	150 18 10½	7 15 0	29 3 0½	49 12 7½	20 16 6
Limerick,	1856,	80 7 2	731 19 3	105 15 7½	15 18 1	23 2 11	77 17 5½	14 5 3
	1857,	168 17 1	558 12 7	77 19 5½	14 14 8	27 1 11	73 6 0	13 12 0
Londonderry,	1856,	144 10 0	107 5 7	123 0 11	3 15 0	23 9 3	—	18 3 0
	1857,	100 8 7	240 18 8	121 7 11	3 15 0	10 11 0	—	1 1 8
Maryborough,	1856,	130 4 5	152 10 4	70 11 7	8 12 0	28 10 10	20 0 10	10 16 6
	1857,	142 17 10	68 17 11	37 1 8	9 18 9	30 8 5	18 18 4	18 12 11
Mullingar,	1856,	53 11 1	11 15 4	40 17 7	—	40 11 5	13 16 0	4 10 5
	1857,	18 6 11	70 8 0	48 1 3	18 13 0	37 6 10	31 17 0	28 10 7
Omagh,	1856,	105 18 10	120 8 10	55 10 5	7 10 0	43 4 11	159 12 0	1 3 3
	1857,	73 14 6	524 15 1	20 14 8	7 10 0	5 15 0	—	3 2 1
Richmond,	1856,	478 10 8	305 14 3	123 13 5	31 5 5	60 19 10	250 12 7	66 10 4
	1857,	484 4 9	678 7 8	130 16 10	35 0 5	67 7 7	271 2 6	109 5 3
Sligo,	1856,	54 0 4	27 0 0	126 6 11	3 0 0	36 3 1	93 18 10	15 8 7
	1857,	104 10 4	102 15 11	48 13 0	19 10 0	36 14 5	87 3 8	37 12 0
Waterford,	1856,	140 14 5	105 8 7	30 12 10	5 0 0	10 3 0	7 15 2	13 0 5
	1857,	177 18 10	94 12 8	43 5 1	5 0 0	20 16 10	0 2 1	14 16 5
General Total,	1856,	2,314 7 1	3,421 10 5	1,086 13 1	206 12 4	540 7 11	1,207 1 7	307 1 1
	1857,	2,793 2 3	4,290 2 7½	954 3 10½	278 6 0	500 15 8½	1,150 4 0	381 19 0½

* This includes £23 16s. salary of the late matron, and not called for by her.   † Overdrawn, £13 8s.

two Years ending 31st March, 1856 and 1857.

EXPENDITURE.

Provisions.			Clothing. Patients.			Clothing. Servants.			Fuel and Light.			Washing.			Salaries of Officers.			Wages of Servants.				Asylums.
£	s.	d.	£	s.	d.	£	s.	d.	£	s.	d.	£	s.	d.	£	s.	d.	£	s.	d.		
1,491	3	3	185	10	0	14	14	0	175	16	0	32	1	1	415	0	0	228	2	8	1856,	Armagh.
1,265	8	2	402	4	10	14	14	0	191	5	10	28	8	3	415	0	0	242	6	0	1857,	
4,705	19	11	487	19	3	115	5	0	499	14	6	64	12	11	573	7	1	420	16	0	1856,	Ballinasloe.
2,646	4	2	481	3	3	118	17	6	608	15	1	63	8	8	569	7	8	432	11	3	1857,	
2,551	0	1	392	7	5	70	0	0	402	16	5	80	18	0	529	3	4	333	15	0	1856,	Belfast.
2,721	18	8	492	4	4	80	0	0	321	5	3	95	18	7	550	0	0	373	19	0	1857,	
1,005	3	2	207	4	2	56	10	10	340	1	2	53	14	7	580	0	0	241	3	11	1856,	Carlow.
1,804	13	2	260	10	0	57	8	9	360	6	5	51	12	9	560	0	0	242	13	0	1857,	
1,441	6	4½	100	7	6	33	5	10	180	8	4	44	10	10	560	0	0	270	14	8	1856,	Clonmel.
1,467	12	4½	187	6	1½	94	1	8	168	7	10	48	11	5	572	11	6	259	0	6	1857,	
3,609	0	0	355	8	10	167	10	5	412	7	8½	97	6	6½	888	17	0	468	5	4	1856,	Cork.
3,282	8	3	444	0	7½	127	17	0½	575	17	0	107	10	0	905	17	8	474	5	11	1857,	
1,308	5	7½	142	16	4	43	16	9	271	5	2	40	11	11	595	14	3	291	2	7	1856,	Kilkenny.
1,178	10	3	230	5	2	70	9	0	249	1	1½	40	8	9½	620	5	1½	241	14	5	1857,	
1,381	13	6½	141	3	0	40	2	5	348	7	10½	37	17	3½	573	6	8	246	10	11	1856,	Killarney.
1,380	16	7	176	13	1½	37	8	8	278	9	7½	52	16	6½	590	0	0	250	3	0	1857,	
3,252	16	2½	399	3	10	43	3	1	373	14	9	104	19	3	690	0	0	513	9	6	1856,	Limerick.
3,297	13	1	311	19	0	48	13	0	340	7	0	95	15	8	709	12	4	521	15	8	1857,	
1,735	7	10	259	6	5	72	13	2	354	12	8	76	6	3	508	16	3	224	3	0	1856,	L. Derry.
1,880	13	8	400	12	2	69	3	11	200	13	0	74	6	7	548	14	6	227	16	4	1857,	
1,697	8	7	245	10	8	54	19	6	253	16	9	67	14	6	567	10	0	236	3	10	1856,	Maryboro'.
1,481	3	10	263	8	9	60	15	7	272	7	8	68	18	5	595	0	0	240	4	0	1857,	
841	6	11	145	10	5½	42	0	0	274	14	11	97	1	7	702	15	4	161	15	7	1856,	Mullingar.
2,059	5	6	344	9	2	44	11	0	164	11	11	40	15	10	605	10	8	240	12	11	1857,	
1,786	14	7	229	4	1	74	0	3	571	13	5	98	16	5	643	6	8	350	0	8	1856,	Omagh.
2,002	5	11	312	15	1	90	4	8	599	0	7	54	0	3	650	0	0	359	10	0	1857,	
6,226	5	7	620	15	5	307	8	6	708	8	2	91	7	3	1,455	2	5	917	15	11	1856,	Richmond.
7,436	8	2	631	11	1	328	4	10	754	13	7	91	2	4	1,474	1	4	992	7	2	1857,	
1,089	18	0	124	12	9	43	16	7	268	2	0	32	0	5	590	0	0	239	17	2	1856,	Sligo.
1,088	17	4	244	2	3	38	0	9	301	0	0	29	15	0	590	0	0	247	5	11	1857,	
1,222	11	7	109	8	2	27	10	7	157	2	3	61	14	8	518	11	10	172	5	1	1856,	Waterford.
1,116	18	9	128	19	2	29	4	11	137	10	1	51	5	0	500	0	0	170	16	11	1857,	
34,128	10	3	4,207	12	10½	1,206	16	11	5,423	1	0½	981	17	0½	10,421	11	7	5,269	6	10	1856,	General Total.
34,995	6	10½	4,021	13	8½	1,259	3	9½	5,793	9	11	989	14	9	10,473	9	4½	5,349	7	0	1857,	

EXPENDITURE.

Comforts. Wine, Beer, and Whiskey.			Medical Diet.			Tobacco and Snuff.			Incidental Expenses.			Total Outlay.			Balance on Hand 31st March each Year.			Daily Average Number of Patients.	Average Cost of each Patient per head per annum on the entire outlay.				Asylums.
£	s.	d.	£	s.	d.	£	s.	d.	£	s.	d.	£	s.	d.	£	s.	d.		£	s.	d.		
—			—			34	4	1	17	5	10	2,877	11	1	410	17	9	134	21	9	5	1856,	Armagh.
—			—			40	1	5	18	17	10	2,700	0	0	241	18	0	140	19	10	11½	1857,	
45	5	8	46	9	1	65	17	4	57	15	1	5,871	5	8	648	0	4	277	21	3	11	1856,	Ballinasloe.
29	15	1	40	18	9	62	7	6	71	11	8	5,724	10	6	571	10	2	301	19	1	0½	1857,	
12	8	6	34	18	2	—			56	14	3	5,428	13	9	430	19	4	291	18	13	1½	1856,	Belfast.
28	15	6	35	0	0	—			76	3	9	6,414	2	7	900	12	1	323	19	10	11½	1857,	
10	7	4	—			10	10	4	52	3	2	3,880	4	11	6	18	5	101	20	0	3½	1856,	Carlow.
12	15	11	—			12	10	0	66	11	11	3,703	7	5	13	8	11	197	10	5	1½	1857,	
2	2	6	10	15	0	23	4	7	44	0	0	3,267	9	10	248	5	1	140	23	6	0¾	1856,	Clonmel.
0	13	10½	—			17	4	7	25	5	4	3,329	4	1	305	0	1	140	23	15	7¾	1857,	
8	3	1	12	10	6	51	15	6	98	12	5	6,835	13	6	322	10	5	407	16	15	10¼	1856,	Cork.
18	10	3	12	14	4	50	18	9	167	4	4	7,027	0	7	151	14	7	433	16	4	0½	1857,	
14	13	2	—			—			48	15	9	2,924	1	5¼	515	6	11½	143	20	8	11¼	1856,	Kilkenny.
23	4	10	—			—			55	19	4½	2,984	13	11	100	18	3½	146½	20	5	10	1857,	
29	10	2½	—			23	1	4	37	12	2½	3,161	5	11	211	8	1	149½	21	15	8	1856,	Killarney.
28	13	1½	—			27	7	5	55	19	4	3,316	16	10	44	10	4	162	21	14	2	1857,	
5	14	2	4	15	0½	34	6	0	44	0	0½	6,524	7	10½	800	8	1	325	20	1	0	1856,	Limerick.
4	3	4	4	18	8½	35	17	2	63	3	11½	6,378	2	4½	757	18	2	330	19	0	6½	1857,	
6	7	3	—			54	14	3	64	8	6	3,705	1	0	476	1	0	201	18	14	7½	1856,	L. Derry.
3	3	3	—			58	2	8	60	8	10	3,807	18	0	610	8	10	204	18	13	3½	1857,	
15	11	0	—			0	19	6	65	5	1	3,644	1	2	518	10	10	104	22	4	4½	1856,	Maryboro'.
23	13	8	—			1	6	6	54	0	3	3,373	3	6	408	8	9	149	22	13	5½	1857,	
4	10	0	2	17	0	—			118	0	6½	2,532	15	8	2	8	0	125	20	8	5½	1856,	Mullingar.
2	8	4	7	0	0	6	3	0	132	12	4	4,260	7	0	40	12	7	176	24	4	1½	1857,	
29	4	0	—			38	11	9	27	0	0	4,274	13	4	533	3	4	187	22	17	2½	1856,	Omagh.
16	0	1	—			37	3	3	28	5	1	4,726	5	3	502	6	4	211	22	7	11½	1857,	
97	7	0	63	0	1	77	17	0	92	7	3	12,072	1	10	241	3	6	538	22	8	0½	1856,	Richmond.
81	18	0	79	6	8	86	8	0	118	13	8	13,751	4	10	208	19	0	610	22	10	10½	1857,	
0	5	0	0	13	7	15	19	7	80	0	5	2,844	13	0	46	17	11	105	27	1	10	1856,	Sligo.
0	0	0	1	13	2	5	0	4	34	19	0	3,025	16	8	259	5	4	126½	23	18	4½	1857,	
24	5	2	1	7	9	21	3	5	36	9	0	2,606	9	11	23	19	0	128	20	16	7½	1856,	Waterford.
31	10	1	7	15	7	17	14	2	36	8	3	2,617	5	3	—			134	21	2	1½	1857,	
311	15	3½	177	13	2½	463	19	10	941	12	3½	72,020	10	8	5,433	4	5½	3,502½	20	14	8	1856,	General Total.
321	0	9	198	7	8½	458	7	6	1,117	14	5	77,433	4	0½	5,443	0	5½	3,773½	20	10	5	1857,	

No. 24.—TABLE showing the Names and Salaries of the prin[cipal...]

Asylums.	Visiting Physicians.	£ s. d.	Resident Physicians and Managers.	£	Allowances.	Matrons.	£	Allowances.
Armagh,	T. Cuming, M.D.,	100 0 0	Thomas Jackson, Manager,	240	Rations, equal in value to £40.	M. Jackson,	75	Rations equal in value to £25.
Ballinasloe,	Thos. Dillon, M.D.,	125 0 0	J. B. M'Kiernan, Manager,	200	Fuel, light, washing, and vegetables.	M. A. Callan,	70	Fuel, light, washing, vegetables.
Belfast,	H. M'Cormac, M.D.,	100 0 0	R. Stewart, M.D.,	275	Furniture, rations, keep of a cow and horse, &c.	M. F. Stewart,	75	Same rations as Resident Physician.
Carlow,	Thos. O'Meara, M.D.,	100 0 0	M. E. White, M.D.,	260	Washing, vegetables, coal, light, and 2 qts. milk, daily.	L. Parsons,	100	Ditto.
Clonmel,	W. J. Shiell, M.D.,	100 0 0	Jas. Flynn, M.D.,	260	Coals, candles, furnished apartments, & garden.	Ellen Crofton,	70	Coals, candles, furnished apartments, vegetables, and ten tons per annum for servant.
Cork,	{Samuel Hobart, M.D., Surgeon,}	100 0 0	Thos. Power, M.D.,	180	Fuel, light, and washing.	M. Clifton,	60	{Rations, fuel, light, and washing.}
Kilkenny,	L. C. Kinchela, M.D.,	100 0 0	Jas. Lalor, M.D.,	200	Fuel, light, washing, and vegetables.	Joanna Lyan,	90	Same as Manager.
Killarney,	W. W. Murphy, M.D.,	100 0 0	M. S. Lawlor, M.D.,	260	Unfurnished apartments, fuel, light, & washing.	M. A. Fulvey,	75	Same as Manager & £5 per annum for servant.
Limerick,	D. O'Callaghan, M.D.,	150 0 0	R. Fitzgerald, M.D.,	200	Bread, milk, coals, candles, and servant.	A. M. Sleeman,	70	Same as Manager.
Londonderry,	B. White, M.D.,	100 0 0	Wm. F. Rogan,	260	Coals, gas, vegetables.	Eliza Grant,	70	Coals, gas, vegetables.
Maryborough,	John Jacob, M.D.,	100 0 0	T. C. Burton, M.D.,	250	Coals, candles, vegetables, washing.	Eliza Abbott,	85	Same as Manager.
Mullingar,	Jos. Ferguson, M.D.,	100 0 0	H. Berkely, M.D.,	260	No allowances.	K. M. Costello,	75	Allowances, value per annum, £18 10s.
Omagh,	H. Thompson, M.D.,	100 0 0	F. J. West,	300	Vegetables, milk.	H. Hudson,	75	Vegetables, milk.
Richmond,	{J. Mollan, M.D., 168 0 4; R. Tuohill, M.D., 168 0 4; J. Banks, M.D., 150 0 0; J. Hughes, Surgeon, 150 0 0}		Samuel Wrigley, Manager,	230	{Fuel, light, and vegetables.}	{C. Wrigley, 80; E. Blundell, Assistant Matron, 40}		{Fuel, light, and rooms. Ditto.}
Sligo,	W. S. Little,	100 0 0	John M'Munn,	260	Fuel, light, washing, milk, and vegetables.	Margt. Benson,	75	Board, fuel, light, washing.
Waterford,	Pierce R. Connolly,	100 0 0	J. Dobbs, Manager,	200	Furniture, coals, and candles.	K. P. Roynan,	70	Furniture, coals, candles.

No. 25.—TABLE showing the Number of Meetings held during Year ended 31st March, 1856, and the Attendance of Governors thereat.

Asylums.	April, 1855.		May, 1855.		June, 1855.		July, 1855.		August, 1855.		Sept., 1855.		October, 1855.		Nov., 1855.		December, 1855.		January, 1856.		February, 1856.		March, 1856.		Total No. of Meetings during the year.	Average attendance of Governors.
	No. of Meetings.	No. of Governors in attendance.	No. of Meetings.	No. of Governors in attendance.	No. of Meetings.	No. of Governors in attendance.	No. of Meetings.	No. of Governors in attendance.	No. of Meetings.	No. of Governors in attendance.	No. of Meetings.	No. of Governors in attendance.	No. of Meetings.	No. of Governors in attendance.	No. of Meetings.	No. of Governors in attendance.	No. of Meetings.	No. of Governors in attendance.	No. of Meetings.	No. of Governors in attendance.	No. of Meetings.	No. of Governors in attendance.	No. of Meetings.	No. of Governors in attendance.		
Armagh,	1	2	1	3	1	6	1	4	1	5	2	{2/5}	1	8	1	3	1	3	1	5	1	5	1	5	13	4
Ballinasloe,	1	1	1	2	1	3	1	2	1	3	1	1	1	2	1	2	1	3	1	2	1	1	1	2	12	2
Belfast,	-	-	1	4	1	6	1	3	1	6	1	7	1	9	2	{8/6}	2	{10/[illegible]}	4	{13/8}	1	5	2	{6/8}	15	7
Carlow,	2	{8/3}	1	9	1	3	1	5	1	3	2	{2/4}	1	4	1	3	2	{[illegible]}	1	4	1	4	1	4	13	3
Clonmel,	-	-	1	5	1	7	1	7	1	5	1	8	1	4	1	7	1	6	1	7	1	5	2	{5/3}	12	6
Cork,	1	11	2	{11/8}	2	{18/9}	1	4	1	5	3	{12/4/17/4}	1	7	1	6	2	{6/5}	1	13	2	{10/3}	[illegible]	[illegible]	18	8
Kilkenny,	1	4	1	3	1	5	1	8	2	{5/2}	3	{[illegible]}	1	5	2	{6/1}	1	4	1	5	1	6	2	{3/3}	17	4
Killarney,	1	5	-	-	1	5	1	8	-	-	4	{[illegible]}	1	5	-	-	1	5	1	4	1	4	1	9	12	5
Limerick,	1	8	1	9	1	4	1	5	1	6	1	{2/[illegible]}	1	3	1	5	1	9	1	7	1	7	1	6	12	5
Londonderry,	1	8	1	13	1	9	1	11	1	11	2	{[illegible]/12}	1	5	1	13	1	4	2	{10/6}	1	13	2	{9/13}	15	10
Maryborough,	1	3	1	2	1	3	1	8	2	{2/4}	2	{[illegible]}	1	5	1	5	-	-	1	5	1	5	1	3	13	3
Mullingar,	-	-	-	-	-	-	2	{4/11}	1	6	2	{[illegible]}	1	5	1	7	1	6	2	{9/3}	1	5	1	7	12	6
Omagh,	1	3	1	5	1	3	1	7	1	8	1	6	1	10	1	11	1	12	1	10	1	8	1	10	12	7
Richmond,	2	{6/4}	2	{4/4}	2	{3/4}	2	{6/2}	3	{[illegible]}	2	{[illegible]}	2	{3/4}	2	{3/3}	2	{4/6}	2	{6/6}	2	{4/7}	2	{5/6}	20	4
Sligo,	1	5	1	2	1	8	1	5	1	3	1	8	1	4	1	5	1	4	1	2	2	8	1	7	13	4
Waterford,	1	6	1	3	1	6	1	3	1	1	1	4	1	4	1	3	1	3	1	2	1	5	1	2	12	3

Officers of District Asylums, 31st March, 1857.

Protestant Chaplains.	£	Roman Catholic Chaplains.	£	Apothecaries.	£	Clerks and Storekeepers.	£	Allowances.
None appointed by Government; one attends from the Primate.		Similarly; one from the Roman Catholic Archbishop.		Vacant, . . .	—	Samuel Parker, .	82	Lodging and diet.
Rev. J. C. Walker, .	40	Rev. J. Kirwan, .	40	J. E. Poyntz, .	30	J. E. Maher, .	35	Fuel, light, washing. &c.
Rev. John Carroll,* .	—	Rev. Patrick Fagan,	—	Jas. Moore, .	50	Robert Lamont,	50	Furnished apartments, rations, and washing.
Rev. Wm. M'Cullagh,*	—							
Rev. T. Trench,	25	Rev. Jas. Hughes, .	25	Henry Montgomery,	30	T. Brennan, .	40	Rations, washing, coal, light, clothing, and premium.
Rev. H. Fry, .	25	Rev. —— Wallace, .	33	Richard Graham, .	30	Edward O'Neill, .	55	Allowances, value £8 per annum.
Rev. C. H. Clifford, .	50	Rev. P. Burton, .	50	W. T. Jones, .	40	W. Renwick, Steward	80	Rations, fuel, light, & washing.
						W. Connell, Clerk, .	55	Ditto.
						J. P. Duggan, Storekp	30	Ditto.
Rev. J. Graves, .	30	Rev. E. Larkin, .	95	John Fitzsimons, .	45	Wheeler O'Flaherty,	60	No allowances.
Rev. T. La Hunte, .	20	Rev. J. Conrihan, .	60	Richard Linnegar, .	30	J. Wallace, .	50	Unfurnished apartments, fuel, light, washing, and rations.
Rev. B. Jacob, .	50	Rev. Michael Malone,	50	John B. Bonchier,	50	James Dobbin, .	40	No allowances.
Rev. W. Craig, .	25	Rev. Edw. Doherty,	25	W. J. Eames, .	30	Thomas Colhoun, .	35	Rations, coals, gas.
Rev. Dr. Denham,†	25	Rev. Dr. Taylor, .	95	Thomas Pilsworth, .	80	T. C. Molloy, .	30	No allowances.
Rev. Thos. Harpur,	25							
Rev. John Hopkins, .	25	Rev. Jas. Moran, .	50	W. Malleton, .	35	James M'Kenna, .	50	Allowances, value per annum, £18 10s.
Rev. R. Swift, .	30	Rev. P. O'Dogherty,	30	Francis Trevor, .	35	John Carson, .	50	Full rations.
Rev. J. Mitchell,*	30							
Rev. A. Leeper,	80	Rev. J. Faulkner, .	100	P. Beatty, Apothecary,	100	J. Fitzsimon, .	80	No allowances.
				J. Atkins, ‡ Clinical	20	J. Nunn, Accountant.	40	Ditto.
				H. Booth, ‡ Clerks ‡	20			
Rev. E. Day, .	30	Rev. P. Boyle, .	40	John Lougheed, .	95	John M'Carthy, .	50	Board, fuel, light, & washing.
Venble. R. Bell,	25	Rev. P. Wall, .	35	John Mackesy, .	30	Thomas Keary, .	55	No allowances.

* These clergymen have not officiated at the Asylum for some time, in consequence of a decision in the Court of Queen's Bench.   ‡ Messrs. Atkins and Booth are allowed fuel, light, and vegetables.
† Presbyterian Chaplain.

No. 26.—TABLE showing the Number of Meetings held during Year ended 31st March, 1857, and the Attendance of Governors thereat.

Asylums.	April, 1856.		May, 1856.		June, 1856.		July, 1856.		August, 1856.		Sept., 1856.		October, 1856.		Nov., 1856.		December, 1856.		January, 1857.		February, 1857.		March, 1857.		Total No. of Meetings during the year.	Average attendance of Governors.
	No. of Meetings	No. of Governors in attendance	No. of Meetings	No. of Governors in attendance	No. of Meetings	No. of Governors in attendance	No. of Meetings	No. of Governors in attendance	No. of Meetings	No. of Governors in attendance	No. of Meetings	No. of Governors in attendance	No. of Meetings	No. of Governors in attendance	No. of Meetings	No. of Governors in attendance	No. of Meetings	No. of Governors in attendance	No. of Meetings	No. of Governors in attendance	No. of Meetings	No. of Governors in attendance	No. of Meetings	No. of Governors in attendance		
Armagh,	1	3	1	4	1	2	1	4	1	4	1	3	1	4	1	3	1	4	1	4	1	5	1	5	12	4
Ballinasloe,	1	3	1	4	1	2	1	2	1	3	1	3	1	4	1	2	1	2	1	6	1	7	2	{8/8}	13	3
Belfast,	1	5	1	7	1	4	1	5	1	6	1	5	1	9	1	2	1	7	1	7	1	7	2	{8}	13	6
Carlow,	4	{4/4}	1	4	1	0	3	{8/3/4}	1	5	1	1	1	5	1	6	1	5	1	3	1	5	1	5	15	4
Clonmel,	1	8	1	6	2	{5/3}	1	3	1	4	2	{6/13}	1	5	1	6	1	5	1	6	2	{9/5}	1	5	15	6
Cork,	1	12	2	{6/8}	1	5	1	5	1	7	1	5	1	6	1	5	2	{1/1/5}	2	{2/4}	1	4	1	5	18	3
Kilkenny,	1	4	1	6	1	4	1	5	1	5	2	{8}	2	{2}	1	4	1	6	1	5	1	5	2	{8}	14	5
Killarney,	2	{4/8}	1	4	1	3	1	5	1	4	1	4	1	6	1	6	1	5	1	4	1	4	1	6	14	6
Limerick,	2	{6/12}	1	8	1	6	1	5	1	5	1	3	2	{14}	1	8	1	6	1	5	1	5	1	5	15	9
Londonderry,	1	9	1	11	1	3	1	7	1	11	1	11	2	{17/6}	1	12	1	20	1	11	1	9	1	6	15	9
Maryborough,	3	{10/10/3}	1	8	1	5	1	7	1	6	1	6	1	8	1	4	1	7	1	6	1	7	1	6	14	6
Mullingar,	1	5	1	5	1	3	1	3	1	3	1	8	1	4	2	{7/3}	1	4	1	7	1	5	1	5	12	6
Omagh,	1	3	1	8	1	3	1	7	1	7	1	7	1	5	2	{10}	1	8	1	6	1	9	1	5	13	4
Richmond,	2	{5/4}	3	{4/5/4}	2	{5/3}	2	{4/5}	2	{5/4}	2	{3/4}	2	{5/4}	2	{5/4}	2	{7/6}	2	{9/7}	2	{5/4}	2	{4/6}	25	5
Sligo,	2	{5/5}	1	4	2	{4/6}	1	6	1	7	1	8	1	8	1	4	1	6	2	{4/9}	1	15	15	5
Waterford,	1	2	1	3	1	6	1	5	1	2	1	8	1	3	1	3	1	5	1	6	1	10	1	4	12	4

No. 27.—NAMES of GOVERNORS who attended Meetings during the Years 1856 and 1857, and the Dates of Appointment.

Name.	Date of Appointment.
ARMAGH.	
His Grace The Primate,	1824.
Rev. James Jones,	1831.
William Paton, Esq., J.P.,	1841.
George Robinson, Esq.,	1847.
Rev. A. Irwin,	1850.
Thomas Dobbin, Esq., J.P.,	1851.
Maxwell Cross, Esq., J.P.,	,,
Francis White, Esq., M.D.,	1852.
John Nugent, Esq., M D,	,,
Most Rev. Archbishop Dixon,	1854.
Right Hon. Lord Rossmore, D.L.,	1855.
William Fowler, Esq., J.P.,	,,
R. H. Dolling, Esq.,	,,
Right Rev. Doctor MacNally,	,,
BALLINASLOE.	
Right Hon. Earl of Clancarty,	Aug. 15, 1833.
Right Hon. Lord Clonbrock,	Dec. 31. 1834.
Walter Lawrence, Esq., J.P.,	,,
Denis Kelly, Esq., D.L.,	,,
Hon. Robert Le Poer Trench, D L.,	July 16, 1844.
Charles Filgate, Esq., J.P.,	,,
James Bell, Esq., J.P.,	,,
H. J. Gascoyne, Esq.,	,,
Right Rev. Doctor Derry,	Sept. 13, 1847.
Francis White, Esq., M.D.,	1852,
John Nugent, Esq., M.D.,	,,
H. J. Potts, Esq.,	Feb. 12, 1855.
BELFAST.	
Mayor of Belfast,	March, 1829.
Sir Robert Bateson, Bart., D.L.,	June, 1829.
William M'Cance, Esq., J.P.,	January, 1836.
R. J. Tennent, Esq., J.P., D.L.,	,,
John Sinclaire, Esq.,	October, 1836.
Right Rev. Bishop Denvir,	,,
Rev. John Edgar, D.D.,	,,
Rev. H. Montgomery, LL.D.,	,,
Very Rev. Dean Stannus,	April. 1842.
Rev. H. Cooke, D.D., LL.D.,	,,
R. B. B. Houston, Esq., J.P., D.L.,	,,
Conway B. Grimshaw, Esq.,	October, 1846.
John Clarke, Esq., J.P.,	Sept., 1847.
John Sharman Crawford, Esq., J.P.,	Nov 1847.
William Dunville, Esq.,	May, 1851.
Rev. T. F Miller,	Dec., 1851.
Francis White, Esq., M.D.,	April, 1852.
John Nugent, Esq., M.D.,	,,
A. J. Macrory, Esq.,	June, 1852
Thomas M'Clure, Esq.,	January, 1856.
CARLOW.	
Sir Thomas Butler, Bart., D.L.,	Dec. 1, 1831.
Samuel Haughton, Esq.,	,,
Rev. James Maher,	Nov. 2, 1837.
Robert Cassidy, Esq.,	Aug. 20, 1839.
Horace Rochfort, Esq.,	May 5, 1843.
Robert Clayton Browne, Esq., D.L.,	Feb. 15, 1847.
Patrick W. Redmond, Esq.,	,,
John Nolan, Esq.,	Oct. 19, 1848.
Hugh Blackney, Esq.,	,,
William F. Burton, Esq., D.L.,	March 7, 1850.
Francis White, Esq., M.D.,	1852,
John Nugent, Esq., M D.,	,,
Henry Bruen, Esq., M.D.,	Dec. 21, 1855
Right Rev. James Walsh, D.D.,	,,
William Ducket, Esq., D.L.,	,,
Philip T. Newton, Esq., D.L.,	,,
John H. Nangle, Esq.,	Jan. 29, 1856.
Thomas FitzGerald, Esq.,	,,
CLONMEL.	
John Bagwell, Esq., D.L.,	1834.
S. Moore, Esq., D.L.,	,,
S. W. Barton, Esq., D.L.,*	,,
Rev. Walter Giles,	1835.
Rev. Dr. Burke,	1836.
Rev. Mr. Baldwin,	,,
C. Bianconi, Esq.,	1841.
Ed Phelan, Esq., M.D.,	,,
Colonel Phipps,	1842.
W. H. Riall, Esq.,	,,
Rev. John Dill,	1843.
Right Hon. Earl Donoughmore,	1849.
Thomas Lalor, Esq.,	,,
Joseph Grubb, Esq.,	,,
Francis White, Esq., M.D.,	1852.
John Nugent, Esq., M.D.,	,,

Name.	Date of Appointment.
CORK.	
Lord Bernard, D.L.,	Oct. 4, 1845.
Sir C. D. O. J. Norreys, Bart.,	,,
Lord Doneraile,	,,
General Burke, J.P.,	,,
Thomas G. French, Esq., J.P.,	Oct. 4, 1845.
G. Standish Barry, Esq., D.L.,	,,
William Coppinger, Esq.,	,,
Horatio Townsend, Esq., D.L.,	,,
Cooper Penrose, Esq.,	,,
F. B. Beamish, Esq., M.P., D.L.,	,,
R Touson Rye, Esq., J.P,	,,
William Fagan, Esq., M.P., D.L.,	,,
James Murphy, Esq.,	,,
James Morrogh, Esq.,	,,
Richard Dowden (Richard), Esq.,	,,
Right Rev. Dr. Delany, R.C.B.	March 13, 1848.
The Very Rev. The Archdeacon of Cork,	,,
The Recorder of Cork,	,,
William J. Sheehy, Esq.,	,,
Major Atkins,	,,
David Leahy Arthur, Esq.,	,,
Lord Bishop of Cork, Cloyne, and Ross,	June 17, 1850.
Denham W. J. Norreys, Esq.,	,,
Francis White, Esq., M.D.,	May 1, 1852.
John Nugent, Esq., M.D.,	,,
Member of Parliament for Borough of Kinsale,	Feb. 18, 1853.
Member of Parliament for Borough of Youghal,	,,
Mayor of City of Cork,	,,
High Sheriff of City of Cork,	,,
Hon. Robert Hare,	,,
Nicholas Dunscombe, Esq.,	,,
William L. Perrier, Esq.,	,,
Sir Thomas Tobin,	,,
S. T. W. French, Esq.,	,,
Henry William O'Donovan, Esq.,	,,
Benjamin S Wood, Esq.,	,,
Robert De La Cour Beamish, Esq.,	,,
William R. Meade, Esq.,	,,
KILKENNY.	
The Earl of Desart,	1852.
Right Hon. W. F. F. Tighe,	,,
Michael Sullivan, Esq., M.P.,	,,
The Hon. C. B. Wandesforde,	,,
Right Rev. James O'Brien, Bishop of Ossory and Ferns,	,,
Sir John Blunden, Bart., D.L.,	,,
William L. Flood, Esq., D.L.,	,,
John Newport Greene, Esq., J.P.,	,,
John B Wandesforde, Esq., J.P.	,,
Edmond Smithwick, Esq., J.P.,	,,
Francis White, Esq., M.D.,	,,
John Nugent, Esq., M.D.,	,,
Peter Connellan, Esq., D.L.,	,,
Colonel Wemyss, D.L.,	,,
Lord James Butler, D.L.,	1855.
James M. Tidmarsh, Esq.,	1856.
William Lanigan, Esq., Mayor, ex officio,	,,
KILLARNEY.	
The Viscount Castlerosse, M.P.,	April 30, 1852.
Daniel C. Coltsmann, Esq., J.P.,	,,
Sir William Godfrey, Bart., D.L.,	,,
Thomas Gallwey, Esq., J.P.,	,,
Henry A. Herbert, Esq., M.P.,	,,
John Leahy, Esq., J.P,	,,
Denis Shine Lawlor, Esq., J.P.,	,,
Daniel Mahony, Esq., J P.,	,,
The M'Gillycuddy of the Reeks, D.L.,	,,
James O'Connell, Esq., J.P.,	,,
Francis White, Esq., M.D.,	,,
John Nugent, Esq., M D.,	,,
James B. Hewson, Esq., J.P.,	Sept. 20, 1853.
The Ven. Archdeacon Forster,	April 4, 1853.
The Right Rev. Dr. Moriarty, R.C.B.,	Nov. 13, 1854.
LIMERICK.	
The Earl of Clare,	Feb. 18, 1822.
Lord Monteagle,	,,
The Mayor of Limerick,	,,
The Very Rev. Dean Kirwin,	,,
Archdeacon Forster,	,,
William Howly, Esq.,	Dec. 15, 1827.
Joseph Gabbett, Esq.,	June 21, 1833.
Thomas Gabbett, Esq.,	,,
William H. Gabbett, Esq.,	,,
Henry Maunsell, Esq.,	,,
John W. Mahony, Esq.,	June 21, 1833.

* Died in November, 1855.

No. 27.—Names of Governors who attended Meetings during the Years 1856 and 1857, and the Dates of Appointment—*continued.*

Name.	Date of Appointment.
LIMERICK—*continued.*	
David J. Wilson, Esq.,	Sept. 30, 1856.
John Singleton, Esq.,	”
Right Rev. Doctor Ryan,	1839.
Michael Farnell, Esq.,	Nov. 1, 1845.
Henry Watson, Esq.,	”
Richard Russell, Esq.,	1847.
Francis Spaight, Esq.,	”
William Hartegan, Esq.,	”
William Gibson, Esq.,	”
Patrick A. Shannon, Esq.,	”
Thomas O'Grady, Esq.,	1849.
William J. Geary, Esq.,	1850.
Thomas Boyce, Esq.,	”
Francis White, Esq., M.D.,	April 26, 1852.
John Nugent, Esq., M.D.,	”
LONDONDERRY.	
Lord Bishop of Derry,	1829.
The Archdeacon of Derry,	”
The Dean of Derry,	”
The Mayor of Derry,	”
Rev. Thomas Lindsay,	1848.
Patrick Gilmour, Esq., J.P.,	”
Sir Robert Ferguson, Bart., M.P.,	1829.
Thomas Scott, Esq., D.L.,	”
William H. Ash, Esq., D.L.,	1830.
John Barre Beresford, Esq., D.L.,	1839.
Rev. William M'Clure,	1845.
Sir H. H. Bruce, Bart.,	1847.
William L. Browne, Esq.,	1849.
Anthony Babington, Esq.,	”
Hervey Nicholson, Esq.,	1853.
Sir Edmund Hayes, Bart., M.P.,	1829.
Sir James Stewart, Bart.,	”
William Fenwick, Esq.,	”
John Hervey, Esq.,	”
Rev. William Knox,	1830.
John Ferguson, Esq.,	1856.
A. J. R. Stewart, Esq.,	1850.
Benjamin G. Humphrey, Esq.,	1832.
Rev. Edward Bowen,	1834.
Robert M'Clintock, Esq.,	1836.
Sir Robert Bateson, Bart.,	”
John V. Stewart, Esq.,	”
Rev. J. M. Staples,	1839.
Lord Lifford,	1845.
Thomas Batt, Esq.,	1855.
Rev. Benjamin B. Gough,	1848.
John Nugent, Esq., M.D.,	1852.
John G. Bowen, Esq.,	1855.
Wybrants Olphert, Esq.,	1856.
Francis Mansfield, Esq.,	”
MARYBOROUGH.	
Viscount De Vesci,	April 6, 1833.
Rev. T. Harpur,	”
A. M. Moss, Esq.,	”
George Adair, Esq.,	March 24, 1835.
Robert Cassidy, Esq.,	March 9, 1838.
J. R. Price, Esq.,	Feb. 2, 1841.
Rev. J. T. Moore,	Aug. 7, 1841.
R. S. Hawksworth, Esq.,	April 12, 1846.
Right Hon. J. W. Fitzpatrick,	Oct. 9, 1830.
Thomas Kemmis, Esq.,	Nov. 10, 1830.
Rev. Dr. Taylor,	May 16, 1855.
D. Thompson, Esq.,	April 22, 1856.
Francis White, Esq., M.D.,	Nov. 10, 1850.
John Nugent, Esq., M.D.,	”
MULLINGAR.	
Edward M'Evoy, Esq., J.P., M.P.,	July 8, 1854.
John Farrell, jun., Esq.,	”
Lord Vox of Harrowden,	”
Right Rev. Dr. Cantwell,	”
Sir P. Nugent, Bart., D.L.,	”
Sir A. Levinge, Bart.,	”
W. P. Urquhart, Esq., M.P.,	”
H. M. Tuite, Esq., D.L.,	”
John C. Lyons, Esq., D.L.,	”
J. W. Berry, Esq., D.L.,	”
George Boyd, Esq., D.L.,	”
Colonel Caulfield,	”
W. H. Magan, Esq., M.P.,	”
Right Rev. Dr. Kilduff,	”
Rev. Mr. Edgeworth,	”
Colonel F. S. Greville, D.L., M.P.,	”
John L. O'Farrell, Esq., D.L.,	”
MULLINGAR—*continued.*	
Henry G. Hughes, Esq., J.P.,	July 8, 1854.
Philip O'Reilly, Esq.,	”
Frederick Jessop, Esq., J.P.,	”
George Evers, Esq.,	”
Francis White, Esq., M.D.,	”
John Nugent, Esq., M.D.,	”
Samuel Winter, Esq.,	1854.
Lord Castlemaine,	”
OMAGH.	
Lord Claud Hamilton,	Sept. 10, 1852.
Hon. A. G. Stuart,	May 24, 1855.
Sir R. A. Ferguson, Bart.,	Oct. 14, 1852.
Robert William Loury, sen., Esq.,	Dec. 11, 1852.
Thomas R. Browne, Esq.,	”
William Ogilby, Esq.,	”
James Anderson, Esq.,	Sept. 10, 1852.
Rev. Henry Tottenham,	Oct. 14, 1852.
Samuel Vesey, Esq.,	Sept. 10, 1852.
Francis Ellis, Esq.,	”
Samuel Galbraith, Esq.,	”
John Humphrey, Esq.,	”
Charles Eccles, Esq.,	”
Francis J. Gervais, Esq.,	”
David White, Esq.,	”
Charles R. Scott, Esq.,	”
George T. Spiller, Esq.,	”
Hon. and Rev. J. C. Maude,	”
Captain M. Archdall,	”
Rev. John G. Porter,	”
William D'Arcy, Esq.,	”
William Archdall, Esq.,	”
John G. O. Porter, Esq.,	”
Robert Archdall, Esq.,	”
John Nugent, Esq., M.D.,	”
RICHMOND.	
The Hon. and Very Rev. the Dean of St. Patrick's,	Feb. 24, 1844.
Sir George Hodson, Bart.,	”
Michael Stanuton, Esq.,	Feb. 15, 1847.
Thomas Hutton, Esq.,	”
The Very Rev. Dr. Yore,	”
John Lentaigne, Esq.,	”
Francis White, Esq., M.D.,	April 26, 1852.
John Nugent, Esq., M.D.,	”
Laurence Waldron, Esq.,	Aug. 2, 1856.
Thomas Lee Norman, Esq.,	”
SLIGO.	
Right Hon. J. Wynne, M.P., Chairman,	Sept. 10, 1852.
George Armstrong, Esq.,	”
Simon Armstrong, Esq.,	”
Sir Robert G. Booth, Bart., M.P.,	”
Lieut.-Colonel Barrett,	”
Richard Brinkley, Esq.,	”
The Earl of Leitrim,	”
C. W. Cooper, Esq.,	”
B. O. Cogan, Esq.,	”
Robert Culbertson, Esq.,	”
J. R. Dickson, Esq.,	”
Major Ffolliott,	”
W. Johnston, Esq.,	”
H. T. Montgomery, Esq., M.P.,	”
John Nugent, Esq., M.D.,	”
F. M. Olpherts, Esq.,	”
Peter O'Connor, Esq.,	”
William Phibbs, Esq.,	Sept. 29, 1852.
Edward Smyth, Esq.,	”
Captain Wood,	”
Colonel J. Whyte,	”
WATERFORD.	
Captain W. S. Doyle,	May 8, 1835.
Henry Denny, Esq.,	Feb. 13, 1836.
James Keating, Esq.,	Oct. 19, 1848.
Very Rev. Edward N. Hoare,	Dec. 8, 1851.
John Power, Esq.,	”
Edward Roberts, Esq.,	”
W. M. Ardagh, Esq.,	”
Charles Newport, Esq.,	Aug. 1, 1853.
Lieutenant-Colonel Edmond Roberts,	”
Rev. Martin Flynn,	”
The Mayor,	”
Francis White, Esq., M.D.,	”
John Nugent, Esq., M.D.,	”
Right Rev. Dr. O'Brien,	April 22, 1856.

APPENDIX D.

No. 1.—RETURN of all Persons in custody in Gaols during the two Years ending 31st March, 1856, and 1857, who were Acquitted of Offences on the ground of Insanity.

GAOL.	TOTAL.			NATURE OF OFFENCE. Homicide.			Felony.			Assault.			Burglary.			Larceny.			Discharged.			Removed to Asylum by Warrant of Lord Lieutenant.			Died.			Remaining in Gaol.		
1856.	M.	F.	T.	M.	F.	T.	M.	F.	T.	M.	F.	T.	M.	F.	T.	M.	F.	T.	M.	F.	T.	M.	F.	T.	M.	F.	T.	M.	F.	T.
Cork City,	–	1	1	–	–	–	–	1	1	–	–	–	–	–	–	–	–	–	–	1	1	–	–	–	–	–	–	–	–	–
Downpatrick,	1	1	2	–	–	–	1	–	1	–	1	1	–	–	–	–	–	–	–	1	1	–	–	–	–	–	–	1	–	1
Tralee,	–	1	1	–	–	–	–	–	–	–	–	–	–	1	1	–	–	–	–	–	–	–	1	1	–	–	–	–	–	–
Tullamore,	1	–	1	–	–	–	1	–	1	–	–	–	–	–	–	–	–	–	–	–	–	1	–	1	–	–	–	–	–	–
Carrick-on-Shannon,	3	–	3	–	–	–	–	–	–	3	–	3	–	–	–	–	–	–	–	–	–	3	–	3	–	–	–	–	–	–
Limerick,	–	1	1	–	–	–	–	–	–	–	–	–	–	–	–	–	1	1	–	–	–	–	1	1	–	–	–	–	–	–
Longford,	1	–	1	–	–	–	1	–	1	–	–	–	–	–	–	–	–	–	–	–	–	1	–	1	–	–	–	–	–	–
Trim,	–	1	1	–	1	1	–	–	–	–	–	–	–	–	–	–	–	–	–	–	–	–	1	1	–	–	–	–	–	–
Sligo,	1	–	1	1	–	1	–	–	–	–	–	–	–	–	–	–	–	–	–	–	–	1	–	1	–	–	–	–	–	–
Waterford,	1	–	1	–	–	–	–	–	–	1	–	1	–	–	–	–	–	–	1	–	1	–	–	–	–	–	–	–	–	–
Mullingar,	1	–	1	–	–	–	–	–	–	1	–	1	–	–	–	–	–	–	–	–	–	1	–	1	–	–	–	–	–	–
Total,	9	5	14	1	1	2	3	1	4	5	1	6	–	1	1	–	1	1	1	2	3	7	3	10	–	–	–	1	–	1

GAOL.	TOTAL.			NATURE OF OFFENCE. Homicide.			Felony.			Assault.			Arson.			Indecently exposing person.			Vagrancy.			Discharged.			Removed to Asylum by Warrant of Lord Lieutenant.			Died.			Remaining in Gaol.		
1857.	M.	F.	T.	M.	F.	T.	M.	F.	T.	M.	F.	T.	M.	F.	T.	M.	F.	T.	M.	F.	T.	M.	F.	T.	M.	F.	T.	M.	F.	T.	M.	F.	T.
Belfast,	1	–	1	–	–	–	–	–	–	1	–	1	–	–	–	–	–	–	–	–	–	–	–	–	–	–	–	–	–	–	1	–	1
Cavan,	1	–	1	1	–	1	–	–	–	–	–	–	–	–	–	–	–	–	–	–	–	–	–	–	1	–	1	–	–	–	–	–	–
Downpatrick,	1	–	1	–	–	–	1	–	1	–	–	–	–	–	–	–	–	–	–	–	–	–	–	–	–	–	–	–	–	–	1	–	1
Kilmainham,	1	–	1	–	–	–	1	–	1	–	–	–	–	–	–	–	–	–	–	–	–	–	–	–	1	–	1	–	–	–	–	–	–
Richmond,	1	–	1	–	–	–	–	–	–	1	–	1	–	–	–	–	–	–	–	–	–	–	–	–	1	–	1	–	–	–	–	–	–
Grangegorman,	–	1	1	–	–	–	–	–	–	–	–	–	–	–	–	–	–	–	–	1	1	–	–	–	–	–	–	–	–	–	–	1	1
Athy,	2	–	2	–	–	–	1	–	1	–	–	–	1	–	1	–	–	–	–	–	–	–	–	–	–	–	–	–	–	–	2	–	2
Car.-on-Shannon,	–	1	1	–	–	–	–	–	–	–	1	1	–	–	–	–	–	–	–	–	–	–	–	–	–	1	1	–	–	–	–	–	–
Limerick County,	1	–	1	–	–	–	–	–	–	1	–	1	–	–	–	–	–	–	–	–	–	–	–	–	–	–	–	–	–	–	1	–	1
Roscommon,	1	–	1	–	–	–	1	–	1	–	–	–	–	–	–	–	–	–	–	–	–	1	–	1	–	–	–	–	–	–	–	–	–
Sligo,	1	–	1	–	–	–	1	–	1	–	–	–	–	–	–	–	–	–	–	–	–	–	–	–	1	–	1	–	–	–	–	–	–
Waterford,	1	–	1	–	–	–	–	–	–	–	–	–	–	–	–	1	–	1	–	–	–	–	–	–	1	–	1	–	–	–	–	–	–
Total,	11	2	13	1	–	1	5	–	5	3	1	4	1	–	1	1	–	1	–	1	1	1	–	1	5	1	6	–	–	–	5	1	6

No. 2.—RETURN of all Persons confined in Gaols during the two Years ending 31st March, 1856, and 1857, who were found Insane on Arraignment, and incapable of pleading.

GAOL.	TOTAL.			NATURE OF OFFENCE. Homicide.			Felony.			Aggravated Assault.			Creating Disturbance.			Discharged.			Removed to Asylum by Warrant of Lord Lieutenant.			Died.			Remaining in Gaol.		
1856.	M.	F.	T.	M.	F.	T.	M.	F.	T.	M.	F.	T.	M.	F.	T.	M.	F.	T.	M.	F.	T.	M.	F.	T.	M.	F.	T.
Carlow,	2	1	3	–	–	–	–	–	–	2	–	2	–	1	1	1	1	2	1	–	1	–	–	–	–	–	–
Lifford,	2	–	2	–	–	–	2	–	2	–	–	–	–	–	–	–	–	–	2	–	2	–	–	–	–	–	–
Kilkenny,	1	–	1	–	–	–	1	–	1	–	–	–	–	–	–	–	–	–	1	–	1	–	–	–	–	–	–
Nenagh,	1	1	2	–	–	–	–	–	–	1	1	2	–	–	–	–	–	–	–	–	–	–	–	–	1	1	2
Total,	6	2	8	–	–	–	3	–	3	3	1	4	–	1	1	1	1	2	4	–	4	–	–	–	1	1	2

GAOL.	TOTAL.			NATURE OF OFFENCE. Homicide.			Felony.			Assault.			Arson.			Larceny.			Removed to Asylum by Warrant of Lord Lieutenant.			Died.			Remaining in Gaol.		
1857.	M.	F.	T.	M.	F.	T.	M.	F.	T.	M.	F.	T.	M.	F.	T.	M.	F.	T.	M.	F.	T.	M.	F.	T.	M.	F.	T.
Carlow,	2	–	2	–	–	–	2	–	2	–	–	–	–	–	–	–	–	–	–	–	–	1	–	1	1	–	1
Naas,	1	–	1	–	–	–	–	–	–	–	–	–	1	–	1	–	–	–	–	–	–	–	–	–	1	–	1
Nenagh,	2	–	2	–	–	–	–	–	–	1	–	1	–	–	–	1	–	1	–	–	–	–	–	–	2	–	2
Mullingar,	1	–	1	1	–	1	–	–	–	–	–	–	–	–	–	–	–	–	1	–	1	–	–	–	–	–	–
Wexford,	–	1	1	–	–	–	–	–	–	–	–	–	–	–	–	–	1	1	–	–	–	–	–	–	–	1	1
Total,	6	1	7	1	–	1	2	–	2	1	–	1	1	–	1	1	1	2	1	–	1	1	–	1	4	1	5

No. 3.—RETURN of all Persons under Sentence of Imprisonment or Transportation in Gaols, who became Insane in Gaol during the two Years ending 31st March, 1856, and 1857.[*]

GAOL.	TOTAL.			Homicide.			Felony.			Aggravated Assault.			Deserter.			Removed to Asylum by Warrant of Lord Lieutenant.			Died.			Remaining in Gaol.		
1856.	M.	F.	T.	M.	F.	T.	M.	F.	T.	M.	F.	T.	M.	F.	T.	M.	F.	T.	M.	F.	T.	M.	F.	T.
Galway County,	1	–	1	1	–	1	–	–	–	–	–	–	–	–	–	1	–	1	–	–	–	–	–	–
Wexford,	1	–	1	–	–	–	–	–	–	–	–	–	1	–	1	–	–	–	–	–	–	1	–	1
Total,	2	–	2	1	–	1	–	–	–	–	–	–	1	–	1	1	–	1	–	–	–	1	–	1

GAOL.	TOTAL.			Homicide.			Felony.			Assault.			Discharged.			Removed to Asylum by Warrant of Lord Lieutenant.			Died.			Remaining in Gaol.		
1857.	M.	F.	T.	M.	F.	T.	M.	F.	T.	M.	F.	T.	M.	F.	T.	M.	F.	T.	M.	F.	T.	M.	F.	T.
Athy,	1	–	1	–	–	–	–	–	–	1	–	1	–	–	–	1	–	1	–	–	–	–	–	–
Limerick County,	1	–	1	–	–	–	–	–	–	1	–	1	–	–	–	1	–	1	–	–	–	–	–	–
Wexford,	1	–	1	–	–	–	–	–	–	1	–	1	1	–	1	–	–	–	–	–	–	–	–	–
Total,	3	–	3	–	–	–	–	–	–	3	–	3	1	–	1	2	–	2	–	–	–	–	–	–

[*] This does not include persons who became insane in Government Prisons.—(See p. 50. Table 8.)

No. 4.—RETURN of Persons committed to Gaols in default of Surety to keep the Peace, during the two Years ending 31st March, 1856, and 1857, who were Insane at the time of committal, or became Insane subsequent thereto.

GAOL.	TOTAL.			Insane on Committal.			Insane subsequent to Committal.			Discharged.			Removed to Asylum by Warrant of Lord Lieutenant.			Died.			Remaining in Gaol.		
1856.	M.	F.	T.	M.	F.	T.	M.	F.	T.	M.	F.	T.	M.	F.	T.	M.	F.	T.	M.	F.	T.
Kilmainham,	1	1	2	1	1	2	–	–	–	–	–	–	1	1	2	–	–	–	–	–	–
Grangegorman,	–	8	8	–	8	8	–	–	–	–	8	8	–	–	–	–	–	–	–	–	–
Tullamore,	1	–	1	–	–	–	1	–	1	–	–	–	1	–	1	–	–	–	–	–	–
Limerick,	2	1	3	2	1	3	–	–	–	–	–	–	2	1	3	–	–	–	–	–	–
Omagh,	2	1	3	2	1	3	–	–	–	2*	–	2	–	1	1	–	–	–	–	–	–
Total,	6	11	17	5	11	16	1	–	1	2	8	10	4	3	7	–	–	–	–	–	.
1857.																					
Cork County,	2	–	2	1	–	1	1	–	1	–	–	–	2	–	2	–	–	–	–	–	–
Cork City,	1	–	1	1	–	1	–	–	–	–	–	–	1	–	1	–	–	–	–	–	–
Lifford,	1	–	1	1	–	1	–	–	–	–	–	–	–	–	–	–	–	–	1	–	1
Downpatrick,	–	1	1	–	1	1	–	–	–	–	–	–	–	1	1	–	–	–	–	–	–
Richmond,	37	–	37	37	–	37	–	–	–	32	–	32	2	–	2	1	–	1	2	–	2
Grangegorman,	–	12	12	–	12	12	–	–	–	–	11	11	–	1	1	–	–	–	–	–	–
Limerick,	–	1	1	–	1	1	–	–	–	–	–	–	–	1	1	–	–	–	–	–	–
Londonderry,	–	2	2	–	2	2	–	–	–	–	–	–	–	2	2	–	–	–	–	–	–
Total,	41	16	57	40	16	56	1	–	1	32	11	43	5	5	10	1	–	1	3	–	3

No. 5.—RETURN of Persons committed to Gaols under the Vagrancy Act, during the two Years ending 31st March, 1856, and 1857, who were Insane on committal, or who became Insane subsequent thereto.

GAOL.	TOTAL.			Insane on Committal.			Insane subsequent to Committal.			Discharged.			Removed to Asylum by Warrant of Lord Lieutenant.			Died.			Remaining in Gaol.		
1856.	M.	F.	T.	M.	F.	T.	M.	F.	T.	M.	F.	T.	M.	F.	T.	M.	F.	T.	M.	F.	T.
Cork City,	1	–	1	1	–	1	–	–	–	1	–	1	–	–	–	–	–	–	–	–	–
Kilmainham,	1	–	1	1	–	1	–	–	–	1†	–	1	–	–	–	–	–	–	–	–	–
Omagh,	–	1	1	–	1	1	–	–	–	–	1	1	–	–	–	–	–	–	–	–	–
Waterford,	–	2	2	–	2	2	–	–	–	–	2	2	–	–	–	–	–	–	–	–	–
Total,	2	3	5	2	3	5	–	–	–	2	3	5	–	–	–	–	–	–	–	–	–
1857.																					
Armagh,	–	1	1	–	1	1	–	–	–	–	1	1	–	–	–	–	–	–	–	–	–
Grangegorman,	–	1	1	–	–	–	–	1	1	–	1	1	–	–	–	–	–	–	–	–	–
Total,	–	2	2	–	1	1	–	1	1	–	2	2	–	–	–	–	–	–	–	–	–

* One of these two cases was admitted out on bail.   † Returned to his friends by order of Lord Lieutenant.

No. 6.—RETURN of all Persons committed as Dangerous Lunatics during the two Years ending 31st March, 1856, and 1857.

GAOL	Remaining in Custody			Committed during year			Total Number in Custody			Removed to Asylum by Warrant of Lord Lieutenant			Discharged, by order of Magistrates on Medical Certificates, cured			Otherwise removed from Gaol			Died			Total Removed, Discharged, and Died			Remaining in Gaol on 31st March		
	M	F	T	M	F	T	M	F	T	M	F	T	M	F	T	M	F	T	M	F	T	M	F	T	M	F	T
1856.																											
Belfast,	1	–	1	11	3	14	12	3	13	8	3	11	–	–	–	–	–	–	1	–	1	9	3	12	3	–	3
Armagh,	1	–	1	3	3	6	4	3	7	4	3	7	–	–	–	–	–	–	–	–	–	4	3	7	–	–	–
Carlow,	–	–	–	4	2	6	4	2	6	1	1	2	1	1	2	–	–	–	–	–	–	2	2	4	2	–	2
Cavan,	–	–	–	9	5	14	9	5	14	7	1	8	–	1	1	–	–	–	1	–	1	8	2	10	1	3	4
Ennis,	–	1	1	12	3	15	12	4	16	9	3	12	2	–	2	–	–	–	–	–	–	11	3	14	1	1	2
Cork County,	–	–	–	13	12	25	13	12	25	9	8	17	3	3	6	–	–	–	1	–	1	13	11	24	–	–	1
Cork City,	–	–	–	2	–	2	2	–	2	1	–	1	1	–	1	–	–	–	–	–	–	2	–	2	–	–	–
Lifford,	7	–	7	15	8	23	22	8	30	5	7	12	5	–	5	–	–	–	–	–	–	13	7	20	9	1	10
Downpatrick,	13	5	18	10	8	18	23	13	36	16	4	20	4	5	9	–	–	–	2	–	2	22	9	31	1	4	5
Kilmainham,	–	–	–	12	8	20	12	8	20	9	2	11	1	1	2	–	–	–	–	–	–	10	3	13	2	5	7
Richmond,	2	–	2	34	–	34	36	–	36	24	–	24	4	–	4	–	–	–	1	–	1	20	–	20	7	–	7
Grangegorman,	–	15	15	–	49	49	–	64	64	–	41	41	–	10	10	–	–	–	–	2	2	–	53	53	–	11	11
Enniskillen,	–	–	–	8	4	12	8	4	12	7	4	11	–	–	–	–	–	–	–	–	–	7	4	11	1	–	1
Galway County,	–	–	–	10	7	17	10	7	17	8	4	12	2	3	5	–	–	–	–	–	–	10	7	17	–	–	–
Galway Town,	–	1	1	6	4	8	6	4	8	5	3	8	3	2	5	–	–	–	–	–	–	6	3	9	–	–	–
Tralee,	–	–	–	1	1	2	1	1	2	1	1	2	–	–	–	–	–	–	–	–	–	1	1	2	–	–	–
Naas,	1	2	3	4	2	6	5	4	9	3	1	4	1	1	2	–	–	–	–	1	1	4	3	7	1	1	2
Athy,	–	–	–	–	–	–	–	–	–	–	–	–	–	–	–	–	–	–	–	–	–	–	–	–	–	–	–
Kilkenny County,	2	2	4	19	7	26	21	9	30	13	6	19	4	1	5	–	–	–	–	–	–	17	7	24	4	2	6
Kilkenny City,	–	–	–	1	–	1	1	–	1	–	–	–	–	–	–	–	–	–	–	–	–	–	–	–	1	–	1
Tullamore,	8	–	8	13	5	18	21	5	26	14	4	18	6	1	7	–	–	–	1	–	1	21	5	26	–	–	–
Carrick-on-Shannon,	4	2	6	6	1	2	5	3	8	4	1	5	1	1	2	–	–	–	–	–	–	5	2	7	–	1	1
Limerick County,	–	–	–	9	4	13	9	4	13	9	2	11	–	1	1	–	–	–	–	–	–	9	3	12	–	1	1
Limerick City,	–	–	–	–	–	–	–	–	–	–	–	–	–	–	–	–	–	–	–	–	–	–	–	–	–	–	–
Londonderry,	–	–	–	8	1	9	8	1	9	3	–	3	1	–	1	1	–	1	1	–	1	6	–	6	2	1	3
Longford,	2	–	2	–	7	7	2	7	9	2	5	7	–	–	–	–	–	–	–	1	1	2	6	8	–	1	1
Dundalk,	–	–	–	8	6	14	8	6	14	4	5	9	2	1	3	–	–	–	–	–	–	6	6	12	2	–	2
Drogheda,	–	–	–	1	4	5	1	4	5	1	4	5	–	2	2	–	–	–	1	–	1	1	3	4	–	2	2
Castlebar,	11	–	11	19	11	30	30	11	41	20	8	28	0	3	3	–	–	–	1	–	1	30	11	41	–	–	–
Trim,	6	9	15	10	7	17	16	10	32	8	14	22	4	2	6	1	–	1	2	–	2	16	10	31	1	–	1
Monaghan,	–	–	–	6	5	11	6	5	11	5	3	8	–	1	1	–	–	–	1	–	1	5	5	13	1	–	1
Maryborough,	5	–	5	12	1	13	17	1	18	10	1	11	1	–	1	–	–	–	–	–	–	17	1	18	–	–	1
Roscommon,	3	1	4	4	4	8	7	5	12	7	4	11	–	–	–	–	–	–	–	–	–	7	4	11	–	1	1
Sligo,	–	–	–	5	4	9	5	4	9	5	4	9	–	–	–	–	–	–	–	–	–	5	4	9	–	–	–
Nenagh,	8	1	9	18	8	26	26	9	35	2	–	2	13	5	18	–	–	–	1	–	1	16	5	21	10	4	14
Clonmel,	4	4	8	12	9	21	16	13	29	4	1	5	5	5	10	–	–	–	1	–	1	9	7	16	7	6	13
Omagh,	–	–	–	1	–	1	1	–	1	1	–	1	–	–	–	–	–	–	–	–	–	1	–	1	–	–	–
Waterford County,	–	–	–	5	1	6	5	1	6	3	1	4	2	–	2	–	–	–	–	–	–	5	1	6	–	–	–
Waterford City,	–	–	–	1	–	1	1	–	1	1	–	1	–	–	–	–	–	–	–	–	–	1	–	1	–	–	–
Mullingar,	1	–	1	12	4	16	13	4	17	10	4	14	2	–	2	–	–	–	–	–	–	12	4	16	1	–	2
Wexford,	10	5	15	17	4	21	27	9	36	2	5	7	7	1	8	–	–	–	1	–	1	10	6	16	17	3	20
Wicklow,	–	1	1	5	6	11	5	7	12	3	5	8	–	–	–	–	–	–	1	–	1	3	6	9	2	1	3
Total,	89	49	138	341	216	557	430	265	695	251	158	409	87	51	138	3	–	3	13	7	20	354	216	570	76	49	125
1857.																											
Belfast,	3	–	3	5	8	13	8	8	16	7	7	14	–	–	–	–	–	–	1	–	1	8	7	15	–	1	1
Armagh,	–	–	–	4	3	7	4	3	7	2	2	4	–	1	1	–	–	–	1	1	2	3	3	6	1	–	1
Carlow,	2	–	2	1	3	3	3	1	3	1	–	1	–	–	–	–	–	–	–	–	–	1	–	1	2	–	2
Cavan,	1	3	4	10	6	16	11	6	20	10	4	14	1	2	3	–	–	–	–	–	–	11	6	17	–	–	3
Ennis,	1	1	2	11	10	21	12	11	23	6	2	8	4	6	10	–	–	–	–	–	–	10	8	18	2	3	5
Cork County,	–	1	1	11	4	15	11	5	16	9	5	14	1	–	1	–	–	–	–	–	–	10	5	15	1	–	1
Cork City,	–	–	–	–	–	–	–	–	–	–	–	–	–	–	–	–	–	–	–	–	–	–	–	–	–	–	–
Lifford,	9	1	10	16	13	29	25	14	39	6	13	22	12	–	12	–	–	–	–	–	–	21	13	34	4	1	5
Downpatrick,	1	4	5	23	5	28	24	9	33	21	7	28	1	2	3	–	–	–	–	–	–	22	9	31	2	–	2
Kilmainham,	2	5	7	15	15	30	17	20	37	6	0	6	2	4	6	1	1	2	–	–	–	12	11	23	5	9	14
Richmond,	7	–	7	37	–	37	44	–	44	28	–	28	6	–	6	–	–	–	–	–	–	34	–	34	1	–	10
Grangegorman,	–	11	11	–	51	51	–	62	62	–	0	0	–	22	22	–	–	–	5	–	5	–	33	33	–	20	29
Enniskillen,	1	–	1	16	4	20	17	4	21	10	3	10	–	–	–	–	–	–	–	–	–	10	3	19	1	1	2
Galway County,	–	–	–	8	6	14	8	6	14	8	6	14	–	–	–	–	–	–	–	–	–	8	6	14	–	–	–
Galway Town,	–	–	–	3	3	6	3	3	6	3	3	6	–	–	–	–	–	–	1	1	2	3	3	6	–	–	–
Tralee,	–	–	–	2	2	2	2	2	2	2	–	2	–	–	–	–	–	–	–	–	–	2	–	2	–	–	–
Naas,	1	1	2	2	2	4	3	3	6	1	3	4	1	–	1	–	–	–	–	–	–	2	3	6	1	–	1
Athy,	–	–	–	4	–	4	4	–	4	2	–	3	–	–	–	–	–	–	–	–	–	2	–	2	2	–	2
Kilkenny County,	4	2	6	14	6	20	18	8	28	4	8	12	9	–	9	–	–	–	–	–	–	13	8	21	5	–	5
Kilkenny City,	1	–	1	1	1	2	2	1	3	1	–	1	1	1	1	–	–	–	–	–	–	1	1	2	1	–	1
Tullamore,	–	–	–	12	5	17	12	5	17	10	5	15	2	–	2	–	–	–	–	–	–	12	5	17	–	–	–
Carrick-on-Shannon,	–	1	1	2	2	4	2	3	6	3	1	2	3	–	3	–	1	1	–	1	1	2	3	5	–	–	–
Limerick County,	–	1	1	16	16	32	16	17	33	9	10	19	1	–	6	–	–	–	–	–	1	10	10	25	6	2	8
Limerick City,	–	–	–	–	–	–	–	–	–	–	–	–	–	–	–	–	–	–	–	–	–	–	–	–	–	–	–
Londonderry,	2	1	3	7	2	9	9	3	12	9	3	12	5	–	5	–	–	–	0	1	7	9	3	12	–	–	–
Longford,	–	1	1	1	6	6	1	7	7	7	0	1	7	–	7	–	–	–	–	–	–	0	1	7	–	–	–
Dundalk,	2	–	2	10	7	17	12	7	19	10	1	7	17	1	1	–	–	–	1	–	1	11	7	18	1	–	1
Drogheda,	–	1	1	1	2	5	1	3	6	8	2	2	1	–	4	–	–	–	–	–	–	2	6	8	–	–	–
Castlebar,	–	–	–	16	21	37	16	21	37	13	20	33	3	1	4	–	–	–	–	–	–	16	21	37	–	–	–
Trim,	1	–	1	14	12	26	15	12	27	12	10	22	–	–	–	–	–	–	–	–	–	12	10	22	3	2	5
Monaghan,	1	–	1	7	2	9	8	2	10	6	2	8	–	–	–	–	–	1	1	–	1	7	2	9	1	–	1
Maryborough,	–	–	–	6	–	6	6	–	6	6	–	6	–	–	–	1	–	1	–	–	–	5	–	5	1	–	1
Roscommon,	–	1	1	11	2	13	11	3	14	11	3	14	–	–	–	–	–	–	–	–	–	11	3	14	–	–	–
Sligo,	–	–	–	7	7	14	7	7	14	7	7	14	–	–	–	–	–	–	–	–	–	7	7	14	–	–	–
Nenagh,	10	4	14	13	8	21	23	12	35	1	2	3	11	4	15	–	–	–	–	–	–	12	6	18	11	6	17
Clonmel,	7	0	18	13	6	19	20	12	32	5	1	6	10	0	10	–	–	–	–	–	–	15	7	22	5	5	10
Omagh,	–	–	–	1	–	1	1	–	1	1	–	1	–	–	–	–	–	–	–	–	–	1	–	1	–	–	–
Waterford County,	–	–	–	2	1	3	2	1	3	2	1	3	–	–	–	–	–	–	–	–	–	2	1	3	–	–	–
Waterford City,	–	–	–	–	–	–	–	–	–	–	–	–	–	–	–	–	–	–	–	–	–	–	–	–	–	–	–
Mullingar,	1	–	1	5	2	7	6	2	8	6	2	8	–	–	–	–	–	–	–	–	–	6	2	8	–	–	–
Wexford,	17	3	20	0	7	10	20	10	30	–	–	–	0	0	0	–	–	–	2	–	2	7	4	11	10	0	25
Wicklow,	2	1	3	8	6	17	10	10	20	0	–	0	0	1	4	–	–	–	–	1	1	7	4	11	3	0	9
Total,	70	49	125	348	253	601	424	302	726	251	154	405	75	63	138	0	1	7	5	10	16	337	228	665	87	74	161

No. 7.—Summary of the foregoing Tables for the two Years ending 31st March, 1856, and 1857.

—	Remaining in Custody.			Committed during year.			Total Number in Custody.			Removed to Asylum by Warrant of Lord Lieutenant.			Discharged, by order of Magistrates on Medical Certificates, cured.			Otherwise removed from Gaol.			Died.			Total Removed, Discharged, and Died.			Remaining in Gaol on 31st March		
1856.	M.	F.	T.	M.	F.	T.	M.	F.	T.	M.	F.	T.	M.	F.	T.	M.	F.	T.	M.	F.	T.	M.	F.	T.	M.	F.	T.
Persons acquitted of offences on the ground of insanity,	6	2	8	3	3	6	9	5	14	7	3	10	1	2	3	–	–	–	–	–	–	8	5	13	1	–	1
Persons found insane on arraignment, and incapable of pleading,	–	–	–	6	2	8	6	2	8	4	–	4	1	1	2	–	–	–	–	–	–	5	1	6	1	1	2
Persons under sentence of imprisonment or transportation, who became insane in gaol,	1	–	1	1	–	1	2	–	2	1	–	1	–	–	–	–	–	–	–	–	–	1	–	1	1	–	1
Persons committed in default of surety to keep the peace, who were insane on, or who became insane subsequent to committal,	–	–	–	6	11	17	6	11	17	4	3	7	2	8	10	–	–	–	–	–	–	6	11	17	–	–	–
Persons committed under the Vagrancy Act, who were insane on, or who became insane subsequent to committal,	–	–	–	2	3	5	2	3	5	–	–	–	2	3	5	–	–	–	–	–	–	2	3	5	–	–	–
Persons committed as dangerous lunatics,	89	49	138	341	216	557	430	265	695	251	158	409	87	51	138	3	–	3	13	7	20	354	216	570	76	49	125
Total,	96	51	147	359	235	594	455	286	741	267	164	431	93	65	158	3	–	3	13	7	20	376	236	612	79	50	129
1857.																											
Persons acquitted of offences on the ground of insanity,	2	–	2	9	2	11	11	2	13	5	1	6	1	–	1	–	–	–	–	–	–	6	1	7	5	1	6
Persons found insane on arraignment, and incapable of pleading,	1	–	1	5	1	6	6	1	7	1	–	1	–	–	–	–	–	–	1	–	1	2	–	2	4	1	5
Persons under sentence of imprisonment or transportation, who became insane in gaol,	–	–	–	3	–	3	3	–	3	2	–	2	1	–	1	–	–	–	–	–	–	3	–	3	–	–	–
Persons committed in default of surety to keep the peace, who were insane on, or who became insane subsequent to committal,	41	16	57	41	16	57	41	16	57	5	5	10	32	11	43	–	–	–	1	–	1	38	16	54	3	–	3
Persons committed under the Vagrancy Act, who were insane on, or who became insane subsequent to committal,	–	–	–	–	2	2	–	2	2	–	–	–	–	2	2	–	–	–	–	–	–	–	2	2	–	–	–
Persons committed as dangerous lunatics,	76	49	125	348	253	601	424	302	726	251	154	405	75	63	138	6	1	7	5	10	15	337	228	565	87	74	161
Total,	79	49	128	406	274	680	485	328	803	264	160	424	109	76	185	6	1	7	7	10	17	386	247	633	99	76	175

No. 8.—Return of all Persons under Sentence of Imprisonment or Transportation in Government Prisons, who became Insane in Prison during the two Years ending 31st March, 1856, and 1857.

Prisons.	Total.			Nature of Offence. Larceny.		Receiving Stolen Goods.		Cow Stealing.		Bigamy.		Burglary.		Felony.		Assault and Wounding.		Malicious Burning.		Vagrancy.		Removed to Asylums by Warrant of Lord Lieutenant.			Died.			Remaining in Prison on 31st March.		
1856.	M.	F.	T.	M.	F.	M.	F.	M.	F.	M.	F.	M.	F.	M.	F.	M.	F.	M.	F.	M.	F.	M.	F.	T.	M.	F.	T.	M.	F.	T.
Spike Island,	3	–	3	1	–	1	–	1	–	–	–	–	–	–	–	–	–	–	–	–	–	2	–	2	–	–	–	1	–	1
Cork,	–	4	4	–	3	–	–	–	–	–	–	–	–	–	–	–	–	–	–	–	1	–	2	2	–	–	–	–	2	2
Philipstown, Mountjoy, Newgate, Smithfield, Grangegorman,	Nil.																													
1857.																														
Spike Island,	*3	–	3	–	–	–	–	1	–	1	–	–	–	–	–	–	–	–	–	–	–	3	–	3	–	–	–	–	–	–
Philipstown,	10	–	10	3	–	–	–	1	–	–	–	2	–	2	–	1	–	1	–	–	–	7	–	7	–	–	–	3	–	3
Cork,	–	†2	2	–	–	–	–	–	–	–	–	–	–	–	–	–	–	–	–	–	–	–	2	2	–	–	–	–	–	–
Mountjoy, Newgate, Smithfield, Grangegorman,	Nil.																													

* This number includes one remaining in Prison on 31st March, 1856.

† Remaining in Prison on 31st March, 1856.

APPENDIX E.

CENTRAL LUNATIC ASYLUM RETURNS.

Admissions, Discharges, and Deaths, during the two Years ending 31st March, 1856 and 1857.

	1856.			1857.		
	Male.	Female.	Total.	Male.	Female.	Total.
In Asylum,	84	42	126	80	43	123
Admitted during the Year	7	2	9	14	3	17
Total,	91	44	135	94	46	140
Discharged during the Year:						
Cured,	*7	1	8	4	2	†6
Improved,	—	—	—	—	—	—
Not Cured,	—	—	—	1	—	‡1
Total Discharged,	7	1	8	5	2	7
Deaths:						
Natural Causes,	4	—	4	5	2	7
Total Discharges and Deaths during the Year,	11	1	12	10	4	14
Remaining in Asylum,	80	43	123	84	42	126

* Of this number, three were discharged by order of the Lord Lieutenant, two were sent back for trial, one returned to County Prison, and one to Convict Depot.

† Of this number, three were discharged, two transmitted to Convict Depots, and one sent for trial.

‡ One transmitted to a Private Asylum.

Classification of Patients in Asylum on 31st March, 1857.

Classification.	Male.	Female.	Total.
Convalescent,	11	7	18
Quiet and Orderly, but Insane,	22	11	33
Moderately Tranquil,	23	6	29
Noisy and Refractory,	21	10	31
Imbecile,	7	8	15
Total,	84	42	126
Epileptics enumerated under the different foregoing heads,	6	2	8
Suicidal ditto,	6	4	10

Form of Disease in those remaining in Asylum on 31st March, 1857.

Form of Disease.	Male.	Female.	Total.
Mania Acute, Chronic,	36	21	57
Melancholia,	15	2	17
Imbecility and Idiocy,	15	8	23
Dementia and other forms of Mental Weakness,	8	3	11
Sane,	10	8	18
Total,	84	42	126

Cause of Death during the two Years ending 31st March, 1856 and 1857.

Cause of Death.	1856.			1857.		
	Male.	Female.	Total.	Male.	Female.	Total.
Tubercular Liver, Jaundice, and Dropsy,	1	—	1	—	—	—
Exhaustion after long fit of Maniacal Excitement and Urinary Disease,	1	—	1	—	—	—
General Paralysis,	2	—	2	—	—	—
Apoplexy,	—	—	—	2	—	2
Dropsy and Heart Disease,	—	—	—	1	1	1
Phthisis,	—	—	—	1	1	2
Caries of Knee-Joint,	—	—	—	1	—	1
Melanotic Tumour of Eye and Neck,	—	—	—	1	—	1
Total Number,	4	—	4	5	2	7

Outlay and Produce of the Farm and Garden for the two Years ending 31st March, 1856 and 1857.

	Amount.		
	1856.		1857.
	£ s. d.		£ s. d.
Outlay,	190 16 11½		343 13 6½
Produce,	301 6 7		418 3 3
Net Profit,	110 10 7½		74 9 8½
	A. R. P.		A. R. P.
Land under Spade Cultivation,	6 3 20		*9 3 37
Land under Plough Cultivation,	9 3 0		11 0 10
Land under Grass Cultivation,	3 0 30		4 0 22
Buildings, Pleasure-grounds, &c.,	3 3 22		3 3 32
Total,	22 3 1		40 0 21

* At the expiration of Mr. Kinehan's lease, 6A. 1R. 20P., statute measure, were added to the farm.

RECEIPTS and EXPENDITURE for the two Years ending 31st March, 1856 and 1857.

RECEIPTS	Amount.			EXPENDITURE.	Amount.		
	1856.		1857.		1856.		1857.
	£ s. d.		£ s. d.		£ s. d.		£ s. d.
Balance on hand, 31st March,	73 1 10½		787 3 11	Provisions,	1,409 19 5		1,302 13 7
Treasury Advances,	4,148 17 4		2,515 15 11	Clothing of Patients,	102 11 7½		160 13 11½
Received for sale of Farm Produce,	110 16 9		108 4 5	" Servants,	63 0 0		60 10 0
" on account of Income Tax,	45 13 4		48 13 4	Fuel and Light,	476 14 2		378 0 10
To amount of Casual Receipts,	11 11 8		23 13 0	Washing,	52 5 2½		37 8 7
				Salaries of Officers,	730 0 0		730 0 0
				Wages of Servants,	357 6 8		364 16 8
				Furniture,	38 18 0		18 14 0
				Repairs and Alterations,	13 7 8		4 19 3½
				Farm and Garden,*	185 0 11½		†245 0 6½
				Medical Comforts, Groceries,	20 5 0		21 7 6
				" Medicines,	26 19 10		15 1 6
				" Wine and Beer,	19 10 0		26 11 6
				" Medical Diet,	33 5 2		36 10 0
				Tobacco and Snuff,	31 4 0		31 10 0
				Incidental Expenses,	51 9 8		46 15 7½
				Total Outlay,	3,505 17 0½		3,475 8 7
				Balance on hand, 31st March,	787 3 11		8 2 0
				Daily average No. of Patients,	125		127
				Average Cost of each Patient per annum on the entire outlay,	£ s. d. 28 10 11		£ s. d. 27 7 3
Total Receipts,	4,393 0 11½		3,483 10 7				

* In the years 1856 and 1857 we purchased nine cows, the cost is included in the accounts of the two years, which rather increases the apparent expense.   † This includes the purchase of cows, referred to at p. 21.

APPENDIX F.

No. 1.—Return of the Number discharged from Private Asylums, and of the Number who died therein, during the Year ending 31st December, 1856.

Name of Asylum.	Remaining in Asylum on 31st December, 1855.			Admitted during year ending 31st December, 1856.			Discharged, &c.															Remaining in Asylum on 31st December, 1856.		
							Cured.			Not cured, but improved.			Incurable.			Died.			Total Discharged and Died.					
	M.	F.	Total	M.	F.	T.	M.	F.	T.	M.	F.	T.	M.	F.	T.	M.	F.	T.	M.	F.	T.	M.	F.	Total.
Retreat, County Armagh, .	12	9	21	7	6	13	2	1	3	3	2	5	·	·	·	·	2	2	5	5	10	14	10	24
Cittadella, County Cork, .	13	8	21	4	4	8	4	2	6	1	3	4	·	·	·	·	·	·	5	5	10	11	8	19
Lindville, " .	24	9	33	6	6	12	2	2	4	6	3	9	·	·	·	·	·	·	8	5	13	22	10	32
Bellvue, County Dublin,	23	10	33	4	1	5	1	1	2	1	·	1	·	·	·	·	·	·	2	1	3	25	10	35
Eagle House, "	9	11	20	2	4	6	·	2	2	1	1	2	·	·	·	3	·	3	4	3	7	8	17	25
Farnham House, "	26	13	39	13	10	23	6	3	9	1	3	4	·	·	·	2	1	3	9	7	16	29	15	44
Hampstead House, "	17	11	28	10	3	13	5	3	8	1	2	3	·	·	·	4	1	5	8	5	13	18	10	28
Hartfield House, "	22	21	43	10	11	21	6	7	13	1	·	1	1	2	3	2	1	3	10	8	18	21	22	43
Jamestown House, "	2	3	5	·	4	4	·	1	1	1	1	2	·	·	·	·	·	·	2	3	5	·	4	4
Lysle House, "	·	6	6	·	4	4	·	·	·	·	2	2	·	·	·	·	2	2	·	2	2	·	8	8
Bloomfield Retreat, "	10	14	24	1	3	4	·	2	2	1	1	2	·	·	·	·	2	2	·	4	4	11	13	24
Midland Retreat, Queen's Co.	11	7	18	3	3	6	1	1	2	1	1	2	1	1	2	·	·	·	2	2	4	12	8	20
Bushy Park, Co Limerick,	5	2	7	2	2	4	1	1	2	1	1	2	·	·	·	·	·	·	2	1	3	5	3	8
Swift's Hospital, Dublin,	73	73	146	7	6	13	·	1	1	1	2	3	·	·	·	2	5	7	3	8	11	76	72	148
Total, . .	247	197	444	63	67	133	24	23	47	18	21	39	2	3	5	15	11	26	59	58	117	250	210	462

No. 2.—Return of the Number of Patients in Private Asylums on 31st December, 1856, classified as to Professions, &c.

Name of Asylum.	Married.			Single.			Previous Occupation or Profession, &c.										Total in Asylum.	Found Lunatic by Inquisition.			Sent by authority of Friends.		
	M.	F.	Total.	M.	F.	Total.	Army.	Navy.	Church.	Law.	Medicine.	Students.	In Trade.	Other Occupations.	Farmers.	No Occupation.		M.	F.	T.	M.	F.	Total.
Retreat, County Armagh, .	1	6	7	13	4	17	1	·	·	·	1	·	8	1	4	11	24	·	1	1	14	9	23
Cittadella, County Cork, .	2	2	4	9	6	15	1	·	·	1	·	·	5	1	·	12	19	2	·	2	8	9	17
Lindville, "	7	4	11	15	6	21	6	·	·	1	1	1	4	1	3	16	32	2	1	3	20	9	29
Bellvue, County Dublin,	6	2	8	19	8	27	5	2	1	2	1	3	1	1	·	20	35	4	2	6	21	8	29
Eagle House, "	2	8	10	9	6	15	·	·	1	1	1	·	2	4	·	21	25	2	·	2	6	17	23
Farnham House, "	4	5	9	25	10	35	4	1	1	1	1	4	2	1	3	24	44	8	3	11	21	12	33
Hampstead House, "	3	5	8	15	5	20	1	·	1	1	1	1	2	1	3	13	28	2	·	2	16	10	26
Hartfield House, "	2	4	11	19	13	32	·	·	7	3	1	·	·	3	4	20	43	5	3	8	16	19	35
Jamestown House, "	·	·	·	·	4	4	·	·	·	·	·	·	·	·	·	4	4	·	1	1	·	3	3
Lysle House, "	·	2	2	·	6	6	·	·	·	·	·	·	·	·	·	8	8	·	·	·	·	8	8
Bloomfield Retreat, "	1	2	3	10	11	21	·	·	1	1	·	·	2	5	2	9	24	1	·	1	10	13	23
Midland Retreat, Queen's Co.	2	3	5	10	5	15	·	·	·	1	2	·	3	2	1	14	20	2	1	3	10	7	17
Bushy Park, Co Limerick,	3	1	4	2	2	4	·	·	·	2	·	·	·	1	1	5	8	·	·	·	5	3	8
Swift's Hospital, Dublin, .	18	8	26	53	64	123	6	·	12	8	3	6	10	22	9	71	148	3	2	5	73	70	143
Total, . .	51	57	108	201	153	354	23	5	24	20	7	14	37	50	29	253	462	31	14	45	221	196	417

APPENDIX G.

QUERIES addressed to the RESIDENT PHYSICIANS and MANAGERS of DISTRICT ASYLUMS, on the subject of MECHANICAL RESTRAINT.

1. Is mechanical restraint used in the asylum?
2. Under what form?
3. How, and by whom directed?
4. What is your opinion on the subject? In a violent case of mania, the patient being physically powerful, would you consider resort to mechanical means, such as a camisole or muffs, more effective and less dangerous in their result than personal coercion of attendants?
5. Do attendants encounter any personal risk in restraining violent patients without resorting to mechanical means, or have they on any occasion suffered injury?
6. What is the practice at present, and what, in your opinion, the best means of treating violent and noisy patients at night, so as to prevent them from injuring themselves and disturbing the rest of others?
7. Has any act of cruelty been committed in the asylum? If so, what was its nature, and what steps were taken to punish the guilty?

REPLIES to QUERIES on the subject of MECHANICAL RESTRAINT.

ARMAGH.

1. Yes.
2. Muff or vest.
3. Manager or Physician.

4. Mechanical restraint is, when judiciously and properly applied.
5. No question they are subject to personal risk.
6. Complete separation from the other patients and from each other, and when violence is present, the strait vest. The department for cases of this nature should be peculiarly fitted up, to meet their afflicted state. There are no padded rooms in this asylum.
7. None, whatever.

THOMAS JACKSON, *Manager.*

BALLINASLOE.

1. Yes; but very seldom, and in violent cases, to prevent the patients injuring themselves, or from taking off blisters or surgical dressings.
2. Chiefly by leather muffs, sometimes the camisole.
3. By the physician, sometimes in the prescription book, at other times by his directions—in my presence, and given out by myself to the attendant, also by myself for violent cases at night; all these occur very rarely.
4. I am of opinion, that restraint by a camisole or muffs is more effective and less dangerous than personal coercion of attendants, which latter causes long struggling of the patient to endeavour to overcome the restraint of attendants. I prefer the muffs to the camisole, as not confining the chest or causing heat, and being more easily put on.
5. The attendants occasionally receive kicks, an odd time a black eye, or an injury in the hand, as a sprained

thumb; but the principal injuries are only scratches and clothes torn; however, none of these occur frequently.

6. Violent cases sometimes occur which would be unsafe to be placed lying in a bedstead, except they were secured; this has, in rare cases, been resorted to in winter to prevent them getting cold; such cases, generally *epileptics*, are placed in a single room with straw, thickly covering over the whole floor. A few padded rooms would be most desirable for such cases, and it would be advantageous, if they could be kept to a moderate temperature in winter by steam or hot-water pipes. Such cases have been frequently benefited by sedatives, as morphine or full doses of opium (after due preparation). Small doses appear to only stimulate and make them more restless; they generally bear larger doses of medicine than others.

7. None.

J. B. M'KIERNAN, *Manager.*

BELFAST.

1. Occasionally.
2. Arm-straps, long sleeves.
3. By attendant in charge, under the direction of the Resident Physician.
4. Mechanical restraint, certainly, in preference to that of attendants, as much more effective, and less irritating to the patient.
5. Very frequently, both as to personal risk and actual injury.
6. Placing them in padded rooms, warm baths, and opiates.
7. Not any.

ROBERT STEWART, M.D., *Resident Physician.*

CARLOW.

1. Yes.
2. Camisole, arm-strap, bed-strap.
3. By the Resident Physician.
4. Due precaution and superintendence being used, I consider it much safer, less exciting, and far less likely to be injurious to apply *proper* and effective mechanical restraint, than to use the personal coercion of attendants; it also irritates the patient far less than a personal struggle would do. It would appear to me that the arguments against the practice, being drawn from the *abuse*, are not valid against the *use* of *proper* restraint.
5. Repeatedly; the attendants are frequently struck and severely injured by violent patients. I have known the teeth struck out, and the eyes blackened. A patient will sometimes suddenly become violent, and, as it were, *run a-muck* through the corridor, striking every one he meets with.
6. The patient is placed in seclusion in the quietest place available at the time. We also use morphine, and, occasionally, small doses of tart. antimonii, very cautiously, and generally with good effect. Considering this to be the best practice, we use it in this asylum. There are no padded rooms here.
7. No act of cruelty has been committed in this asylum.

M. E. WHITE, M.D., *Resident Physician.*

CENTRAL CRIMINAL LUNATIC ASYLUM, DUNDRUM.

1. Very rarely, indeed.
2. A leather girdle, to which broad soft straps are sewed, which pass before and confine the wrists.
3. By the Resident Physician.
4. I consider the above means as much easier to be borne, to be much less irritating to the patient, much less liable to give occasion to bruises, or resistance on the part of the patient, or violence or injury on the part of attendants, than any manual restraint whatever; whilst it allows the patient full scope for exercise in the open air. One or both wrists may be restrained by it, as may be necessary.
5. We have not had any injury of any moment done to an attendant. The means above stated clearly diminish the risk of injury to attendants and patients.
6. It would be desirable to have some few chambers

more shut out from the general corridors, to prevent the great inconvenience and annoyance caused by noisy patients. In a few instances, we occasionally find one noisy person causes excitement, and prevents others sleeping.

7. There has not been any report of cruelty being committed by any of the attendants.

WM. CORBET, M.D., *Resident Physician.*

CLONMEL.

1. In one case only.
2. A waist belt *by day*, confining one arm.
3. By the resident and visiting medical officers, and by special order of successive boards.
4. By all means. But in this asylum a few hours' seclusion frequently are sufficient for all purposes, unless in suicidal tendencies.
5. Heretofore one patient injured parties in the service of this asylum, but from the precautions now taken he cannot do so.
6. There should be, as in the well-arranged asylums of America, an hospital detached, with a few cells, wherein such cases might be secluded, so as to prevent the irritation and want of rest now occasioned by violent and noisy patients; they soon sink to rest where not irritated by others equally noisy.
7. None within these many years.

JAMES FLYNN, M.D., *Resident Physician.*

CORK.

1. It is, to a very limited extent.
2. Strait vest—wrist-band attached to girdle.
3. Mostly ordered by physician, but occasionally, in his absence, by head superintendent or matron.
4. My opinion is, that it cannot be altogether dispensed with. In the case above adduced, I would prefer mechanical restraint to that of coercion by attendants, as less irritating to the patient, and more safe for both patient and attendants, but would have recourse to seclusion in the padded cell in preference to either. I find mechanical restraint indispensable in cases determined to remain in an upright position day and night, without clothing, if permitted; in cases when patients have a propensity to knock their heads against the wall; in cases so wild as not to permit of their being allowed at large without danger to the other patients and attendants. A case of this kind was about a month under restraint for this cause within the year, and was since sent out perfectly cured. In cases requiring to be blistered, the jacket is, surely, better than coercion by attendants, as well as in cases inclined to bite themselves, which is not unusual; there are other cases that may be adduced. The very few subjected to restraint during the year shows the practice is not carried to any objectionable extent whatever.
5. They have frequently suffered some injuries, and had their clothing torn and face scratched, but nothing more severe has occurred since my appointment.
6. In noisy, sleepless cases I cautiously administer some preparation of opium, and repeat the dose in three hours, if ineffectual, occasionally combining camphor and antimony; if intending to injure themselves, their mattress is laid on the floor of the padded cell, and they are put to sleep there for the night.
7. No act of cruelty has occurred.

THOMAS POWER, M.D., *Resident Physician.*

KILKENNY.

1. No.
4. I have not had occasion to use either mechanical restraint or personal coercion by attendants for some years; but on theoretical principles, I think mechanical restraint would often be more effective and less dangerous than the personal coercion of attendants, particularly if the period for which either were considered advisable should be at all protracted.
5. I do not possess data for an accurate opinion.

6. So exercising your patients by day as to secure their rest at night; and if this cannot be accomplished, I do not think we possess satisfactory means to effect the objects referred to.

7. No. No act beyond one punishable by a slight fine, and not for a long time.

Jos. LALOR, M.D., *Resident Physician.*

KILLARNEY.

1. Not for the last two years, with the exception of using muffs on the hands during the application of leeches, or the operation of shaving the head, when the patient's state calls for such aid.

3. Used under the direction of the physicians.

4. In the case put, I consider mechanical means, such as described, applied under the directions of the physician, as more effective and less dangerous in their result than personal co-rcion of attendants.

5. The attendants do encounter personal risk frequently. I witnessed last year a serious injury escaped, more by a lucky chance than by the coolness and courage which the attendants displayed, when three powerful attendants were in presence of a violent maniac.

6. If there are grounds to apprehend that a violent patient will injure himself in the night, he is watched all night by an attendant. Sedatives and baths being used, as the indications of each individual case call for. I do not know any other way of treating a violent patient at night than as one would in the day time, viz., by keeping him under efficient observation. But it must be remarked, this system of treatment, to be efficiently carried out, calls for a larger staff of attendants than exists in this asylum. I believe that an economy of labour as to attendants, and a greater security as to a certain class of patients, might be arrived at by the organization of dormitories (something like the wards in hospitals) upon a plan which would allow, say three attendants to observe and control a large number of lunatics at night.

7. I do not believe that any act of cruelty has been committed in this asylum since its opening.

M. S. LAWLOR, M.D., *Resident Physician.*

LIMERICK.

1. Rarely.
2. Strait waistcoat.
3. Generally, Resident Physician.
4. I am of opinion that restraint is sometimes absolutely necessary.
5. They do, and have suffered sometimes.
6. It is sometimes necessary to put on muffs or strait jackets.
7. None.

ROBERT FITZGERALD, M.D., *Resident Physician.*

LONDONDERRY.

1. It is, to a small extent.
2. The camisole.
3. By the Resident Physician.
4. Were this asylum properly constructed, I think I could entirely dispense with mechanical restraint. I allude to the proper construction of sleeping rooms for violent patients, so that they could not injure themselves, even if unrestrained. I have seen violent patients hurt themselves very much against the walls of their rooms. I consider the camisole and muffs more effective, and less dangerous in their result, than personal coercion of attendants.
5. On several occasions the attendants have suffered injury, when endeavouring to manage violent patients, prior to putting them into restraint, one attendant almost lost his life on one occasion.
6. Violent and noisy patients are kept in single rooms, if very violent, the bedstead is taken out, and the bed placed on the floor; if the patient will not lie in bed, I put on him an overall made of ticken, and lined with flannel, laced up the back so that he cannot take it off.
7. I do not know of any.

WM. F. ROGAN, M.D., *Resident Physician.*

MARYBOROUGH.

APPENDIX G.

Mechanical Restraint.

1. No mechanical restraint is allowed in the asylum.

4. My opinion is, that the use of the camisole, and muffs,—or either, is likely to be more effective, and less dangerous to patients,—in a case such as here described —than personal coercion of attendants.

5. Attendants do encounter personal risk in restraining violent cases, and they have on several occasions suffered injury.

6. The present practice' consists of topical bloodletting, exhibition of solution of tartarized antimony, cold effusion on the head. No other means are adopted to prevent patients from injuring themselves except leaving attendants in the room with them, and removing all articles likely to be used as offensive weapons. The rest of other patients is constantly disturbed by patients violent at night. A night-watch goes round every hour on the male and female side of the house, and is supposed to visit each patient at each round. My opinion is, that the use of sedative medicines carefully administered, together with the judicious application of mechanical restraint, would be found very serviceable in treating the violent and noisy patients at night. I omitted to mention, that sedatives are occasionally ordered by the Visiting Physician, when patients exhibit signs of restlessness, or refuse to remain in bed during the night.

7. A patient, named Richard Ramsbottom, charged an assistant keeper, named Patrick Cashen, with assaulting him while in bed, and striking him with a stick, whereby a bone in Ramsbottom's right arm was broken. Cashen was tried at quarter sessions, and sentenced to pay a fine of £3, or imprisonment. William Patten, keeper, and Patrick Cashen, assistant keeper, were dismissed; the former for not reporting the circumstances to the manager at the time.

T. C. BURTON, M.D., *Resident Physician.*

MULLINGAR.

1. Yes.
2. Muffs, and strong gloves.
3. By the physicians.
4. I have long and carefully considered this subject, and, in my opinion, cases occasionally arise in which resort to mechanical means, such as those mentioned, must be had, being less injurious to the patient than personal coercion, which at best cannot be satisfactorily modified.
5. They do, and have on some occasions suffered injury.
6. I know no means better suited for this purpose than a padded room, under the supervision of an attendant, such room, of course, being apart from the ordinary dormitories.
7. No act of cruelty, to my knowledge, has been committed in the asylum since its opening.

H. BERKELEY, M.D., *Resident Physician.*

OMAGH.

1. Yes.
2. Strait waistcoat, muffs, and beds of peculiar construction, where violent patients are put to sleep at night, to prevent them from breaking windows and doing other violence.
3. Solely by the Resident Physician, and regulated by him as to time and necessity.
4. Provided the mechanical restraint is under the supervision of manager, I consider it more effective and less dangerous in its result than personal coercion of attendants.
5. Yes.
6. In some cases soporifics have been tried, particularly chloroform. Padded ward, and the locked-down bed already alluded to. The douche bath is also found highly beneficial in this class of patients.
7. None.

F. J. WEST, M.D., *Resident Physician.*

RICHMOND.

1. Seldom, except in cases of great necessity.
2. Strait vest or muffs.

3. In general by the Physicians, and in their absence, by manager.

4. In a case physically powerful, mechanical means will prevent injury to both patient and servant, such as muffs or camisole. The strait vest is very seldom used.

5. They do, but that is much avoided by getting a few servants to attend in restraining violent patients, by seclusion, or with camisole. They occasionally get a black eye from patients who get into a sudden paroxysm.

6. Our general practice is to place a violent patient on a straw bed on the floor, confined in a chancellor, to prevent them from injuring themselves. The Physicians frequently give sleeping draughts to prevent them from disturbing the rest of other patients.

7. No. A servant at the male side in a scuffle with a patient gave him a black eye, for which he was punished by the Board by fine and stopping his pass.

SAMUEL WRIGLEY, *Manager.*

SLIGO.

1. Not at all for the last seven months.

4. I would prefer occasional seclusion in padded rooms, and supervision of confidential attendants.

5. No instance.

6. Separation, surveillance: in extreme cases, padded rooms, and careful night watching.

7. No.

JOHN M'MUNN, *Resident Physician.*

WATERFORD.

1. Yes.

2. Strait waistcoat and body strap.

3. By the Manager and Physician.

4. I consider personal coercion of attendants most objectionable, it is irritating to both parties. When mechanical means are applied, the patient becomes tranquil with few exceptions.

5. Yes; they have been beaten, bit, and kicked, their clothes torn off them, struck by tins, &c., &c.

6. They are placed in single cells, and we are obliged to bear with their noise, and, according to the degree of violence, body-strap or strait waistcoats are used. I believe this to be the best means of treating this class.

7. None.

JOHN DOBBS, *Manager.*

RULES and REGULATIONS to be strictly observed by the Domestics of the RICHMOND LUNATIC ASYLUM.—1815.

" To allow every patient all the latitude of personal liberty consistent with safety.

" To proportion the degree of coercion to the obvious necessity of the case.

" To use mildness of manner, or firmness, as occasion may require.

" Every cause of irritation, real or imaginary, is to be carefully avoided.

" The requests of patients, however extravagant, are to be taken graciously into consideration, and withheld under some plausible pretext, or postponed to a more convenient opportunity.

" All violence or ill-treatment of the patients is strictly prohibited, under any provocation, and shall be punished in the most exemplary manner.

" The mildest acts of conciliation are to be the constant practice in this hospital.

" These laws are of fundamental importance, and essential to the prudent and successful management of this institution."

APPENDIX H.

REPORT of INSPECTORS on a MEMORIAL from the GRAND JURY of the Co. Wexford, for a new asylum for that county.

Office of Lunatic Asylums, Dublin Castle,
July 29, 1856.

The Inspectors have the honour to report, with reference to the accompanying memorial, from the Grand Jury of the County Carlow to His Excellency the Lord Lieutenant—

That the Carlow Asylum was opened in 1832 for the reception of 104 patients belonging to the district comprised in the counties of Carlow, Kildare, Wexford, and Kilkenny.

That the last-named county was constituted a district in itself in 1852, on the erection of an asylum (already full) near the City of Kilkenny, for 160 lunatics.

The Carlow Asylum, without any structural additions to the original building, contains at present 200 patients; it is consequently over-crowded, and has no chapel or infirmary accommodation.

Of the 200 patients in the Carlow Asylum, eighty-six belong to Wexford; which county has further in its prisons twenty-six dangerous lunatics, besides sixty-four at large and in poorhouses. Independent of the above, there are forty outstanding lunatics in the counties of Carlow and Kildare, and five in the gaols of the latter county.

It is thus evident, beyond the shadow of a doubt, that fresh asylum accommodation is required for the three counties attached to the existing Carlow institution. That accommodation must be effected in one of two ways; either by enlarging the Carlow Asylum, which would also be attended with considerable expense, or by converting the large, distant, and almost insulated County of Wexford into a district for itself.

The latter plan would seem the most equitable, and practically good, and therefore most economical arrangement.

FRANCIS WHITE.
JOHN NUGENT.

To Colonel Larcom, Dublin Castle.

To HIS EXCELLENCY GEORGE WILLIAM FREDERICK, EARL of CARLISLE, LORD LIEUTENANT and GENERAL GOVERNOR of IRELAND.

The Memorial of the Grand Jury of the County of Wexford, assembled at the Spring Assizes, 1856.

Humbly showeth—

That the County of Wexford is at present comprised in the Carlow district for the reception of the insane poor.

That there are upwards of ninety lunatics from the County of Wexford now confined in the district hospital, in Carlow; and that in consequence of deficiency of accommodation many are retained in the several union workhouses; and eleven more are now confined in the county gaol of Wexford.

That under the existing local distribution of districts, much inconvenience and expense is occasioned from the over-crowding of the county gaol, and the cost of transmission of lunatics to the district hospital in Carlow.

That the number of lunatics from the County of Wexford largely exceeds that of those from the other counties comprised in said district.

And your Memorialists, therefore, pray, that the County of Wexford may be created a separate district for the reception of insane poor, under the provisions of the Act of 1st and 2nd George IV., chap. 33.

That an hospital for the reception of insane poor may be built within the County of Wexford.

That the sum of money contributed by the County of Wexford for building the district hospital in Carlow may be repaid to the said County of Wexford by Her Majesty's Government; and such further sum may be advanced on loan by Her Majesty's Government free of interest (such loan to be repaid by the said County of Wexford, in instalments, extending over the term of twenty years), as may be required for building an asylum for insane poor within the County of Wexford, containing such accommodation as may be estimated to be necessary.

And your Memorialists will ever pray.

JOHN H. TALBOT, *Foreman,*
For self and Fellows.

LETTERS of INSPECTORS on the subject of ADDITIONAL ASYLUM ACCOMMODATION.

Office of Lunatic Asylums, Dublin Castle,
November 7, 1856.

MY LORDS AND GENTLEMEN,—I regretted not being able to attend, as I intimated my intention of doing so to the manager, at the last meeting of your Board; and finding that I cannot be present at the next, from an official engagement elsewhere, I am now induced to submit on paper, for your consideration, what otherwise I should have brought personally before you. The question of enlarged accommodation for the lunatic poor of the Armagh district, comprising three counties, and already referred to, is one which, from increasing exigencies, ought not to be longer postponed. Whether that accommodation is to be attained by additions to the existing asylum, or by erecting as suggested in the last report of the Inspectors, suitable buildings of a less costly character, but otherwise commodious, and containing the requisites for the maintenance and well-being of persons labouring under insanity of a more manageable, or chronic type, thus leaving the original establishment to its legitimate object—that of a curative hospital for mental diseases: but in either alternative I deem it highly advisable that we should not overlook present marked deficiencies. The laundry department is now so bad, so worn out, and altogether so unfit for use; that it should undergo a thorough repair, and be furnished accordingly. To effect which, some competent builder might submit to the Board a plan for its better lighting, and ventilation; with the addition, too, of a good airy drying-room. An Act just passed, authorizes Governors, with the sanction of the Executive, to make structural alterations or additions. The kitchen, though not so unfavourably circumstanced, admits of much improvement. Then as to an infirmary, baths, water-closets, &c., they are *greatly* needed—*nothing* can be more unsuitable than the privies now in use. It appears to me, that at no considerable expense, an ample and continuous supply of water could be raised to command every portion of the establishment. There are minor details, which it is unnecessary to bring at present before you, as in the progress of more general alterations they can be attended to. With regard, however, to clothing and bedding, I would most respectfully propose, that the servants us elsewhere, be clad in livery, they thus have a more cleanly and orderly appearance. The bedding itself is for the most part good, but the covering is thin, worn, and insufficient for the severity of winter. In conclusion, may I take this opportunity to state, that on my visitations to the Armagh Asylum, I have had every reason to be satisfied at the manner in which the manager and matron fulfilled their duties, and the anxiety evinced by them for the comforts of the persons under their charge. I would also record my sense of the successful and valuable services rendered by Dr. Cumming in his capacity of Visiting Physician,

And have the honour to be, my Lords and Gentlemen,

Your obedient servant,
JOHN NUGENT.

The Governors of the Armagh Asylum.

Office of Lunatic Asylums, Dublin Castle,
March 16, 1857.

MY LORDS AND GENTLEMEN,—After the meeting of the Board on Friday last. I made a minute inspection of the Derry District Asylum. I found the patients duly attended to, well clad, and comfortable; and the corridors, day-rooms, and bed-rooms, all in good order. The general sanitary state of the inmates was very satisfactory—two male patients were confined to bed (labouring under partial paralysis), and three females, one of them in hectic fever, another suffering from dysentery, and the third from a slight ulcer on the foot.

Most of the female lunatics were industriously employed: the day being unfavourable to out-door labour, the men, at the time of my inspection, were not occupied; but I anticipate that the present Resident Physician, Dr. Rogan, will devise means for general employment when the weather interferes with field labour.

As a committee of the Governors is about to examine into the condition of the apartments allocated to the manager and matron, with a view to their improvement, I would respectfully urge on it the propriety of making extended inquiry into the necessities of the establishment, which, in my opinion, requires much in the way of repairs and additions. For example, the laundry is too limited for so large an asylum: various articles in it are worn out, such as the mangles, which, I am told, cut the linen; the

drying apparatus is deficient, and the sewers adjoining are most offensive, and from a want of proper ventilation. cannot but act injuriously: at the other side too —close by the provision room, and leading to the kitchen—I would observe there is a privy. All through the establishment, nothing can be more unsatisfactory than the condition of the necessaries.

With regard to the lavatories, there is an obvious necessity for their construction. As it is, the patients are washed and shaved, in wet weather, in the day-rooms—in dry weather, out of doors. On this head, therefore, totally irrespective of any further arrangement regarding the lunatics of the present district, the existing buildings clearly require repairs and improvements.

The stairs in various parts of the house, particularly those leading to No 5 division, should be looked after, as well as the flooring in some of the day-rooms.

I would further direct the attention of the committee to the useless iron bolts affixed to the cell doors, which have been positively injurious to the plastering along the corridors.

The wood work all through the asylum is in need of being re-painted. Many of the bedsteads are old, broken, and dangerous. The bath-room, at the male side, notwithstanding the money lately expended on it, is unfinished, and in a sanitary point of view, useless; for being in an open yard there should be a covered passage of some kind leading to it. In the central building the lower apartments are dark, gloomy, and dilapidated; they might, at little expense, by throwing into them more air and light, be made very available for general purposes; a second kitchen could be easily made there, besides a couple of workshops. At present there is but *one* kitchen for the Resident Physician, the matron, and the use of the infirmary.

One apartment is also used at present for a drying-room, but until a new stove is substituted for the highly dangerous one in use, I would recommend that, no matter at what inconvenience, clothes should not be dried there.

I shall not trespass further on the attention of the Committee, but conclude by simply stating that, in throwing out these suggestions, I am only prompted by a desire to aid the Governors in carrying out improvements beneficial to the establishment at large.

I have the honour to be, my Lords and Gentlemen,

Your obedient servant,
JOHN NUGENT.

To the Board of Governors of the
Londonderry District Lunatic Asylum.

Office of Lunatic Asylums, Dublin Castle,
February 6, 1857.

MY LORDS AND GENTLEMEN,—The daily increasing pressure for admission into the Richmond District Asylum induces me to suggest to you the necessity of meeting the difficulty by converting, as far as possible, every apartment in both institutions to the most useful purposes. I have already proposed to place six beds in one of the two rooms on the second story, female side, adjoining the main building of the old house.

I minutely examined, on Wednesday last, the capabilities of the new Asylum, and I find from six to eight rooms can, without much outlay, be rendered available on the ground and upper corridors leading from the kitchen. I had long considered that these rooms might be well occupied; however, pending the decision of the Treasury on the claims put forward by the Board, on the report of Mr. Wilkinson, the Architect, I thought it would be premature to move in the business. Their Lordships having awarded a certain sum for definite purposes, and the arrangements now as between Government and Governors in reference to the past being concluded, I deem the present an appropriate opportunity to recommend to the Board the utility of at once examining into my proposition of rendering the apartments in question habitable for patients and attendants. Prepa-

I

APPENDIX H.
——
Additional Asylum accommodation

ratory to so doing, however, it would be necessary to have a competent professional man, probably Mr. Wilkinson, to meet one or two gentlemen deputed by the Board, and see with him how far the proposition of converting useless and unoccupied into useful and habitable apartments might be carried out; the result of which would be, to render from thirty to forty additional be is available. The condition of the infirmary is so unsatisfactory in every respect that no time should now be lost in improving the sewerage, chimneys, ventilation, &c., &c., so as to make it a suitable locality for invalids.

A system has been adopted in some county asylums which I would strongly recommend the Richmond Board to imitate, namely, to convert (as can be done), some large room near the kitchen into a refectory for the field and out-door labourers: thus the corridors will be kept clean and dry, food will be afforded comfortably and warm, and better order and more regularity established.

I have the honour to be, my Lords and Gentlemen,
Your obedient servant,
JOHN NUGENT.

To the Governors of the
Richmond District Lunatic Asylum.

Clonmel Asylum,
March 28, 1856.

It affords me great pleasure to report in the most favourable terms on the condition of the Clonmel District Asylum, which I visited on this day. I deem it simply a duty to state, that the judicious management of the patients is not exceeded by that of any other institution in this country.

I regret to observe that the asylum is by no means equal to the requirements of the district: 140 beds are very far from being sufficient for a population of about 320,000.

The consequence is, that the gaols, much to the interruption of all discipline, are crowded with dangerous lunatics. In the prison here there are sixteen lunatic patients, besides those in Nenagh Gaol.

An ample quantity of land is now attached to this asylum for out-door employment, and I would therefore strongly urge upon Government the necessity of enlarging the institution for the reception of 100 additional patients.

JOHN NUGENT.

On the foregoing recommendation, plans were prepared, and transmitted, with resolutions of Governors, to the Executive. A lengthened correspondence took place between the several authorities—the Board, the Government, and the Commissioners of Public Works —and which correspondence was eventually referred to the Inspectors, who reported thereon as follows :—

Office of Lunatic Asylums, Dublin Castle,
July 25, 1826.

With reference to the accompanying file of papers, a resumé is simply stated for the information of Government.

On the 28th March one of the Inspectors entered a Report (a copy of which is annexed), in the Clonmel Asylum Journal, stating his opinion that there should be additional accommodation for at least 100 patients. That Report was communicated on the 29th to the Under Secretary, who, on the 31st, directed the Resident Physician to submit it to the Local Board

On the 4th of April, by order of the Local Board, the Resident Physician transmitted to the Under Secretary certain plans and specifications for the enlargement, which plans were submitted to the Board of Works on the 26th.

On the 3rd of June the Commissioners of Public Works reported to the Under Secretary, setting forth their objections to certain propositions. These objections were communicated to the Local Board for its consideration, by the Under Secretary, on the 6th of June, together with plans and observations from the Architect of the Board of Works.

On the 4th of July one of the Inspectors went down to compare the two plans, as to the availability of the existing buildings at Clonmel, and their peculiar site; after which he reported a *second time*, approving, *under certain modifications* (much, too, on the score of economy), of the original plan submitted by the Local Board, but disapproving of it, inasmuch as the accommodation thereby proposed was not sufficient

Without a desire for entering into any thing like a difference, either with the Board of Governors or Grand Jury, the Inspectors feel bound to adhere to their recommendation, that an increased, and in every respect a *suitable accommodation* for at least 100 patients, should be provided in the Clonmel District Asylum. And they are further of opinion that, whoever the architect may be, or however small his estimate, the buildings should be substantial, and appropriately finished, under Governmental supervision; and that while economy should be regarded, it should be done so legitimately, considering the beneficial *objects* for which lunatic institutions are intended.

The appointment of a limited number of servants, and the saving thereby, as referred to by the Grand Jury, is not the question at issue, but the absolute necessity and extent of accommodation.

Grand Jurors are, no doubt, bound to look after the economic expenditure of public money; but on a subject like the present, they cannot be regarded as sole judges of the requirements.

Independent of dormitories, and other accessories, extra day-rooms will certainly be needed for the reception of 100 patients; and also suitable airing yards. The latter may, however, be said to exist, as the side gardens and terraces may, at a very trifling expense, be admirably adapted for the purpose.

Besides the absolute enlargement for the patients themselves, there are other structural additions and alterations which it would be advisable to take into consideration, in regard to a chapel, laundry, &c., &c., and which might all be undertaken at the same time.

In conclusion, the Inspectors beg to repeat, whilst now leaving the question to the decision of the Executive, that their desire has been to combine utility with every possible economy, and to disarm local prejudice as far as they were able; and for these reasons they felt indisposed to recommend the plans of the Board of Works—so much more architectural, finished, and ornamental—apprehensive of the opposition they might meet from the local authorities.

JOHN NUGENT.

To Colonel Larcom,
Dublin Castle.

APPENDIX I.

REPORTS of INSPECTOR relative to removal of House of Industry Patients to Lucan Spa.

Office of Lunatic Asylums, Dublin Castle,
19th January, 1857.

SIR,—I minutely inspected the house formerly known as the Lucan Spa Hotel, for the purpose of judging of its suitableness to be converted into a residence for 105 lunatics, at present located in the Hardwicke cells. The concern, generally, is in substantial repair; the roof and flooring unexceptionable, though untenanted for nearly five years; each apartment above the basement story is remarkably dry. The rooms are large, airy, and commodious; four of them—convertible into day or sitting rooms—vary from about 30 to 40, by 25, and are about 18 feet in height. There are, moreover, excellent dormitories, and a few single rooms; altogether capable of accommodating 120 inmates. The site itself is proverbially salubrious; and attached to the concerns are from four to five acres of ground. To render the house, however, satisfactorily habitable, the walls throughout should be whitewashed, the wood-work repaired and re-painted, and a variety of minor improvements effected. Above all, the windows should be efficiently secured, internally, by high iron trellises, or strong wire-work.

With regard to the separation of the sexes, it can be easily attained, by allocating the ground floor to the males, numbering thirty-four. The second and third stories are amply sufficient for the females; whilst from the first landing-place on the stairs an egress can be made to their airing yard, by changing the lobby window into a doorway, and throwing an arch from it to the field, which rises immediately in rere of the building.

As yet nothing like airing courts exist. These, if Dr. Stewart's proposal be accepted, should be at once commenced, or at least, within a fortnight or three weeks. As to the relative position of the concern at large, its front faces the high-road; close by the left wing (in fact within a few yards), and running parallel with the windows is an avenue leading to eight private houses, called the crescent, which lie about 120 yards to the back. These three sides of the building are exposed.

If Government proposed taking the establishment, it might, perhaps, be a consideration with it, whether, under those circumstances, the residence of lunatics in such a neighbourhood might not give cause of umbrage. Dr. Stewart, who acts for himself alone, informs me that he unreservedly communicated to the proprietor the object he had in view, in seeking a lease of the Lucan Spa Hotel.

I have, &c., &c.,
JOHN NUGENT.

To Colonel Larcom,
Dublin Castle.

Office of Lunatic Asylums, Dublin Castle,
2nd February, 1857.

SIR,—Herewith I have the honour to return the various documents you sent me with reference to the proposition of placing 105 lunatics belonging to the old House of Industry under the charge of Dr. Stewart, at a sum of £25 per head per annum. These documents, save on two points, appear to me sufficiently intelligible. I shall, therefore, endeavour to afford the necessary information with reference to them. 1st, as to the exactness of the number of patients (105) chargeable to the Treasury, I would beg to observe, that the 11th Geo. IV. repealed the Act 55th Geo. III., and transformed the Richmond Asylum from a general asylum for the country at large, into a district institution to be supported by Grand Jury presentments. Subsequently the lunatics belonging to the House of Industry, who were located in the Hardwicke cells, were sent to Island-bridge.

In the year 1844, in consequence of the number of urgent cases for admission, it became necessary to remove a certain portion of chronic incurable cases to the Island-bridge Establishment, where there was room; and which establishment was then under the control of the Poor Law Commissioners, who expended the necessary sums for the maintenance of *all* the inmates; and an Act, 9 and 10 Vict., was passed, authorizing the Poor Law Commissioners to demand, from the district of the Richmond, by Grand Jury presentments, such moneys as might be expended by them for the care, superintendence, and maintenance of the lunatic poor so removed from the Richmond Asylum. The *modus operandi* was this: suppose five vacancies occurred in the Poor Law, or rather the Government Department, at Island-bridge, or at the Hardwicke cells, and that it was desirable to remove five chronic cases from the asylum, the Inspectors submitted the wish to the Poor Law Commissioners. On their sanction being given, the five patients were transmitted, and duly charged from the day of reception of the immediate counties of the district to which the individual belonged—the Government being repaid through the Poor Law Commissioners. To meet this expenditure, the Poor Law Commissioners estimated,

APPENDIX I.

Removal of patients to Lucan Spa.

annually, a probable contingency sufficient to cover all the beds at Island-bridge, and the Hardwicke cells, as there was a certain draft from the Richmond to fill them.

Thus, then, the last estimate, 1855-6, was for 178 at Island-bridge, and 99 at the Hardwicke cells, or a total of 277; of whom I believe 116 were *bonâ fide* original House of Industry lunatics. The other Richmond patients were paid for as above stated, and pretty much on the same principle as in District Asylums. In the latter, the Treasury advancing on estimate, quarterly, in the former annually. These facts would seem to have been overlooked in the accompanying letter. Last year we took back all our former patients, leaving behind 111, now reduced to 104.

With reference to the charge proposed by Dr. Stewart—£25—I think your letter to the Treasury places the question in the clearest light. The loss at first is met by the subsequent gain, and irresponsibility of the Treasury to any party on the score of tenancy for the future. As to the proposition of placing the Hardwicke and Island-bridge patients in the Richmond, I apprehend it would be altogether out of the question. This Asylum was erected for the lunatic poor of the district; and even were it legal, there is no possibility of admitting the former, as it is already in a state of congestion, if I may use the expression.

I have, &c., &c.,
JOHN NUGENT.

To Colonel Larcom,
Dublin Castle.

APPENDIX J.

APPENDIX J.

Case of Margaret M'Hugh.

CASE of MARGARET M'HUGH, a Lunatic, removed from Carrick-on-Shannon Gaol to the District Asylum at Sligo.

Office of Lunatic Asylums, Dublin Castle,
December 26, 1856.

SIR,—I am directed by the Inspectors to call your attention to the case of Margaret M'Hugh, who was transmitted from the gaol under your control to the Sligo Asylum on the 23rd instant, and whose death, *on the very day after her admission*, is thus referred to by the Visiting Physician of that institution, under date of 24th:—" *Died*—Margaret M'Hugh, a poor, " emaciated wretch, covered with filth and vermin, " arrived here in a state of great exhaustion, re-" quiring wine and strong beef tea, notwithstanding " which she sank rapidly, and died twenty-four hours " after admission. I consider that it was extremely " imprudent and injudicious to send this woman a " distance of twenty-seven miles in such a state, and " in *such weather*."

The Inspectors coincide with the Visiting Physician in the opinion he expresses, and would wish to impress upon you, that they consider the carelessness displayed in the state of her person highly censurable.

I am, Sir, your obedient servant,

(Signed) W. M. HENNESSY, *pro Chief Clerk.*

To the Deputy Governor
Carrick-on-Shannon Gaol.

Office of Inspector-General of Prisons,
Dublin Castle, January 2, 1857.

GENTLEMEN,—I am directed by the Inspector-General of Prisons to call your attention to the accompanying letter of the Local Inspector of the County of Leitrim Gaol, and to request that you will furnish them with a copy of the communication received by you from the Visiting Physician of the Lunatic Asylum of Sligo, or with any other evidence bearing upon the condition of the lunatic, Margaret M'Hugh.

I am, Gentlemen, your very obedient servant,
JOHN W. GREGG.

To the Inspectors of Lunatic Asylums,
Upper Castle-yard.

Carrick-on-Shannon Gaol, December 27, 1856.

Gentlemen,—I beg leave to enclose a copy of a communication this day received by the Acting-Governor of this prison, from the Inspectors of Lunatic Asylums, with reference to Margaret M'Hugh, transmitted from this gaol to Sligo Lunatic Asylum, on the 22nd inst.; and as it is calculated to cast censure on this prison and its officers, I think unjustly. I wish to apprize you of the facts.—The matron of this gaol is ready to prove that, during Margaret M'Hugh's confinement, she was kept in a cleanly condition, being every day carefully washed; and the night previous to her removal to Sligo she was also washed, and the morning of her removal supplied with *clean clothing from the store*, that could not have contained vermin, as stated by the Physician of the asylum. The policeman who took charge of Margaret M'Hugh will also prove that she was *warmly clothed*, and that the day was not unfavourable to her removal; and the Medical Officer is also ready to give evidence, which will be at variance with the statement of the Physician of the Sligo Lunatic Asylum, as regards her condition, and that though she was in a weakly state, still there was no grounds for her being described as "filthy and covered with vermin."

Under these circumstances, I would ask you to suggest what course should be adopted in order to relieve this establishment of the censure cast on it by the Inspectors of Lunatic Asylums, grounded on the representations made by the Physician of the Sligo Lunatic Asylum.

I am, Gentlemen, your obedient servant,
WM. PEYTON, Local Inspector.
To the Inspectors-General of Prisons.

Office of Lunatic Asylums, Dublin Castle,
January 3, 1857.

Gentlemen,—With reference to your communication of yesterday's date, calling the attention of the Inspectors to copy of a letter, therewith transmitted, from the Local Inspector of Carrick-on-Shannon Gaol, dated 27th ult., and requesting to be furnished with a copy of any communication received at this office from the Visiting Physician of Sligo Lunatic Asylum, or with any other evidence bearing upon the condition of the lunatic, Margaret M'Hugh, transmitted to that asylum from the Carrick-on-Shannon Gaol, on the 22nd ult, I am directed by Dr Nugent to send you the *original* reports of the visiting physician on her admission and death, which form the only evidence the Inspectors possess on the subject

I am also to request you will be so good as to return these documents at your convenience.

I am, Gentlemen, your obedient servant,
W. J. CORBET, *Chief Clerk.*
The Inspectors-General of Prisons.

Office of Lunatic Asylums, Dublin Castle,
January 3, 1857.

Sir,—I am directed by the Inspectors, in transmitting to you the accompanying letter from the Inspectors-General of Prisons, together with a communication from the Local Inspector of Carrick-on-Shannon Gaol, in the case of Margaret M'Hugh, to request you will furnish them with any further information on the subject, at your earliest convenience. Please return the enclosure.

I am, Sir, your obedient servant,
W. J. CORBET, *Chief Clerk.*
To the Visiting Physician of the
District Lunatic Asylum, at Sligo.

Caldwell Place, Sligo, January 4, 1857.

Sir,—I have the honour to acknowledge the receipt of your letter of the 2nd instant, (No. 8), transmitting communications from the Inspector-General of Prisons, and from the Local Inspector of Carrick-on-Shannon gaol, relative to my report of the death of the lunatic, Margaret M'Hugh, dated December 24, 1856.

I immediately submitted all the documents referred to to the Resident Physician, Dr. M'Munn, who intends to bring the case before the Governors on the next Board day (Wednesday, the 7th inst.), together with my report thereon, for a thorough investigation.

I have the honour to be, Sir, your obedient servant,
WILLIAM SWAYNE LITTLE, A.B., M.D.,
Visiting Physician to Asylum, Surgeon of
Sligo County Infirmary.
To W. J. Corbet, Esq.,
Office of Lunatic Asylums, Dublin Castle.

Office of Inspectors-General of Prisons,
Dublin Castle, January 9, 1857.

Gentlemen,—I am directed by the Inspectors-General of Prisons to transmit to you, for your information, the accompanying copy of the proceedings of the Board of Superintendence of the gaol at Carrick-on-Shannon, at an investigation held by them on the 7th inst., into the charge of neglect, in the case of Margaret M'Hugh, brought by the Visiting Physician of Sligo Lunatic Asylum against the prison officers.

I am, Gentlemen, your very obedient servant,
JOHN W. GREGG.

To the Inspectors of Lunatic Asylums,
Dublin Castle.

At a meeting of the Board of Superintendence of Carrick-on-Shannon gaol, held this 7th day of January, 1857, present, The Earl of Leitrim, in the chair; John A. Dickson, Esq., J.P.; E. K. Tenison, Esq., J.P.; Pierce Simpson, Esq., J.P.; Captain Burchall, J.P.; F. Waldron, Esq., J.P.; Colonel Cox. J.P.; the Board proceeded to inquire into the truth of statements set forward in a letter from the office of Lunatic Asylums Dublin Castle, dated 26th December, 1856.

Mary Anne Bourns, sworn—I am matron of the gaol of Carrick-on-Shannon; I recollect Margaret M'Hugh, who was an insane prisoner under my charge: I recollect Mr Sweeny giving me orders to have Margaret M'Hugh prepared to go to the Lunatic Asylum at Sligo, on the 22nd December, 1856. I got her washed and cleaned, and had clean clothes put on her; she left me quite well, free from sores or vermin: I have seen her every day while in my charge undressed, washed, and dressed again; during the time she had been under my charge she never had any vermin on her: when she first came under my charge I had her own clothes washed and put into store, and when she was leaving the prison, her own were taken out of the store and put on her; and I put on her, besides, a bed-gown belonging to the gaol

Abraham G. Swane, sworn—I am Medical Officer of the gaol of Carrick-on-Shannon. I recollect Margaret M'Hugh, she was confined in gaol for some months past as a lunatic. I saw her regularly twice a-week since her committal, and on several occasions I prescribed for her. She was a delicate woman. I saw her on the Saturday previous to her leaving the gaol, December 20th. She was in a good state of health, and in a state fit to travel to Sligo. I never saw her naked, but any opportunity I had to observe her I did not see any signs of vermin about her, nor did I hear of any sores upon her at the time of her leaving my charge. From the woman's habits I can easily understand that, on her arrival in Sligo, she may have been in a dirty state. It would have been my duty to have retained her if I had not considered [her] to be in a fit state to be removed. Frequent applications were made that she should be removed, the first of which was about four months ago.

The Board of Superintendence is of opinion that Margaret M'Hugh ought to have been removed from this gaol to the lunatic asylum at Sligo at a much earlier period, and that there is no blame to be attached to the officers of this prison for her having been removed on the 22nd December, 1856, and the Board of Superintendence is of opinion that the charges brought against the officers of this gaol are without foundation.

The Board cannot close their proceedings without animadverting, in the strongest possible manner, on the extreme impropriety of a letter having been addressed to the Acting-Governor of this gaol, dated from the Office of Lunatic Asylums, Dublin Castle, containing such serious charges as are contained in the letter now before the Board, without its being signed by either of the Inspectors of Lunatic Asylums—this letter being signed by a person totally unknown to the Board.

The Local Inspector is directed to send a copy of the foregoing opinion, and the evidence, to the Inspectors of Prisons.

(Signed,)   LEITRIM, J.P., *Chairman.*

Office of Lunatic Asylums, Dublin Castle,
January 10, 1856.

Sir,—Referring to the case of Margaret M'Hugh, I am directed by the Inspectors to transmit to you, with a request that it will be submitted to the Board of Superintendence at its first meeting, the following resolution. passed by the Board of Governors of the Sligo Asylum, at their meeting on Wednesday, the 7th instant: present—The Right Hon. John Wynne, Lieutenant of the County, in the chair; William Phibbs, Esq., D.L.; Captain Wood, J.P.; Peter O'Connor, Esq., J.P.; F. M. Olpherts, Esq., J.P.; C. Cooper, Esq., D.L.; Major Ffolliott; Bernard O. Cogan, Esq., J.P.:—

"The Governors having inspected the clothes in which the woman who left Carrick-on-Shannon, at five o'clock on a December morning, reached this asylum, are of opinion that the visiting physician would not have fulfilled his duty if he had not made the report referred to; and as the character of the officers of Carrick-on-Shannon Gaol is affected by this report, request that a full investigation may be made into the matter by the Inspectors of Lunatic Asylums."

The Inspectors further desire me to observe, with regard to an opinion of the Board of Superintendence, as conveyed to the Inspectors-General of Prisons, in a communication signed by the Earl of Leitrim as chairman, on the 7th inst.—" That Margaret M'Hugh ought to have been removed from this gaol to the asylum at Sligo at a much earlier period;" the delay did not originate in this office, but was occasioned by irregularities connected with her imprisonment.

By reference to letters officially directed to the Governor of the gaol at Carrick-on-Shannon, it will appear that the first intimation relative to her was transmitted to this office on the 31st July, 1856, she having been committed for trial for an assault on the 1st of that month.

On the 1st of August a letter was written by direction of the Inspectors, requesting a copy of her committal, in duplicate, together with the usual medical certificate, in order that a warrant might be issued for her removal to the asylum. Of this letter no notice was taken, and she remained in prison until the ensuing quarter sessions, when she was acquitted on the ground of insanity. Being informed of the fact (through the report of the Assistant Barrister), the Inspectors addressed a second letter to the Governor of the gaol, on the 27th October, requiring the necessary papers to be forwarded to this office; and on the 7th November, copies of committal, without medical certificate, were received. These papers being themselves irregular, were returned for correction same day; inasmuch as it was represented that Margaret M'Hugh was charged on the 1st January, 1856, for an assault which was alleged to have been committed on the 6th June, 1856. No notice having been taken of this communication either, the Governor was written to on the 19th November, directing, *inter alia*, his attention to the communication of the 7th. On the 21st a reply was given, mentioning the facts of committal, trial, &c., but the required papers were not furnished in a complete form till the 9th December.

A warrant was thereupon issued, and transmitted on the 12th to the asylum, an order for the lunatic's removal being forwarded at the same time to the Governor of the gaol, who " being inexperienced,"* applied for further information to the Inspectors, on the 14th. On the 16th they communicated with him, drawing his attention to the instructions contained in the order for the lunatic's removal, as laid down by the Chief Secretary, and on the 22nd the removal was effected.

The circumstances occurring subsequently have already been under the consideration of the Board, and the Inspectors do not wish now to comment upon them.

In conclusion, and referring to that part of the proceedings of the Board, in which it is pleased to animadvert on the Inspectors, I am directed by them to state, that feeling themselves competent to conduct the business of their office, and to regulate its correspondence, they do not hold themselves responsible to any authority but that of Government for the system adopted by them.

It is their habit, without meaning the slightest disrespect to the official gentlemen with whom they communicate in the course of business, to do so in a manner that could give no just cause of umbrage, and similarly to that which is practised in other departments of the public service.

I am, Sir, your obedient servant,

W. J. CORBET, *Chief Clerk.*

The Governor of the Gaol at
Carrick-on-Shannon.

* The former Governor had just been dismissed for misconduct.

APPENDIX K.

CORRESPONDENCE on the subject of SUPERANNUATION, under 19 and 20 Vict.

Superannuation.

Limerick District Lunatic Asylum,
Limerick, September 8, 1856.

GENTLEMEN,—At the Meeting of the Board, this day, a case has occurred, respecting which my colleagues were desirous that I should obtain your opinion, as the decision which may be taken on the present occasion may govern the conduct of the Board in future.

It is an application for a superannuation allowance for a keeper, who has served during twenty-eight years in this establishment. He is between sixty-five and seventy years of age, he is incapable of performing his official duties, by reason of age and infirmity, and he has obtained a certificate of good conduct from the Governor and the Medical Attendant of the asylum.

The application has been made under the provisions of the 19th and 20th Vict., c. 99, which refers to the 4th and 5th Wm. 4, c. 24, s. 3, for the scale of allowance. The salary received by the applicant was £16 16s., seven-twelfths of which would be £9 16s. But in addition to this salary the applicant calculates the value of the diet and clothing to which he was entitled, at £9 2s., and £3 4s. respectively, making, together with the salary, £29 2s. 6d.

We are desirous of knowing whether you consider that the diet and clothing should be taken into account, and the superannuation based on £16 16s., or on £29 2s. 6d. You will observe that in the s. 9 4th and 5th Wm. 4, c. 24, the scale is fixed in reference, not to salary only, but to salary and *emoluments*. Does the latter word include diet and clothing?

Requesting your answer to above, I have the honour to be, Gentlemen,

Your very obedient,
MONTEAGLE, Chairman.

To the Inspectors-General.

Office of Lunatic Asylums, Dublin Castle,
September 13, 1856.

MY LORD,—I had the honour to receive your letter, addressed to the Inspectors, on the 8th instant, inquiring whether, in their opinion, diet and clothing come within the category of emoluments in regard to the superannuation of servants attached to District Lunatic Asylums, we would answer in the affirmative; and would, therefore, in the immediate instance your Lordship refers to, namely, that of a keeper, who has served twenty-eight years in the district institution, at Limerick, estimate his superannuation, both on the annual wages of £16 16s., and on the aggregate of diet and clothing £12 6s., altogether £29 2s. In calculating the payment of attendants when hired by the Board of Governors, we are aware that diet and clothing are taken into account, otherwise 11d. a day, or sixteen guineas a-year would be no fair remuneration for a keeper, considering the duties he has to perform.

We therefore think, in equity, such an attendant, whether he has been remunerated in kind, or money, has a right to the value of his past services, as so required.

Of course I need not add, that the strictest attention of the Board of Governors should be paid when submitting a proposal for superannuation, to the character, sobriety, age, state of health, and length of service of the individual.

I have the honour to subscribe myself your Lordship's obedient servant,

JOHN NUGENT.

To Lord Monteagle, &c., &c.

Limerick District Lunatic Asylum,
October 9, 1856.

GENTLEMEN,—I beg to inform you that, at the last Meeting of the Board of Governors, Michael O'Shea, a superannuated officer of this asylum, was granted an allowance of seven-twelfths of his salary and emoluments.

I therefore request to be informed, as a guidance for the future, how same is to be paid, whether monthly, quarterly, or per annum.

I should be also glad to know if the man is entitled to pay from the date of the passing of the Act.

I am, &c., &c.

(Signed)   ROBT. FITZGERALD, M.D.

To the Inspectors of Lunatic Asylums,
Dublin Castle.

———

Office of Lunatic Asylums, Dublin Castle,
October 10, 1856.

SIR,—In reply to your communication of the 9th instant, inquiring how the allowance granted by the Board of Governors, at their last Meeting, to Michael O'Shea, a superannuated officer, is to be paid, whether monthly, quarterly, or yearly, I am directed by the Inspectors to inform you, that the Act 19th and 20th Vict., cap. 99, provides that such pensions "shall, respectively, be advanced, paid, presented for, and raised, in like manner as any other monies advanced, or raised, for supporting and maintaining such asylums;" but no mention is made as to the period of payments. It therefore rests with the Board of Governors to decide, as they think fit, on the matter.

I am, however, to observe, that by the 3rd clause of the Act, it is necessary to submit every case, together with such resolution as the Governors may have come to thereon, to the Inspectors, for investigation and approval, before any payment can legally be made.

I am to add that Dr. Nugent's letter to Lord Monteagle, on the subject of superannuation, was merely an explanatory one; and the formal approval of the Inspectors in this, as in every other case of a like nature, has therefore to be obtained, as directed by the Act.

I am, Sir, your very obedient servant,

W. J. CORBET, *Chief Clerk.*

To the Resident Physician of the
District Lunatic Asylum at Limerick.

———

Limerick District Lunatic Asylum,
11th October, 1856.

GENTLEMEN,—Michael O'Shea's superannuation case having been brought before the Board of Governors on three several occasions, and Dr. Nugent's letter to Lord Monteagle having been presented to the Governors at their last meeting, it was taken for granted that the matter had received the formal approval of the Inspectors; and certificates having been obtained from the Visiting and Resident Physicians as to O'Shea's bad state of health, and his good conduct during the period of twenty-eight years that he served in the asylum, he was ordered to receive one month's pay. Therefore, under those circumstances, you will, I trust, he kind enough to say what are to be the future proceedings in this particular case.

I am, Gentlemen, your obedient servant,

(Signed)   ROBERT FITZGERALD.

The Inspectors, Lunatic Asylums.

———

Office of Lunatic Asylums,
Dublin Castle, 15th October, 1856.

SIR,—I am directed by the Inspectors to acknowledge the receipt of your communication of the 11th instant, in the case of Michael O'Shea, and to state, that the course indicated by the statute, as mentioned in a letter which I addressed to you by their direction on the 8th instant, is as follows—namely: "When an officer applies to be superannuated, or when the Board of Governors are of opinion that any such officer is no longer able to perform the duties of his office properly and efficiently, the case is brought formally before the Board, who consider the claims of the applicant, and decide upon the amount of pension within the limits specified by law. A substantive resolution, embodying all the particulars, should then be recorded, and transmitted to the Inspectors for their approval."

I am to add, that it is necessary to take this course in the present case, as it would be contrary to all precedent to give an anticipatory approval to any act of the Board; and although Dr. Nugent signified, in general and explanatory terms, how the beneficial provisions of the Superannuation Act could be extended to Michael O'Shea, you will observe that the opinion expressed by him was not intended to interfere with the formal mode of procedure as laid down by that Act.

I am, Sir, your obedient servant,

W. J. CORBET, *Chief Clerk.*

To the Resident Physician of the
District Lunatic Asylum, at Limerick.

———

To the Board of Governors of the Limerick District Lunatic Asylum. The humble memorial of Michael O'Shea

SHOWETH,—That your memorialist has been for a period of twenty-eight years employed as keeper in said asylum.

That during that period he has discharged his duties to the entire satisfaction of the Managers and Physicians of said asylum, who can bear testimony to his uniform kindness to the patients who have been intrusted to his charge.

That memorialist is at present incapable, from ill health, to discharge his duties, and therefore most humbly hopes that your Honourable Board will take his case into your humane consideration, and grant him a yearly allowance in consideration of the length of time he has been in the public service.

That your memorialist received as a salary, for each year, a sum of £16 16s., which, with a sum of £9 2s. average value of diet, and £3 4s. for clothes, making in the whole a sum of £29 2s. 6d. for each year.

Memorialist therefore humbly hopes your Honourable Board will be pleased to grant him said yearly allowance.

And memorialist, as in duty bound, will ever pray.

MICHAEL O'SHEA.

We certify that the memorialist, Michael O'Shea, has been twenty-eight years in this asylum; and it is our belief that he performed his duties with diligence and fidelity during that period.

DAVID O'CALLAGHAN, *Visiting Physician.*
ROBERT FITZGERALD, *Resident Physician.*

Minute of the Board of Governors of the Limerick District Lunatic Asylum, at meeting held November 3, 1856.

Letters from the Inspectors of Lunatic Asylums, relative to Michael O'Shea, the late keeper's superannuation allowance having been read and considered—It was resolved, that this Board recommend to the Inspectors of Lunatic Asylums the payment of Michael O'Shea's superannuation allowance, from the date of the passing of the Act, on seven-twelfths of his salary, and value of rations, &c.; and that they also submit for the consideration of the Inspectors, whether the officer in question has a right to claim any such superannuation from the time he was unable to discharge his duties as keeper, up to the passing of the Act, 19 and 20 Vic., cap. 99.

JOHN SINGLETON, *Chairman.*

———

Office of Lunatic Asylums, Dublin Castle,
November 8, 1856.

SIR,—I am directed by the Inspectors to acknowledge the receipt of a resolution of the Board of Governors, enclosing a memorial from Michael O'Shea, praying for a superannuation allowance, in respect to his services as an attendant in the Limerick District Lunatic Asylum for a period of twenty-eight years; and which resolution recommends the payment of an allowance to him from the date of the passing of the Act (July 29, 1856), of seven-twelfths of his salary and emoluments, which, together, are estimated at £29 2s.; and to state, that the Inspectors approve of the proposal of the Board—the amount of pension payable to Michael O'Shea, calculated on the above scale, being £16 19s. 6d.

I am to add that, in the opinion of the Inspectors, no claim for superannuation prior to the passing of the Act can be entertained.

I am, Sir, your obedient servant,

W. J. CORBET, *Chief Clerk.*

To the Resident Physician of the
District Lunatic Asylum, at Limerick.

Dublin Castle, January 23, 1857.

My Lords and Gentlemen,—In accordance with a resolution passed on the 12th December, 1856, by the Governors of the Londonderry District Asylum, allocating to Mr. Cluff, after a period of continued service in that Institution over twenty-five years, a superannuation, amounting to a sum of £120 a-year, in lieu of past salary and allowances; and in the case of Mrs. Cluff, the matron, for a similar period of service, and in lieu of same, a superannuation amounting to the annual sum of £64 3s. 4d.; and, as this resolution in pursuance of the provisions of the Act, 19 and 20 Vict., cap. 99, has been submitted for the approval of the Inspectors, or one of them, I have the honour to state for the information of the Board, that I hereby approve the superannuations as proposed in the resolutions above referred to—namely, £120 per annum to Mr. David Cluff; and £64 3s. 4d. to his wife, Mrs. E. Cluff—such superannuation to date from the period of their respective retirements.

I have the honour to be, my Lords and Gentlemen, respectfully,

JOHN NUGENT.

The Board of Governors of the
Londonderry Asylum.

APPENDIX L.

CASE on behalf of the CROWN as to the ADMISSION of PATIENTS into the CENTRAL CRIMINAL ASYLUM, DUNDRUM, who have become insane subsequently to their conviction; for the opinion of the Right Honourable the ATTORNEY-GENERAL, and the SOLICITOR-GENERAL.

10th December, 1856.—By a letter of this date, from the Under Secretary, the Crown Solicitor has been directed to obtain the opinion of the Law Officers of the Crown on a question raised by the Inspectors of Lunatic Asylums relating to patients in the Central Criminal Asylum, at Dundrum, who have, or are reputed to have become insane subsequently to their convictions, and removed from Government Prisons to the Asylum in question.

From a return furnished to the Chief Secretary by Doctor Nugent, Inspector of Lunatic Asylums, it appears that at present there are twenty-four patients in the Lunatic Asylum, at Dundrum, who have been sent there from Government Prisons in consequence of their having become insane (or so reputed to have become) subsequent to their convictions for offences for which they were sentenced to penal servitude or transportation.

In explanation of the subject, Doctor Nugent has addressed a letter to the Chief Secretary, of which the following is a copy:—

December 3rd, 1856, Lunatic Asylums.

SIR,—The accompanying memorandum is copied from a report I requested from the Physicians of the Central Asylum; the observations in *italics* are by me, and explanatory. I am anxious you should consider the question of the length of time, or rather what should be the termination of confinement in the Central or Governmental Institution at Dundrum.

The 12th section, 8th and 9th Victoria, chapter 107, enacts that the Lord Lieutenant may direct the transmission of persons under sentence of imprisonment or transportation to the Central Asylum, there to remain till the close (if he thought fit) of their final servitude.

Twenty-four of the existing inmates, out of 127 at Dundrum, come under the category of imprisonment or transportation.

I believe, by a late Statute, the period of imprisonment is diminished (unless for reasons to the reverse), for example, from seven to four years, how will this regulation affect lunatics in the Central Asylum? Should not they, subsequent to the close of their legal confinement there, if still uncured, be sent to the asylums of their respective districts? On the other hand, should the continuance of their insanity, after the regular period of penal servitude, be deemed as a rule sufficient cause

for their being supported by Government, there will be a never-ending accumulation of lunatics in Dundrum.

The object of my application is two-fold—1st to know whether the diminution of the time of penal servitude, as regards the criminals in gaols, is to hold good with reference to lunatics? 2nd, whether (there of course being now and then exceptional cases) lunatics who have filled their full term of confinement elsewhere, and at the Central Asylum, are not to be discharged from the latter? The Asylum being now in operation five years, the question is one of practical importance.

I have given a list in *full*, &c., of the convicts from Governmental Prisons, and beg to subscribe myself,

Your obedient servant,
JOHN NUGENT.

To the Right Hon. E. Horsman, &c., &c.

APPENDIX L.

Cases submitted for the opinion of the Attorney-General.

LIST of PATIENTS in the CENTRAL CRIMINAL ASYLUM, DUNDRUM, who have or are reputed to have become insane, subsequently to their conviction, and have been removed from GOVERNMENT PRISONS.

1. "Burke, James, convicted in 1850, of larceny; sentence not stated. Certified to have been, in March, 1854, a dangerous lunatic for two years, by Dr. Corr, Philipstown. He is a wild, savage man, at times violent, and of unsound mind.

"*This man was sentenced to seven years' transportation: if sane, he would have been liberated, as his penal servitude has expired.*"

2. "Bonner, James, convicted of larceny, May, 1852; sentence, seven years. Twice before in gaol. Bonner is of unsound mind.

"*Similarly circumstanced as the preceding case.*"

3. "Byrne, John, convicted TEN TIMES; sentence not stated. He is insane, and subject to frequent exacerbations of his malady.

"*Sentence, seven years' transportation, Dec., 1851; similar case.*"

4. "Canty, Thomas, convicted in 1850; sentence, fourteen years. Was in Bermuda, where he is said to have had sunstroke. He is subject to periodical mania, and scarcely at any time quite sane.

"*Eight years of penal servitude unexpired.*"

5. "Comerford, John, convicted in 1850, of sheep stealing; sentence not stated. Certified to have been, for the last month, a dangerous lunatic. November 10th, 1853. Comerford is violent, self-willed; has been at times noisy by night and day; has refused food for days successively; is disposed to resist authority, and has been put into the cold bath for insolence and disobedience. We are often *disposed to think he feigns insanity.*

"*Convicted in 1850, ten years' transportation. This man is not, in my opinion, insane, at least, he displays no manifestation of a diseased mind at present, neither do I think he feigns; his is of a wayward, uncontrollable temperament.*"

6. "Dixon, John, convicted June, 1851; sentenced, ten years; admitted August 9, 1856. Certified by medical officer of Philipstown Convict Prison to be of unsound mind. Dixon is passionate, and of very limited understanding. He is of unsound mind.

"*A case for detention.*"

7. "Duane, Maryanne, convicted of arson, 1851-2; sentence not stated. She is at times subject to violent passions; at all times of weak intellect.

"*Acquitted on ground of insanity.*"

8. "Gleeson, Michael, convicted April, 1850. Certified to be insane July 11, 1853. Admitted Aug. 31, 1853. Gleeson for a considerable time seemed to be convalescent, but of an obstinate character. Having had a quarrel with another patient, Uriah Worthington, he made a murderous attack on him, premeditated and carried out with cunning. Subsequent to this he became mopish, and as if with very little mind; will smile if asked a question, and not reply; obstinately lie in bed for days, and scream if attempts are made to get him up. He has made several attacks on other patients with plates or tins, without much obvious notice.

"*Seven years' transportation. This is obviously a case requiring great attention and care. Under any circumstances this lunatic should be detained where he is.*"

9. "Hayes, Michael, convicted, 1849, of robbery from the person; sentence not stated. Came here, believed to be a malingerer. He is, however, insane, and has become *much more manageable and quiet since he came here.*

"*Seven years' transportation. Time expired.*"

10. "Hyland, John, convicted 1850, cow stealing; sentence, ten years."

11. "Lee, Eliza, (case as No. 1), felony; no sentence. No precise information given us. Of extreme ill-temper; almost constantly in quarrels, very abusive; has no illusions, no false perceptions; speaks correctly, and is very revengeful.

"*Sent from Grangegorman Prison on the opening of the Asylum. Term of penal servitude expired.*"

12. "Carthy, Margaret; no date of conviction nor sentence known. Was subject to fits of epilepsy. She seems to be now free of it, and not insane; perhaps at times getting into a passion without cause, and in some respects weak-minded.

"*Convicted in 1850; violent assault. Time expired.*"

APPENDIX L.

Cases submitted for the opinion of the Attorney-General.

13. "M'Night, James, convicted May, 1850, *larceny*. No account of his sentence. He is insane.

Incompetent to plead.

"*Is this a fit case to be continued in asylum after six years.*"

14. "Murphy (or Credon), Mary, convicted December. 1852, stealing; sentence not given to us. She is *not insane*, but impulsive and passionate.

Similar query to 13.

"*Sentence, seven years.*"

15. "Maher, Patrick, convicted 1849; sentence, fourteen years. Was in Bermuda, sent back in 1855 as a dangerous lunatic. Maher is insane, noisy, and troublesome, of little or no usefulness.

"*Seven years of servitude unpassed.*"

16. "Mullanophy, Michael, convicted 1850; sentence, fifteen years, cow stealing. He seems *very mischievous* and insane, incapable of being made of any use.

"*Nine years of servitude remaining.*"

17. "M'Loughlin, Thomas, convicted of larcenies; sentence, four years, from January, 1855. He answers questions reasonably, but seems of a wayward disposition. He was very frequently in gaol.

"*Three years of servitude remaining.*"

18. "Reilly, Margaret, convicted 18 2. larceny; *sentence not stated.* She is of obstinate disposition, but not of weak mind or insane. She was suicidal in disposition.

"*Seven years' transportation; two remain.*"

19. "Reilly, Mary, convicted February, 1854, *vagrancy;* sentence, four years. She is subject to violent passion, and not of strong mind.

"*Her vagrant habits were probably far less criminal than indications of a weak mind, rendering her a fit object for a District Asylum, or even a poorhouse.*"

20. "Roovey, Mary. committal 1846; sentence not stated. She is quarrelsome, passionate. but has no false perceptions.

"*The most inveterate disposition to commit larceny, attempting to rob even in prison.*"

21. "Sullivan, Mary; nothing known of conviction or sentence. She seems of weak intellect, otherwise not insane. She does *not speak English.*

"*Convicted January,* 1853, *larceny, seven years' transportation. Ought to be sent to Kerry, her native county, where in the asylum she would have some one to speak to.*"

22. "Sullivan, Patrick. convicted July, 1853; sentence, seven years. He is quite idiotic.

"*He appears to me to have been originally of the weakest mind.*"

23. "Waters, Catherine. committal 1853; sentence not stated. She is of a wild, irregular disposition and conduct. Subject to fits of passion.

Sentenced to seven years' transportation; period of four years not quite terminated."

24. "Williams, William, convicted April, 1854; sentence. four years, for felony of a *sheet.* He is insane, but quiet and likely to be useful. *From Newgate Prison, sent to asylum 27th October.*"

"*Is such a patient to be supported by Government, at an expense of £26 per annum, until he recovers, or is he to be discharged (if he lives so long) uncured in April,* 1858?"

(Signed),   WILLIAM CORBETT, }
ROBERT HARRISON, } *Physicians.*

Central Asylum, 28th *November.*

From a perusal of the return of the twenty-four patients furnished by Doctor Nugent, it will be seen that the period of sentence of imprisonment, in some instances, has expired, whilst in others it has not; and in one case the following extract is made therefrom:—

"Williams, William, convicted April, 1854, sentence four years, for felony of a sheet. He is insane, but quiet and likely to be useful. From Newgate Prison, sent to asylum 27th October.

Is such a patient to be supported by Government, at an expense of £26 per annum, until he recovers, or is he to be discharged (if he lives so long) uncured in April, 1858?"

The 8th section 8th and 9th Vict., cap 107, enacts. That so soon as the Central Asylum shall be erected and fit for the reception of lunatics, it shall be lawful for the Lord Lieutenant to order and direct that all criminal lunatics then in custody in any lunatic asylum or gaol, or who shall thereafter be in custody, shall be removed without delay to such Central Asylum, and shall be kept therein so long as such criminal lunatics respectively shall be detained in custody.

The 12th section enacts that it shall be lawful for the Lord Lieutenant, by warrant under his hand, to order that any person who may be under any sentence of imprisonment or transportation in any gaol or place of confinement, or in any District Asylum. and in respect of whom it shall be certified by two physicians that such person is or has become insane, shall be removed to the said Central Asylum: and every person so removed shall remain under confinement in said Asylum so long as such person shall remain subject to be continued in custody, or until it shall be duly certified to the Lord Lieutenant that such person has become of sound mind, whereupon the Lord Lieutenant, if such person shall remain subject to be continued in custody, to issue his warrant to the keeper having the care of any such asylum, directing that such person shall be remitted to the prison or other place of confinement from which he or she shall have been taken; or if such person shall be entitled to his or her discharge, to direct the discharge accordingly

16th and 17th Vict., cap. 99. sec. 4, which appears to be the Act referred to by Doctor Nugent, enacts. That instead of transportation for seven years, penal servitude for four years. Transportation exceeding seven years, and not exceeding ten years, penal servitude not exceeding six years. Transportation exceeding ten years, and not exceeding fifteen years, penal servitude not less than six. and not exceeding eight years. Transportation exceeding fifteen years, penal servitude for any term not less than six, and not exceeding ten years. Transportation for the term of life, penal servitude for life.

You are requested to consider this case, and give your opinion as to the disposal of lunatic prisoners in the Central Asylum, at Dundrum. in instances where the periods of their sentences of imprisonment or transportation have expired; whether, notwithstanding the continuance of their insanity, they are to be discharged therefrom or sent to the lunatic asylums of their respective districts; and what should be the termination to confinement in the Central or Government Institution at Dundrum.

OPINION.

We are of opinion, that prisoners who after sentence of transportation or imprisonment have become insane, and have been removed under the 12th sec. of 8th and 9th Vict., cap. 107, to the Central Asylum, must remain there until the period of imprisonment shall have expired, or until it shall have been duly certified that they have become of sound mind.

When the period of transportation or imprisonment has elapsed, the prisoner is entitled to his discharge, and should not be longer detained at the Central Asylum. If, however, he continues of unsound mind, he should not be cast loose upon the world, but should be dealt with under 8th and 9th Vict. cap. 107, sec. 10, if a dangerous lunatic, or restored to the care of his friends or sent to the District Asylum.

J. D. FITZGERALD.
J. CHRISTIAN.

20th *December,* 1856.

CASE on behalf of the CROWN with respect to MATHEW HAZARD, a CRIMINAL LUNATIC, for the opinion of the Right Honourable the ATTORNEY-GENERAL, and the SOLICITOR-GENERAL.

12th *December*, 1856 —By a letter of this date, from the Under Secretary, the Crown Solicitor is directed to bring under the consideration of the Law Officers of the Crown a communication, addressed to Government by the Inspectors of Lunatic Asylums, in relation to a criminal lunatic, named Mathew Hazard, confined in the Downpatrick prison; and in reference to a case recently submitted to the Law Officers of the Crown, with respect to criminal lunatics in that institution.

It appears that in May, 1854, Mathew Hazard was committed to Downpatrick Gaol on a warrant from William Gregg, Esq, a Justice of the Peace of the County Down, to take his trial at the next following quarter sessions, at Newtownards, on a charge of having cattle in his possession, knowing them to have been stolen. Hazard was tried for the offence, but acquitted on the grounds of insanity, and ordered by the Court to be kept in custody till the pleasure of the Lord Lieutenant was known. The question of his being placed in the Central Lunatic Asylum, at Dundrum, is more fully explained in a communication from Dr. Nugent, one of the Inspectors of Lunatic Asylums, of which the following is a copy:—

Lunatic Asylum Office, Dublin Castle,
November 8, 1856.

Sir,—I have the honour to submit the accompanying case of Mathew Hazard for your consideration, with reference to the practical bearing of the Statute, by which the Central Asylum at Dundrum was created, under the 8 & 9 Vic., cap. 107, for the reception of lunatics charged with offences in Ireland, in order that by this, an extreme case, the question may be decided, whether every individual committing a misdemeanor, or being at the time unwittingly engaged in an act contrary to law, at the instigation of others, if acquitted on the plea of insanity, no matter how trivial in itself the offence or act may have been, must necessarily, under the provisions of the Act, the 8th clause particularly, be transmitted to the Central Asylum? In other words, whether the law on this head be mandatory, or whether His Excellency enjoys a discretionary power?

It may, however, be well to observe here, that the 61st Rule, for the management of the Asylum, passed in Council (and it is to be presumed, approved of by the then Law Officers of the Crown), gives authority to the Lord Lieutenant to re-transfer from the Central Asylum "lunatics charged with minor offences, to the institutions where they came;" the inference would thus be that, a priori, he is not obliged to send to.

Mathew Hazard was tried at the Newtownards quarter sessions, on the 26th June, 1854, and acquitted of the charges against him on the plea of insanity.

On the 29th, the Inspectors were informed of the particulars, and, subsequently, in reply to an application for his removal to the Dundrum Asylum, a letter was addressed from this office to R. Heron, Esq., J.P., Chairman of the Board of Superintendence of the Down Gaol, "that as regards the criminal lunatics, the Central Asylum has even more than its full number of inmates."

The Governors of the Belfast Asylum opposed the admission of any criminal lunatic into their Asylum. Vacancies, no doubt, occurred since the 29th June, 1854, in the Dundrum establishment, but which the Inspectors retained for important and serious cases, involving attempts at life, &c. &c. A bed may soon be at the disposal of Government, and as there appears no urgent application for it, the assizes, too, being remote, I deem it a good opportunity to bring In re Hazard, the present question before you. By a reference to the Fifth Report of the Inspectors, page 10, you will learn the course adopted by them with regard to the first admission of criminal lunatics into the Dundrum Asylum.

The system approved of by Lord Clarendon, and acted on in detail under the cognizance of his Under-Secretary, Sir Thomas Redington, has been the Rule since pursued in this office, and, I believe, with satisfactory results.

In our Sixth and Seventh Report we have again (pages 15 and 16) referred to the subject.

In the case of Mathew Hazard, there appears no tendency whatever to malevolent or violent feelings against property or person. Should, however, the decision of the Executive be to place him and all persons acquitted, on the plea of insanity, of trivial misdemeanors, in Government institutions, I apprehend that as the law now stands, in the course of a few years a very large additional expense will be entailed on the State. The number of so-called dangerous lunatics annually committed to prison, under magisterial warrants, will no doubt surprise you: within the last year, in the source of ten months, we have entered in our books, with all their individual particulars, 530; of these, 344 have been transferred through this office to District Asylums.

The difference was discharged, or remains, I may say, altogether fluctuating in the gaols of four districts.

Now the committal of dangerous lunatics, as they are denominated, is under one of two heads, either as "denoting derangement, and a purpose of committing an indictable crime," or, as frequently happens, of having committed what the attesting parties call an assault, and which, of course, becomes to a sane person an indictable offence.

All, then, a magistrate, if he pleases, has to do, knowing that a criminal lunatic (when acquitted, &c.,) will be maintained by Government during the full period of his lunacy, is, to take informations and send the case to quarter sessions, where the party acquitted on the plea of insanity will be manufactured into a state convict, at a cost, if he lives, as he likely will, on an average of twenty years, of some five or six hundred pounds to the Treasury.

The intentions of the 8th & 9th Vict., cap. 107, are good, but practically, from what I believe, much abused; at all events, the county of Down is fairly represented at Dundrum, sending five members to it.

I have the honour to be, Sir,
Your obedient servant,
John Nugent.

To the Right Hon. E. Horsman, &c., &c.

The 8th section, 8 & 9 Vic., cap. 107, enacts, that wherever and so soon as the Central Asylum shall be erected and fit for the reception of criminal lunatics, it shall be lawful for the Lord Lieutenant to order that all criminal lunatics then in custody in any lunatic asylum or gaol, or who shall thereafter be in custody or gaol, shall be removed without delay to such Central Asylum, and kept there so long as such criminal lunatic shall be detained in custody.

The 12th section provides for cases of criminal lunatics under sentence of transportation or imprisonment, and enacts, that the Lord Lieutenant, if he shall so think fit, shall issue his warrant, ordering and directing their removal to such Central Asylum.

The 13th section enacts, that it shall be lawful to receive, maintain, and take care of, within every District Lunatic Asylum, any number of lunatic poor whatsoever, for the reception and accommodation of whom such asylum shall or may afford space and capacity.

You are requested to consider this case and give your opinion, whether every individual committing a misdemeanor, or being at the time unwittingly engaged in an act contrary to law, if acquitted on the ground of insanity, no matter how trivial the offence or act may be, he must necessarily, under the provisions of the Act above referred to, be transmitted to the Central Asylum at Dundrum; and whether the law is compulsory on the subject, or discretionary in His Excellency, to make an order for the removal of the insane prisoners to said Central Asylum.

OPINION.

We are of opinion, that His Excellency is entitled to exercise a discretion in making orders under the Act, and that it is not mandatory upon him to make an order in each particular case.

J. D. Fitzgerald.
J. Christian.

20th Decem'er, 1856.

Case submitted for the consideration of Government, with a view to the discharge or removal of persons detained in the Central Lunatic Asylum, Dundrum, who are reported to be of sane mind, with the Resident and Visiting Physicians' Certificate, and the Inspector's Observations—Under consideration.

Office of Lunatic Asylums, Dublin Castle.
March 21, 1857.

Sir,—I have the honour to transmit to you a list of persons at present detained in the Central Asylum at Dundrum who are certified to be of sound mind by the resident and visiting physicians, and who have already memorialed for, or personally solicited their discharge, in order that it be submitted to the Lord Lieutenant for his decision in their regard. His Excellency will perceive that some of those individuals were charged with offences of a very grave character, and that a necessity may arise for a reference to documents not in this office.

In submitting such cases for the consideration of his Excellency, the Inspectors can only express their belief for the present, and their expectation in the permanency of each cure. It is satisfactory to be enabled to state that no relapse has occurred to any patient heretofore discharged from this institution. As there is a pressure for admittance into the Central Asylum from government prisons, it would be desirable to have some vacancies.

John Nugent.

To Colonel Larcom.

[List.

K

APPENDIX L. LIST of Persons detained in the Central Lunatic Asylum, Dundrum, referred to in preceding Letter.

Physicians' Certificate.	Inspector's Observations.
Margaret Reilly, detained in the Asylum since the 12th September, 1853, is now of sane mind; the charge against her is larceny; she seems to be self-willed and passionate, and on one occasion attempted suicide, having got into some quarrel. For the last year she has been quiet and orderly.	Convicted in 1852; penal confinement over. Her sister ready to receive her.
Mary Cullen, received into the Asylum on the 5th October, 1850, is perfectly sane of mind, and has been so during her sojourn here.	Poisoned some of her family; acquitted on the plea of lunacy. Very doubtful whether she was ever insane. This woman is urgent for her liberty. I promised, but without holding out any hope, that I would mention her case. I do so, but cannot recommend her discharge.
Mary Creedon, otherwise Murphy, received into the Asylum on the 8th June, 1853, is now of sane mind. For a considerable time she was subject to break out into violent passions and to get into quarrels, but she has become much more steady and amenable. The charge against her is for stealing cloth. Her friends are willing to receive and protect her if she be liberated.	Might be discharged.
Michael Frederick Fox, detained in the Asylum from the 21st November, 1850, is of sane mind, and since he was admitted has not shown any symptoms of being really insane. It is questionable whether his detention in a lunatic asylum is a proper course as regards him.	This man, in my opinion, was not insane; and if he committed any future offence, would be clearly responsible.—[Discharged a pistol, containing wadding only, to frighten his solicitor, as he states.]
Roger M'Donnell, detained in the Asylum since the 2nd September, 1851, is now of sane mind, and has not shown any symptoms of insanity for the last two years and a half. His conduct, while under our observation, has been quiet and becoming almost uniformly.	The history of this case is as follows:—Roger M'Donnell had ever held a good character. One day, walking along the road, near Kilnay, he met a man whom he had never seen before (his mind, for a short time previous, he represents as being very uneasy), he passed the man, and, walking on some few yards, saw a cudgel on the ground, he seized it, and with a sudden homicidal impulse, turned round on the stranger, whom he immediately killed —inflicting seven wounds on his head. He, then, ran a distance of three or four miles to Cavan, where, from his extraordinary conduct in the street, he was arrested. He was subsequently tried for the murder, and acquitted on the score of insanity. By warrant transferred to the Armagh Asylum, he escaped from it, went to America, returned in a year, and gave himself up at the Asylum, whence he was brought to Dundrum.
William Bladdin, detained in the Asylum since the 19th July, 1852, is perfectly sane, and we have not observed any sign of his being insane since he came under our observation. His conduct has been quiet, blameless, and obedient since his coming.	Might be liberated. Accused of gross indecency.
Honoria Ryan, detained in the Asylum since the 9th September, 1854, is now of sane mind, and has been so without any interruption for nearly two years. Her conduct has been very quiet and proper, whilst in health, in this Asylum.	A respectable married woman; infanticide (child, three months old,) while labouring under puerperal mania. Might be discharged, family ready to receive her.—[Now a widow.]
Cornelius Crowly, detained in the Asylum since the 15th October, 1850, is of sane mind; and his conduct, whilst under our observation, has been in general very correct and proper; on one or two occasions during his residence here there was a manifestation of hasty and violent temper, but he never otherwise showed any symptoms of insanity as far as we have seen or heard	This man is most urgent for his discharge—but was not tried, incompetent to plead when arraigned. Homicide of his wife.

APPENDIX M.

CORRESPONDENCE relative to PATIENTS refusing to work in the CENTRAL ASYLUM, DUNDRUM.

Central Asylum, September 19, 1856.

GENTLEMEN,—It has occurred here that patients who were fitted for employment, taking into account their bodily powers as well as their understanding, have, from time to time, refused to do work appointed for them, saying that they were supported by the Government, and were not compellable to do any work; in fact, they think they may decide such a matter as they think most agreeable to themselves, and continue in the enjoyment of all the privileges of well-behaved patients. Now, as we have not professedly any restraints or punishments calculated to meet such cases, and as it is advisable that no such idea should exist in any one's mind who is capable of knowing right from wrong, as that he is to be judge of how far he is to obey or refuse obedience to authority, some duly recognised penalties should be applicable to such persons. What I would beg to suggest is, that a lower scale of diet should be fixed on for such persons as long as they remain in a state of contumacy, restraining them, either wholly or in part, for such period as may be deemed necessary, from meat; and if they prove very refractory, cutting off one meal in the day of any food they may be allowed. In addition to this, it might be authorized that they might be secluded for twenty-four hours at a time, if their disobedience should be deemed sufficient to authorize such a proceeding.

May I beg you will consider this matter, and let me have your instructions upon it.

I remain, Gentlemen, your obedient servant,

WM. CORBET.

To the Inspectors of Lunatic Asylums, &c.

Office of Lunatic Asylums, Dublin Castle, September 21, 1856.

SIR,—In reply to your letter of the 19th inst., respecting an unwillingness on the part of certain patients in the Central Asylum to render themselves useful to the institution, when fully able to be so, and who, perfectly cognizant of what is right and what is wrong, evince a spirit of contumacy, I think, so far as the question of diet is concerned, your proposition a good one. The dietary of the Dundrum Asylum is above that in other establishments for the insane, and therefore admits of diminution, certainly so as to animal food. I should, therefore, in refractory cases such as you refer to, diminish the quantity of animal food usually given, substituting for it some other, but always ample, and in such manner as you may deem most advisable and economical. I do not think, however, on principle, we could resort to confinement, or any direct punishment, in a lunatic asylum.

I am, Sir, your obedient servant,

J. NUGENT.

Dr. Corbet, Resident Physician, Central Asylum.

RULES and REGULATIONS for the Government of the CENTRAL LUNATIC ASYLUM at DUNDRUM, ordered and established by the LORD LIEUTENANT and COUNCIL of IRELAND, August 22, 1850.

1. In order to effect the better management and control of the Central Asylum at Dundrum for the reception of insane persons charged with offences in Ireland, the Inspectors of Lunatic Asylums shall visit that establishment together, or separately, once in each month, or oftener if they shall think proper.

2. On each monthly visitation the Inspectors or Inspector shall specially examine into the health, appearance, and conduct of the patients then confined in the asylum, and note in a book, to be called "The

Inspectors' Report Book," such observations as may be deemed useful for the information of Government; and they shall on such visits make all the inquiries directed by the Statute 8 & 9 Victoria, cap. 107.

3. The Inspectors shall investigate all complaints, and be empowered to suspend all officers or servants, on the charges being proved, and shall forthwith report thereupon for the information of the Lord Lieutenant.

4. The Inspectors are to report half-yearly to the Chief or Under Secretary the general state of the Institution, the number of inmates, &c., &c., with particular reference to such cases as they may deem it advisable to notice; and on the recovery of every lunatic they are to submit to the Chief or Under Secretary the name of the individual so recovered; the offence with which charged, if untried, or of which acquitted on the plea of insanity; together with the general character and conduct of such individual, for the information of the Lord Lieutenant.

5. The Inspectors shall jointly or separately examine, on each monthly visitation, the accounts of the asylum, checking and comparing the various vouchers and receipts given and received by the Governor during the preceding month, which documents are to be duly initialed by both or either of them.

6. All requisitions for the advance of money from the Treasury for the support of the asylum, by way of estimate, as well as for the payment of the sums already expended, shall be investigated by the Inspectors, and by them transmitted to the Chief or Under Secretary.

7. The Inspectors shall advertise for, receive, and select all tenders for contracts for the Central Asylum at Dundrum, at their office in the Castle.

8. *Visiting Physician.*—The Visiting Physician to the Dundrum Central Asylum is to attend three times a week, or oftener if required, entering on each occasion the date and period of his visit. Whilst going through the house he is to be accompanied by the Resident Physician, with whom he shall consult as to the medical and moral treatment of the patients, and order such regimen, &c., &c., as he shall think fit.

9. In conjunction with the Resident Physician he shall keep, at the asylum, a registry or history of the symptoms and treatment of the patients; and, on the reception of any lunatic, sign the official return which is to be forwarded to the office of the Inspectors.

10. He is, when requiring absence for more than a week, to notify his intention to the Inspectors, that suitable provision may be made in case of need.

11. In all cases of the death of a patient he is to examine as far as possible into the physical causes connected with the insanity of the deceased, and make an entry in the Registry of the asylum, of the *post mortem* appearances, with any observations he may deem useful thereon, for the advance of science, and the utility of such lectures as he may be called on to deliver, pursuant to the Statute.

12. *Governor and Resident Physician.*—The Governor and Resident Physician shall, under the control of the Inspectors, regulate the entire establishment, and shall devote his best exertions to its successful management; at no period absenting himself for more than two consecutive days without previous notification to the Inspectors, so as to enable them to make arrangements during his absence.

13. He shall be most particular in the regularity with which the various books of the asylum are kept, and be responsible for all moneys placed to his credit, as well as for the accuracy of his disbursements and receipts.

14. He shall have his books always ready for inspection, and the monthly accounts duly prepared for examination at the Audit Office. He shall submit all vouchers, as well as a list of any furniture or other articles that may be required, to the Inspectors, and through them convey every communication connected with the establishment to the Chief or Under Secretary.

15. He is to see that the strictest order be observed in every department; that all the attendants and servants conduct themselves with propriety, and that the utmost cleanliness and decorum be regarded by them in their dress and habits of life.

16. He is to attend the Visiting Physician through the wards, and conduct, in unison with him, the mental and physical treatment of the patients, and assist with him in keeping the Medical Journal, or "Case Book."

17. In the absence of the Visiting Physician he shall act as the general director of the whole medical department of the institution, and be responsible for its due administration.

18. He shall inspect the corridors and apartments every forenoon and evening, and give such directions as he may think fit to the attendants with reference to the treatment of the lunatics, and direct the attention of the matron to any irregularity or misconduct that may occur within her department.

19. He shall exercise a general supervision over the various articles contracted for as to quality and quantity, and if deficient on either point, forbid their delivery, and procure a supply elsewhere at the contractor's expense.

20. He is at all times, and in all places, to encourage habits of industry amongst the lunatics, and have them engaged as much as possible in out-door work, but under the most cautious observation.

21. *The Matron.*—The Matron shall exercise immediate superintendence, but in position subordinate to the Governor, over the female department of the Dundrum Asylum.

22. She is to take particular care that cleanliness and good ventilation are attended to.

23. She is to look after the inner-clothing, bedding, linen, &c., of the patients and attendants, that they be kept in good repair, and shall take care that without the slightest waste there is a regular supply of sheeting, stockings, shirts, &c., &c.; and she is to be particular as to the order in which the kitchen, laundry, pantry, and dairy are kept.

24. She shall accompany the Physician when visiting the female side of the asylum, both morning and evening, and report to him any irregularity or cause of complaint she may notice.

25. She is to reside constantly in the asylum, and to employ the female patients as advantageously as possible to themselves and to the establishment.

26. *Clerk and Storekeeper.*—The Clerk and Storekeeper is to attend regularly at a quarter to eight o'clock in the morning, and remain in the asylum till four, P.M. (time of meals excepted).

27. He shall have charge of the stores of the establishment, be accountable for the quantity and quality received by him, and keep an accurate return of the amount issued.

28. He is to sign the pass-book kept by the various contractors for milk, bread, meat, &c., &c., on the delivery of the articles, and to sign the receipts for every other article employed for consumption by the patients and servants, or for the general use of the house.

29. He is to make an entry of the different materials issued by him for the purpose of manufacture, and keep an exact inventory of the furniture.

30. In the daily delivery of food to the Cook or assistants, he shall be particular that the quantity be proportionate to the demand in the different divisions as specified in the Dietary Book.

31. As clerk he shall attend daily in the Governor's office, to assist in drawing out official documents, writing letters, &c., &c., and to keep all accounts, fiscal or other, connected with the Dundrum Asylum.

32. *The Chaplains.*—The Chaplains are to attend at the Dundrum Asylum on Sundays and Holidays to officiate according to their respective creeds: they are moreover to visit the institution once in the week, at least, to administer religious instructions to those susceptible of its influence. They shall, in case of illness, attend at any time when noticed to do so.

33. *The Apothecary.*—The Apothecary is to visit the asylum regularly three times in the week, and as often as his services may be required by the Governor.

34. He is to make up all prescriptions with the greatest accuracy, and copy them into a book, to be called the "Prescription Book," to be kept in the asylum; he is to be answerable for the due administration of the medicines ordered.

35. *The Cook.*—The Cook shall take care that in the morning at half after seven o'clock, the kitchen be in regular order, the fires lighted, and every thing prepared for her business; she shall receive from the Storekeeper the different articles to be prepared as food for the patients and attendants, and be particular as to the quantity required; she shall be responsible that the meals are properly and fully dressed at the particular periods specified for delivery.

36. She shall keep all the utensils employed by her with the greatest cleanliness, and never omit, before retiring to rest, to have the boilers well scoured, and the kitchen and scullery thoroughly ventilated and purified.

37. *The Laundress.*—The Laundress shall take charge of the patients employed by her, and when their business is over shall see that they return to the safe keeping of the attendants in their respective divisions.

38. She shall keep a book, to be called the "Laundry Book," in which are to be entered, under separate heads, the various articles, soap, blue, starch, &c., &c., received by her from the Storekeeper; and also a book containing an exact list of the foul clothes to be washed and returned by her weekly to the Matron.

39. *Servants and Attendants.*—Both male and female are responsible to the Governor for their good conduct, for habits of cleanliness, order, and subordination, as well as for the most unvarying humanity towards the lunatics placed under their charge.

40. They shall never absent themselves from their divisions so as to leave the patients unguarded, or attempt coercion, restraint, or confinement, without the Physician's sanction.

41. In the morning they are to see that the patients are properly cleaned and washed—at night that due regard be paid to their comfort, and that they retire decently to rest.

42. They are to be present when the patients are at meals, and repeat Grace before each repast; they shall pay particular attention to the clothing and becoming appearance of the patients, and contribute all in their power, both in and out of doors, to their amusement and occupation.

43. They shall be answerable for the safe keeping of the lunatics under their respective care, and in the event of escape, shall be either at the expense of the re-capture, or be discharged, should negligence appear to have been the cause.

44. They are to report daily to the Governor the conditions of their wards and corridors, and keep a diary in reference to the patients, towards whom they are expected to conduct themselves in the most humane and considerate manner, so as to engage their confidence and affection.

45. No servant or attendant will be permitted egress from the institution, and no admission to their friends without the Governor's sanction; and on no account will children be allowed to reside in the asylum.

46. *The Porter.*—The Porter is to have charge of the hall and adjoining public apartments; he is to see that they are kept with neatness and order.

47. He is to record in the "Porter's Book" the names of strangers, the visiting friends to the patients, as well as the attendance of the different officers of the asylum.

48. When called on he shall assist in taking charge of the male lunatics, and render himself generally useful.

49. In the morning, during the summer months, that is, at half-past five o'clock, to ring the bell to call up the servants and attendants; during the winter, at a quarter to seven.

50. At night he is to see that all the doors are locked, and the different yards duly protected, in summer, at nine o'clock, P.M.; and in winter, at eight, P.M. He shall deposit all the keys intrusted to him with the Governor.

51. *Gardener and Land Steward.*—The Gardener and Land Steward is to report himself present to the Porter during the summer months at seven o'clock in the morning, and to remain till six, P.M. In the winter months, that is, from the 1st October to the 1st March at eight o'clock, A.M., and to remain till four, P.M.

52. He shall take charge of all the implements used on the farm, and be accountable for them. He is to superintend the lunatics when employed on the grounds, and to assist the attendants generally in the care and observation of them.

53. He shall make no purchase whatever of seeds, shrubs, &c., &c., without a written direction from the Governor; neither shall he employ labourers without an order to do so

54. He is to have a Farm and Garden Book of the expenditure and produce in his department, and accurately enter in it the amount of vegetables delivered by him from time to time for the use of the asylum.

55. He shall be responsible for the neatness, order, and cultivation of the grounds, and the good condition of the farm.

56. *General Regulations as to the Patients.*—Patients on admission shall be washed, cleaned, &c., &c.; and when examined as to bodily health by the Physician, are to be placed in the division most suitable to the general symptoms of their mental affection; and if not already decently attired, are to be clad in the costume of the institution.

57. The hours for rising and retiring to bed shall be, in summer and winter respectively: in the former, half-past six o'clock, A.M., and half-past eight, P.M.; in the latter, half-past seven, A.M., and eight, P.M. The general hours for meals shall be: breakfast, half-past eight, A.M.; dinner, half-past one, P.M.; supper, half-past six, P.M.

58. The friends of the patients may be admitted on Tuesdays, from ten o'clock, A.M., to twelve o'clock; on Thursdays, from three to five, P.M., under the control of the Governor; but no stranger shall be allowed to visit without an order from the Chief or Under Secretary, or from the Inspectors.

59. Patients night and morning to join, so far as practicable, in common prayer; and on Sundays and Holidays of obligation to attend the religious worship of their respective creeds.

60. On no account whatever, without an express order in writing from the Chief or Under Secretary, will criminal lunatics be permitted to leave the precincts of the asylum.

61. As lunatics, charged with minor offences, may be transferred from District Asylums to the Central, they shall, at the discretion of his Excellency, and on the report of the Inspectors, be subject to be sent back to the institutions from whence they came.

62. Any servant or attendant who is guilty of harshness towards a lunatic in the Dundrum Asylum, either in language, by upbraiding the unfortunate individual with the offence committed, or by an act of violence, shall be liable to immediate dismissal, and the loss of all wages due at the time.

(Signed)   Francis White.
           John Nugent.